DIANA WAS OUT OF BED, reaching for the pistol before she realized what had awakened her. It came again. The crash of the fort's cannon.

"Get up," she shouted. "To the cellar." Her fingers needed no instructions. The pistol was cocked, powder poured from the small horn into the pan, and the weapon put down to half cock while she watched the flurry from Ruth and her two children. She turned to the loft— and saw and heard nothing. She was at the top of the ladder. Brian and Farrell were gone. As were their coats, which should have hung behind the kitchen door.

Ruth was starting to keen in panic. There wasn't time. She jerked the woman toward the door and told Samuel to get everyone into the cellar. Load the rifle and shotgun. Kill anybody who opened the trap. She pulled her coat around her shoulders and was almost out the door. No. You won't save anyone if your feet freeze. She forced them into boots, then grabbed the pouch with pistol balls and powder horn. Then out the door.

She couldn't find any footprints in the muck. A thick fog hampered her search. Think, woman. The creek? It was one of their favorite playgrounds, although what they could be doing at this hour of the morning was unknown. But both of them of late had been behaving like there was some great secret. Maybe the creek. She could think of no other possibilities. The creek was nearly in the middle of

Cherry Valley—in the same direction the screams and battle sounds came from.

The sleet was now coming in drifting sheets, with clear patches between. The rising wind was driving the fog out of the valley. She stumbled through the fields, deep in mire, and tore her hands and clothes pulling herself across the stone fences.

Suddenly Diana went to her knees and threw up. Damn you, woman. Damn this child in my belly. I have no time to be sick. She refused to allow her body its dictates and ran on…

About The Authors:

International bestselling authors and screenwriters Allan Cole and the late Chris Bunch were collaborators for nearly twenty years. Together, and separately, they published over forty novels and sold more than 150 TV and movie screenplays.

Their most noteworthy collaborations produced the eight-book Sten series (http://tinyurl.com/3go7w5n) hailed as "landmark science fiction" by Publishers Weekly, among others as well as the The Far Kingdoms series.

Their other notable works are a series of historical novels about America's wars - of which this is one. And Freedom Bird, set during the Summer Of Love.

For details about Allan's life and work, see his homepage at http://www.acole.com. Both authors are also listed at Wikipedia.com and IMBD.com

Other books in this series can be found at Amazon.com and other major booksites. Audiobook versions of this novel- narrated by Scott Larson - can be found at Audible.com, Amazon.com and I-Tunes.

And be sure to visit his popular blog - My Hollywood MisAdventures - to read humorous tales of his years in Tinsel Town, along with his late partner, Chris Bunch. The MisAdventures are at: http://www.allan-cole.blogspot.com/

* * * *

Books In This Series:
A Reckoning For Kings
A Daughter Of Liberty
The Wars Of The Shannons
Freedom Bird

A Daughter Of Liberty

Book Two Of The Shannon Trilogy

By Allan Cole and Chris Bunch

For
Kathryn and Karen
The late Leo L. Bunch
Elizabeth R. Bunch
The late Margaret Regina Guinan
And
The Irish

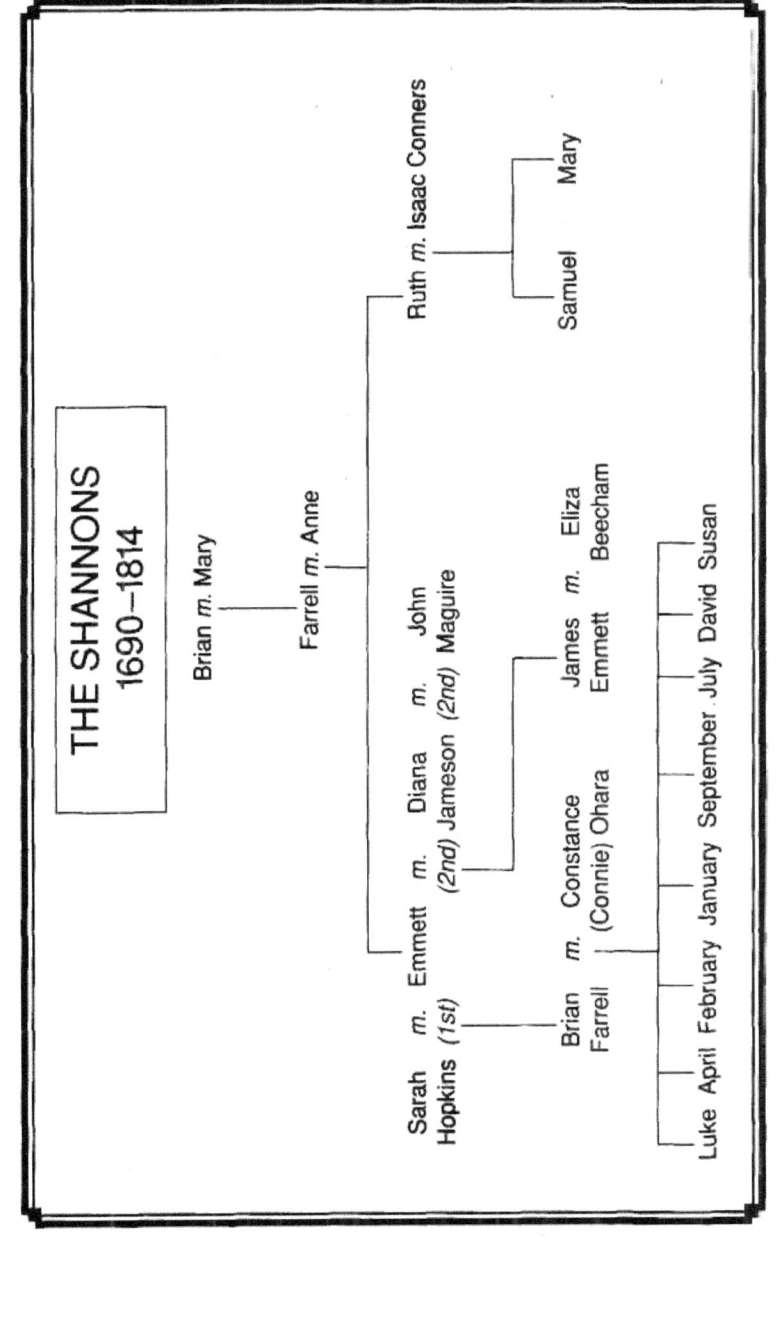

THE SHANNONS
1690–1814

Brian *m.* Mary

Farrell *m.* Anne

Ruth *m.* Isaac Conners

Samuel   Mary

Sarah *m.* Emmett *m.* Diana *m.* John
Hopkins (1st)   (2nd) Jameson (2nd) Maguire

James *m.* Eliza
Emmett   Beecham

Brian *m.* Constance
Farrell   (Connie) Ohara

Luke April February January September July David Susan

America in 1778

The New York Frontier

PROLOGUE

THUNDER, SUMMER THUNDER swept aside the morning's heat-curtain and echoed down the glen and across the river. But lightning and rain would not follow to break the heat.

The thunder came from huge, massed drums. Behind the drums, ten abreast, came the Dutch Guards.

Brian O Seannachain wiped sweat-slick palms dry on his dirty jerkin and braced his pike against the ground.

He hoped that from this day forward Ireland would be free of the foreign king, his German God and his bloody-handed soldiers. That after this day Brian could find his way back, back away from this heat-drenched tidal river named the An Boin, back to his own lands and his own river, the Shannon.

For centuries, his family had farmed the rich land along that river some boasters claimed bore their name. They worked the land through good times when peace hung over Ireland and the men with bloody swords busied themselves in other lands with their killing and the O Seannachains' scythe was a tool for harvesting and the pike was hidden rusting in the thatch. In good times there was food, some for the day and for the winter.

But there were other times, times of famine. And there were times of fear, when the soldiers came across the land. Then the O Seannachains fought. Fought the Romans, the Vikings, the Normans for independence. Then came the English, and the land itself bled. King John. Henry. Elizabeth. Cromwell. Each time the English, quicker with the sword and the lash, won.

Now, on this hell-baking July day, one thousand six hundred and eighty-nine years after the birth of Our Savior, another battle was to be fought. The last one, some said. Between the Dutch William of Orange, William the chosen Protestant king of England, and James II, the Stuart, the Catholic, dethroned in England, renamed king by a Dublin Parliament.

Drumthunder crashing closer now. Screaming, pain-screaming anger-screaming as the English and their gallow-glasses waded into the neck-deep water of the ford toward Brian and the Irish line. Thud of carbines, dull in the heat. Across the river the crash-crash-crash of cannon, and there was a man pulling himself out of the water toward him, using a handful of willows for a hold, baskethilt sword waving, most unwarlike, peruke and hat sogging down over his face, and his hands flung wide, pitching the long sword high into the air as a musket ball caught him.

A horse screamed beside Brian. There were other horses, armed men astride them, being kicked through the river. Brian set his mind and his feet firm—cavalry would not charge, he had learned in the months past in the long dreary retreat from the north, any man or thing that stood firm. But if you turned and ran, you would be ridden down and take a sword, pike or ball in the back. Brian knew this—others did not. He saw the ripple as men shouted. Ran. Banners were cast down, cast away with weapons for ease of flight. He warned himself to not be thinking of that. Concern himself only with this small yardage that was his battlefield. His life, his death would be found here, as white cannon smoke and dust closed the horizons in. A sword cut across his arm, but it was nothing and numb and Brian fought on, stepping aside once, twice, again as the Irish cavalry charged through the lines against the English, Sarsfield's happy banner flashing in the stilly sun, until shouts broke his mind. Shouts that the flank was turned, James had fled, save yourselves my sons, my lads, save yourselves, and the dust lifted.

Brian saw horsemen, English horsemen, crash into the Irish line on the left, wails and the line broke. Broke, and crumbled back, back toward the narrow pass of Duleek toward Dublin and screams from a man Brian had followed north from the River Shannon into battlehell to run, run, we can fight again another day, and then that man went down.

Brian was running, trying to watch over his shoulder, cavalry, good Irish cavalry holding the ground, even charging the Englishmen as the foot soldiers fled and looming just up in front of him a man shouting something in a tongue that was not Gaelic nor English. Brian slashed with his pike, and the man fell back.

Brian heard hooves behind him, turned, saw cavalry sweeping across this battleground that was becoming a shambles and pain seared, burnt, numbed, and he stumbled, 'most fell, turned, seeing that man he'd but touched pull his sword free, free from Brian's left side, drawback for the killing slash and Brian put the pike through his face.

Christ to lie down just to bleed awhile, Christ for some water, Christ how dry the world is and the sound of battle waver on him. No, he thought. No you will not. You will not fall, you will not stretch yourself on this battlefield for them to find and slaughter you like they have so many of your friends before. You are moving, damn you, damn you. One foot. Now then, another. You can do it. Get that damned pike up; see the horseman pull his mount away from the wavering, threatening bloodred tip. Clear now. Clear for the pass. Away from this river and this hell. For home. For the Shannon. But there will not be safety there, because this day is the end. Hide yourself, Brian O Seannachain. Hide yourself well, in the marshes, in the empty moors, in the cities, and then you will hide yourself on foreign shores.

That day in July, 1690, began the Flight of the Wild Geese. Irishmen, driven out of their country. Driven to France, to Germany, to Spain... and to America.

One of them was a pikeman. His name became, in the language of the conqueror, Brian Shannon. He came with only his wits, the clothes he wore, and the passion to find a land where no man would be his master. It was a poor legacy for the Shannons. But it was all he had.

BOOK ONE:

VALLEY FORGE
WINTER-SPRING, 1778

CHAPTER ONE

ON FEBRUARY 22, 1778, Private Emmett Shannon, Fourth New York Regiment, deserted the Continental Army at Valley Forge. He had not suddenly joined the ranks of the summer soldiers and sunshine patriots so loathed by Tom Paine. The Royal Brute of Britain and his bullies were still insufficiently punished—and Emmett had generations of Irish forebears to revenge.

Nor had physical hardship broken him: twenty pounds lighter, canvas pants flapping in the icy wind, a hacking cough, the half-gill of rice and tablespoon of vinegar that had been his Thanksgiving meal—these were expected in a campaign. He'd learned that the first time he went a-soldiering, almost fifteen years before. Even as a civilian wandering the frontier, he'd known far harsher winters and suffered shorter rations in his thirty-five years. But it was time to go home. His fingers touched the letter folded into a pocket of his hunting shirt, which had arrived two days earlier.

Dear Brother Emmett,
The council has taken our goods and property for debt. We have no furnishings. Not even a bed. Nor do we have wood to last the winter. I fear there will be not food enough to last one half of that. Your two sons are gravely ill and my own children are failing. I do not care for myself, but your poor wife must be crying in Heaven to see such a sight. Please come home soon or I fear we shall all be dead.
Your loving sister, Ruth

His sister was of a flighty disposition, prone to make a tempest out of a chimney rattler. But whatever was happening in Cherry Valley obviously needed some attention.

It made perfect sense to Emmett that the Committee of Public Safety would persecute the sister and children of a widower fighting for their own cause; or what had become the committee's cause after the destruction of British general Burgoyne at Saratoga. These brave Patriots in Cherry Valley needed an example to show their new fervor.

But this was how the war was being waged, Shannon and his fellow soldiers agreed. The loudest of the Patriots seemed content to let others do the actual fighting while they concentrated on profit. For instance, here at Valley Forge the army was starving, but the burghers just beyond a foraging party's range were untouched by the war and fat as fireside cats. Only the soldiers suffered.

Before the war, Valley Forge had been the home of Quaker farmers and a prosperous iron forge and gristmill. It made perfect sense to the starving, miserable revolutionary soldiers that this hellhole, originally one of William Penn's properties, had been named the Manor of Mount Joy. Of course, Mount Joy itself was within the campsite and Mount Misery just outside it.

It was a natural fortress. General Washington, with his surveyor's eye for terrain, had chosen it as the best possible location for the battered Continental Army's winter quarters. About sixteen miles from British-occupied Philadelphia, it had a creek-swollen gorge on its west, the Schuylkill River guarding its borders on the north and east, and steep bluffs on the south. If Lord Howe—commander of the British forces occupying Philadelphia—tired of his mistress's bed and marched out to battle, the American army would face him from a four-foot-deep trench, with earth mounded behind it; earthen forts prepared as strongholds, and a line of sharpened stakes beyond the trenches. A strong position, far better than most of the hasty defenses the Americans had fought from earlier in the war.

The defenses of Valley Forge might be properly laid out, but there was almost no one fit enough to man them in the event of a battle. About eleven thousand men marched into winter quarters at Valley Forge on December 19. There were less than four thousand left. By February, Valley Forge was a sewer of nearly two thousand acres. When the weather rose above freezing, as it had regularly and unpredictably that winter, the residue of a half-trained indifferently led army thawed and stank, from shit to garbage to the hundreds of dead horses.

The soldiers themselves felt abandoned by their leaders, politicians, and countrymen.

Emmett Shannon himself had been unpaid for three months. His captain had announced, rather dryly, just after New Year's Day, that the ever-generous Continental Congress had authorized an extra month's pay for any officer or man who would soldier on through the winter. That, too, had never been paid.

On paper the Continental Army was well fed. Each soldier was authorized, daily, a pound of bread, a pound of meat or salt fish, a pint of milk, a quart of beer, a quart of peas, a quart of beans, and butter. Shannon, waiting for dusk in the reeking murk of his hut, tried to find some humor in that. He had last tasted beef, he calculated, a week ago. Rancid salt beef it was, too. No rations at all had been issued for the last three days. The hooting and cawing had gone up and down the company streets, and then the chants of "No meat, no coat, no flour, no soldier." Shannon didn't bother to join in—that put no victuals on his table. Eventually the chants died away, and there was silence except for the wind snarling outside, whistling through the indifferently mud-caulked timbers of the hut.

Emmett Shannon reconsidered his careful plans for desertion while he waited. The current penalty, he'd heard, was five hundred lashes on the bare back, well laid on. Such a punishment, if he was caught, was unlikely to be carried out. Nor would the previously proclaimed penalty of a hundred lashes. Those unfortunates who'd been stripped and striped in front of their regiment were fairly committed villains who'd also struck an officer—in one case with a ramrod—stolen, or been imbecile enough to head for the British lines at Philadelphia to join up, only to be captured by

Allan Cole & Chris Bunch

their former comrades. But Emmett preferred not to play the odds.

The first and most important step was getting rid of his damned musket. In a way, Emmett was sorry to part with the ten-pound Tower musket that the British called a Brown Bess, for a stupidly sentimental reason: it had been made at, and was stamped behind the lock, DUBLIN CASTLE; about the closest he would ever come to his grandfather's homeland.

But there was no place for sentiment. Shannon gathered musket and the six-pound metal cartridge box filled with balls, powder, and accessories. He headed out from his brigade's position along the bluff into Woodford's brigade, sited across Baptist Road, one of the five rutted trails into Valley Forge.

Eventually he encountered one of Morgan's riflemen who was equipped with a particularly well-mounted and - maintained Pennsylvania long rifle. He offered a trade and was greeted with immediate and total suspicion.

The rifle may have been legendary among the myth-makers, balladeers, and propagandists. But none of them had ever stood on a bare field, discharged one round at the onrushing enemy, and then realized that the British line would be on them before they would be able to reload. On them with needle-sharp, triangular, seventeen-inch bayonets.

After that first engagement, any rifleman who survived was eager to acquire a Brown Bess from a dead Britisher.

A musket and a rifle looked a bit the same. Each was about five feet long and weighed about ten pounds. Both were loaded at the muzzle. Gunpowder, either poured by eye or spilled from a paper tube, went in first. Then the ball—a round cartridge of hand-poured lead about three-quarters of an inch in diameter—was put down the barrel on top of the powder. Both the musket and rifle ball would be wrapped in a greased linen or buckskin patch. Loose gunpowder was sprinkled in a pan that inletted into the barrel's base. When the trigger was pulled, the hammer, which actually was a tiny vise holding a piece of flint, would fall and strike sparks from the pan cover—called the frizzen—set off the powder in the pan, and the weapon would fire.

The weapons were very similar—but there were two major differences. Both differences killed riflemen. The musket barrel was a smooth pipe. A ball could be—and in an emergency was—simply dropped down on top of the powder, the weapon hastily lifted and fired. That would work, if the musket ball did not simply roll out of the barrel before the powder went off.

The rifle was a more sophisticated weapon. Its tube was grooved, so the ball would spin as it exited, and gain accuracy. The rifle ball, in turn, was cast so that it fit tightly into the barrel. A rifleman sometimes had to use both his ramrod and a small mallet as well to drive the load home. In that time, a Hessian Jaeger would have wreaked the martyrdom of Saint Sebastian on the unfortunate man. For some unknown reason, no rifles had yet been equipped for bayonets. So, once the first ball was discharged, the rifleman's sophisticated instrument of death was nothing more than a club.

So Shannon's offer to Morgan's man was far too good to be believed. The man examined the musket with the care of a horse trader being offered a blind spavined nag with glanders. But he could find no fault. He therefore growled for an explanation. Shannon, smiling guilelessly, gave him one. He had been told off by his sergeant for a foraging party, which would range up toward New Jersey. Shannon had plans of assassinating a deer. "No deer closer'n thirty miles," the rifleman said.

"My deer'll have just two plain horns," Shannon said. "One t'either side of its skull."

A smile flickered across the rifleman's face. "And if you yanked its tail, it'd bawl," he suggested.

"It might," Shannon said.

"The Dutchmen could stand to lose a bullock or two," the man said, and handed over the rifle and shot pouch. That

Allan Cole & Chris Bunch

was the hardest part. The rest of the supplies Shannon had amassed were either slung around his body or fit handily in the brown, hairy goatskin knapsack acquired from a very dead British grenadier while doing a bit of thoughtful corpse-looting after Saratoga.

There wasn't much to take. For clothing Shannon had a pair of moccasins he'd sewn up early in January, hide traded to him by one of the regiment's butchers; leggings; his deerskin hunting shirt; a ragged pair of pants he'd made from tent canvas—quite explicitly against Washington's orders when the tents were turned in to the quartermaster some months earlier; his rifleman's slouch hat; and a blanket, worn Indian-style, for a coat. A second blanket was rolled and tied across his knapsack.

One thing he would not need was the tarred rope around his waist. Emmett, being a man who had occasionally made his way selling medicine, had scientifically protected himself with the rope against the vapors this fever camp would produce. But now, heading away from the pollution, this would not be necessary.

Shannon heard the tootle and rattle start from behind his hut, down below on Gulph Road. It was time to go. He picked up his rifle and shouldered his pack. He stumbled, nearly fell, and swore. Normally the barrel-chested man carried around 150 pounds on his five-foot, seven-inch frame. No longer. He was in no shape to be walking across the valley, let alone the hundreds of miles to his home. But there was no choice. He walked away without looking back.

There was a cluster of soldiers trailing up the road around the artillery brigade's cannons, vaguely following the sound of music. The music came from the cannoneers' fife and drum corps, and the group was marching in what they thought a proper military formation toward General Washington's quarters in the Potts House. It was the General's birthday, and this was the best his army could do to celebrate.

May you have many more, Shannon thought to himself as he wove his way through the throng. Loathing officers, he respected the general. A rich, slave-owning bastard from Virginia he might be, but he knew how to soldier. He'd been down in the muck and the mire like any rifleman. He'll win this war, Shannon thought, in spite of the fools in the Congress. Maybe when we lick the British he'll lead the army on York or wherever the sons of bitches are hiding. Emmett joined a ragged cheer for the general, then moved on, toward Fort Washington. He found an abandoned breastwork to hide in, and waited. It was freezing, even out of the wind. But Shannon was used to being cold.

Eventually, at sunset, the drumroll started down the line, then went through the second line, the artillery, and the reserve.

Retreat. It got darker and colder. Again the drumbeat sounded through the camp. Tap too. Nine of the clock.

Shannon gave it another estimated hour, until whatever sentry was on guard should be frozen through, then crept on toward the frozen Schuylkill River. Staying low, eyes widened, looking for a patch of black in the blackness that would mark the sentry, he saw nothing. Then he heard movement as the man came up from a huddle, dropping the blanket he'd had around his shoulders, and there was the click of a musket being brought to full cock.

"Halt," came the challenge. "Who comes there?" Then: "Orkney."

"Otway," answered Shannon. He'd been given the night's password by his sergeant.

"Advance one." Shannon walked toward him. "What's your business?"

"Damned sergeant told me to reinforce the sentry out on the bridge," Shannon said.

"Shit." The sentry was unimpressed. "They reinforce, they send four men. And the corp'ral of the guard."

"Not when the sergeant throws a knave and you hold a king, they don't," Shannon said.

Allan Cole & Chris Bunch

Silence, while the sentry considered the story. Shannon moved closer to the man. He'd rather not . . . but his fingers touched the tomahawk in his belt. The sentry was very young. His clothes were even more ragged than Emmett's. Over his shoulders were the remains of a British greatcoat. His head was bare.

Shannon looked down. The sentry was standing on his tricorner hat. He shifted frequently from naked foot to naked foot. Poor lad, Shannon thought. Shoes without soles. He wondered if there was blood on the frozen ground. "You're deserting," the young man said. The tomahawk was reversed in Shannon's fingers. With luck, he'd be able to knock the man unconscious with the flat, and not kill him.

"Wish't I could as well," the young man added suddenly. "But . . ." and Shannon could see the man's head move. Gesturing downriver. Toward Philadelphia. "Understand the king's got a few troops in the city. Hell. I don't even know if I've got a home to go back to." Shannon had nothing to say. "Better you get moving," the sentry said. "My sergeant's been known to check his posts right around this time. Hopin' to catch us sleeping. Wish't I could. Too damned cold."

"You take a care," Shannon said softly.

"Care or anything else comes my way."

Emmett Shannon slid toward the river, and down it to the ice. He unhooked the cross strap of his knapsack so he could dump it if he went through. Holding his rifle in front of him, he moved out onto the ice. Ten feet from the shore, it groaned. Shannon thought he saw a rock in the dimness, moved toward it, found firmer footing, and continued on. His foot broke through. Shannon flailed back. His foot came out of the water and he was safe. Then rising blackness in front of him, the opposite shore—with no waiting British patrols. He had made his escape. Now for Cherry Valley, far to the north, and west from Albany, on the New York frontier.

CHAPTER TWO

EMMETT'S MOST IMMEDIATE concern was to put miles between his tender skin and Valley Forge. An American patrol would return him to the encampment for punishment. If he encountered British soldiers, the best he could hope for was to be captured by regular infantrymen. Neither the mounted infantrymen called dragoons nor the German mercenaries everyone called Hessians took much interest in prisoners.

His plans were limited by geography. The roads around Valley Forge led mostly east toward occupied Philadelphia or west toward the frontiers. Shannon did not dare strike due north across rough terrain. A frontiersman he may have been, but one of the fabled long hunters he wasn't. Certainly not in the dead of winter. Plus he had neither map nor compass. So he determined to take the road that somewhat paralleled the Schuylkill River, past Reading. Then the road curved north and west toward Bethlehem. He would follow that route through the pass in the Kittatiny Mountains, and cross the East Branch of the Delaware into New York. From there he intended to strike again northeast to the Hudson and follow that river, even though it led through the wasteland of the Neutral Ground to Albany, and then the final road west to his home. It would have been simpler if British forces weren't lurking across the roads to his northeast. That would be a far more direct route; a direct route, most likely, to one of the British prison hulks in New York Harbor. If he had wanted to starve or die of the fevers, Shannon thought, he could have remained at Valley Forge and saved himself this walk.

He moved on—slowly and cautiously. His progress wasn't helped by the weather. Two days after he deserted, the storm broke. Snow and sleet slashed down, and his slow movement became a plod. He took a large chance and followed the road, to pick up speed. Emmett cursed the weather—until it saved his life.

* * * *

Shannon heard the jingle of harness in time to roll off the rutted road into a shallow frozen runnel. He kept his head low, broadcasting thoughts that he was nothing more than an uninteresting rock as the riders passed. Emmett waited until he was sure there was no rear guard before he dared a look. There were about fifteen of them. It might have been possible to think they were nothing more than a group of civilian drovers, headed for shelter. But since when did drovers wear identical cloaks? Or have saddlery the same? Let alone the dimly glimpsed flash of a saber's scabbard on the rearmost rider.

British dragoons. Their supposed purpose was for reconnaissance. Essentially they were mounted infantrymen. Ride to battle, dismount, skirmish, and then get out. In fact, they were used as scroungers, thieves, raiders, and ambush experts. On both sides dragoons tended to be somewhat casual about obeying the laws of man, the military, or God Himself. They were armed with three-foot-long sabers, the shortened muskets called musketoons, a pistol or two if the trooper had managed to liberate one, plus whatever other weapons they fancied. They tended to be skilled in the use of all of them. The infantry equivalent of the dragoons were the rangers, who had an equally questionable reputation among the line units. These, Emmett thought, were probably an ambush element, clumsily disguised, trying to waylay any of the Continental Army's foraging expeditions. Or maybe foraging on their own. Dragoons tended to keep their own counsel.

Emmett was not that terrified. Especially after seeing the backs of the dragoons disappear into the storm.

There had been dragoons, after all, at Saratoga that summer. They'd been on foot, wading through the swamps called the Drowned Lands in twelve-pound horse boots, and lugging carbines and yard-long, basket-hilted sabers. Each one of them also carried a halter, intended for the horse to be won somewhere in America. They were part of the eight-thousand-man British army invading from Canada. The army was led by Gentleman Johnny Burgoyne, he of the florid face, the vast concern for his soldiers' welfare, the mistress, and the thirty carts of personal belongings. Among his forces were some of the proudest regiments of the British army, German mercenaries, Loyalists, Canadian frontiersmen, and nearly four hundred Indians.

Burgoyne fought south, taking casualties in a hundred little nameless skirmishes, dragging his army through the swamps. The damned rebels had destroyed the few roads that existed. His men stumbled through the wilderness, bewildered, mosquito- and snake-bitten, and starving. Moving his army twenty miles through virgin wilderness took him twenty-six days. His Indian allies contributed to the war effort by murdering the fiancée of one of his Tory officers, then deserting in a snit.

Burgoyne's march went on. Eventually he stumbled to the Hudson, where the main rebel army waited, under an ambitious schemer named Gates, near a minuscule village called Saratoga. The Americans were camped on top of Bemis Heights, a steep plateau surrounded by woods that was completely fortified.

Burgoyne split his army into three columns and sent them forward into the attack on a brisk, frosty fall day.

Turkey gobbles rattled from the thick brush. Daniel Morgan's Virginia riflemen used bird sounds to signal. The gold-braided officers and pike-carrying noncommissioned officers were the first to go down under the spatter of rifle fire. The British sent in backup troops, and the nightmare began, hours of screaming, blood, sallies, countersallies, and death.

Emmett had been part of that nightmare. By now he had a story assembled as to what happened to him that day—how his company had gone against the light infantry, been shelled flat by the British, then had gone on and taken the guns. It all

Allan Cole & Chris Bunch

happened. But Shannon's real memories had, at least to his mind, little of the reach of an epic. In fact, he'd realized later, they bore closer resemblance to what his grandfather had told him in fits and starts about his own career as a soldier.

There was a sergeant shouting at them, and they were up, muskets charged, running forward. A scream of "fire" and Emmett was staring down the barrel of his Bess and the trigger was pulled. Jolt against his shoulder and a cloud of white. Unsure of what he'd shot at, he was running forward again. A bawl from someone to halt and reload, and Emmett was ramming a fresh charge and ball down the barrel of the musket, trying to remember if he hadn't done this moments ago, and if so and he hadn't fired, the musket was going to explode. Then seeing the man next to him— Garrity, he remembered—grunt gently, look at the gout of blood where his arm had been, and then fall forward.

Another man—Emmett could not, for his life, remember his name—was staggering, spraying blood from his throat, for all the world like a slaughtered chicken, and ahead of them were billowed white clouds that might have been storm signals at sea but were not, and then came the blast, the blast that sent his hat spinning and Emmett stumbling. A man was coming at him, shouting something, and all Emmett could see was the stabbing needle of the bayonet. Somehow Emmett had his musket sideways and the needle shoved away and he and the man were chest to chest. Emmett's knee came up, and the man screamed, doubled. Emmett struck with the musket butt, and the man was on his back. Emmett had his musket up, butt lifted to crash downward to finish the kill, and there was another scream. Turning, he saw a Britisher pulling his bayonet out of the body of Fraser, who—he remembered—he still owed a flask of rum to, and the redcoat was pulling back for the finishing stroke. Emmett's musket went off, and the ball blew out the Englishman's guts.

Someone was shouting at him now to retreat. Pull back. Emmett was running back the way he had come as a line of

British infantrymen lockstepped forward. The line suddenly vanished in a crash of cannon fire—theirs, ours?—and someone else was crying the charge yet again, and Emmett was headed back the way he had come. He remembered the rattle of harness, the screams of a horse and thunder of wheels. But maybe that had come before, because he was told later that they charged once more against four British cannon.

But if that were so, who had slaughtered the British soldiers? And why would anyone charge into cannon fire? It made no sense, but he found himself at a run, his bayonet aimed at a matross's chest, and that cannoneer trying to block his thrust with a ramrod, and the bayonet thumping home, and the sound of the matross's last breath whistling, most clear, as he died. Which Emmett should not have been able to hear.

The day went on. Hours—so Shannon guessed—hours of stumbling up and down that hill, over the softness of bodies, and hearing the shatter of cannon fire. He could put none of it in order. The first he could remember, when time began once more, was his lunged thrust pulled aside as the red haze lifted and he saw the face of a corporal-Atkins, it was, Second Company—shouting at him that they were pulling back. "Back, you Irish bastard!" Shannon had turned and stumbled away. Uphill away. He was heading in the right direction, he guessed. All he was really aware of was a great thirst. Pouring mountain rivers of water, and him lying underneath them.

He got his drink, back atop Bemis Heights. And was told what had happened. The British hadn't been beaten. But six hundred of them lay out there on the slopes below the plateau. He could hear their screams and groans, fading down as the freezing wind whispered over the battlefield and night closed in. At daybreak a heavy mist, and each side went out to bury the dead and bring in the wounded. British and Colonial troops would stumble into each other, wordlessly

Allan Cole & Chris Bunch

stare, and then backstep into the fog. There'd been enough death.

Burgoyne decided not to count the number of his dead, but held in place, entrenched his position and called the battle a victory. Some days after that, surrounded, Burgoyne sent some soldiers out to see what would happen. The American forces, led by one of the most brilliant officers of the revolt, Benedict Arnold, counterattacked. At the end of the day Gentleman Johnny's troops—bearskins, sabers, and traditions—were driven back against the Hudson. Ten days later, after negotiations—and the only person in America who could pose more nobly than Burgoyne was Granny Gates—Burgoyne surrendered 5,700 of Britain's formerly-finest soldiers. He had been trapped by a force more than three times his number.

Shannon thought, as he trudged on through the storm, at least he had been part of that. His unit, the Fourth New York, had been detached from Gates's army and ordered to march south in fall, just in time to go into winter quarters at Valley Forge.

South, away from Cherry Valley. Shannon was unsure if he would have enlisted at all if he'd known he would be serving far from his home. He'd joined for the bounty—but also to protect his people and farm against the Loyalists and the Indian butchers they controlled from across the border.

Never mind, Emmett thought, bringing himself back to this icy Schuylkill road. The matter is done.

* * * *

Emmett Shannon was traveling light. His rifle he carried ready and primed in one hand. The hunting bag he'd gotten from Morgan's rifleman was particularly fine. The bag was built so the powder horn was slung below it. The horn was three-quarters full of powder. The leather bullet pouch inside the bag held twenty-six balls. It was more than enough ammunition. The bullets were for hunting or, at worst, delaying an enemy until Emmett could disappear into the woods.

In the rifle's patch box were the necessary cleaning and maintenance tools for his rifle. Stuck in his worn leather belt were his tomahawk and the horn-handled nine-inch-bladed knife Emmett had forged from a file years earlier.

Around his neck he carried his drinking cup. Also slung was his small camp kettle—tinned iron—in a dirty linen pouch, as was a one-quart tin British canteen, half full of rum. He would need that for medication. The rest of his gear was carried in the hairy knapsack: a wooden plate, a spoon, a jackknife, flint and steel; a rolled skin pouch, in case he needed to carry water. His provisions: one and one-third pounds of Indian meal, one pint of dried peas, about a pint of rice, a hunk of dirty salt. Not much, but the best he had been able to acquire.

At least his medical supplies were adequate. Emmett was proud of what he carried. He had clean linen, to serve either for bandages or spare rifle patches. A bit of soft soap-made of ashes and dirty tallow. He had a half pint of vinegar, alder, oak bark for fever tea, sumac, horseradish roots, and mustard seed. Plus some Glauber's purging salts in a twist of paper. He wished he had been able to steal some opium or tobacco.

But he also wished he could have obtained a surrey, a change of horses, and a cavalry escort home. Emmett Shannon, hunched under his blanket coat, looking less like a shaman than a starveling, traveled on through the storm.

* * * *

On the sixth day after he deserted, the weather broke. Frozen slush became muddy slush. But there were tiny spots of green on the trees. Maybe spring would come early this year, Emmett hoped, as he rolled his blanket coat onto his pack and moved on again. By now he should be beyond most of any army's tentacles. He felt well enough to mutter a song to himself:

* * * *

"How brave you went out with your muskets all bright And thought to befrighten the folks with the sight But when you got there how they powdered your pums And all the way

Allan Cole & Chris Bunch

home how they peppered your bums. And is it not, honeys, a comical—"

* * * *

He broke off, rifle coming up as he crouched and doubled off to the side of the track. Voices ahead. Emmett moved farther away from the road, into cover. Then he slid forward, toward the voices. The road below him dropped away, into a small hollow. There were three men, sweat-stained and spattered with mud. One man was doing most of the swearing. Four unhitched draft horses stared disinterestedly at what was going on. The four-wheeled wagon sat canted, one end of its box supported by a braced wagon jack. The shattered remains of a wheel lay to one side. Two of the men were muscling a new wheel onto the axletree.

Shannon's hands on the rifle stock were white. He had no use for teamsters. At least not those that made the run from Reading to Valley Forge. Thieves and profiteers they were, at best. "Lean into it, sods," shouted the vocal one, and Emmett knew their roles. The one doing the least and shouting the most was the wagon master, prosperity having spilled his gut over the front of his breeches; the other two were bound-out servants.

The wheel slid into place. The wagon master took a large wooden mallet from the wagon. "We've been miring ourselves since Reading," the man said. "Mought as well lighten the load now." The mallet swung—and the bung came out of the first barrel. Brine poured out, and Emmett had a gut-searing, memory taste of putrid beef from other barrels deliberately smashed on their way to Valley Forge by other thieving teamsters. The wagon master stepped to another barrel and the mallet came up and fury overtook Emmett. His rifle locked into his shoulder, his finger pressing, then the flash of powder and the smack of recoil as the ball took the wagon master just above the eyebrows and ripped away most of the skull. The echoes of the shot rang around the tiny hollow.

CHAPTER THREE

SHANNON FORKED THE hunk of salt beef from the swimming mass of boiled peas. He bit into one end and sawed off a piece with his knife. It was the first meat he'd eaten in weeks, but he forced himself to chew slowly. He could not afford the waste of vomiting. Emmett softened a piece of fire cake in the stew of peas. The fire cake was made of Indian meal—more husks and grit than corn—mixed with water. He ate gingerly, sifting through the mush with his tongue for bits of millstone. A broken tooth could greatly lessen his chances of reaching Cherry Valley.

All these things he did without thought—not tasting the food, or enjoying the fire's warmth, or even feeling the fingers of cold creeping around it, numbing the unprotected edges of his body. Outside his shallow cave the storm was raging. Just beyond the glow of the fire the mouth of the cave was a sheet of white—streaked with shifting streaks of night. The heated air inside the cave was an imperfect seal against the wind that fluttered in a constant drumbeat, like distant cannon fire.

Emmett was appalled at himself. What he had done was murder—there was no other word for it—and he could feel the jagged-edged wound on his soul. He ran the sequence of events over and over again. As the wagon master knocked the bung from the beef barrel, and the preserving brine spilled to the ground, Shannon saw the rage overtake his shadow self: the rifle coming up in one smooth motion, sights fixing on the bloated face, finger tightening, hammer falling, the flash of the pan, then the weapon bucking as it hurled its missile, the teamster falling away from view. He'd swiftly reloaded and the rifle had come up, sniffing for another victim. Shouts of terror from the teamster's servants had brought him back to a formless reality. But the rifle barrel hadn't wavered until the men had scurried off the trail and disappeared into the trees.

What troubled Shannon almost more than the murder was that at no point had there been any control. No moment of hesitation. It was as if a blacksmith had knocked out a critical gap in the rows of teeth encircling a gear, and the millstone had jumped from coarse to fine with none of the niceties of the middle grades.

After the men had fled, he had numbed forward until he was standing over the teamster's body. The top of the man's head was missing, and Emmett had turned away with a fit of dry heaves. He'd steadied himself, wiped the spittle from his mouth and taken stock of the situation. The man was dead, and Shannon knew that later he would mourn him. But death had also brought opportunity, and if he did not seize on every chance that fell his way, he would not survive.

Feeling like a thief, he had filled the pockets of his hunting shirt with beef. As he turned to leave he saw a large horseman's bag on the wagon seat. The leather was finely tooled, the buckles and fastenings thick brass—a little rich for a wagon master. He snagged the bag and hefted it. The weight suggested contents of value. He'd heard distant cries in the woods, and ran.

Now, Emmett's fork jarred against the wooden plate. He looked down, startled to see he'd emptied it. The kettle was on its side, scraped clean. He must have filled his plate again, eaten, and then wiped the edges of the kettle with fire cake until he had consumed every morsel. All this and no memory of it. He found it amusing, laughed aloud, then frowned. He touched an experimental finger to cheek. The flesh was dry, hot. Ah, Christ save him. It was the fever. Just thinking it made him shudder, and he wasn't sure whether the chill he felt was real or imagined. Another shudder and he realized there was no imagining to it. He fished out his medical kit, oddly grateful he now had a problem he could actually do something about.

He shook ground alder and oak bark into his cup. He mixed it in vinegar and drank, wishing again he had some laudanum to stiffen the elixir. Emmett decided he'd also better dose himself with a rum. He dug out his flask, extracted the cork and sipped. It quick-fused to his stomach, kicking like a rampart gun. Shannon grinned, a bit tipsy already. He thought about the teamster . . . this time with a shrug. He tucked the incident into a lockbox far in the corner of his mind. But just before he stowed it away, he promised himself that someday he would find a means of atonement. no matter how meager.

Emmett dragged over the horseman's bag and opened it for the first time. On top was a large, squat, corked jug. Well, buss my sweet Irish ass, Shannon, lad…could it be…? He pulled the cork with his teeth, and the small cave filled with heady fumes. He laughed again—with no fever in it this time—and took a long, gasping pull. He felt his ears flame as he choked the sweetish liquid down, then held the jug away from him, staring in disbelief. It was good old reliable Jersey Jack, straight from the stills of the Pine Barrens, where old men worked their cider artistry out of sight of the tax laws. He pawed through the bag to see what else he could find Next was a large pair of linen drawers. Expensive—and very dirty. Emmett held them up. The pouch could not have belonged to the teamster. The drawers would have fit the teamster and his two servants ... at the same time. The wagon master would meet his Maker with more sins than mere supply fraud to worry about.

He dug into the pouch once more, feeling less like a robber cackling over his loot than a birthday child. He uncovered a pistol and its powder and brass shot. The barrel was brass as well, and the butt and sideplate handworked silver. It must have belonged to an officer or a rich man. At the bottom of the bag was a broad oilskin packet. He opened it. Emmett's eyes glittered at the next gift from Heaven staring up at him: money!

Allan Cole & Chris Bunch

His fingers trembled as he counted it. Christ help me, it's twenty-five dollars I'm holding in my hands. No, it couldn't be. It must be Satan mocking me. But the bills were perfect Continental dollars printed in . . . He peered closer at one of the bills . . . spelling out the letters carefully: P-H-I-L-A-D-E-L-P-H-I-A. It was spelled correctly. Aw, shit on your leggings and call them brown linen! They were counterfeit. Guaranteed.

Shannon, an old hand at spotting a coiners' fraud, knew that on real Continental dollars the city was misspelled: PHILADELPKIA. Not only was the absence of the K a giveaway, but these bills were too well made. He considered . . . No. It wasn't worth the chance. Penalties were severe: starting with flogging and branding the thumbs. The punishments after that depended on how many coiners had been recently pissing on Congress's money. Emmett almost tossed the bills into the fire, but after reconsidering he wrapped them back up. He could always use extra paper. For wiping his bum or starting fires. Whatever, it was sure to be twenty-five dollars exclusively spent.

Despite his fever and the guilt nibbling at the edge of his conscience, the whole thing put him in a much better mood. He pushed the logs closer into the fire and curled up beside it. He pulled the jug into his arms for easy reach and tucked the blankets around him. After a few more sips he even began to imagine he was warm, and drifted off into a light sleep.

* * * *

Emmett grew up with his father's easy laughter, his mother's dare-the-law Catholic piety, his sister's nervous wit, and his grandfather's brooding presence beside the hearth.

Long after the old man was dead, Emmett could still see him sitting there in his heavy chair. Never drunk, but sipping steadily at his grog and staring into the fire. Sometimes he would mutter a name aloud. His face would blacken and he'd growl a Gaelic curse and drink more deeply. The split-board chair would groan under his weight as he shifted like an old dog grumbling at ancient slights. The family would fall silent until the creaking stopped and Grandfather Shannon found comfort in his fire again.

Emmett didn't know who he was cursing. Or if it was one man or many. Or even if it was not a man at all, but circumstances. He did notice, however, that when the great stirring began, his grandfather always kept an eye fixed on one point in the hearth. As if it was from there that a great danger threatened. In time Emmett took for granted something powerful and frightening must be there or his grandfather wouldn't keep such close watch. It worried him until he realized that whatever it was, it feared his grandfather more than the old man feared it. Otherwise he couldn't keep it pinned in the hearth with a mere glower.

When he was too big to carry but still too small to walk very far, Emmett's mother began leaving him at home on market day in his grandfather's care. At first he was intimidated. He cried as his mother stepped outside the door into the full rumble of traffic, shouting crowds, bawling animals, and pealing bells that was Market Day in Boston. But his mother pushed him back, gave him the look that said weep and die, so he stifled his sobs and shuffled off to a cluttered corner of the one-room shack his grandfather owned and shared with the family.

The shack hung from a small rocky rise above a narrow street that led to the docks. There were few other homes or even shacks on that street. Mostly it was a mixture of warehouses, blacksmiths, wheelwrights, chandleries, and a grog shop where his father spent his time between spurts of casual labor—parking carriages in the theater district or digging the occasional ditch. Behind the shack was a vegetable garden that struggled on rocky soil. The shack itself was about thirty by forty-five feet. During the day the center of the room was empty, save the old man's hearthside chair. All of the family's other belongings were crammed against the walls, to be dragged out when needed: a table and several log slab chairs for dinner, mattresses with straw ticking, old chests with clothing and bedding stacked inside and on top, a jumble of tools and parts for repairs, jugs, bottles and tinware of odd variety, his mother's two spinning wheels, the large loom for linen, as well as sacks and kegs of food stuffs.

The room smelled of a mixture of drying herbs, with the sharp edge of damp baby flannels when his sister was still in diapers, mixed in with sweet pudding bubbling on the hearth; or, in good times, roasting birds—usually sparrows, robins, or pigeons. Not so nice-smelling was the ever-present jug of milk souring for cheese. Sanitation of several slop jars which were dumped daily into two kegs in the cellar, along with other offal. Once a week (in theory) the kegs were set next to the sewer ditch which ran along the middle of the street for pickup by the city slop wagons.

Water was hauled in pails by his mother from a public fountain several long streets away, where the heavy washing-up of kitchen utensils was also done. Laundry was carried weekly to a larger fountain even farther away. The lighting was mostly nonexistent: even the burned gristle-smelling yellow tallow candles were very dear during Shannon's childhood—when all the colonies were sorely pinched for funds. In the day, weather permitting, there was only the open front door and one window—with paper set in the frame—to let in light.

It was in this gloom and clutter that Emmett hid from his grandfather. He sat behind his mother's spinning wheel feeling sorry for himself, wondering what he would do when he had to use the slop jar. If someone had asked why he was frightened, he couldn't have said. His grandfather had never struck him or even chastised his behavior aloud. If Emmett was too noisy, or doing something he shouldn't, the old man would only fix him with that furrowed-brow stare of disapproval. Emmett's heart would stop, as would his misbehavior.

He ducked his head quickly when he heard the heavy scrape of the old man's chair. Footsteps. Then his hand was taken and he was being led to the hearth, where a small stool was drawn up near his grandfather's chair. He was seated. Emmett was too afraid to move as he heard other sounds of the old man bustling about, but when the great chair creaked again under his grandfather's weight he dared a peek. His grandfather was toasting two slices of bread over the fire. Could one of them be for Emmett? When the toast was done, the old man placed them on a plate. He dipped out chicken fat with a ladle and smeared it on the toast. Emmett's mouth watered. Then he saw his grandfather pick up a stone jug of milk—warming by the fire—and pour out a single cupful. Silently the old man passed the plate and the cup to him. Emmett took them, bit into the toast and washed down the salty goodstufT with a milk.

He looked up at his grandfather. The old man nodded at him and then took a sip from his jug. "Are ya at ease, young Emmett?" the old man asked. Emmett didn't know what to say, so he just bobbed his head. "That's nice," the old man said. And went back to staring into the fire. Then the old man began to speak. He didn't look at Emmett but into the fire and Emmett wasn't sure who his grandfather was addressing. So he just listened.

The old man seemed to be talking about fighting and soldiers and things, so it promised adventure. But Emmett couldn't make out who was fighting whom and exactly what soldiers were involved, or even when it all happened. Sometimes the old man shifted from fighting soldiers to escaping soldiers. It didn't matter. It was all very exciting. Especially some of the bits about escaping. There was a long, hungry trek home, but from where, to where, Emmett couldn't tell. He finally got the nerve to ask a question. He pointed to the fearful spot on the far side of the hearth. "What's there, Grandfather?"

"William's men," he answered, flat. "Don't turn your back on them, young Emmett," he warned. "Not ever."

Allan Cole & Chris Bunch

"I won't, Grandfather," Emmett promised. And he meant it. Whatever Williamsmen was, if he met up with it, he'd keep close watch just like his grandfather.

"Another thing," his grandfather went on, "if they get through the line after ya, don't wave your pike about like some lad chasing lambs from the gorse. Get the butt set good, and take your man low. In the belly, if you can. When you get him to earth, give your pike a full twist before you wrench it free."

"Yes, Grandfather," Shannon said, frowning in concentration as he gave his imaginary pike a good full twist and then pulled. "Even if you believe in your heart the man can be nothing else but dead, still keep your eye on him. He may be only taking a small rest from the fighting. Or, worse, playacting. Then, whilst your back is turned ..." The old man gingerly touched his side in painful memory. Emmett had seen his grandfather shirtless many times when he washed up. Even in his twilight, his grandfather was built like a cooper. Although not tall, he had arms and legs that seemed the size of a ship's mast. His chest was the breadth of a hogshead of nails. But on his left side, below the rib-cage, was the large maw of an old wound. Still angry red after all these years.

His grandfather fell silent, and Emmett finished his small meal. As soon as he was done, his grandfather took up his plate and cup, rinsed them clean and put them away. He sat down and didn't speak until Emmett's mother came home. From then on Emmett eagerly awaited Market Day. He never made the mistake again of eating so quickly, because as soon as he was done, his grandfather would repeat the ritual. Cleaning up, followed by silence.

There were more stories about fighting and fleeing in a place called "Ourland." And the Williamsmen wasn't a thing, but the soldiers of some king. The Kingsmen. Two rivers were mentioned over and over again: the Boyne and . . . the Shannon? Had the king's soldiers stolen a river from his grandfather? Emmett burned with hatred for the king and his thieving minions. After the fighting and the final escape across the ocean, there was a woman. His grandfather's voice was edged with aching years of mourning when he spoke of her. Her name was Mary. She was Emmett's grandmother. She'd died a long time ago. The old man had never touched another woman since.

"My mother? She was a saint," Emmett's father had said when asked. "She had a laugh like the church bells. And smart! She taught your grandfather to read. And she could do sums as well."

"What happened to her?" Emmett asked.

"She died giving birth to your father," Emmett's mother said. "Thank the Lord he was the only child they bred. For with no woman in the house—" She broke off, concerned that anything else she said would be taken as criticism of her father-in-law. Although he was a puzzlement to her and she was wary of his moods, she clearly liked and admired the old man.

About a year after the Market-Day stories began, Shannon's mother decided it was time for him to learn to read. The only book the family owned was forbidden. It was the Catholic prayer book, Garden of the Soul, and besides being illegal, if lost or damaged it would be impossible to replace. Shannon's mother kept it hidden beneath the linen. Every evening she used to read aloud to the family. So Shannon found it strange when she pulled it out one morning and sat him in her lap. She tried to coax him into memorizing some of the squiggles on the page. Emmett became fitful and squirmed. She held him tighter and Emmett fidgeted and whined to be let down to play.

"Young Emmett!" It was his grandfather's voice. For the first time he was speaking sharply. Emmett turned to see the old man glowering at him. He motioned for the boy to come to his side. His mother set him free. Reluctantly Emmett dragged his feet over to his grandfather's chair. The old man placed a heavy hand on his shoulder. "Listen close to me, lad," his grandfather said. "You must learn to read. From me

Allan Cole & Chris Bunch

forward, every Shannon reads, do you understand? Otherwise
we are nothing more than teagues, or animals, and you will
have no rights before the Kingsmen. And if you do not read,
young Emmett, then do not breed." His grandfather turned
back to his fire and his jug.

Shannon shrank to the safety of his mother's lap and put
up with the boredom of the squiggles. The next Market Day
the ritual changed. As soon as the snack was ready and the
little stool dragged up and Emmett perched upon it,
Shannon's grandfather pulled out the dreaded book.

"Read to me, young Emmett," he commanded.

Emmett hesitated, not knowing what to do. This was
ridiculous. He couldn't read! He was only a child! This was
the height of unfairness. His grandfather pressed the book at
him again. "Read," he said, "or there will be no tales of
soldiers."

Emmett opened the book and haltingly began to read.
From then on the reading became part of the ritual. Nearly a
year later, when his grandfather fell very ill, Shannon had
mastered the book, and his mother was saving money to buy
a primer.

At his graveside, Shannon learned his grandfather's
name.

It was Brian.

* * * *

Shannon bleared awake in darkness and cold. The fire
had died and the storm was raging so fiercely he couldn't tell
if it was day or night. His flesh was still feverish, and he
shivered with the sudden chill that had awakened him. His
head throbbed and every joint in his body ached with the
flux. He got the fire going with his now meager supply of
fuel and prepared himself another dose of bark and vinegar
tea. Despite his illness, he was so ravenous he wolfed down
the greasy, salt beef cold. He eased the soreness in his throat
with cider. Emmett recorked the bottle and huddled in his
blankets against the chill. He stared out into the storm,
waiting for the fire's feeble warmth to bring relief.

* * * *

Farrell Shannon looked at life through the rosy glow of
an only child who had never known want—despite the
endless series of disasters that struck Boston throughout his
life. No matter how bad the times, Emmett's father always
managed to struggle along. Farrell Shannon always believed
that any day now his ship would come in. For such a thing to
ever happen would be magical in the extreme—since the man
never had enough money for a seabag, let alone a cargo. No
matter, it was the idea of the ship that seized Farrell's mind
At any moment God would shower him with riches, that was
all. It would take no real effort on his part. It was this vision
that kept the family at the edge of poverty, for he would
spend his last penny on a whim, and trust to Providence.
Unfortunately, when the old man died, so did Providence.

He sold the shack and found new quarters off Back
Street near the Mill Pond. It was still a one-room shack, but
far larger: two windows, better garden soil, and in the winter
a clear view of the mills surrounding the pond. In the spring
and summer, however, the pond became ripe with filth and
mosquitoes.

Emmett stayed away from home longer and longer
during these months. The real attraction was that Emmett was
a quick student of the street. With his muscular build and
quick feet, he was adopted into the young gangs of
apprentices and indentured lads who infested the waterfront
between Clarke's Ship Yard and the Long Wharf. They
preyed on the booziest and nastiest leather aprons, or press
gang members who strayed from the pack. But the injuries
were never more than bruises, the larceny always petty, and
the targets so universally disliked there was never any
retaliation from the city elders. Besides, there were far
greater threats to the peace than a few mischievous boys. For
every man laboring on the docks, there were six more with
aching bellies and slim hope of work. These were the
teagues, usually Irish, always willing to make up a mob.

Allan Cole & Chris Bunch

Emmett thrived in this atmosphere. Each passing week made him better with his fists, quicker on his feet, and faster with his brain. Soon he was able to smooth-talk his way in or out of any situation. His youth actually increased his status with the gang, and his share of the spoils grew accordingly. Although he didn't realize it, there just weren't that many children his age. They were either nearly toddlers, or four or five years older.

Emmett's reign as a miniature terror ended five months before his father's death. It was on November 5—Guy Fawkes Day in England, but Pope's Day in Boston. The celebration to commemorate the thwarting of the Catholic "conspiracy" in 1685 was a particular favorite of the Boston poor, since on this day the world was turned upside down. It was the Colonial version of Fool's Day, where villains donned the rags of nobility, and the upper classes were mocked without fear of reprisal. The day was marked by serious drinking, brawls, fireworks, and a big parade, with the leaders of the mob bearing an effigy of the Pope—to be burned amid wild cheers and brawls on the main square.

Emmett had always been too young to participate before, but this year he not only joined the parade with his gang friends, but found himself being pushed to the front. "So there I was in all my youthful glory," he told his wife Sarah many years later. "Drunk as a rat that fell into the punch and screaming for the Devil himself to speed the journey of all Papists to hell. How was I to know I was a Papist myself?

"My mother, bless her soul, raised us to be good Christians, but when we were young, she didn't say exactly what kind of Christian she had in mind. We did not attend church, but this was not strange to our neighbors. Neither did most of them. But then, they did not belong to an outlawed faith, so what did they have to fear?

"The parade was making its jolly way to the fireworks at Long Wharf, and as we turned the corner at Fish Street, I saw my mother. But not before she spied me. I don't know why I knew what I was doing was a sin—besides the drunkenness, I mean—but I knew it soon as I saw her face. It was too late to hide, and where do you run when it's your mother seeking you? Eventually, you have to go home. In my family, if it was my mother you angered, the longer you delayed the punishment, the worse it was.

I shook off my friends and stepped out of the crowd. I stood there and waited for her to come. But she didn't. She merely stared at me with that hurt on her face that made a son wish he were for the boiling oil for the pain he had caused the woman who had borne him. Finally, I burst into tears. I crawled to her in my shame. It was like it was only the two of us in the world, and not the streets with its thousands.

"She did not say a word, but turned for home. I followed her, and thought she looked so small, with her shoulders down and her walk so brisk her skirts set up a stiff breeze.

"When we returned home, she got out the book and sat in her chair and began to read the prayers to herself. I sat in the corner and watched, not daring to speak. My father and sister ate and went to bed. But she prayed all night and I sat up with her until daybreak. Finally, when she had calmed herself—or found whatever answers she was seeking in the book—she called me to her side. She explained in a gentle voice that we were Catholics. That the Pope was our Holy Father, and that we were the keepers of the True Faith—in hiding like the poor martyrs that the Romans fed to the lions.

"I often think of that morning. Not for the reason that she showed me the Path. Because after thirty years in this life, I have little faith in the next. But because that is how I remember her. Her face so solemn, her golden curls under her dust cap, her voice like a song as she spoke. Ah, forgive me. I'll be weeping Irish tears next. It must be my father speaking in me."

Emmett stayed closer to home after that. He probably wouldn't have had much choice anyway. The times had worsened and the shipyards lay empty and prices and taxes began to spiral. Farrell Shannon said Boston was stricken with the "galloping consumption," but he didn't say it with the usual booming laugh at his own joke. He was worried and was spending less time at the tavern with his chums and more time looking for work.

There was little point in the search, for the taxes were driving the leather aprons out by the droves, and soon the streets where the tanners, blacksmiths, coopers, bakers, and gunsmiths worked fell silent. Only Anne Shannon's constantly spinning wheel and chuffing broadloom kept the family from starvation. In one of those strange quirks of business, the foreign trade created a boom in linen, while the rest of the city's trades went begging.

Disaster heaped upon disaster in January when the smallpox came. It chewed through the town like a rodent kept from the grain by soft wood. The General Court fled to Cambridge in March. By May refugees were flooding outlying towns. The Shannon family was not among them. They did not have the means to flee.

Farrell Shannon died in April. But not of the pox. With the spring came the foul odor of the Mill Pond and the swarms of insect torment. He died of malarial fever. "It's a wonder he didn't kill us all, bringing us to that house," Emmett recalled. "The air was so putrid, it had to be diseased. My mother made us all wear flannel masks dipped in vinegar about our faces. She put tarred rope all over. Spent precious pennies buying sweet stuff to burn. It was that which saved us, I'm sure. Except for my father, none of us got the fever. But I don't know what spared us from the pox. It must have been one of those miracles my mother was always talking about.

"Although if there is a greater miracle for fever than Jesuits' Bark, I'd be greatly surprised."

* * * *

During a break in the storm, he crawled out of the cave to replenish his fuel. He was dizzy and disoriented and had to stop twice to spew up his guts. Although he had only stumbled twenty or thirty yards in his search, he nearly lost his way on the return. Shannon made more food and forced it down. After it seemed that it would stay in place, he built a triple dose of his bark remedy. He fell into a deep sleep and only groaned slightly when the wind returned in full force.

* * * *

At thirteen Emmett Shannon was indentured to a Scots-Irish carpenter and put into the sawpit. For two years he stood at the bottom of the pit and endured a constant shower of choking sawdust as a series of luckier boys balanced on the top and worked the other end of the saw. For a year and a half he pleaded to his master for promotion— or at the very least, relief—but the man just laughed or growled, depending on his mood. Then he beat Emmett. He always seemed to be in the mood for that. For the next six months, Emmett brooded and waited for his chance. Sometimes he thought his only hope was murder. Eventually he realized there was no hope and he would serve the full seven years of his contract at the bottom of the pit—if his lungs permitted him to live that long. The reason—and Shannon became positive of this—was the carpenter had found religion during the Great Awakening and suspected Emmett of being Catholic. This put him on the level just below a slave, for a slave at least had value, since he would never be free.

Anne Shannon had no choice in her son's indenture. For the poor of Boston the years after Farrell's death became bleaker. A group of linen traders formed an association to aid the poor. This consisted of forcing widows into workhouses—where they saw their wages devoured by inflated costs for their keep—to produce linen for the ever-richening foreign market. It also meant the forced indenture of their children. But Anne, like others among Boston's many hundreds of widows, was a fiercely stubborn woman. She refused to leave her home—it belonged to her, didn't it? Instead, she kept plying her wheel and loom—kept from the workhouse because of the city's greed for her craft.

Emmett's sister Ruth was safe for a while. It could be argued she was too young to be taken from her mother. But there were no excuses for Emmett. At thirteen his chest was

Allan Cole & Chris Bunch

already bursting the seams of his shirt, and his biceps were quickly catching up. He was for hard labor. Anne begged for time. She argued he could read and do sums as well as any son of the rich—which was true, thanks to his grandfather's insistence—and that she could find him a better position than that of bale carrier.

She came home glowing with excitement. She'd secured him a promise of indenture to a carpenter. For a moment a bit of her husband's rosy misview crept in. This would be an enormous step upward for the Shannon family. After seven years of indenture, Emmett could boast of having the full skills of a carpenter! A leather apron for the Shannons! Poverty would be forever swept behind them. With a skilled male in the family, they could buy the nicest of homes, plenty of food, a good marriage for Ruth, and perhaps—if the future was kind—Emmett might someday join the ranks of the city fathers.

Instead he went into the pit. The only skill he learned was a method of breathing that kept his lungs partly clear. He slept in the tool shed and was fed the same scraps the carpenter's wife fed to their pig. Although he lived just half a mile from his mother's home, he rarely saw his family. During all that time, Shannon never whispered a word of his fate to his mother. She had enough troubles.

On Easter Sunday, near the end of his second year, Emmett spent the day with his family. A half a dozen other Catholics dared the law to crowd into the room for a rare service. It consisted of a simple reading from the Garden of the Soul, performed by Emmett's mother since everyone agreed she by far had the best voice and delivery, and then a few prayers. There was no mass, because there was no priest. Shannon had never met one, and among the others, only his mother had attended a service conducted by a priest. That man was an itinerant seller of notions and remedies and a barely literate transport from Ireland. Just the same, Anne Shannon said, it gave her comfort to receive the Host for the one and only time in her life. For the most part, Catholics had to be satisfied with "Hearing The Mass In Spirit." The group quietly discussed this and other matters, and then furtively left for their own homes shortly after dark.

"I don't know how she guessed it," Shannon told his wife, "but as soon as they left, she began pressing me, and finally my tongue was wagging and I was all but sobbing as I told her of my mistreatment. My mother told me to run. But how could I abandon her and Ruth? I would be shamed for the rest of my life. Then she told me the news she was holding back.

"She had lost her final appeal to the merchants' association. The two of them were for the workhouse. 'Then we all must run,' I cried! But she said it was no use. With them to burden me, they would soon catch up to us and bring us back. The penalty would be seven more years of indenture. 'Then I shall stay,' I said. But she told me I would be a fool. She made me promise to be careful. To be patient despite my age. And only to bolt when there was little chance of capture. After I promised, we prayed together—my mother, Ruth, and I. Then I returned to my master. It was the last time I was ever to see her."

"Three weeks later Shannon got his chance. His master was drunk, and Emmett was escorting him home from a tavern, trying to dodge his blows and keep the man upright at the same time. They were turning the corner at Ann Street— an appropriate name for what happened next— when they encountered a Royal Navy press gang, and from the glowering look on the sergeant's face, they had spent futile hours trying to snare a few men for a crew. Shannon's mind leapt to a memory of the taunts he used to yell during his days with the gang. He screamed an obscenity involving the king. The sergeant stared at him, in awe at his daring.

Shannon gave his master a hard shove. "Run!" he shouted. "They're on us!" Shannon grew wings on his feet and flew down the street. An enormous freight wagon loomed up. He rolled under it. The heavy wheels barely cleared him, and he was on his feet and ducking into an alley.

Allan Cole & Chris Bunch

Only then did he stop to peer around the corner. The sergeant had his master by the throat and was belaboring him about the head and shoulders. But no one was looking for him. A few minutes later, Emmett saw them hustling the carpenter away. He guessed it would take several days for his master to sort things out. Perhaps even a little longer, considering how foul the obscenities he had shouted.

By dawn the next day Shannon had a full pack of stolen food and necessaries and was nearly twelve miles from Boston. The roads were full of widows and their children—refugees from the frontier wars—fleeing from the poverty of the wilderness to the poverty of the city. So no one noticed a teenage boy trodding in the opposite direction. Shannon wanted to warn them they would find nothing but heartlessness and a swift warning out from the Boston merchants. But he kept his peace.

Years later his sister told him it took two weeks for his master to be released. By then Emmett was earning a few pennies chopping wood at a small frontier farm some miles east of Albany.

CHAPTER FOUR

AFTER THE SAWPITS of Boston, Shannon wanted no man as his master. He spent the next three years wandering the New York frontier, living by his wits and strong back. He traveled from village to farm to town, always trying to skirt the tides of "George's War"—another of the seemingly never-ending struggles against the French and their Indian allies. He specialized in the dirty, hard-labor jobs—putting in a month or two at a mill, doing scut work at a blacksmith shop, helping farmers clear new land or getting in the harvest.

During this time, Emmett Shannon never appeared on a town's official rolls, usually finding bed and board at his place of work, or living in the squalor of the squatters' camps that ringed any well-off farming village. He learned no skills of great value, preferring the freedom of moving on whenever he chose, to laboring in the lower ranks of some leather apron's trade. The free life he enjoyed was easy to maintain during these years because the toll of the Indian wars made male labor of any type exceedingly scarce; so scarce, he was constantly offered opportunities to stay on in some village and make a life.

"I may have been young and a fool," Shannon later told Sarah, "but I wasn't that great a fool. I saw how others like me were treated. When you arrived in a town you were greeted with great enthusiasm at the tavern. Everyone cozying up to you for your services. But if a man was stupid enough to remain and take their damned redemption contract, it was short rations and hard labor next, with a stick across the shoulders to keep you quick.

"I never met a traveling man who was allowed to join the village circle. No money, no land, no vote. If you came in poor, you would remain poor. So I was always treated well. What else could they do? One harsh word and I was gone down the road to the next man who needed me."

A few years short of his majority, a different kind of opportunity knocked. In return for the promise of land— rich, New York border land—he was recruited by a ranger company to fight the Frenchies and their Indian allies. It proved to be a mistake.

It was the offer of real land that clouded his view. With land, he would instantly become a man to be reckoned with. The land would enfranchise him, give him a say in matters. He would be the first Shannon who could stand tall in any circle. His advice would be sought, his opinion valued. More importantly, he would be able to free his mother and sister from the poverty of Boston. Not that the few letters he received from his mother were complaining; she was the sort who took on any burden and tried to put a good face on it. Emmett realized the only hope his little family had for a future rested on him. The term of enlistment was for three years.

"I was so green that it is a wonder I managed to survive the first months, much less live out my term of contract," Shannon said. "A religious man would say it was a miracle. But if the truth be known, it was because I was a gifted murderer. 1 learned quickly, made few errors—and those I did make, I was lucky enough to escape and wise enough not to repeat."

He also discovered he had a minor talent in medicine. "It was fright that quickened my wits," Shannon said to his wife. "After a fight, with the wounded all around groaning and praying for death or mercy, the doctors would walk through the field with nothing but a lancet. They'd bleed you on the spot, if you let them. If you survived that and made it to the tent, they'd want to dose with the ten-and-ten. This was a purgative. For horses. They would do this every three hours, followed by massive bleeding each time. It was the rare man who survived that.

"In a battle, chances are only two men will fall if a hundred charge. In a doctor's hands, the number will be twenty-five out of a hundred. What was left of us, the plagues got. That's how most of us died: bled by the doctor, starved by the quartermaster, or fried by the fever."

Emmett developed his own theories and kit bag of medicines—relying on proven herbs, quantities of healthy foods—which meant no purging or bleeding—backed up by burning pure-smelling things to drive away the little animals of disease that lived in foul air, or, as a last resort, trapping them on tarred rope.

The treaties of peace were signed, violated, and signed again before his enlistment was finally up. Shannon presented himself to a British lieutenant for his wages and the document that deeded him the promised land. The man slowly counted out the shillings he was owed. Then he stopped. Next, instead of the deed, the lieutenant slid over a brimming cup of rum.

"I'll not be wanting that, thank you just the same," Shannon said. "I'll have my promise, redeemed, if you please."

The officer laughed. He pushed over a slender sack that chinked with coin. "I'm buying you out," the lieutenant said. "Haven't you been told? Ah, but you're a ranger. They're always the last to get the word. You don't want land, son. It would be worthless in your hands. Besides, the plot is small and poor."

"Then why would you be buying it, sir?" Shannon asked the obvious.

The British officer's face turned bloodred with anger at being questioned. Through stiff lips and bristling moustache he gave Shannon the ultimatum: sell out now, or there would be nothing at all for him tomorrow. That the man lived beyond the next few seconds was only because Emmett had learned to keep his temper under control during these last years.

"What could I do?" he asked Sarah. "He and the other king's men made it plain: sign over the land or get the back of their hand. It should have been no great marvel to me," Shannon said. "During those three years of war, I kept on hearing my grandfather's voice warning me—'Never turn your back on the king's men.' And here I was fighting for the king's men. Ah, well, in some things the Shannons are slow to learn."

What upset him far more than the cheating was the response to the letter he'd written his mother and sister in anticipation of his newfound status as a landowner. It was the first letter he had been able to write in over two years. The letter said he would be sending for them as soon as he mustered out. It would be hard work at first, he told them, but after that they would never agonize over the price of bread or firewood again.

A week following the incident with the lieutenant, while he worried over how he would break the sad news to his family, Emmett got a tragic reprieve. It was a letter from Ruth. His mother had died a few months before in the smallpox epidemic that swept Boston that year.

Finally, Ruth said she wouldn't be joining him, either, but thanks for the kind offer. She had married. From the description of the man—reading between the glowing adjectives of praise—he sounded exactly like their father. His name was Isaac Conners.

Once again the Ship of the Shannons had foundered.

* * * *

Shannon woke, drenched in sweat and ravenous. His fever had broken. The storm roared on outside the cave. He stumbled out for more firewood, cooked and ate. He built up the fire, then sleep smashed down on him. He was out for nearly twenty-four hours.

* * * *

The first time Emmett saw Cherry Valley, he did not notice the town's small jealousies. He was on a scouting expedition to the springs well past the town. It was during George's War, in early summer, and his party sat under the trees at a small tavern on the edge of town. He thought he had never seen such a pleasant little community—in the distance he could see smoke rising from the chimney of a farmhouse and smell the smells of something delicious cooking for dinner. The traffic past the tavern was unhurried, and everyone was smiling and well-fed. The innkeeper even stood Shannon's group a round, and his wife packed them a double brace of cold bird and a meat pie for the trail.

Later he often thought of Cherry Valley as a hazy ideal. He envisioned himself being part of a town like that once he had his farm. Even after the British lieutenant robbed him of the dreams of landed respectability, Shannon had kept the brief hours in Cherry Valley safe from the cynical probing of his mind.

Emmett returned to wandering after his mustering out. He spent six years traveling the roads of New York, but this time as a trader, tinkerer, and apothecary. No longer did he earn his bread with hard labor, but depended on charm and the voluminous knapsack on his back. The frontier was becoming more self-reliant, and the cities of the East were buying more than they were selling. Still, frontier life was isolated. The settlers sometimes wondered if they were missing something living far from the coast in these empty lands.

Emmett specialized in creating a small need and then fulfilling it. With a lonely farm wife he might talk about city life, mentioning perhaps some elegant woman he had seen outside a fine shop and the bit of lace that added just the perfect touch to her costume. Then he would recall he had the very same piece of lace in his pack, and he would draw it out slowly, temptingly. The farm wife could never have the costume, but she could have the lace. She could keep it in her drawer with some cloves or some spiced-apple cachet, and when a friend visited, she could slip it from its nesting place—slowly and temptingly like Shannon—and paint that picture of the elegant city woman for her friend. It was a way of dressing up her dreams.

At a tavern Emmett might perform the same magic with a gleaming pocketknife or a pouch of brandy-cured tobacco from some exotic Virginia plantation home. With such a

Allan Cole & Chris Bunch

knife a man could imagine whittling the most wondrous toys—with moving, wooden-clockwork parts for his children—toys that Shannon remembered seeing at a fair. With the tobacco he could light up and inhale smoky reflections of a man at leisure in his library.

It was his herbs and medicines that really opened people up to Emmett. You could tell when he spoke there was no blarney in these products. He wasn't selling Seneca Oil or miracle cures from the Spanish Lands. People began to look forward to his irregular visits, and they delighted in feeding him, putting him up in their softest beds and filling him in on the major details of their lives since they last had met. In the winter months he might take a contract as a scout, traveling from town to town and fort to fort. He would stay at a prosperous farm, drink hot cider and let himself be enticed into the barn by the pretty girls.

During those days, if you asked, his customers would tell you Emmett Shannon was a man who was a marvel with a story. He always had the freshest, most interesting news and gossip—or at least he told it so it seemed that way. But if they reflected, they would realize that in the time he spent with them, they'd done most of the talking. Emmett was a man who could listen, and give a person the impression that he was as great a chatterbox as they. Finally they would tell you Emmett was a man who seemed to have no aim, no goal but the next lovely stop in the road.

He came to Cherry Valley again. It was in the summer of the new decade. The tavern had been replaced by one much larger. The traffic in and out was constant, the folk more prosperous. There was a town center now, complete with a new church and school. Shannon noticed all this idly: he had no intention of staying more than that night. His real business was in another farm community well beyond Cherry Valley.

The next morning he strolled out of town, leading his packhorse. He paused to lean on a fence at the western edge of town. It protected a vast, rich meadow. Just beyond was a gate opening on a path that wound through weeping willows and cherry trees. The path ended at a sprawling farmhouse. There was a drumming of hooves on rich grass just to his right.

Shannon turned to see a vision. A girl was riding bareback on a fat brown horse. Her skirts were at her knees and she kicked the horse's flanks with naked heels. Her face and arms and legs were milk-white, and she had long black hair that streamed out behind her in the wind. It was like the myth of Molly Brant come true. In local legend this was how Sir William Johnson—founder of the entire Mohawk Valley some forty years before—had met the Indian princess who was to become his wife. Shannon's girl on horseback was no myth and no Indian. She was Scots-Irish and she had a sprinkle of freckles on her nose. Her name was Sarah Hopkins. In three months she would be his wife.

First he had to get past her father. Sarah was an only child whose father had never remarried after her mother's premature death. Unlike Shannon's grandfather, there was nothing tragic/romantic about Alex Hopkins's decision to live the permanent life as a widower. People said he was as tight-fisted as a Dutchman. Emmett approached his courtship of Sarah Hopkins like a man waging border warfare. The moment he saw her thundering past him on the horse, the picture blended with his long-ago dream of Cherry Valley. This would be his wife. For the first time he set a goal and went after it with a will.

The town elders were happy to hire him as a scout. There were Indian fears about—all nonsense—mainly caused by the area's steady encroachment on farms already owned by Indian families who had put aside their tomahawks and breechclouts for trousers and the plow. Shannon sold off all his goods—bargaining shrewdly to amass capital—and laid siege to Mr. Hopkins. At the tavern, he always bought the man a round or three. Hopkins favored a bit of opium in his ale, but was too stingy to pay the extra penny, so Shannon made sure the drink was spiked the way he liked it. He listened intently to the man's tales—mostly complaints of

Allan Cole & Chris Bunch

how his neighbors were always trying to cheat him—and always frowned or smiled at the right point.

Eventually Hopkins invited him home to share a meal—bribed with a promised bottle of good brandy. Sarah helped serve the dinner, and politely sat on a stool by her father's chair as the man droned on and on. By the time the bottle was three-fourths gone, the fire was dwindling and the room was growing cold. No matter: Hopkins was drunk and snoring, his feet dangling close to the grate.

Sarah had kept her eyes modestly low during all this, but she finally raised them in protest when her father let out a loud snore. She found Emmett staring at her, smiling. His eyes were clear, his hand steady as he reached over and let his hand rest on her arm. She glanced worriedly at his glass and saw with a start that it was full—realizing the drinking that night had been done only by her father.

"I want you for my wife, Sarah Hopkins," was all Shannon said. Then he rose and left the house.

Sarah confessed later she had sat by the cold fire long after he left, wondering who this Emmett Shannon could be. "I want you for my wife," indeed. The man must be mad. And the next time she saw him she would tell him so. Give him a very large piece of her mind. She remembered his dazzling smile, the clear blue eyes, and the place on her arm where he had touched her suddenly grew warm.

Everyone in Cherry Valley said it was a grand wedding—considering it was the daughter of Alex Hopkins who was wed. It should have been: Shannon paid for it himself.

On their wedding night she came to him in a plain white cotton shift, her black hair tumbling to her waist. There was no nervousness or hesitancy: she gave a long, deep sigh as she came into his arms, and it was as if they had been lovers forever.

Emmett had a dream in his hands. It was a dream with soft arms and thighs and a full, throaty chuckle. It was probably for this reason that his mind was clouded when

Alex Hopkins made his offer of a large, uncleared parcel of land that lay at the edge of his farm. It would be his and Sarah's, in return for Shannon's labors on the Hopkins farm proper. Emmett pushed aside his memories of redemption farmers who toiled for entire generations and died with arthritic limbs and empty bellies.

It was also for Sarah's sake he did his best to ignore Hopkins's loudly stated views that everything that was English was good and noble and everything American a poor, degenerate shadow. His best usually came in a poor second. They had heated, almost violent arguments. Sarah would pull them apart and take Emmett home to their split-board shack, and soothe him with her voice and soft fingers stroking his temples.

Shannon's marriage and monetary alliance with Hopkins put him at odds with the town. Tavern debates over the shackles the motherland was throwing over her stepchildren would be silenced when Emmett entered. Suspicious eyes followed as he took his drink to a solitary corner. Emmett couldn't agree with them more. He knew firsthand the arrogant British opinion that her colonies were some kind of an obscene child, born out of wedlock in a cold bed with not even an old gramer to tend it. Never mind that thousands of Colonials had died taking up arms against the French in defense of the mother country. Somebody had to pay the enormous cost of George's War, and the king was determined it wouldn't be him.

Emmett witnessed deprivation spreading across the land as the colonies tried to struggle out of the pit that follows any great war. Prices and taxes climbed the mountain hand-in-hand. Even on the frontier the roads were swarming with refugees from the poverty of the cities, desperate to find some kind of life. Cherry Valley accepted some—in bondage. The rest were warned out before the alms laws forced them to assume the burden of their support. The refugees moved on, and few knew or cared what happened to them.

pg. 57

Allan Cole & Chris Bunch

Church also kept Shannon apart. Although he was not a religious man, he remained stubbornly Catholic, and any time he was even tempted to soothe his neighbors into accepting him by attending services, he would remember his mother's stricken face when she saw him marching at the head of the Pope's Day parade.

Sarah, like most of the people of Cherry Valley, was only semiliterate. But she quickly warmed to the idea of books and the lives they revealed when Emmett began reading to her aloud. They would sit by the fire at nights and Shannon would open whatever volume he managed to obtain and he would weave tales for her with his rich voice— which was very much like his mother's, but with a deeper timbre. The stories would always end in tender lovemaking: the kind people remember for the rest of their lives. She promised when their children were born, they would learn to read as well as their father. She even suggested Shannon find a copy of Garden of the Soul. Their children would be introduced to both their religions. When they were older, they could make up their own minds.

Their first child was born in the autumn of 1772. It was a boy. They named him Brian. The pregnancy was easy, and Sarah said the birth pains were nothing at all and she was anxious to have another—a companion for Brian—as soon as possible. Shannon made her wait another year.

The work on the two farms was some of the hardest he had ever done in his life—rivaling even the sawpits. His own parcel was like Hopkins himself—stubborn and resisting. It would take weeks to clear a few yards, and he never knew so many rocks could hide in dirt. Emmett found that he was a very poor farmer. He never had time to work his own land. Hopkins always kept him doing his own bidding to pay off Shannon's debt. The man kept a careful accounting of Emmett's days and subtracted them from his books. But the amount owed never dwindled.

Things didn't get easier after Brian was born. Emmett got a desperate letter from his sister Ruth. As Shannon suspected, the man she married proved to be a wastrel. Isaac Conners had gone off "a-pirating," abandoning her with two children. He hadn't been heard from since. Despite this, Ruth still loved the man and was reluctant to leave. It took a firm letter to his sister to convince her of the hopelessness of her position.

Emmett added to his shack and brought her to the farm. Although the two women took an instant liking to each other, Ruth was no help to Sarah at all. She was a Boston girl through and through, and shrank from farm squalor.

"At least the air is healthy and clear and we never lack for victuals," Shannon would argue.

His sister would sniff the breeze suspiciously. "If you call this air," she would say dismissively. "It seems a little thin to me." Then they would all laugh and Ruth would go back to spoiling whatever task she was performing.

The hardship didn't prey on Emmett. He was too much in love with Sarah, and trusted somehow things would get better—although he worried if this wasn't his father creeping into him.

Their second child came in the spring of 1774. It was another boy, and they both had agreed beforehand that they would name him Farrell. Actually it was Sarah who insisted on this. She wanted to honor his parents. If it had been a girl, they would have named her Anne.

Something went wrong. The midwife came out of the room carrying his son swathed in cloths. Her lips were compressed, her face pinched, and she was shaking her head. "She's dying," the old gramer said. That simple. That flat.

In shock, Emmett stumbled into the room. The bed sheets were red and Sarah lay pale and quiet. Asleep, or. . . ? Shannon sat on the bed and took her limp hand. Suddenly she opened her eyes and looked at him, her eyes wild in fright. She gripped his hand—hard. Then she died without a word.

Her death rocked what little faith Shannon had. If God wanted children, he told his sister, why did He make women suffer so much? And why did He kill them? He had seen women dying in childbirth all of his life, but it had never registered as such a terrible penalty. Midwives' sayings, like "a tooth for every child," came into awful focus. His sister hushed him and said it was just so, that women accepted the burden God had written for them. For her sake Shannon pretended he was comforted.

The next three years went by in a blur. He dragged himself to his labors each day, not even bothering to argue with Hopkins that the poor parcel he was struggling to pay off was all that he would ever own, and that with Sarah's death he lost any call on her father's rich farm.

From the East came wild rumors, fueled equally by hope and pessimism. The king relented. No he didn't. War was imminent. The colonies were content.

Alex Hopkins's was the loudest voice of all. He mocked majority views in Cherry Valley. Without England, America was nothing. The king only demanded what was rightfully his. The people should respect his wishes. They had no right to question. On and on. Shannon saw this was no casual tavern debate. People were tending to their knives and rifles and choosing sides. He feared if his father-in-law went much further, he would rouse a mob that would sack and burn both farms. Shannon could also see people weighing each other's holdings.

If war broke out, he was sure there would be quick excuses to use the law as a thief, or account settler. Alex Hopkins had many people who itched for revenge.

War. And the fever gripped Cherry Valley. Committees were stripped of Loyalists and re-formed by "Patriots." The Committee of Safety would preside over all others. A militia was raised, and there was much parading and marching up and down the village square. Shannon noticed when the marching was over everyone drifted off home or to the inns to get drunk. There was no intent to actually send the militia anywhere. It would be kept in Cherry Valley "to protect the homeland." As far as individual sacrifice, it was to be the war with the Frenchies all over again. Stay safe at home and profit from the struggle of others. So when asked, Emmett refused to join the militia. Some grumbled at this, but after so many years of shedding blood, the Cherry Valley militia was a line of hypocrisy he would not cross.

As for Alex Hopkins, his complaints grew louder. The man was insane, but there was no arguing with him. He boasted of his loyalty to the king, gloated at every Colonial failure, swore that any day now the effort would collapse and the traitors would all pay. He got his mob; sanctioned by the Committee of Safety. The men seized his holdings and his animals for the public good. Some men eyed Shannon's own poor land, but he stood at the fence line, his rifle ready, and they wisely left him alone.

Hopkins managed to flee, and in the luck of the truly insane, he found a warm reward waiting for him in Quebec, where he sat out the troubles in great ease, mocking his former friends in Cherry Valley.

Shannon was left destitute. His own land could not support his family. Before, the gap had always been filled by the food he earned on Hopkins's farm. Now, with his awful skills and impoverished soil, Emmett hadn't a hope.

A recruiter for the Fourth New York Regiment came to Cherry Valley in January of 1777. The bounty for a three-year enlistment would provide a solution for Emmett's family. Plus, he would be able to send his wages home so they would never want. Shannon ignored the whisper of experience in his mind and signed. Besides, when he saw the recruiter, he realized just how angry a man he had become.

He took his rifle and set off to kill the Kingsmen for his grandfather.

After three days the weather broke. Shannon kicked the remains of the fire apart, packed up his goods and set off in the clear, cold air. He felt refreshed and ready, and he set a pace that would gobble up the miles. He was in a hurry to get home.

Allan Cole & Chris Bunch

CHAPTER FIVE

TWO DAYS BEYOND Reading, Emmett lay on his belly, rethinking his strategy. After the storm he'd had two days of cold weather, and then blessed warmth had come. The last of the teamster's beef, then one meal grudgingly provided by a farmer after Emmett lugged water enough to float a frigate, plus an unwatched chicken house on Reading's outskirts, had supplied him so far.

But now was the time for redrawing rations. Across the road and up a rise lay the farm he had planned to use for his victualing as far back as Valley Forge. The problem now, Emmett thought, catching and killing a louse caught by the afternoon sun, was that someone else appeared to have gotten here first. Smoke still curled up from the ruined farmhouse and outbuildings.

Shannon had seen this farm months earlier, when he'd been detailed with seven other men, a sergeant, and a brainless ensign, to forage. The problem was, General Washington was a gentleman. His soldiers didn't know— and wouldn't have given a damn if they had—that everyone from Washington up through the Continental Congress was scared spitless their army might be thought similar to the scoundrels of King George. British soldiers were infamous looters, thieves, gamblers, and drunkards, known for quartering themselves in civilian homes without payment. If this meant the Continental Army would be honest and sober, sleeping in the snow if necessary, so be it. It also meant that any foraging party had to pay—on the spot—for supplies. But payment would be in worthless paper currency, and the British paid in gold. It did not matter to the farmers around Valley Forge that selling anything to the enemy was a court-martial offense. Mostly canny Germans, they knew they could outthink or outhide anything from any army, having generations of experience against the larcenous armies and rulers of their homelands. Why should America be different?

Shannon's foraging party had seen the prosperous farm from a distance and, licking their lips, instantly defined the moment as a belated payday, especially since their cretinous ensign was still back at the last inn. Supposedly he wanted to have his horse reshod. Actually, they knew he'd lingered because there was still rum in the cask, and the keeper's wife seemed interested in talking to him about a personal matter.

It had not gone as simply as they'd thought. The farmer was not only a brawny man with a rifle close at hand, but there were at least ten others—sons, farmhands, and others equally uncooperative. A handful of mastiffs growled in the background. "Nein, nein," the farmer kept saying. "We have no beeves for sale. Spanish fever. And raiders. Terrible. I do not know how me und mein kinder will live out the year."

Shannon thought they could probably live on the accumulated fat around their midsections, but said nothing. Instead, he concentrated on getting within musket-butt range of the nearest farmhand. If the soldiers hadn't been so hungry, thirsty, and angry at seeing another Dutch Clever Fellow in action, they might have found this confrontation in a frozen farmyard funny. But in a few seconds it might be even less funny, as Shannon saw his sergeant's hand close around his sword grip.

Then the ensign clattered up in a drunken babble of orders, cautions, and gentility. Of course the good farmer—Mister van Voteffer—was telling the truth. Of course the soldiers of the Continental Congress would never behave like the rascally Britishers. Of course . . .

Of course the foraging party marched—or rather slunk—back down the hill with nothing. That farm had been a frequent topic of conversation when they returned to Valley Forge. Emmett remembered it very, very well. It had been his intention to scout the farm by day. Somewhere there would be an unguarded steer. And there must be a springhouse about. But the smoke and destruction made him wish he could change his plans. If there had been any food at all in his knapsack, Emmett might have kept moving. But there

Allan Cole & Chris Bunch

was not. Readying his rifle, he moved toward the ruins, using all the cover he could. Not only could the raiders still be in residence at the farm, but Emmett had no desire to see what he expected to find atop the hill. George's War, plus his experiences on the frontiers, had satisfied whatever interest he had in massacre postmortems.

The first body lay on its back outside the farmyard. Shannon ignored it as he waited for any movement around the farm. There was none. He slid up to the body. One of the farmer's strong young men lying dead in mid-shout and blood-soaked mud, a bullet wound in the stomach.

Shannon stepped into the yard. The mastiffs lay dead around it. He looked at two of the bodies, one knifed, the other's skull cloven with a tomahawk. Indians? This far east? Shannon looked farther.

In the center of the yard lay a large, overturned black iron kettle. Spilled out of the kettle were the remains of a stew or soup. And in the stew's remains was a small body. The farm's house cat. Nicely parboiled. It must have been a capital jest. Shannon hoped the animal'd clawed hell out of whoever had flung it into the pot.

Just outside the main house's entrance lay another body. A woman. Shannon choked, his throat dry. She had not died easily. He pulled the ragged shift down over her legs.

The woman had been blond, but there were only fringes of hair around her neck. She'd been scalped. Shannon could not bear to turn the body over and see her face. He found four other bodies around the ruins. Two of them—one woman and one probably long-haired man—had also been scalped.

Shannon started looking for tracks. He found them on the lee side of the hill. A herd of cattle had been moved away from the farmhouse toward the road. He scoured the edge of the cattle prints and found a clear print in the mud, of a shod horse. Recently shod. He followed the tracks down the hill, toward the road. They turned northeast, away from Reading, and in the direction he must travel.

Shannon considered. If the raiders—he thought there had been eight, maybe nine of them—were Indians, they most likely would have taken their spoils and headed west. Probably off the roads. He was starting to figure out who had butchered the farmers, and got confirmation on a careful sweep outside the farmyard. He found a dead bullock, killed with a rifle ball in the forehead. Indians, even if they had firearms, would have cut the animal's throat, not wasting powder or shot. The animal had been gutted and rough-butchered. There was enough meat gone, Shannon estimated, for steaks for about nine men.

The raiders weren't Indians. Indians would have either stayed around the carcass, feasting until there was nothing but bones, or else carried the rest of the meat off with them. They wasted nothing. Only white men gave themselves this luxury.

Shannon shivered—and it was not from the wind or the sudden chill as the sun was obscured by heavy clouds. He knew men such as these. Renegades. Some were pro-English Loyalists, grown on the frontiers among the Indians. They fought as the tribesmen did. Their privilege. And when they were caught, they would die as they'd killed others. But there were far worse monsters on the frontiers. Men who chose the Indian way of war because they loved the torture, the ambush murder and the bloody raiding. Outlaws no side would claim.

In his wanderings, Shannon had met some of them, and counted himself lucky he'd never had anything they wanted. They grouped in small parties or operated by themselves, sometimes with, sometimes without, Indian allies. They were men lost to God and the Devil. Any man caught by them would find eventual death very welcome. And a woman . . . Shannon stopped thinking about that, and about the body in the farmyard, and puzzled over his own problem. The raiders were moving north. Eventually he might encounter them. That might not be a problem—they would have little interest in a tattered traveler. His problem was more immediate. He had only found six bodies. Even allowing for some burnt to

pg. 65

cinders in the fired buildings, there were still live farmers. Farmers who, if they returned to the farm, would see him and draw immediate, obvious, and lethal conclusions.

Emmett thought on. The previous two days—just travel time to Reading—had been warm, and the German farmer would have probably wanted to go to market. The raiders would have waited until the farmers were out of hearing before they moved in.

Shannon blew on a charred beam, and sparks glowed. Assuming the farmers left at first light, the raiders would have waited until . . . noon, maybe, until they attacked. Noon yesterday. Then they . . . took what they wanted, he thought hastily. Spent the night in the farmhouse, and burnt the farm just before dawn as they fled. The farmers, now, would have reached Reading sometime today. They would do their marketing this day or probably tomorrow. Most likely they would stay in town tomorrow night, then return, unless the farmer was unusually parsimonious and unwilling to pay for an inn. In which case they could be returning now.

Emmett, boy, you had better be long down that road and leaving no tracks. Then he realized: that wind and those clouds. Again the weather was breaking. He might have more time than he'd thought. He started scouting to see if the raiders had left some scraps. He scuffed carefully around the house, looking at the ground. A beam groaned and sagged. Emmett burnt his fingers shoving it out of the way. The entrance to the root cellar. Very good. That would give him shelter.

Shannon felt someone's eyes on him. The hell. He did not believe in banshees, either. But he kept his rifle ready as he dragged the bodies to a sagging shed and arranged them as neatly as he knew how. He muttered a prayer when he finished. He found that springhouse. The raiders had smashed almost everything. But he did find a crock of milk, not even soured. The steer's carcass was more than fresh enough. He cut several steaks and started back to his quarters. He thought he could still feel those eyes.

Shannon moved underground. It was quite plush, he decided. More than enough potatoes for his kettle. He bent a twisted iron tire into a broiling rack. The sawdust the potatoes were stored in would make a perfect bed. His fire was built near the entrance, with enough of a draw to keep the smoke from suffocating him. Tomorrow, he thought, he would see if those Jesus-abandoned butchers had left anything for an honest man. He turned to his steak, which was sizzling most appetizingly. He heard the cough from just outside.

In a flurry of sawdust Shannon rolled across the cellar, and had his rifle cocked and aimed at the entrance. The cough came again. An experimental, self-announcing sort of cough. "I hear you," Emmett said. He picked up his knife.

Tattered shoes. Sacking-wrapped legs. Breeches even shabbier than Emmett's own. The ruins of a once-blue uniform coat. Next appeared a pair of hands. Quite empty. Palms up. Shannon scuttled back against the far wall. The man stooped into the cellar. Emmett knew him by his moustaches. Great drooping bedraggled tusks. Behind them hollow eyes and starving cheeks.

At one time the man might have looked quite fearsome, wearing his brass mitre of a cap, bayoneted musket at the charge, part of a deadly blue line. The man was tall, and if well-fed, would be an ox. At the moment all he looked like was one more Hessian deserter. There were thousands of them on the loose in the colonies. "Freund," the man said, attempting a smile.

Shannon did not lower the rifle. Perhaps he was a friend now, since Shannon was the one holding the rifle. But at Washington Heights the Germans had butchered American prisoners. Even their lords the British thought the Hessian legions, led like cattle, were cowardly, dirty peasants. The fact that the Germans held the center of the line at Saratoga and had saved the legendary Black Watch from being obliterated during Howe's attack on the Continental Army did not matter. The British seldom let truth stand in the way of a decent prejudice.

Unlike most Americans, Emmett Shannon didn't actively loathe the German mercenaries. Any more than that neighbor's bull who'd tried to gore him. En masse, under orders, the Hessians were lethal. Shannon had more than one friend who'd dropped with a ball in him in battle, and whose bayonet-spitted body had been recovered later. But he'd also seen what happened when they were broken or when their officers or sergeants were killed. The comparison to cattle was quite apt.

Shannon lowered the rifle, feeling a little disgusted. First there had been the wagon master. Next, being witness to the butchery outside. He was determined he'd return to Cherry Valley as a man, not a murderer. This poor bastard, shivering in fear and cold across from him, had no weapon. Not even a knife to eat with. He was barely more than a boy, Shannon realized. Some poor dumb farmer whose prince had sold him to the British. He eased his rifle's hammer to half cock and set it on the bag of potatoes beside him, still close at hand. Shannon picked up the knife—and the Hessian's eyes gaped in terror and his hands came up once more.

"No, no, you dumb Dutchman," and Shannon, burning his fingers in the process, sawed his steak in half. He dumped the meat on a bit of board, and handed it across. Then it was his turn to gape. Christ, he'd thought he was hungry. The German simply engulfed the steak. Shannon put another steak on his broiler, lifted a potato from the boil and passed it to the Hessian. They ate in silence, no sound but the hiss of the wind outside and the crackle of the fire. Watching each other warily. The German finished and wiped his hands on his coat. "Danke."

Shannon grunted. The German tapped himself on the chest. "Johann. Von Knyphausen."

Nein, my "freund." You are not a von, Emmett thought. A bare-arse peasant just like himself. Then he got it. The von whatever was this German's commander—that Dutch general whose name nobody got right.

"Shannon." Emmett, said, thumping his chest. He no longer belonged to anybody's damned army.

The German tried sign language, pointing at Emmett . . . fingers mimicking walking . . . and then hands together and head rested on them. Shannon nodded. Yes. He was going home. The Hessian gabbled on, gesturing wildly. Shannon got something called an Anspach something or other, and the man kept repeating "heimweh."

Shannon shrugged, not understanding.

They stared at each other.

The German tried again, pointed to Shannon, pointed to himself. Two sets of walking fingers. A questioning look. Like hell, Shannon thought. The German was even more poorly equipped than he was. And Shannon somehow had the idea his sister would not be pleased to be presented with her own pet Dutchman when they reached Cherry Valley. He picked up his knife and casually began stropping it on his moccasin sole, appearing to think about the proposition. Finally he looked up and, trying to put regret on his face, shook his head. The German's face went stony. Then turned into a smile. Another gabble, then, without ceremony, he picked up some sacking, pulled it over himself for a blanket, and lay down.

Shannon waited until the man's breathing became regular, then he banked the fire and got ready for sleep. He considered, and his hand moved out, toward the wall. He found the haft of a broken hoe he'd seen earlier, and, in the blackness, propped the haft across two potato sacks. He lay back, thinking he'd best stay awake for another hour or so. His body decided differently, and Emmett blanked out.

He bolted awake as the hoe slammed into his legs and a body crashed. A muffled curse, and Emmett saw a flash—the bastard must've hidden a knife—as he rolled sideways, hand grabbing the rifle by the barrel and sweeping it out like a scythe. Impact, and a shout of pain. Emmett had his

Allan Cole & Chris Bunch

tomahawk up and slicing into the darkness. Nothing. Breathing, and suddenly a scrabble, as of some huge rat. Moonlight gleamed down the steps, and Emmett saw the bulk of the Hessian scuttle up them. He went after the German.

The storm had broken for a moment, and cold moonlight blazed as Emmett burst out of the cellar. Running, stumbling down the hill, toward the fence, was the Hessian. There was plenty of time. Emmett eased his breathing, brought the rifle to full cock and sighted. The Hessian's back was centered in the vee notch. Emmett held his breath, put slow pressure on the trigger.

He lowered the weapon. His finger came off the trigger. He watched as the Hessian dove over the fence and, staggering, disappeared into the brush. Emmett was panting as if he'd run for miles. He looked up at the sky and nodded. Perhaps now the murder of the wagon master would be a lighter load.

CHAPTER SIX

SHANNON SLEPT NO more that night. He also froze. He knew that Johann the Hessian would never return. In fact, he'd probably freeze to death in the snow. But he hadn't survived thirty-five years by believing what he knew was necessarily what happened. So the fire stayed glowing brightly in the root cellar below, while he huddled in his blankets, gun ready, waiting for dawn.

It came as a gray through the whirling snow. Chilled through, Emmett took a chance and went down into the cellar and built up his fire. He slowly melted snow in his kettle and had a hot drink. More snow was melted, and he dumped chunks of beef and potatoes into the pot for breakfast. Then, one eye on the lowering horizon, waiting for the farmers to return, he searched the ruins.

The two-story main farmhouse had collapsed on itself. All that remained was the wreckage of a few blackened walls. Shannon oriented himself, found the main entrance and walked through, imagining he was in the half-remembered and now mentally reconstructed house. Nothing in the ruined hall. A crunching spill of china in the parlor. Then his first discovery—a large, charred wooden case. He tomahawked the chest open, and a smile grew across his face. He muttered a prayer, a thank-you and a vow never to murder any Germans or anybody else who crossed his trail—unless they deserved it—as he lifted out: underclothing! Heavy trousers! A linen shirt! They smelled of smoke, but there were only a few burn holes marring them. Then a great miracle—a half-caped horseman's overcoat! Why wasn't somebody wearing it? Maybe it was the wrong color or fashion. Maybe he was too fat to fit. Emmett had never lived in a world where any of these was an option, but he assumed every sort of riches on the part of the absent van VotefTer. Emmett searched on, and found a pair of work boots. Praying once more, he doffed his moccasins and tried the boots. They almost fit. Back to the chest, and he found two scarves that would serve as stockings.

The next "room"—or above it—would have been a bedchamber. Burnt, wet feathers. And the ruins of blankets. Ruined for civilization perhaps. But perfectly fine for him. His own lice carriers would stay here. Emmett again oriented himself and strode over beams toward the kitchen, where he found a trove. Under the burnt slab of the huge kitchen table he found not only a broken-stemmed clay churchwarden, but an unsinged pouch, half full of leaf tobacco. He was tempted to stop for a smoke—but the morning was moving on. A baked ball. Shannon broke it apart and scooped flour into his knapsack. Kettles, pots, broken glass, cutlery, and then an un-smashed, corked cruet. He uncorked it and sniffed: vinegar. This was where the farmer had kept his medicines. At that point Emmett went on his hands and knees, sorting inch by inch through the debris. He found what he was hoping for— a small black brick that might have been charcoal. It was not. The resin on the brick's surface, bubbled up by the heat of the flames, smelled most sweet. Opium.

That was enough luck for Emmett. He took dried peas and beans, plus four potatoes from the root cellar. He scrabbled through the ruined smokehouse and found a double handful of now doubly dried beef, forced all this into his bulging knapsack, and went away from the nightmare farm, through the driving snow.

Emmett eventually was forced to shelter on a lee slope, pushing himself under the snow-laden boughs of a tree to its trunk. One blanket made a tent. He didn't dare light a fire— even if he'd been able to find, somewhere, dry wood. But, thinking of his treasures, he gnawed dried beef and a raw potato, and slept rough but content.

He woke to rain, and forced himself to strip raw. He stood for a few icy moments in the downpour, rubbing himself with the last of the Valley Forge soap. Luxuriously, he dressed in the new undergarments and pants of cloth, instead of the crotch-grating canvas. He beat his hunting shirt against a tree, at least terrifying its lice, and tugged it back on. Then the wonderful warmth of that coat, with a blanket over his shoulders. Even wet, the wool was heaven. Shannon shouldered his gear and moved back onto the road, almost content with his lot.

* * * *

His pace quickened the next few days as the weather grew warmer. The continuing, occasional rain was tolerable. Also, he ate well, not from the provisions from the farm, but on fresh beef. The first calf surprised him. Dead beside the trail, its skull cloven by a hatchet.

The renegades.

They were on this road, still ahead of him but moving fast—faster than he could travel on foot. Any animal that slowed would be killed and, if the renegades had a moment, quick-butchered. That provided not only a moving quartermaster for Emmett, but reassurance that as long as he found dead steers, and, as the weather continued above freezing, hoof-prints, he didn't have to worry.

He vaguely hoped the renegades would continue their successful escape until, perhaps, the Hudson. At which point a patrol of regulators would encounter them. It did not take that long. Emmett was moving along quite briskly on a bright, chilly morning, the road paralleling a thawing swamp, when he smelled cow shit.

At first it reminded him of home, then he realized its meaning and went into the brush once more. Cow shit did not stink forever, at least not in this weather. After a time he moved toward the stink.

The head helped him understand what had happened. It leered down, dirty and bearded. A spike had been driven through its forehead, fixing it to a tree trunk. Below that someone had axed bark from the tree and knife-carved: COW BOYS WARND.

Shannon quartered the small clearing beside the road, once again reading tracks. He returned to the nailed head. Odd that he had not found the body that would have gone

Allan Cole & Chris Bunch

with it. Odder still that he had a vague recollection that the face—or at least what remained of it between the spike and the .75 ball that had gone in through the temple—was somewhat familiar.

He dug out the stub of a pipe, crumbled leaf tobacco into it, and sparked the tobacco to life. The hoof- and footprints on the ground, the blood trails, the cow shit, set the scene for him. The renegades had driven their cattle here. Maybe this happened at dawn, after they'd nighted in this place. Or perhaps they were taking a meal. Others had come down the road toward them—from Easton. Militia? Regulators? British or American dragoons? Perhaps a bigger band of thieves? The last was unlikely, because of the warning carved into the tree.

Questions would have been shouted. Rifles would have come up from across saddlebows. One man killed—the man whose skull would bleach on that tree. Other men were shot. Shannon found two, possibly three blood trails. Horse tracks scattered into the swamp.

The renegades had lost the skirmish—else the head would not have been where it was. Whoever had won had gathered the cattle and pushed back the way they came.

Satisfied, Emmett knocked out his pipe and started out once more. On the one hand, he was pleased the renegades had met vengeance and sorry that every one of them was not decorating a tree. But on the other, this meant the band's survivors, if they regrouped, would be leaving almost no trace, without the cattle. They could be moving ahead, or— and Emmett inadvertently glanced behind him—following him.

The dawning spring suddenly meant nothing. Shannon moved onward, rifle at half cock, ready for battle.

CHAPTER SEVEN

A FEW MILES southwest of Bethlehem, Shannon began getting worried. In every direction he looked there were long plumes of chimney smoke. Then he heard the sharp clip-clop of hooves and the creak of carriage springs and he dived off the road and snuggled behind a tree. A sulky came sweeping around the bend. On it was a prosperous-looking young farmer, dressed as if he were going a-courting. The sulky was a flat-bed carriage with an old, overstuffed easy chair attached to it. The farmer sprawled lazily in the chair with his feet up and every once in a while gave a gentle flick of the whip to encourage his fat little mare. Civilization was looming near.

With bodies behind him, murderers who knew where, and another party of spoilers roaming about whose intentions Emmett could only guess at, he decided to give the town a pass. It was not the time or place to get caught out and trust to bluff. He found an old Indian trail that seemed to suit his purposes. Somewhere between Bethlehem and Nazareth he became lost. It didn't worry him. He knew he was in the center of a vague triangle formed by Bethlehem, Easton, and Nazareth. If he bore east, he should hook up with the Delaware again.

He spotted deer sign heading toward the fork of a creek and decided to follow—visions of a venison supper luring him on. He was thinking how good its liver would taste stewed in onions when he heard something heavy, slowly thudding—as if in a wind—wood against wood. But the day was still and clear—some hours yet from the breezes of evening. He slipped forward, and then the trail crossed a narrow, deeply rutted road. He took the road. It became a path that wound through a small, empty field. On the other side were two oddly long and narrow buildings. The sound was coming from the farthest building.

Shannon hesitated and almost turned away, back toward the Indian trail. Then he looked at the field again; it wasn't as empty as he thought. It was pocked with long mounds, dirt rounded and patted down. Graves. There were nearly twenty of them, and all were fresh; but not all of them were full. Six stood yawning, waiting for some promised burden.

In the center of the graveyard lay what someone had obviously meant to be a large marker—laboriously carved from wood. Shannon stopped and stood above it, staring. Someone had tried to carve a name upon it but had only managed a shaky T. From a few other scratches he realized that only one name—and that a single word—must have been intended. He looked around for some sign of another tombstone; there was nothing. Was this to be the only one? Why?

The thudding sound had stopped, but now it began again. This time it was quicker, in a sort of flurry, as if someone feared they were using up a last burst of energy. Shannon headed for the source of the sound.

He found her, small and weeping, struggling for her bed. A churning paddle lay near her, underneath a window—the source of the sound. There was the putrid smell of corpses all around him, and the girl screamed when he knelt down to help her. His eyes weeping with the odor, he lifted the girl to the bed. He had to turn away when he saw her face. She could be no more than thirteen, and her face and bare arms and legs were a mass of dripping, pus-filled sores. It was smallpox.

He turned back to her. She was writhing and moaning on the bed, babbling and pleading; but what, Shannon couldn't make out.

"Rest easy," he soothed, "it's only Emmett." He pulled filthy blankets around her, trying to gentle her out. Then her eyes opened wide and she gripped his wrists in fierce manacles.

I renounce thee, Satan," she shouted. "I renounce thee, renounce thee, renounce ..."

Her hands loosened and she fell back, unconscious. Shannon patted the horror that was once someone's little girl and began investigating the room—doing his best to keep the instinctual terror of the pox from him and agonizing about what he could possibly do. Intellectually he knew he was safe—he had bitten the fear back after his mother died and had himself inoculated at the first opportunity. Part of him refused to believe this magical protection and screamed to run, run, run.

In the long single room there were many beds. Three were occupied—by corpses. All of them were women, but much older than the girl. In the other building—identical to the first—he found two more decaying bodies ... of middle-aged men. Shannon knew the answer to the riddle of the empty graves. There were six for those who remained. But there was no one to bury them. A scattering of outlying sheds, abandoned tools, barrows, and a forge told him the people had been working at some kind of mining operation—probably iron. The poverty he saw meant they were working on redemption for some absentee owner living in leisure in one of the large towns he had been trying to avoid. But all this still left the most basic questions unanswered: Who were they? What did the T on the grave marker stand for?

Emmett was hurrying back to the girl when he heard the jolting sound of many horses.

He met them at the edge of the graveyard, his rifle at full cock and the pan primed with fresh powder. The men danced their horses around him, but Shannon kept his rifle swinging, always aimed at the leader. There were four men leading two extra horses. The horses' flanks were streaming sweat, and the men had the red-eyed look about them of a long, desperate flight. Shannon caught flashes at their belts of fresh scalps.

It was the raiders.

* * * *

Emmett got his back to the stone wall of the spring-house, forcing the men into a single, horizontal line. One

Allan Cole & Chris Bunch

raider, a pinch-faced little man wearing a filthy Indian blanket, kicked his horse closer, as if toying with the idea of crushing Shannon against the wall. Emmett steadied his aim on the leader's chest, finger tightening on the trigger. This man was huge and looked even bigger draped in a voluminous horseman's caped coat styled a bit like Emmett's, but with red piping that set off the streaming red woolen woman's scarf wrapped about his neck. His long, black hair was tied back with a piece of scarlet ribbon. He wore laced leather leggings, engulfed in a rich pair of cavalry officer's boots with real silver spurs glinting at the heels.

The whole effect was topped off by a big slouch hat with a green parrot's feather poking out of the band. White teeth gleamed at Shannon through a black bush of a beard. Emmett remembered the head on the post with its vaguely familiar face. Now, he knew that man—just as he knew the one before him.

Tell them I don't like horse stink, Frenchy," Shannon said.

The grin vanished in the beard as Frenchy McShane leaned forward to peer at Emmett with green eyes that sat like polished stones at the end of twin tunnels. Then the beard exploded with a loud, bellowing laugh. "Well, kiss me and call me a fat squaw whore, if it isn't Emmett Shannon," Frenchy said. "Take a care, boys, you're looking at an old mate of mine. He's the trickiest obscene child this side of the Mohawk."

He kicked his horse closer, but remained at a respectful distance. Emmett noticed Pinched Face and the others calming their animals. He eased the hammer to half cock and let the butt of the rifle droop, but kept his finger on the trigger; the half-ounce ball would take McShane just below the beard.

Frenchy didn't miss this and he laughed again. "I'll wager you've spiced your load with a little buckshot," Frenchy said.

Shannon grinned back just as mirthlessly. "You know me, McShane." With Frenchy there was never any reason not to lie.

Emmett took note of the two spare horses. They were both saddled, and loaded with their riders' gear. "I expect it was your sign I saw a few days back," Emmett said. "Although then there were more of you driving cattle in a terrible rush."

"We encountered an intolerant bunch," Frenchy said. "Most covetous sons of bitches you ever saw. Unfortunately, there were too many of them for our argument to carry. So we let them keep the cows."

Shannon motioned with the rifle at the spare horses. "Looks like they got a little more than cows, Frenchy," he said.

"I'll only mourn one. And not for long at that."

"They put Bill Grady's head on a stump," Shannon said.

"Suspected they might," McShane said.

Then he paused, looking Shannon up and down. "I won't ask you what you're doing in these parts," he said. "It isn't any of my concern. However, unless my guesser's resigned on me from too much rum, you're headed back for the Mohawk."

"That was my intention," Shannon said.

In that case," McShane said, "maybe you'd like to ride with us for a while. I'll be honest with you, Emmett. The profits haven't been much this trip. But I expect to make up for it when we get into the Neutral Ground."

Shannon kept his peace, but Frenchy didn't seem to notice and went on. "I'll tell you, this is one war I'm getting to admire. I never was that happy before with the pickings up on the border. But things are getting pretty fine, if I do say so. We're blessed with a Congress that's got its head wedged up a bullock's ass far as it can go, and a king who's climbed all the way in.

"Every place I go all I see is fat farms and big moneybags with no one to tell you, 'No, Frenchy McShane, you cannot take that. It belongs to another.' Good Lord, man, these times no one even knows which side you're on, or dares ask, providing you keep powder and ball handy."

Emmett knew what McShane was getting at. He had first run into him during George's War, where the big Scots-Irishman had won the name Frenchy for his habit of switching sides whenever it suited him. Shake a bag of gold at him and McShane became a fierce ally for your cause. Unfortunately, you had to be most careful your enemy didn't press another, heftier bag his way during an inconvenient moment. Otherwise you would be on the wrong end of a "French trade."

In the years after the war, Shannon saw him sporadically, but heard of him often; all of it was bad. There were stories about settlers who hired Frenchy to guide them west—and vanished. Rumors that Frenchy—just to keep his murderous hand in—went raiding with the Indians for recreation.

McShane leaned back in his saddle, letting his big cloak fall open. He was fingering something at his belt. "Of course, I can't guarantee our takings, but we can always pick up a dozen scalps or so to tide us over. The bounty on scalps has gone up along with everything else in this war.

"You recall how good I am with scalps, don't you, Emmett? White or Indian, doesn't matter to me. Why, with a little weathering I defy any man to tell the difference when McShane's got done with his art."

Shannon finally realized what Frenchy was fingering on his belt. He saw a wrinkled knot trailing long, blond hair. It was the scalp of the woman at the Dutchman's farm.

"What's your decision?" McShane asked. "Shall we give them all hell together?"

Shannon pretended to chew this over a long moment, then shook his head. "As much as I'd like to, Frenchy," he said, "I'll have to say no. I've got some important private business, and it would be wrong of me to say it would not interfere."

The easy friendliness dropped from McShane. He looked over at the shacks. "Something in those sheds," he said, "wouldn't be part of your private business, would it? I'd hate to introduce you to my boys here as an old mate and then have to face them and humbly confess I was wrong and you're a greedy cheat."

"It isn't anything like that," Emmett said. "And I wouldn't go in there, if I were you. There's pox about."

Frenchy startled back, barely able to cover his fright. Then he glowered at Shannon, angry and disbelieving. "I suppose you're going to tell me that you've been inoculated and are safe? And I'll have to take your word there's nothing of value about?"

Shannon didn't answer, he simply let his rifle slide up and pulled the hammer back to full cock. From long experience Emmett knew there was no sense arguing with a man like Frenchy McShane when things came to this pass.

In Shannon's mind McShane was already dead, Pinched Face had been clubbed off the horse, and he was choosing which of the remaining two he would tomahawk first, when a scream split the air like shot. Everyone whirled, nearly losing their horses. Then the men were reining back hard and the horses were dancing back, choking for air with their necks nearly bowed in half.

The girl was standing in the doorway of the women's quarters, shrieking. "I renounce thee ... I renounce thee . . . !"

Frenchy fought his fear under control. He gave Emmett a look of grudging respect. "If there's anything there, mate, you're welcome to it and God bless."

The raiders vanished in a cascade of mud.

* * * *

Emmett made a clean bed for the girl in the shack that housed the forge, and pumped up the fire until the room was glowing and warm against the night. Brandy laced with opium put her in a groaning sleep, while he washed her and dressed her in a clean gown he'd found. He sprinkled lavender flakes in the water he washed her with, and did his

Allan Cole & Chris Bunch

best to brush the tangles from her hair, tying the limp locks with bright blue ribbon. Then he sat by her side, sipping steadily at the cider. There was nothing else he could do. If God was kind and he was generous with the laudanum, she would drift off for good sometime in the night.

Despite his mother's teachings, Shannon was cynical about the mercifulness of Heaven. In fact, as he thought about it, he realized that he had long ago lost what little faith she had instilled in him. If Sarah had lived—ah, bugger it! How many bargains, Emmett Shannon, have you tried to make? And not one taken. When Sarah lay dying, he had prayed: take me instead! I'm the sinful one. The doubter. The one with blood on his hands. Maybe that was the trouble. Maybe God was waiting until he piled up a sufficiency of sins so he would be as welcome in Hell as the likes of Frenchy McShane.

As he stared at the sleeping girl, Shannon decided he had little fear of Hell. What could be worse than this? Then he thought about his mother. How long did she suffer? Did she look like this? Did anyone sit with her until she died? Not likely. It would take more than a saint to dare the pox. And what are you doing here, Emmett? Measuring your brow for a halo? Don't give yourself airs, you're at no risk. If it's sainthood you want, kill the child now. That would be the act of a merciful man.

He got out the pistol, loaded and primed it, and studied the girl, figuring where best to put the ball. Then he lost his nerve and, calling himself every kind of a coward, put the pistol aside and took up the cider again.

* * * *

On this night God and Emmett Shannon came to a small understanding about the nature of mercy.

He must have slept for a while, because suddenly he found himself starting up at the sound of her voice. "Mother Wettstein! Mother Wettstein!" The girl was sitting up, her eyes staring past him into the shadows.

Emmett tried to hush her and feed her some more of the potion, but she pushed it weakly away. He tried again, but she pulled her head back sharply and some of the mixture spilled on the blankets. "Mother Wettstein," she cried again. "Please, Mother Wettstein!"

Shannon didn't know what to do, so he just said: "She's here."

The girl nodded and lay back. She touched her head and her heart. "I renounce thee, Satan," she said. Very firm. "I renounce thee." Again she made the gesture to the head and the heart. A blessing? What?

Part of the puzzle began coming to him. The separate quarters for men and women. There were no young people except the girl. Was it some religious order? A vow of chastity? Shannon had heard of such things. A covenant. Swearing off all but the plainest of livelihoods. Some made a practice of adopting children so the covenant wouldn't die off. Was this what was happening here? Was the girl the last . . . He found it difficult to allow himself to complete the thought.

"Mother Wettstein. Please, Mother Wettstein!"

But he had to. When the girl died, it was likely she was the very last of her kind. No human being could be more alone than this. To die with a stranger at your side and no one to know your history.

"I renounce thee ... I renounce thee."

The plea was accompanied by the sign at the head and her heart. She wanted to be baptized. She was saying she knew Satan and was making the adult choice of renouncing him, and now she was begging for Shannon to purify her soul. He couldn't think of the words. Even if he could, they would be Catholic. Was the ritual any good for people who weren't Catholic? Would the girl hate him if she knew? Don't be a fool, Emmett. You don't believe any of this anyway. Then it struck him this might be the greatest evil of all: to perform a baptism and be empty of all faith.

"I renounce—"

Allan Cole & Chris Bunch

Shannon drew some water and took it to her. She was quiet now, as if she realized what he was doing. He couldn't think of any proper words, so he sprinkled her with water and said: "Dear Heavenly Father, if you're listening now, please have mercy on this child. Don't blame her for my ignorance, and please, Lord, if you have any pity in your— ah, I'm sorry for that. Pay no attention to this heathen and let this poor girl find peace."

He sprinkled a little more water, hoping it was enough, and as an afterthought crossed himself as humbly as he could. The girl smiled and he felt a little better. She was quiet for a few moments. Then she began pitching and moaning again.

"What's troubling you, lass?" he asked.

"No . . . one will . . . know!"

Oh, he could see it now: for some reason she was ashamed.

"I won't tell," he said.

Her hands were on his wrists again, strong and desperate. "No! Tell. Please, tell. Tell someone."

"Tell them what? What should I tell them?"

No answer. Just the hard grip. Then, "Tell them! Tell them Wettstein! Tell them Klee! Francis Klee. And Leonhard. And Alfred. All Klees! All Klees!"

Emmett's heart was near bursting. He wanted to help, but how? Think, Shannon, think. What's she trying to say?

"Moira," the girl cried. "Tell them Moira. Moira Werner. And Charles. Yes, Charles . . . Charles . . . Gutkind. Gutkind. Charles Gutkind. And Henri. Not . . . forget . . . No. Henri, too. Henri Gutkind ..."

It was a list of names. But— Oh, don't be such a stupid man, Emmett Shannon. They're the names of the people here. She wants you to know all the names and tell someone. Write it down, maybe. So no one will forget.

Otherwise, the covenant will be lost to history forever.

"Tell me the rest, lass," he said. "I'll remember. I promise to God I'll remember."

Shannon listened for half an hour and more, committing the names to memory. He almost wept when he learned the girl's name. It was Anne, like his mother's.

Finally she was done.

She fell back into the bed like a whirling dervish had caught her and was sucking her down.

But what of the people themselves? What was the name of the covenant?

This time it was Emmett who gripped another's wrists, ignoring the sores breaking and running under his palms.

"Who are you?" he demanded. "Who are your people?"

She tried to answer, but words wouldn't come. She shook her head hard, trying to get it out.

"It starts with a T," Shannon pressed. "On the marker. A T. T . . . T . . . T . . . What's the rest?"

Suddenly the girl smiled. For the first time since he had come to this terrible place, she looked at him and knew he was there. Anne opened her mouth and began to form the word . . .

Shannon buried them all the next day. He set the buildings ablaze so that no one else would stumble on this place and have the pox wriggle into their flesh and burst through again in great, weeping sores.

He placed the wooden marker firmly in the ground.

There was still only the letter T upon it.

Allan Cole & Chris Bunch

CHAPTER EIGHT

EMMETT REGAINED THE main road after Easton. Now the country rose steep, wild and desolate. If he had a map, it might've been labeled with a variation of the old mariners' charts—Heer Bee Outlaws. He went through the gap in the Kittatinys just at dawn, moving as fast as caution would allow.

He relaxed enough to stake out a creek just at dusk and ambushed a young buck. It was his first venison, Emmett decided from his camp buried deep in the brush, for entirely too long. He gave himself a holiday on the following day, while he jerked the rest of the deer's meat over a green-wood fire. The brush and tree cover was heavy enough so almost no smoke could be seen from the road. He hung that damned hunting shirt in the smoke cloud, in the rather futile hope that some more of his lice would expire and spent the rest of the day sprawled in the sun. The sudden shower that night didn't disturb him. He slept warm and almost dry.

The next day he felt himself a new man. Of what stock? he wryly wondered. Let us see now. English? Not a chance, even though it would bring wealth. Dutch? They seemed to enjoy their riches damned little. Scots-Irish? With their long faces and droning services? Hardly. Perhaps an Indian. No. A Jew? Shannon had met only one in his life, a rather nice fellow, who compared his mother's spare religious services to his own people's. No one here in America seemed to bother them. But remembering circumcision, he decided to stay a Shannon. Emmett chuckled at his own bare humor. At least thoughts such as these passed the miles under his boots painlessly.

There were not many settlers in this country. Here and there would be a log hut, with farmland scraped from the wilderness. The handful of travelers he met on the road greeted him warily, hands never far from their weapons. There were a few villages on the route—rough clusters of half a dozen shacks, not much different from the redemption village below Easton. The road roughly paralleled the Delaware, but often veered inland for miles. Where it met the water, there might be a tiny mill. Shannon was not at home in this wilderness. Although not a man of the city, his experience on the frontier had been intermittent, and he thought the occasional cleared farm much brighter to his eyes than a roaring waterfall hung around with thickets.

At a river bend there was a small ferry. The riverbank had been recut to make a gentler slope. There was a shack for the ferryman, a ramshackle raft large enough for one farm wagon and its unhitched single team, two corralled oxen for the towrope, and a small boat. No people. Emmett walked to the river and looked across to the far bank. Possibly swimmable. But the current was too swift for comfort here, and certainly it would be deep. Perhaps he could find some planking, or even a dead log he could lash his gear onto. Certainly the ferry was not for him. Ferrymen, from Charon forward, required payment.

"You're for the crossing," came the voice behind him.

Emmett spun—and gaped. The heavy man in his fifties was suitable for gaping. He moved on wooden crutches, one crutch propped under the stump of an arm. He had also been scalped.

Very thoroughly. Whoever had taken his hair had not only ripped away most of the man's scalp, but taken the man's ears with it. Some men, Emmett had heard, survived being scalped. But he'd never thought to meet such a man, and now wished his thinking had proven true. Most of the man's skull was scarred and barren. A couple of tufts grew out near where his ears had been. Without support, his cheeks draped like those of a hound.

Shannon tried to cover his horror and failed. The man smiled. He must've been used to it. Shannon had the thought that perhaps now he even welcomed the reaction.

"Fivepence," the man said. "Good hard currency, and I'll root the boy out and have him row you across." Shannon

Allan Cole & Chris Bunch

shook his head. The only money he had was the forgeries still wrapped in the teamster's pouch. "A rough swim, boy. Man drowned last summer tryin' it."

"Don't look like I've a choice," Emmett said.

The man cupped one hand behind one of the holes in his skull. "Speak slow, son. Since the Sauks went an' relieved me of my echo boards, talk takes a while to get through." He thoughtfully stroked his chops. "You're a soldier."

"Enlistment's expired."

The man smiled, making his face slightly more horrible. "Don't matter a curse to me if you're takin' French leave. Least you're headin' home with what looks like all your parts." Emmett chose not to say anything. "God damned army," the man muttered. "Use you up. Spit you out. And send you home to beg by the door. Happened to me. Happen to all of you fightin', minute we send the redcoats howl in' home."

Emmett saw a glimmer. The man wanted to talk. Maybe he'd not be swimming the Delaware. "Happened to me already," he said. "King's officer grabbed m'promised land the last time by."

"You served afore?"

"I did. Looks like I didn't learn enough first time around."

"Too early for a pannikin?" the man asked.

"Like to," Emmett said. "But I'd best try to get across before it gets later."

"Rest easy, boy. Ain't no way I'd charge a man who burnt powder 'gainst the red 'uns. Eventually my pet idiot'll get tired of chasin' pigs or his own tail out there and come back. He'll take you 'crost."

Emmett followed the man to the porch of his shack, where an already heavily sampled jug of rum sat. Introductions, after the first sear of alcohol, followed. The man's name was Brewster.

"You're headed?"

"Up near Albany. Place called Cherry Valley."

" 'Pears like you're havin' to work your way north."

Emmett grinned. He was wearing better clothes now than when he left Valley Forge, but he had to admit they were a little road-battered. "A man could always use a little coin in his purse."

"You listen to advice?"

"Never turn it down."

"After you cross, you'll hit civilization. Roads're straight. Fences maintained proper. Cattle's fat, and so're the folks. All the housin's got fresh paint, least on the parts you see from the road. Town's called New Kent. Looks a place that should've been named New Eden."

"Looks?" Shannon asked, already getting an idea of what Brewster was going to warn him about.

"Looks is right," Brewster said, reclaiming the jug. "You done any travelin'?"

"Some."

"Maybe you'll follow when I tell you that New Kent's got exactly fifty-three shares. Fifty for the settlers, one for the church, one for ministers, one for the school. Each share ran out 'bout a thousand acres, give or take what the surveyor'd take when he laid out the land.

"Facts're real interesting," Brewster went on, seemingly in an aside. "Tell you anything more when I say last census there warn't but about two thousand people? Legal people, anyway."

"Shit."

"Ee-yup. Town got settled by rich folk, lookin' to grab some land, hang on it a bit and then sell. Didn't work out that way, so they decided they was gonna build it up. 'Course that meant they'd need people who knew which end of a shovel went in th' dirt. And they got 'em, promising 'em the world, a vote in the town affairs, fat oxen an' their daughters. Mebbe should've said fat daughters an' oxen. Rum fuddles a man real easy. Got some fat asses down there, some on four legs, some on two."

A Daughter Of Liberty

"I've been in towns like those," Shannon said, and then, echoing something he'd told his wife years earlier, "but I never got stupid enough to take their damned redemption contracts."

"You looked a man of sense. Problem is, they got a real nasty habit in New Kent of warnin' out people who don't dance to their hornpipes."

"Wouldn't be the first time I've been warned out."

"Mebbe. But these people mean it. They don't mean linger on till plantin' or harvest or hog-killin' time is over. They mean get your butt down th' road now, an' maybe here's a charge'a birdshot or some tar and feathers t' help you on your way."

"Mmm." Emmett considered.

"All I'm suggestin' is that maybe, while we're sittin' here, enjoyin' this rum an' this spring day, you might want to strip off an' clean up. Bucket out the back. Look inside the shack, there's a fresh-stropped razor an' soap. Got some sulfur you can burn, if you got creatures in that fine huntin' shirt of yours. What story you come up with so's not to sound like some wanderin' wastrel's your concern. But figger least I can do is help you look t' match th' story."

Emmett swallowed rum and eyed Brewster suspiciously. "Don't mean to insult the offer, but it's been my experience ain't but few who help somebody out of pure goodness."

"Ain't goodness at all. Those people over there think 'cause their folks brought over some gold an' some fancy names an' dress, this land's God-given to them. But they ain't never the ones who'll cut the roads, make th' farms or hammer th' steel. Just like there weren't no gentry at Mackinac. Except that shitsack officer who said there ain't gonna be trouble with Indians 'cause they're playin' at games.

"You know," Brewster observed, somewhat irrelevantly, "sound of havin' your scalp lifted, from the inside, is just like bubbles poppin'."

Shannon's stomach turned slightly.

"You start cleanin' up. And thinkin' 'bout what you plan to tell those swells in New Kent, with their committee an' paradin' militia they use to run squatters off open land. Mebbe you can figure out some flash that'll get you their gold. Hope you get some of their hide for me."

By the time Brewster's "idiot"—a truly retarded hulk of a young man—showed up, Shannon was clean, neat, fed, and drunk as a judge. The boatman deposited him on the far bank. Shannon turned and waved across the river at Brewster. But he seemed collapsed on his porch and oblivious. Emmett took his example, made it as far as the hilltop and a clump of brush, spread out his blanket and passed out cold…

* * * *

The skeleton must have been hung up years ago. A lot of the bones lay scattered on the path below the tree, or were absent, carried away by wolves or dogs. Mummified skin still clung in bits around the skull and below the rib cage. Emmett couldn't begin to estimate how long it had been there—the rusting chain the skeleton dangled from was buried in the growing wood of the tree. An escaped slave? A thief? Who knew. Maybe even somebody who hadn't taken being warned out that seriously.

Welcome to New Kent, Shannon thought.

It was, Shannon had to agree, a beautiful village. Painted. Laid out by a geometer. The cattle pastured outside the village were grain fed. The village meeting house, set near the square, was more than large enough to accommodate those pious folk who fit the town's description of proper citizens. In that square, under a lowering sky, the militia drilled. Even from this distance, Shannon could see they were all uniformed. And they had music—the twitter of a fife and the clatter of a drum came up to him. Shannon smiled: at first the feral expression of a fox who's just realized the chicken run is open, then forming into an open, ingenuous grin; the grin of a man anyone would be sure to trust his last shilling and youngest daughter to.

Allan Cole & Chris Bunch

A Daughter Of Liberty

Shannon took out the pistol he'd originally planned for trading stock and stuck it, unloaded—not wanting to shoot his bollocks off for the sake of authenticity—into his belt. He started for New Kent.

The first building on the town's outskirts was to be avoided, Brewster had told him. An inn. An inn where the keeper watered the ale, sold short portions, and sold venison for beef. Emmett Shannon headed, unerringly, for that first inn.

CHAPTER NINE

DIANA JAMESON FINISHED itemizing exactly what was wrong with New Kent, her master, life, and being fifteen at about the same time the Black Lamb's last window was spotless. Another silly task—it would rain in a few moments, and then tomorrow Rhoda would have her out cleaning them all over again.

She can have me cleaning them twice a day until Midsummer's Eve and I still will not call the bitch Mrs. Hatch. Rhoda was eighteen, Nate Hatch's recently married fourth wife, and determined she would get respect due her from any bondswoman.

Rain spattered down. Diana saw the militia break formation and scurry into the meeting house. Three men mounted horses and galloped for the Black Lamb. One of them would be Saul Hatch.

Saul—Nate's youngest son and a widower—had begun looking for a second wife. Another baby producer and cook was what it would be. Saul, ten years older than Diana, had cordially ignored the bonded child. But now Diana was beddable and Saul was available. With spring his courting had begun. So far it had consisted of little more than Saul loudly bragging on how prosperous the gristmill was, how important he would be, and the fine things he'd fetch his new wife from England once the damnable war was over. For New Kent the wedding was as good as announced. Diana thought otherwise. However, she wasn't sure how to implement her plan. But implemented it would be, she thought. If not tomorrow, then very soon after.

The horsemen reined up in front of the inn: Saul, "Captain" Beebe—selectman and commander of the militia—and Mister Marsh. Once a minister, Marsh had found being justice of the peace more to his liking. He didn't despise the increased profits either. In his most landed-gentry manner, Saul tossed his horse's reins to Diana. "Stable these out of the wet, would you, love."

Love. Diana burned. "Yes, milord Hatch, sir." Diana curtsied deeply and blinked her blue eyes at him.

Saul's smile—which Diana thought resembled a hog awaiting his slops—fed her sarcasm. He went into the Black Lamb. Captain Beebe laughed, nudged Marsh, and they trooped into the inn. Diana collected reins and started for the stable. Nate—Mister Hatch—would no doubt have something to say about her behavior. But not for very much longer.

She returned to see a solitary traveler coming toward her. He approached the porch, swept his battered hat off, bowed and smiled broadly. "I have a complaint about your town, milady. Your skies appear to leak."

Diana found a smile on her face. There'd been few of those of late. "Come out of the rain and don't waste the miladies," she said. "My master and his wife set the rates."

Emmett stepped onto the porch and shook off the wet. He eyed the girl standing next to him. Red hair. Very red. A small thing, she was. Under five feet. Freckles. Pretty, Emmett thought. In a few years there'll be many sparking around her even if she is the scullery maid.

Diana eyed him skeptically. Maybe a soldier, maybe just a wandering freeman. Not as poor as most that come by, she thought, looking at the travel-battered but still expensive-looking cloak, and at Emmett's rifle.

"The Black Lamb's a fine name for an inn," Emmett offered.

Diana, for some unknown reason, decided to warn him. Most likely he'd go inside, report what she'd said to Nate, and she'd be for a harsh scolding and .added work. "You might be thinking about what happens to lambs when they grow," she said.

"They make a fine stew."

"They also are sheared."

"Ah."

"I won't say there's better taverns in New Kent," Diana said. "But at least either of the other two will pour a more honest measure. And have feathers in the mattresses no more than a year or two old."

"No, milady," Emmett disagreed. "From the first moment I saw that fine sign, this sturdy building, and your smile, I knew this place was for me."

"Nobody cautions a fool but once," she said.

"Ah," Emmett said. "But am I fool or flash?" Smiling, he walked into the Black Lamb.

* * * *

Emmett closed the door behind him and let his eyes adjust. There were four men. Behind the bar, the host; blubber-butted, with a tallowy, drooping complexion fringed by a gray brush around his chops. The other three wore uniforms: glossy black shoes with shiny brass buckles, pure white leggings, breeches and smallcoat; blue coats with bright red facings, gold shoulder knots and buttons. Their tricorner hats, set atop the bar, were red-edged and fitted with enormous drooping feathers. The silver-mounted smallswords were carried on shoulder belts with silver buckles. As grand, Emmett thought, as the last time he'd seen General George himself at a review.

But those smallswords, Emmett thought—best divest yourselves of them, lads, because if you ever run across the lobsterbacks, the blades will get in your way and trip you when you flee. Which, being militia, you will. Not that this far from the war you'll ever have to worry about the British.

The three men were near the window, looking at something the oldest man was holding to the light. Of the three, Emmett decided one must be related to the innkeeper; the other was red-faced and wore enough braid to be an officer; and the third reminded him of a justice who'd once warned him out of a village.

Emmett was puzzling how he could maintain his yet-to-be-mounted role without having to spend any money, when he caught a bit of conversation. "A coiner's work, certain,"

Allan Cole & Chris Bunch

the older man said. "The ink is smeared. And the fool who made the plates didn't have enough sense to spell Philadelphia as it is."

Emmett laughed. Loudly enough for the four to turn. Now the entrance, he thought. Holding his rifle so the light reflected the brass working on his lock, he tossed back his cloak and strode forward. "Good afternoon, gentle sirs."

The tapster: "Not all that good, I'm afraid."

"Ah, but it is," Emmett corrected. "Once you're inside with a fire and a tankard of flip in the prospect. Soldiers such as ourselves need little more."

Emmett waited for a response. It came from the reddest-faced man, who puzzled, then noted the pistol in Emmett's belt and stepped forward, holding out his hand. "Captain Beebe, Lieutenant."

Lieutenant? Hell, Emmett thought he was distinguished enough for a captaincy. But better a green cockade than none at all. "Shannon," Emmett said. "With Captain McLane's company."

"Your glory," the younger version of the innkeeper said, looking at Emmett critically, "shines more brightly than your uniform."

"When you're scouting in front of the whole army," Emmett said, "sometimes it don't pay to look all that much like a soldier." He was pleased his tongue had not lost its glibness.

"Plus m'damned horse shied on me ten miles back," he went on, "and I rolled off, and the poor beast went on over a cliff face. Horse trader who sold me the animal claimed she was direct line from Old Snip. But he was from Jersey and probably lyin'. Anyway, lost my saddlebags and everything except what I had tucked in this knapsack I took off a lobsterback after Trenton."

"So you're looking for a remount?"

"Eventually. After I give you people a hand. And after we toast General Washington, the Continental Congress, and damnation to King George."

A mutter of approval and they all turned to the bar. Hatch shifted, edgy.

Emmett let the silence grow for a moment—just enough to get uncomfortable. Behind him he heard Diana walk into the taproom. Then: "I may be afoot and dressed like a tramp," he said heartily. "But I can still hold my place."

He dug into the bottom of the teamster's pouch, took out the oilskin packet and drew out a handful of those beautiful forgeries. "Keeper, a quart of your best whisk—" From the corner of his eye, Emmett saw Diana shake her head in warning. Emmett caught himself. ". . . rum. Rum's the drink for a day such as this."

Toasts and introductions followed. Emmett was pleased he'd called all four of the men with fair accuracy. He leaned back in his chair. It was enough so he could see the girl, who was busying herself with the inside of the windows and staying within earshot. She definitely will break some hearts when she comes of age, he thought.

"You said something a few moments ago about coming to the assistance of New Kent, Lieutenant Shannon?" asked Mister Marsh in a slightly inquisitorial tone.

"Can't see what we need," Beebe added. "Town's on its course. Any problems we could have, the militia'll clean 'em up faster'n we burn out a squatter." He laughed.

"It's not just New Kent, Captain," Shannon said. "It's this whole county. There's trouble coming." Appropriate menace: "The British are coming."

The reaction was all Emmett could have hoped for. Saul looked out the window, Marsh and Beebe half rose, and Nate Hatch glanced down and to the side. Were I a thief, Emmett thought, I would now know where his cash box is.

"But we're a long way from Philadelphia," Marsh said.

"That you are. Also a long way from New York. But then, Kingston was quite a distance from General Clinton's bailiwick." Silence. Kingston, third biggest city in New York, had been burnt to ashes the previous fall. It lay on the Hudson River only a few days from New Kent.

Allan Cole & Chris Bunch

Panic: "When? How many?"

"Calm yourselves, gentlemen. Our spies say they're still readying their forces. Gen'ral Washington himself told Captain McLane to send out his best scouts. Warn the people. Captain McLane gave us additional orders that if we saw fit, we could stay on for a few weeks if we found a town that might need the talents of a scout."

"Well, we certainly could use someone like you."

Believed you might, Emmett thought. Fancy folk don't like to be running around in the bushes where nobody's going to admire you. Those fancy whites get dirty out in the forest. This was why Emmett had frequently been able to pay his keep acting as a ranger for villages like New Kent.

****

Across the room Diana had her head turned. The British? How could these people believe this cheapjack's patter? He was no better than a tinker. She thought,—and then thought again. Why should she care?

She grinned as she realized: of course these fools like the Hatches, Marshes, and Beebes would believe him. Weren't they in their own way at least as crooked, with their liberty poles, but sending no one to fight; their fervent toasts to the Congress, but selling supplies to the British; or their whinings of poverty when anyone attempted to collect a tax? Good, she thought. I hope you find a way to get them. Down to their last shilling.

She looked again at Emmett. You can tell, she thought, that wherever he's from they know how to keep the Hatches and those like them in their place. Not like New Kent. Then: I wonder if his wife takes proper care of him.

* * * *

"If you're willing to stay a day or so," Captain Beebe was saying, "perhaps you'll do us the honor of reviewing the men."

"The honor'd be mine," Emmett said. "As I was coming into town I saw some glimpses of them in the square before the rain started. Fine-looking group you have, sir."

"Thank you. Tomorrow's Market Day. We planned a review. It'll be quite impressive for the farmers. Although I don't know if it'll be the same for you. Having been part of General Washington's army and all."

Yes. The raggedy-ass, barefoot, freezing, starving Continental Army. "Not at all, Major. I once heard General Washington himself say that he judges his soldiers by how they march, not how many of them there are."

"Damned fine words," Saul said, lifting his glass. "That's the spirit that won Trenton."

And lost Quebec, Long Island, and Paoli, Emmett thought. Market Day, hmm? Emmett saw the way clear. The militia would march up and down, the farmers would get drunk and cheer. Any contributions would be humbly accepted by Lieutenant Shannon. It wouldn't be much, Emmett thought. He knew tightfists like New Kent well. But any hard cash would be welcome. He'd also exchange as much of the counterfeit Continentals as he could before moving on. And, maybe when he did, he actually would have a horse.

The door swung open. Emmett, feeling pleased with the hand dealt, turned, about to offer the newcomer, whoever he was, a drink. His mouth closed. The woman hobbling toward the bar wore rags. A filthy shawl covered her head. She passed by a window—and Emmett's stomach turned. Her left cheek was burnt deep with a scar—made by a white-hot poker. The scar roughly scribed the letter R. The woman did not speak, but went behind the bar, lifted the trap, and went down into the cellar.

Emmett breathed deeply and drank rum. He was doing his best to control himself. "You still brand your runaways?" his voice most neutral.

"Haven't had to since Runner Mary," Beebe said, motioning toward the cellar. "The other servants learned from what happened."

"It was intolerable," Marsh added. "She would run, and we would find her and bring her back. Nothing seemed to convince her. Whippings. Adding to her time of service. As soon as her mistress turned her back, she would run once more. This was our last hope. Fortunately, it worked satisfactorily. Now she's free. Makes soap, such as it is. I believe she lives somewhere outside the town. Among the squatters."

"Almost a pity," Beebe said. "She was quite a respectable-looking woman before that."

"She was," Saul agreed. "I remember looking at her when I was . . . oh, Diana's age. She would've been five years up on me. And thinking thoughts that, pardon me, Justice Marsh, I wouldn't mention if you were still in the pulpit."

"You still should not," Marsh said. "When I renounced the cloth, I did not give up my convictions."

Emmett turned and looked as the woman came back up from the cellar carrying a basket of ashes. He would have thought her to be in her fifties. Nate Hatch's age. Instead . . . maybe thirty? Sweet Holy Jesus, Emmett thought, turning away. I would trade ten years more in Purgatory if the damned British were on their way with flame and bayonet.

Diana saw Emmett's face and the look of black rage. His eyes met hers for just one breath, and from the flicker, she realized the same emotions must be at play on her own face.

She found herself measuring the man a bit differently than before.

CHAPTER TEN

THE NIGHTMARE HAD started a few weeks after Gramer Fahey died, and it had continued almost every night without relief for the past two months.

In the dream, Diana was standing in the main room of the Black Lamb with Saul Hatch's plump proprietary arm about her waist. She was his wife, and she could already feel a child kicking in her guts. The room was always full of New Kent's elite, and there was a jolly fire glowing in the hearth. People were drinking and eating and laughing at Nate Hatch's barnyard jests.

Another Diana—her "real" self—watched the scene from another part of the room. She looked with disgust at the self-satisfied smiles on the faces of the good people of New Kent. Then, with growing horror, she saw an identical look on her own face—the Diana who had Saul's arm about her waist. She moved closer, saw the vacant look in her eyes, the puffy pouches bulging under them, and a trail of grease on her chin from the pork joint that rested in the platter on the inn's main table.

It was a portrait right out of a political broadside, with pigs or forest apes dressed in village finery and mocking the pretensions of the landed class. Diana fit in perfectly with all the other pigs.

She saw her other self grab a joint and tear off a chunk of flesh. Still laughing, the woman gobbled the chunk down. Suddenly she gave a strangled gasp as the pork stuck in her throat. Her face turned scarlet and her eyes frogged from their sockets. The other Diana grabbed at her throat, waving wildly at the others, begging for help. But the Hatches and their friends laughed all the harder as she fell to the floor, kicking and clawing at rough boards, trailing blood from ripped nails. Somehow Diana became the woman on the floor, choking to death and peering up at bleary, laughing faces crowding over her and drinking in all the air in the room.

The dream always ended the same: Diana bolting up in her bed screaming for Gramer Fahey—who never came because she was a corpse now; lying in state on a broad board table on the other side of Diana's room, dressed in her Sunday finest, her arms crossed on her breast.

Something black sat chittering on her face, and Diana knew it was a rat, but she had to get up just the same, to move closer . . . closer . . . closer . . . and the rat turned to her so she could see it full on. It had heavy jowls and a ruff of white beard rimming its chin. The rat had the face of Nate Hatch!

* * * *

Diana never screamed when she awoke for real, because when the nightmare first began she became fearful the others would know how deeply she suffered from the old woman's death. They would use her grief as a weapon against her and pester her to distraction for details. To guard against a scream, she always tucked a corner of her blanket into her mouth before she went to sleep, and gripped it so tight during the night that her jaws felt swollen and bruised in the morning.

What disturbed her most about the nightmare was that she knew how easy it would be for the dream to become a reality. Since Saul's wife had died six months before, the pressure had been growing. To New Kent, Diana was the obvious choice to take the dead woman's place as mother to Saul's brood of five and head of the household at the Hatch mill. It would be an honor to her.

Diana's indentured status would end when she took to the marriage bed, and at fifteen she was young and strong enough to add at least a third of a score to Saul's virile name.

That is, if she managed to live through that many, because she knew Saul would pump one out of her every ten or eleven months without relief, until she had not a tooth in her mouth and her bones felt like they were going to crack when winter winds blew. That was what had happened to Saul's first wife. She had died at twenty-three, bearing Hatch child number five—and half a year short of her fifth wedding anniversary.

The subject of the Hatch men's virility had become a quiet jest in the town since Nate married the eighteen-year-old Rhoda Parker. The wedding had been a bit of a mockery, with lush Rhoda—who came from a far poorer family—marrying fat old Nate Hatch.

For months, when Nate was in his cups, he would make not too subtle jokes about his prowess. But Rhoda's belly was stubbornly refusing to swell. Now the boasting had stopped and Rhoda could be seen giving her husband a look of disgust that did not speak well for bedded bliss.

Oddly, Rhoda's hard-won knowledge of the Hatch failings was no aid to Diana at all. Instead, Rhoda had become part of the pressure on her to give Saul some hope. If it were just the fact that Rhoda wanted her out of the household, she could understand.

Diana was well-aware that her newly blooming figure was drawing the attention of the young males of New Kent, as well as longing looks and furtive fumbles from Rhoda's husband; just as she knew that if it weren't for Gramer Fahey, Nate would have trapped her in the barn and had her praying with her knees up years ago—before she had even a promise of a figure. No, it wasn't fear of Nate Hatch's near-senile lust that worried Rhoda. Diana was sure the good Mrs. Hatch just wanted her to join the misery.

Gramer Fahey was seventy years of age when the infant Diana Jameson had been brought from Philadelphia to New Kent. It was an act of charity—the Hatches always pounded at her—for them to take this "obscene child" in to raise.

They said her mother was a dirty little wench who was always betraying her mistress's trust, until she finally got caught out. But even then the good Quaker people she worked for cared only for their serving girl's reputation. The Quaker family had sought and found aid from their distant

Allan Cole & Chris Bunch

cousin, Nate Hatch and his wife, who had a slave to wet-nurse the child and agreed to hide the shame that was Diana in their own merciful keeping.

In turn for raising her to Christian womanhood, all they asked was that she share in their labors until she reached majority. What this translated to was that Diana was required by indenture law to work at any task, no matter how hard, and to eat any rations, no matter how unfit, until she was eighteen.

* * * *

Diana had no memory of her mother. She had died when Diana was still in flannels. It was the protection of Abigail Fahey—the mother of Nate's first wife and grandmother to the first six Hatch children—that made life tolerable for Diana. As the most respected midwife in New Kent, Gramer Fahey was a woman of uncommon prestige. There were few children in the area she hadn't boiled up sheets for, or eased the pain of their mothers. Her knowledge of medicine was vast, her tenderness legendary.

Diana was nearly plucked from the wet nurse's nipple when the slave—whose name was Sandra—caught the eye of a traveling dealer who bought her for the Boston market. It was then that Gramer Fahey took little Diana under her wing and raised her with the help of a succession of young servants. Later, Diana realized she was a surrogate for the brood of children the woman never had. At sixteen she produced her only daughter—Nate's future wife—and in the bloody aftermath of fevers and infections, lost the ability to bear any others. A year later her husband died—how, she never explained—leaving her destitute.

These two events pushed Gramer Fahey into an intense study of medicine, with an emphasis on child bearing and child rearing. It was a study that jumped from dusty volumes to Indian villages to midwives and back to the books again. She became so expert, she could charge the highest prices for her services and not expect an argument. Nor did anyone dare criticize her when she offered the same services for free to the poor.

The final tragedy—the death of her own daughter in childbirth—set her in stone. In all the years that followed, Gramer Fahey dedicated herself to shoring up the women of New Kent. She would lend them funds when their husbands drank what little they had away; she would tend their injuries when the same men took out their bitterness on them; give them shelter when they were abandoned; or nurse them through the early months of their widowhood.

Diana and Abigail Fahey made an odd pair: sometimes they behaved like mother and daughter; sometimes like sisters, with whispered confidences on dark nights; sometimes like teacher and student, poring over primers and Bible; and sometimes they behaved like two equals—mature peers—who strolled the marketplace, bargaining haughtily for the table.

Gramer Fahey told Diana hundreds of stories, but her favorites were those from Abigail's own girlhood. In each of the stories, she always found some common chord that applied to Diana's current life. Later Diana realized, with a shock, that the childhood the stories came from occurred in the previous century. Yet, the old woman viewed things with an eye as fresh as today—but with a reasoned perspective of a great distance.

A few months before Abigail died, Diana started a little book containing some of the things the old woman told her.

* * * *

On child bearing: "After my first, I spent nearly twenty-five years cursing my barrenness. Then when I saw the lot of the women around me, I spent the next forty praising God for His gift. My barrenness freed me to think for myself."

On romance: "There'll come a time when these loutish boys suddenly appear handsome and you'll weigh their every word as if it's a treasure from some great scholar. But it's only the cock in your eye you're seeing, not really them.

Allan Cole & Chris Bunch

After, it will be the same louts from New Kent you're looking at. Don't bed a New Kent boy, Diana. Promise me."

At the time, the promise was no trouble at all. But lately she was beginning to realize what Gramer Fahey meant by having a "cock in your eye," and was grateful that she was also raised never to break a vow.

On sex: "I still miss it, even though I had to give it up so young. New Kent is not the place to spread your knees and keep your independence. But in other places there are discreet ways a woman can leap into a man's bed as eagerly as a witch to the Devil's Sabbath and not chance her reputation. As for getting caught out, there's little reason in these times. I have means, which I'll teach you when you're older, so that you can have pleasure without fear—wedded or not."

On independence: "If you live past your child-bearing years, you can expect a long life. But you cannot and should not also expect the protection of a man. He'll die in war, or the plague, or just go away. Once we've survived the change, there's few men who will outlive us. So you must have some means of earning your own keep, so that you can be your own woman, no matter what path the Lord leads you to."

On men: "You'll think from my nattering that I view men as the enemy. There is some truth to that, but only if you are weak or foolish enough to choose the wrong man. I know the thinking here is that sooner wed, less time for sin. But this is a great falsehood. Take your time, Diana dear, take your time. And if you're wondering about that special man—the one they talk about in stories, who sweeps women away in great romantic fashion—I don't know if such a man exists. However, I can tell you this . . . There's none being bred here in New Kent that will test my notions."

* * * *

Gramer Fahey could never see a life for Diana in New Kent. She urged that as soon as her period of indenture lapsed, she move on to some city—"not Boston, it's nothing but widows and squalor"—like Philadelphia or New York.

106

It was to this end that the old woman pointed Diana's entire education. No book crept through town in a traveler's pocket without being sniffed out by Gramer Fahey and then judged for its worth. "It's the witch in me," she used to say. "I can smell printer's ink in a snowstorm."

Just as importantly, Gramer Fahey also sniffed out a talent in Diana that promised to pay: her eye for beauty. Before Diana even knew her letters, she was sketching crude copies of pictures from the primer. Then anything and everything became her subject: broken milk stools, cows, trees, and a dozen cats who were driven to feline insanity from being constantly prodded and poked into poses for young Diana.

The most interesting thing, the old woman noted, was that Diana always found a way to make the object she was drawing appear more comely than it did in real life. "You don't want to be an artist, Diana, dear," she said. "Only the wives of royal governors and merchant princes are allowed to be artists or poets, and no one ever pays them. No, it's the needle you must take up. That's the way to your fortune."

By taking up the needle, Gramer Fahey did not mean mindless sewing of farmers' breeches, or coarse dresses hacked together by a squatter's wife. She meant fine clothing cut from the best bolts of silk and cotton and linen, dyed with the richest of colors and graced with the most elegant of lace. From the moment the idea came to her, until years later when she fell fatally ill, Gramer Fahey taught Diana every trick she had learned over a lifetime with the needle.

It wasn't an easy course: months would go by when Diana would grow childishly bored and impatient with the detailed work the old woman insisted on. "Front or back, the stitches should look the same," Gramer Fahey said. "If you wear the dress inside out, only the seams—not your needlework—should give it away."

The turning point came when Diana was twelve. Abigail convinced her she should take on some project that would test all of the skills she had learned so far. It should be something that she could keep forever, to hand on to her own daughter, or the woman who married her son. It was a comforter. A child-sized comforter—just four feet by three. They planned it together, but it was up to Diana to construct.

The project took her months. For a time there seemed to be no odd-shaped or colored swatch of material that was safe from Diana. She gathered hundreds of pieces of cloth together and then sifted and refined and cut and sewed and tossed them aside in disgust at her clumsiness. But then it all came together and the comforter was done in a smooth rush. It had a broad band of blue surrounding a deep, rich red— "the color of your lovely hair, Diana, dear." Through the whole thing she worked an intricate pattern of colors and cloth that pleased the eye close up, but turned out to be an even more eye-pleasing forest scene when viewed from afar.

Gramer Fahey studied it for a long time. The suspense was maddening. But the old woman just nodded and mumbled and looked. Finally came the ultimate test. She turned it over. It was exactly the same. No matter how closely one looked, not one stitch revealed where or even if it had been tied off.

"It's the most stunning bit of needlecraft I've ever seen," Abigail said. "I don't know a woman in New Kent who could match it."

Diana had lived on that moment of praise ever since. It was what kept her from fatal error when Nate Hatch cheated her of her inheritance.

Gramer Fahey kept a heavy leather bag of coin and currency in her sewing chest. In it she had her own money and what Diana was beginning to earn from her needlework. They both knew it would take no excuse at all for Nate to seize anything the girl earned to pay for the bread he begrudged her every day.

As Nate Hatch saw it, the long, hard hours she worked for him didn't count against more than a crumb—"especially in these hard times of rising prices and tight-fisted customers who expect a glass of the best for naught." All of his indentured servants—and slaves, when he had them—were required to turn over their excess earnings to their master. Diana was exempted, but only because of Gramer Fahey. Hatch feared not only the old woman's tongue, which could be worse than a forger's rasp, but the power of opinion she wielded in New Kent.

The money was to be used by Diana when she was eighteen to finance the new life Gramer Fahey saw for her. If the old woman died first, Diana was to inherit. If she chose, she could use part of the money to buy out the rest of her contract and leave then. All of the Hatches knew this. Abigail Fahey had made it plain to them so there could be no mistake.

After Gramer Fahey was buried and the family returned from the services, the first thing Nate Hatch did when they entered the inn was march upstairs to the old woman's room. Diana listened in dread as she heard his heavy footsteps clomping around and the trunk being dragged open.

A few minutes later Nate marched back down again, holding up the big leather bag. He came right up to Diana, towering over her, menacing. "I'll be keeping this," he said, "and there will be no argument about it. Is this understood?"

Diana was too stunned to say anything at first, but then as it began to dawn, her mouth came open to protest.

Nate thundered at her before she could speak: "Is it understood?"

Her mouth snapped shut. She had never been struck by any of the Hatches—they wouldn't dare when Abigail was alive—but she had seen them administer brutal beatings to other servants. At that moment Diana knew if she spoke she would soon be lying on the floor, with only a broken jaw if she were lucky.

Even then Diana was too stubborn to give them the satisfaction of a nod of agreement. Instead, her heart thundering against her ribs, fear and anger pounding at her temples, she whirled and stalked out of the room.

Nothing was ever said about the matter afterwards.

Allan Cole & Chris Bunch

A Daughter Of Liberty

Except, that was when Saul Hatch began to call.
It was then that Diana determined to run.

CHAPTER ELEVEN

DIANA STOOD OVER Abigail's great trunk, her mouth dry, her heart leaping. The trunk stood in what was once Gramer Fahey's room, now put into service for paying guests. The young Irish lieutenant's few belongings were dumped in one corner. Downstairs, Diana could hear the boasting voices of New Kent's aristocracy entertaining Lieutenant Shannon.

In Shannon's absence there was nothing unusual about Diana's presence. She could say she was cleaning. Just as innocent was her going through the trunk; all she wanted was a portion of her sewing kit. Her sewing things were nothing anyone in this house coveted. But to Diana the kit was symbolic—a final act of defiance. For weeks she'd been hiding things in her own room—clothing, food for several days—and now all that was left were the tools to win a living after she'd escaped New Kent.

She forced calmness and opened the trunk. On top was the comforter. Diana fingered it, remembering each stitch and the praise she had won from Abigail. Although it was small and made for a child, it would be foolish to carry—it was still too bulky. If all went well, this would be the last time she saw it. Diana rummaged about, forcing herself to ignore the memories that leapt up as she encountered each item. Finally she came to her kit; she sorted it, discarding all but the most necessary items. These she put into a silken scarf she could hide in her bodice.

Diana's plan was simple: she would run tomorrow after everyone left for Market Day. In the excitement, she'd not be missed for hours. If the Hatch men drank to habit, she might have as long as the following day. Much thought had gone into what she would do next. She'd discarded the romantic notion of disguising herself as a boy. Under the circumstances, a helpless female would be a better ploy. She'd travel swiftly for a few days, then post herself on the main road. There she'd await an appropriate wagon bearing goods from the New Kent market; a merchant traveling to Easton with his family.

She'd say she was from a nearby farm—with a sick mother and father. Their situation was so desperate, she'd explain, her family was forced to trust their innocent daughter to seek help from the farm's absentee owner—a man of noted distinction and compassion who lived near Easton. No one would suspect her, or refuse her tearful pleas. Once in Easton, she intended to vanish into the swollen population of refugees, where she was certain a young, pretty thing with a talent for needlecraft could easily earn her keep. Eventually she'd make her way to Philadelphia—the city of her unfortunate birth. But Philadelphia would have to wait until the British were driven out.

Her heart fluttered as she heard boot heels thumping up the stairs. Quickly she tucked her booty into her dress and then, ostentatiously, began pawing through her sewing kit. "Please forgive the intrusion, Lieutenant," she said over her shoulder, "but I had to fetch a few things. I'll only be a moment."

Shannon entered the room as she turned, and she saw from the big, gleaming smile on his face that her presence was no intrusion at all. "You're far sweeter company than I've been keeping of late," he said.

She sensed his eyes flickering over her, but this barely raised a blush; his look was merely admiring, nothing threatening or expectant. But there was no sense testing him by lingering. She started past. "They're all probably in a dither downstairs," she said, "wondering where I've gotten myself off to."

"No, lass," Emmett said, "I doubt that very much. When I left, everyone was pretty well taken by drink. I don't think you'll be missed at all. In fact, if I were you, I'd take myself off for a little bit of a lie-down until supper." He politely stepped out of her way.

Emmett watched her go by, wishing there was some way he could delay her . . . call her back. It had nothing to do with lust. He despised men who played the rogue's game with indentured women. But she looked and smelled so nice, and her voice was so gentle after months of barked orders from harsh sergeants' throats. And he'd sensed something strong pass between them during the encounter with the poor branded woman. Isn't it a fine world, Emmett Shannon, when two human beings cannot even speak?

Then he found himself goggling in amazement when Diana paused in the hallway.

Diana's thinking was along the same line: Shannon was handsome, in a raggedy, underfed sort of way. But she'd seen handsome men in her short life, just as she'd seen many a rogue with a smooth tongue ply his trade in the Black Lamb. Some were caught out; many weren't. Considering the nature of New Kent—especially the Hatches—she didn't care. But in that moment when the two had exchanged looks across the shambling figure of Runaway Mary, her shame burned on her cheek, Diana thought she saw someone like herself. Unlike Emmett, Diana always spoke her mind. Although now as she found herself looking into his wide, blue eyes, which seemed almost out of place in his weathered face, she hesitated ... as if on the edge of something exciting—unexpected.

"Who are you?" she finally blurted out. She caught herself in the act of covering her mouth as if she were trying to catch the blunt question, but was a little too late.

Emmett stared a moment, then flushed under his leathery skin. Then he broke into a laugh that warmed the distance between them. At that moment Diana lost her heart.

"Don't," she said. Unconsciously she held up a small hand that Emmett thought looked like a fine, white dove.

Emmett stopped laughing and stepped back into the room. He moved to Abigail's trunk and sat on the lid. Diana followed, perching on the bed. She sat quietly as Shannon gathered his thoughts, or courage—she wasn't sure which.

Finally he shook his head and smiled that smile of his. "I'm not a lieutenant, miss," he said.

"Diana."

Allan Cole & Chris Bunch

"Ah . . . Diana. I like that. But I'm no lieutenant, Diana."

"I guessed that."

"But there's no lie to my name. It's Emmett Shannon. And I'm a private in General Washington's army—or at least I was. Now I'm . . . aw, to hell with it. 1 don't know why I'm telling you this. I'm not drunk. To make a short tale of it, I'm a deserter." He looked at her and saw no surprise or disdain. "Does it matter?" he asked.

"Why should it? It's not my war. I belong to my master, and no one seeks my opinion of this or that or any fine thing."

"Still, I wouldn't want you to think poorly of me," Shannon said. "I have my reasons for what I've done."

Without thinking, he reached into his hunting shirt and pulled out the letter from his sister. He passed it to her. It was an odd act for Shannon, who had been raised to reveal nothing of his or his family's business. Why he gave her the letter, he couldn't say, but he watched anxiously as she read.

Finally she finished, folded the letter back up and returned it to him. "I would desert as well," she said, and her voice was so fierce in his defense that it startled him.

Diana was equally surprised at her intensity; also at her conflicting emotions. She pitied Shannon and his family. She guessed what they were going through, if Emmett's town was anything like New Kent. She also felt strangely exalted learning that his wife was dead. It was a stupid feeling, especially since after tomorrow—while Shannon was unwittingly aiding her in her flight by adding more excitement to Market Day—she'd never lay eyes upon him again. Stupid or not, the feeling nestled close to her like a kitten. Also she was now feeling vaguely guilty, thinking she had tricked him out of a confidence that was dangerous to reveal.

She looked at the confusion on his face and saw he was thinking the same. "I'm going to run, too," she blurted, scaring herself, but glad as soon as she said it. "I can't bear it any longer. So, I'm running . . . tomorrow . . . while they're all out making a fuss and fools of themselves. They can all be damned, and they'll never see the back of me."

Emmett was frightened for her . . . more than anyone before in his life—except when his wife lay dying. He thought of the mummified remains of the slave hanging from chains on the outskirts of New Kent. Of the broken, branded woman the good citizens gloated over and named Runner Mary.

"They'll catch you," he said, "and bring you back. It'll just make things worse."

"Oh, ho! So you can desert, but I must remain in my master's keep? Is that how you see it?"

Shannon thought of the sawpit and his decision to run at just about her age. He understood all too well. But . . . "You're just a little thing," he said. "Don't be angry at me for saying that. You don't know what's happening. Things are mad."

He thought of the redemption village and the child dying of smallpox. He thought of Frenchy McShane and Bill Grady's head on the post. He thought of the Dutchman's farm and all the dead and the woman lying spread-eagled in the snow and her hair at Frenchy's belt. How could he explain all this? He looked at her face: defiant, determined, plain Scots-Irish stubborn. It appeared even more so, framed by her thick red hair. This was not a woman to debate once she had made up her mind.

"Do you have a good plan?" he asked.

"Yes." So flat and final, he almost believed her.

"Stay just off the road so you can hide as quick as a thrust if a wrong one appears," he said. "Do you promise you'll do that for me?"

She just nodded, yes.

"I'll make a good show for them," he said. "I'll drill and train every man in New Kent so hard they won't be able to stand for a week, much less chase after an errant scullery maid."

Allan Cole & Chris Bunch

Diana stood up. A bargain had been struck between them, although she wasn't sure it was the one she would have wished under different circumstances. They stared at each other, wanting there to be more to say. But there wasn't. Diana took a step toward Emmett, and for a moment he thought she was about to kiss him and his heart hammered for the kiss, but then she just said "Thank you" and was gone.

CHAPTER TWELVE

DIANA PRODDED THE banked coals to life, then closed
the stove's firebox door and stood shivering in the predawn
chill.

Outside the inn she heard a slight clatter and a mutter.
Another drunk, she thought. Someone who'd stumbled out of
the taproom and found the nearest straw to sleep in. Diana
walked to the half door that opened onto the stable yard and
pushed the curtain aside to see whether the wakening drunk
was unknown or poor, in which case he was to be ignored; or
one of Nate's friends, in which case she'd best make a
whiskey toddy to brace him for the new day.

Gray fog hung low over the yard and climbed the hill
beyond the town. The clouds, as she'd once heard a child say,
were walking. She saw something move toward her through
the mist. Diana flattened back against the wall. Two soldiers.
Wearing red coats. She thought they were giants—then
realized both men wore tall, black helmets. They carried
long, bayoneted rifles as if they were spears. The British!

Diana waited for musket butts to hammer in the barred
door. Nothing happened. She chanced another look and saw
more soldiers advancing toward, and then past, the inn.

Noiseless in bare feet, she ran upstairs into Emmett's
bedchamber. He was sleeping heavily, curled on one side of
the bed. She shook him, and Emmett woke. Muzzy from the
night before.

"The British!"

"Eh?"

"The British are outside!"

"Jesus, lass. That's a story I—"

"No. Look."

She dragged him—Emmett stumbling, not aware of his
near-nakedness—to the window and twitched the linen
curtain away. Emmett saw a halberd-carrying sergeant wave

a squad forward, and in a moment he was away from the window.

"What do we do?" Diana was still whispering.

Emmett's mind spun through rum fumes, and then he was dragging his clothes on.

"Do I wake up Hatch?"

Emmett pulled on his boots, not bothering with foot-cloths. Diana was trying to keep from tears. Emmett sucked air, feeling his heart hammer; he calmed a little. "No. Don't wake anybody up," he hissed.

"But-"

"But nothing. They're lobsterbacks, right enough. Here to loot, I'd gamble." He gave her a close look, to be sure she would thoroughly understand what he was going to say next. "There's nobody standing against them now. Which is the best thing that could happen. They'll move to the center of town and take formation. Then they'll loose a volley and wake everyone up."

Emmett was nearly dressed. "They'll levy New Kent for what they need: horses, provender, the liquor. If Hatch has a brain, he'll roll his whiskey outside, and maybe save his inn. As long as no one fights back, you'll have your lives. With luck, they won't fire the town."

"What about you?"

"Me they'd shoot. Or hang. But I won't be here. I'll be out the back and gone across the hills before they come back with their searchers. One man, fleeing afoot with nothing of value, is beneath their worries."

Emmett was on his knees, shoveling his supplies into the pack. Maybe he'd best leave the rifle. Look even more innocent. Calm yourself, Emmett. Don't run off like a spooked yearling. Then he saw Diana had left the room. There was no time for farewells. What might have been would never be. He was halfway down the stairs when he heard a scuffle behind him. It was Diana, clutching her shoes and a canvas carrying bag. His mouth opened, and she motioned silence and brushed past him into the kitchen. There, still in a whisper: "I'm going with you!"

"The hell you are! If you're for a runaway, now's not the time, with troops out, blood and loot in their eye."

Diana was putting on her shoes. Emmett Shannon was looking for a closet to shove her into and something to block its doors while he cut and ran, when he heard the first dull thud through the mist. Coming from near the village square.

"Christ! That's done it!"

Four ... no, five single shots, then the slam of a volley. Some goddamned villager must've been still awake to see the red coats, and had his musket at hand. The volley, sounding like a single, huge blunderbuss going off, would have been from the British line. More spattered shots—the British skirmishers or maybe some confused colonialists. New Kent was fighting back. Shannon heard the shout of orders and the thud of running feet past the inn. He grabbed Diana's arm.

"Now you're coming."

The British were no more prone to atrocity and rape than any other army. Unless they were opposed. That would produce the terror. Shannon had the back door open and Diana out, into the stable yard. She followed him, running, across to the stables. Shannon thought for a moment, then thumbed his rifle's frizzen open and sprinkled powder into it.

"You're going to fight them!" A bit of pride.

Emmett didn't bother with an answer. He dribbled powder from the horn on a pile of dry hay under the eaves of the stable, turned the rifle to the side and snapped the trigger. Sparks flew, and the powder and hay caught. He shouted for Diana to free the horses. Emmett flung a handful of burning hay into one stall. A horse neighed in panic and bolted out. Emmett pulled more clumps and pitched them into the other stalls. The yard was a wild confusion of panicked horses, rearing and whinnying. The dry interiors of the stalls exploded into flame, and the horses bolted toward Emmett— he shouted, waving his rifle—then spun and plunged out of the stable yard, toward open country.

Allan Cole & Chris Bunch

"Now we run." Diana hesitated, not sure, now frightened.

"I'm not mad," Shannon said. "There's not a soldier serving, even a Britisher, that'll let a horse go past him. Not unless he wants to live with the sergeant's boot for a backside. Now be quiet! Try to do what I do."

Crouched, they scuttled off in the wake of the horses, straight toward the ridge and away from the paths. Emmett heard the shouts of soldiers from the hill in front of him. Behind him there came the double crash of volleyed fire inside New Kent. But Shannon's eyes, ears, and mind had no time for whatever was happening in the village. He was thinking only of what could be in the brush line ahead of him, his empty rifle, whether there would be redcoat vedettes on horseback in the valley beyond the hill, and that damned young woman panting along in his footsteps.

* * * *

The smokeboil that had been New Kent could still be seen five miles beyond the village. Emmett lay on his stomach, looking down at the main road. He wondered from which direction the British had come. Actually, he was trying to think of other matters rather than what to do about Diana. He turned, hearing a metallic clink, saw what Diana was doing and groaned. The clink came from a handful of coins.

Gold.

Diana finished counting, added the pile to a stack of currency and stuffed it all into Abigail Fahey's money sack. The sack went into her canvas bag.

"My inheritance."

"I'm pleased you trust me enough to let me see it," Emmett said dryly. "But that brings up a question. If you had this inheritance—and I'll not ask how it came that a bonded servant would have someone leave her gold—why didn't you buy your way out? Instead of running with me?"

"Hatch stole it. So I took it back. Just before we ran."

"Oh." Emmett saw no reason to disbelieve her. Certainly Hatch was the kind that would steal from any person in his power. But this now changed Shannon's thinking. He had thought that perhaps before they reached the Hudson and he turned toward Cherry Valley, they might encounter a small village or farm where Diana could be left. Willing labor, in these times, was scarce. But no longer. Not with that gold. Someone in the Hatch family—even if Nate ended up spitted on a British bayonet—must know of the money. A runaway might or might not be advertised— but one who had stolen would certainly be hunted. With a reward. He would probably be responsible for her, Emmett thought with a touch of gloom, until . . . until, Christ, it could be Albany. He didn't know how far up the Hudson the barbarism of the Neutral Ground had spread. But he thought the worst. Then he smiled.

Diana, waiting for a reaction to the gold and her statement, returned the smile. Tentatively.

"I was just thinking," Emmett said, "that maybe you're luck for me. If you hadn't kicked me out of my stupor, I might this moment be swinging on the end of a British noose."

He stood and helped Diana up. Her tentative smile grew firm.

"I hope you'll be the same for me," she said.

Allan Cole & Chris Bunch

CHAPTER THIRTEEN

EMMETT SHIFTED ON the hard wooden bench. There
was scant room on the little dray, and his muscles were
cramping keeping a modest distance from the soft, feminine
form beside him. Diana seemed unaware. She was bright-
faced and scrubbed, craning this way and that as she took in
the sights along the road. A faint, lavender smell rose from
her—she was still fresh from her morning wash at the creek a
few miles back.

Shannon had glossed over what had to have been the
only realistic fate of New Kent. He didn't know if she
believed him, or if she was pushing it from her mind. Either
way, Diana was unforcedly cheery and viewing everything
she saw on the road to Albany as an adventure. She seemed
satisfied with Shannon's immediate plans for her. Among his
friends in Albany, he'd said, was a prominent merchant
family he knew would be delighted to take Diana in. With
her "inheritance," she could set herself up and leave any
long-range planning until after the war.

Emmett and Diana were three days out of New Kent.
Moving at a lazy pace on their rickety dray, with a few bags
of feed for Horse and provisions they stowed in the back,
they seemed to be nothing more than a couple off to visit the
wife's family.

Emmett shifted again, wishing he had a pair of the
padded drawers green horsemen used until their rumps were
callused. Ahead, the short, heavily muscled and light-brained
farm horse plodded contentedly along—moving in a slow,
endless pace which could not be hurried even with a fresh
switch.

The animal was their first shared joke. After they'd
purchased it, they'd spent an hour seeking a name to fit its
personality. But there is dull-witted and then there is dull-
witted. So they decided to just call it "Horse."

After New Kent they'd traveled hard for two days. Diana gamely kept up, but it would be foolish to continue afoot farther, even on the main road. She was wearing her most durable frock, but her shoes, although sturdy, were made for the town, not long walking. A tight-fisted backwoods farmer had provided the solution. They came upon his small, lush spread, with its tidy stone house the evening of the second day. Until Shannon offered to room or board, the farmer refused them even the shelter of a musty stack of hay. Even then, his greedy eyes measured as his wife spooned up bowls of thin gruel and cut crusts of hard bread for their supper. His wife was no better. Diana saw her hide the salt cellar and instead pull out a threadbare sack containing only a few rocks of dirty salt. Shannon decided a little fleecing was in order, and was surprised how quickly Diana picked up the game.

As usual, he spiced the dish he was cooking with heavy drams of the truth. Diana aided and abetted him as he described the British attack on New Kent and then painted a pitiful tale of how he and his poor wife—left with barely a stitch—were now making their way to family in Albany. Diana stretched the two days into four, inventing detail upon detail of their harrowing flight through the wilds, with British patrols and brambles blocking a path even wild hogs couldn't penetrate.

"So you can see the trouble we're in, sir," Shannon said, "all we possess gone in flames, and many miles between us and the safety and comfort of our family's bosom."

The farmer and his wife tsked, tsked and said what a pity, but the ways of the Lord are strange and wonderful, and besides, what could be done?

"When we approached your fine place," Diana said, "we noticed that you had an abundancy of animals for a farm this size—especially horses." Too quick, lass, Shannon thought as the couple reacted in alarm—smiles fading, lips compressing. "We were both saying how very sad people had to work so hard to gain the little that we could see, only to lose it in an instant to the British. Isn't that so, Emmett, dear?"

Emmett buried a harrumph of surprise in a cup of water, then nodded vigorously: yes, dear, how pitiful, but true.

"They're not many miles behind us," Shannon said, "sweeping through the countryside for their booty. And it's horses they prize the most, yes indeed. Horses."

He looked full into the farmer's shocked face. Then he let his eyes widen in brilliant inspiration. "Perhaps we could help one another," he said.

"Aha." This was as far as the farmer would go. But it was an interested "aha," Shannon thought.

"If you worked all night, you could hide most of your goods. But the animals pose a different problem. The British will know they're about and hunt until they find them. We, on the other hand, have a need of transportation and the means to pay. We could possibly spare a little cash for a horse and a dray; they prize drays as well—almost above wagons. For the officers, you understand."

"Ah." Emmett sensed growing committal, but still some doubt.

"We could leave you a receipt of purchase you could show them," Diana came in. "Put as much as you want on it, and you'll have proof there's nary a beast about." She turned to Emmett. "What do you think, dear? You're much wiser in these things."

Emmett pretended to ponder it carefully. Finally he gave a big, wide smile. "There's no reason it shouldn't work," he said. "The British are notorious fools about official-looking papers. You'd think they were Dutchmen. What's your thinking, sir?"

The farmer's thinking was eager. Before they knew it, he'd sold them the beast destined to be called "Horse," the dray, feed for the animal and provisions for them. Shannon also talked the farm woman out of a good, sturdy riding cloak with a hood on it for Diana. They came to the matter of payment. Diana hefted out her fat, leather purse. But the chink of coin brought no joy to the farmer's face. He was feeling gloomy, because he had been forced to keep the prices he was charging fair. Otherwise, no one would believe the receipt. For a moment Shannon thought the man might let his sense of injustice outweigh everything else and back out on the contract.

He fumbled out his sheaf of counterfeit bills and pretended he was going to pay with these instead of coin. The farmer refused. Currency, he said, had nowhere near the value of coin. Shannon acted hurt. Then he offered a slightly larger currency-to-coin ratio. It was the farmer's turn to appear hurt. It went back and forth, until the farmer had boosted the exchange rate up and Shannon humbly hung his head to his proven master in bargaining and gave up the last bill he had to his name. Diana said nothing during this final bargaining, and Shannon wondered if she knew the currency was worthless as a rich man's promise.

The next morning the two of them harnessed up the dray and drove off without a word to the couple, pretending to be still smarting and angry over the arrangement. When they were well out of hearing distance, Diana burst into laughter.

"You're not a kind man at all, Emmett Shannon," she said.

"Oh? I think I'm the kindest fellow you'll ever meet," he said. "A mean man would have laughed in that farmer's face when the papers were signed."

"I think you're bending a point until it looks like the back of that poor beast we bought," she said, still laughing. "Now, own up. Admit I'm right."

"Not until you admit," Emmett said, "how you loved every moment of it. You've a talent for it, Diana, and if you played dice with the Devil ... I wouldn't put a penny on the Devil!"

* * * *

"Have you ever visited Philadelphia?" Diana asked. "I mean, the Philadelphia with an H, not a K." She flashed him

Allan Cole & Chris Bunch

a malicious grin, and now Emmett knew she was well aware of his little currency deception.

"No, I haven't."

"Well, wouldn't it be like Boston? It's a city of great size, isn't it?"

"You don't want to go to Boston," Shannon said. "It's a city of cold hearts. And you've never seen such poverty."

When he saw her expression darken, Emmett gave himself a kick. Where's your sense, man? The woman doesn't want to hear that. She's wanting a little glamour in her dreams just now.

"Actually," he said after a moment, "city life has a great deal to be spoken for. There's always new and different folks about. Discussing thousands of things."

"Like what?"

"Like what? Oh, uh . . . the theater, say."

Diana was suitably impressed. "You've been to the theater?"

"Well, I'd be lying to you if I said I had. It's much too expensive. But my father used to care for the carriages of the theater folk, and he'd take me along to see all the grand people."

From the glow in Diana's eyes, he knew he was getting back on the right path. "But there's lots of other amusements. Some of them at no cost at all. Why, when the ships came in from the West Indies, we all used to troop down to the wharfs. There'd be monkeys and wondrous birds. I saw a bear from the far north one time. It was pure white, like the snow and ice they say always covers the land up there.

"And on Clarke's Wharf you could visit a circus in the summer. One time I saw a famous acrobat, direct from England. And you'd call me a liar if I described his feats. There was a woman on Clarke's Wharf—Mrs. Hiller, I believe—who had wax figures of the grandest people of Europe. They were dressed so fashionably, and people who knew said they were identical in every feature. There was another waxworks not far away that was a bit more of a

126

scandal. The man who owned the collection had on display the image of the Countess of Heininburg, who reputedly had three hundred and sixty-five children at one birth."

Diana's lower jaw almost dropped. "Three hundred and . . . That can't be true."

"He had the figures there just the same. The countess and all her babes. I never saw for myself. My mother would have forbidden it."

"How did the countess . . . ? Oh, never mind. Still, it sounds very grand. A great occasion every day. What did the people look like? What did they wear?"

"Quite fashionable, as you can imagine," Shannon said.

Diana's left eyebrow twitched, and he realized she wouldn't be satisfied so easily. She'd want specifics. She was no farm wife who would be awed by a smooth tongue and talk of a "bit of lace." He'd seen a lace maker's pillow in her kit.

Emmett stumbled for description. "Uh . . . well, the ladies wore, uh . . . bows?" Diana nodded, encouraging. "Right. There were lots of bows on 'em. And, uh . . . ruffles?" Another nod. "Yes, bows and ruffles. They were covered with the stuff. And, uh . . . their dresses were all kind of tucked in . . . here . . . and, uh . . . billowy, thereabouts . . . uh, you know, like . . ." He made helpless, wavy gestures with his hands.

"You mean flounces?" Diana said.

"That's it! Flounces, they were. All bows and ruffles and flounces." Shannon was exhausted by all this. He glanced over at Diana, as if expecting congratulations.

"They sound daft to me," she said.

Emmett sighed. "So they were," he said. "So they were."

* * * *

As the days went by, they became easier with each other, unguarded in their thinking. Emmett and Diana were a little like a brother and sister who have rediscovered one another as adults and become friends. Not so sibling like was the growing sexual tension between them. But they both did their

Allan Cole & Chris Bunch

best to keep it at a distance, as if afraid it would spoil the rich broth they were cooking up together. This tension might seize them in a pause in conversation, or become the dark shadow behind an innocent touch. Once it was merely the unusual heat of an afternoon, when the sun bore up the sticky scent of pine and they both found their voices growing heavy and thick. Emmett leaned closer, and Diana found herself sagging back for him, and then she was flushing and turning away and Emmett busied himself with his pipe, spilling tobacco through trembling fingers.

Mostly they just talked; endlessly and about everything. Diana told Emmett about life in New Kent, the scandal of her birth and the powerful influence of Abigail Fahey. When Diana talked about the Hatches, Emmett grew so unreasonably furious, he wanted to turn back then and hunt them down for punishment. She reacted with equal fury when he told her about the sawpits, the cheating British officer, the petty and misplaced revenge of his Cherry Valley neighbors. When he talked about his dead wife, Sarah, she drew him out on the subject—asking questions of some detail; for what purpose, she didn't know.

She was also curious about his grandfather, and it wasn't just because of the effect two old people had on each of them. Shannon understood it was because Diana—born on the wrong side of the hedge—was a person whose beginnings were nearly as obscure to her as a slave from the African coast. If asked, she would have said this was only partially the explanation. To her it was mostly because the old man had reached directly over Emmett's poor, gentle father to gift him with the few things he treasured most. Brian Shannon's belief in the great importance of the ability to read struck her like a commandment that should be carved on a stone tablet.

They made camp early one day. The harness and the dray needed fussing over, and Horse's slow pace seemed even wearier. Diana took the opportunity to tend to her own things, such as whip-stitching a few rents in her garments.

As Shannon reached to hang the harness from a branch, the back of his hunting shirt gave way in a great ragged tear. He greeted it with a soldier's oath he cut off in mid-obscenity when he saw her laughing face. "I've patched it a hundred times," he said, "but it keeps getting the better of me. What's worse, the tear gets larger each time. Soon I'll be naked as Adam."

Diana had him remove it and examined the marks of endless patching. "You can't mend it this way," she sniffed.

"Ah, she gives herself away," Shannon mocked. "Underneath all that prettiness, the woman's sharp as a new stitch. I myself would never have guessed I was doing it all wrong."

Diana shook her head at his weak humor. "It's just that you cannot use needle and thread to right a bit of leather that's gone wrong this way," she said.

She showed him the old marks of the needle on the shirt. "With cloth," she said, "it would be different. Cloth heals itself, as we like to say. But leather is flesh, after all, and when you pierce it with a needle, the wound is permanent because there is no living thing underneath to grow it back."

"Then it's hopeless. My future is clear. I'm faced with burned skin by day and nights of trembling cold."

Diana didn't answer. Instead, she dug for her kit and drew out a small amber-colored stick. She had Emmett fetch two clean rocks from the creek and set them heating on the fire. She chipped a few slivers from her stick into a tin cup and put it near the fire. As the chips melted, Diana cleaned up the worst of the jaggedness with a sharp blade from her sewing kit, and then deftly constructed a patch out of a piece of the shirt's tail. Then she pulled the cup away from the fire. The chips inside had melted into a mass of goo. She stirred it with a stick, testing the consistency.

"What kind of glue is that?"

"It's just Diana's famous tailor's elixir. Handed down from generations of ancient Senecas. That's all."

Allan Cole & Chris Bunch

"Right. A secret between us at last. Well, let's just see how this ancient brew works and if there's a fortune in your future."

With a clean twig she drew a bead along the edges of the patch and then on the shirt. She maneuvered the patch into place and then used the hot stones as a press. Emmett had to squint hard to see where the old tear had been. He was amazed at her skill and talked about it over the next few hours.

Near evening he remembered something. "Do you recall me telling you about the waxworks on Clarke's Wharf?"

"You mean the one with the countess and her three hundred sixty-five babes? In shuddering detail!"

"No, no. The one maintained by Mrs. Hiller."

"Yes."

"Well, I didn't tell you all about it. She made a good deal of money from the waxworks. But she made even more with her skill with a needle. She was well-known for miles about. Still, this was not the true genius of our dear Mrs. Hiller.

What she did was open a school of needlework. It was for all the daughters of the rich merchants and leather aprons in Boston. The school was very expensive, but as you know, if the rich find something to be fashionable, it becomes as great a need for them as a poor man wanting bread.

"Well, with that in mind—Mrs. Hiller's success, I mean— wouldn't that hold a possibility for you? Once you get set up in Albany, or Philadelphia, or wherever your heart takes you, couldn't you use your skill to start such a school?"

"Me?" Diana was astounded. "But I'm just a—"

"Don't be silly," Shannon said. "It doesn't rest easy with you. Why should you tell anyone from this day on where you came from? Or how? Or why? Your particulars are your own business, and if you give that great cold stare I know you have in you, they'll be ashamed they ever asked. Besides, greater men and women than you and I come from humbler places and more scandalous births.

"The point I'm trying to reach, Diana, is that you will do very well, I'm sure. But you'll have to work like a servant to get anywhere. Unless you find some way to make yourself a darling of the rich. Then everything you do will bring back gold instead of silver. Otherwise . . . the harder the labor, the meaner the pay, is the firm rule in this life."

Diana had to admit he made sense. Then she brought the conversation around to what he saw in his future.

"I'm no good as a farmer," he admitted. "I'd be better in some business where I could use my wits."

"Then, perhaps you should consider the city," Diana said hopefully, feeling an odd tick of hope in her heart. "From what you said about Boston, that's out, I suppose. But there's always—"

"Not one of those eastern flea holes," Shannon broke in. "Their narrowness would stifle me. I'd choke in their high-nosed Tory air."

"Then where?"

"Pittsburgh," he said. "That's the place for me."

He told her about Pittsburgh, the rough-hewn town along the Monongahela River in the Pennsylvania wilderness. People asked no prying questions of another in such a place. It was already growing—with rich land all about, and iron as well—but more important was the river trade. Shannon believed that in the future the city would number more than a thousand residents and there would be opportunity for a man who could use his wits.

Diana had heard travelers' tales about Pittsburgh and she had other thoughts than Emmett's. But she didn't say anything about them. Instead: "Why not go there, then?"

Shannon groaned. How could he ever accumulate the funds for such a venture? His farm was worthless, and there would be the added cost of setting up a household for his two sons, his sister and her son and daughter.

"Oh, I'm not too sure about that," Diana said, sounding wiser than her years. But she had kept her ears open and her mind darting during her time at the Black Lamb. "You claim

pg. 131

Allan Cole & Chris Bunch

the farm is worthless. I'd be speaking over myself to argue. But didn't you say it was on the crossroads, at the edge of the town?"

Shannon nodded, this was true.

"Then it's a perfect place for an inn," she said, excited. "There's a fortune to be made at any crossroads. That's one thing I learned from Nate Hatch! So it's easy, then. You start an inn . . . build up the business . . . sell it for a handsome ..."

She went on, happily planning Shannon's future. Building the inn stone by stone; where the hearth would go; how many rooms; the food; the drink. Shannon just lay back, listening. It was amazing. No matter how far you had to dig through her excited words, there was always a hard grit of Tightness about what she said.

They slept closer that night.

* * * *

The following evening, Shannon pulled the dray deep into the woods. They were nearing Kingston and it was time for caution. It was so dark under the trees, they couldn't see beyond the edge of their tiny campfire. Shannon got the oil lamp from the dray, filled it, and set it atop a rock to widen their small circle of light.

After they ate, they sat close together and listened to the stream that gurgled a few feet away, but in the darkness seemed to come from someplace far away. Then there was a slight shift of the breeze and the smell of moss drew them nearer to the stream's warm shallows.

Diana found herself staring at the glow of the oil lamp. Insects flashed at the lamp, their trails looking like sparks flying off into the night. She felt Emmett turn, and she looked at him. He seemed so sad, she wanted to tell him there was nothing . . . nothing ... to be sad about.

Emmett marveled how her hair shone so deep red and black in the firelight, and as Diana fell back, the hot scent of lavender rose up to embrace him.

* * * *

The next day would have been bewildering to any poor sane man or woman who had never been as fatally smitten as Diana and Emmett. In the manner of lovers, volumes of things were taken for granted—all without discussion. As they loaded the dray, it was assumed Diana was continuing with Shannon to Cherry Valley. They kept on planning the inn, its eventual sale and their new life-to-be in Pittsburgh. When the town grew as Emmett predicted, Diana would have her sewing school there, and Emmett was wondering about opening a waxworks exhibit annex, like the one developed by Mrs. Hiller on Clarke's Wharf.

Suddenly Diana stopped. "What are your sons' names?" she asked.

"Brian and Farrell," Shannon said. "Brian's the oldest."

"Ah. For your grandfather and your father," she said. "They'll both read as well as a schoolmaster, I promise you." And then she picked up the previous conversation in midstream.

A little later, each thinking private, pleasant thoughts under a drowsy afternoon sun, she asked: "Is your religion important to you?"

"No, not like most people," Emmett said after a moment's thought. "But I'll stick to being Catholic. First off, I despise churches, and if you're Catholic there aren't any to attend, are there? But mostly because the British have been trying to whip it out of us for hundreds of years. Anything they hate so much has to have something to say for itself, don't you think?"

Diana nodded, thinking this over a bit. She had even less religious feelings than Shannon; being raised by an old cynic like Abigail assured that. She didn't know anything about Catholics, but she was willing to give it a try. "What about Brian and Farrell?" she asked.

Emmett thought about this, then raised an eyebrow. "I don't know. What do you think?"

"They'll be Catholics like their father," she said firmly. Then: "Do you think your sister Ruth will like me?"

Allan Cole & Chris Bunch

Shannon laughed. "There's no trouble there," he said. "A person would have to work very hard indeed to get on the wrong side of my sister. It's her fault and failing at the same time. She goes along too easily with people . . . not because she's afraid they won't like her, but because she's so . . . so . . . warm, I guess you'd call it."

It was only early afternoon when they made camp again. Even so, they were barely in time and Horse had to stand patiently in harness until evening.

CHAPTER FOURTEEN

KINGSTON WAS A city of the dead. Emmett and Diana looked down on the gray-black wasteland. There was only one house still standing, and it appeared abandoned. Broken chimneys stuck up from still-blackened timbers in orderly rows. Here and there were the shells of stone houses, or sometimes just a still-standing wall or two. Near the center of the desolation was a taller pile of rubble with a shattered vee of unburnt wood beside it, across what would have been the street. A church, Emmett guessed. Another ruin. A courthouse? They saw no people in the ruins. The bluff the town had been built on sloped down across wetland to the Hudson River, a couple of miles away.

"I wonder," Diana said quietly, "if New Kent looks like this now."

Shannon didn't answer. His mind was busy peopling the landscape. Here there would have been a marketplace. There would have been Dutch farmers and their wives and children moving goods toward it. Standing outside taverns, talking to townsfolk, bargaining with merchants, gossiping, running across the village green. But now, nothing.

Approaching Kingston, they'd passed abandoned huts where desperate people must have taken hasty shelter. Shannon wondered where those people were now. Even the streams were dead, still ash-choked. A bird warbled from a tree, and both of them started. Emmett clucked and Horse began moving again. The creak of the cartwheels was unbearably loud in the stillness all around them.

"I wonder how long it'll take them to rebuild?" Diana said. Emmett thought maybe it would never happen. As a boy he'd heard a sailor claim he'd seen great stone cities, buried in the jungles of Mexico and again in Africa near the island of Madecass. From the tale, they were desolate. Abandoned. He had listened to a church lecturer returned from the Holy Land, who said the great cities of the Bible were now nothing but huts and Arabs. He himself had seen crumbling stockade villages once used by the Iroquois. Maybe Kingston would just return to the forest.

He shivered, thinking of Cherry Valley, and beyond it the thousands of miles of mountains and wilderness, stretching to the Western Ocean. It drew him—and scared him. Then he wondered how Diana would find Cherry Valley. He knew she saw it as a smaller version of New Kent. But New Kent was civilization itself compared to Emmett's home. What would she think on her first Market Day, when she realized that half of the marketgoers were wild forest Indians? Or when she saw a farmer plowing a field, his musket propped against the rail fence not far distant? Or parents worried when children were out of earshot or sight? That, he thought, will have to take care of itself. First we have to catch the rabbit.

He jumped down and led Horse through the least-blocked street. Here was a lump of melted iron. A stove, Emmett realized, blown out of a house when the building exploded. Here would have been someone's garden. A low bush had managed to produce a single flower. Emmett picked it and gave it to Diana, bowing low. She managed a smile. Farther on, Emmett heard mews, and saw movement in a ruin as three mottled kittens scurried into hiding. Emmett wondered what their mother had lived on during the winter.

There were bits of a recruiting poster on a tottering wall. Emmett could make out that it was calling for Intrepid Heroes. Surely, he thought. Come and join the Revolution. Burn a Loyalist out because the British burnt you. Bayonet a lobsterback prisoner because a friend was found slashed to death. Shoot a teamster, he reminded himself, because you had to live on spoiled rations. Be a hero, lads. It's a right honorable trade.

"What are you thinking?" Diana asked.

Emmett shook himself back to Kingston. "I was just musing," he said. "If I should have me another son, and he takes his first step with his left leg like soldiers do when they march ofT, I'll break it in six places." A rat stared insolently at them, not moving as the cart passed.

Emmett pushed well away from the road when it was time to make camp. They ate a cold meal, not willing to chance a fire. Emmett rubbed Horse down, fed and watered him, then replaced the harness. He would only have to hook up the traces and they could be moving instantly. He felt slightly sorry for the beast—but better having to worry about it being galled in a few days than wasting time if raiders came on them. The road now led almost due north, following the west bank of the Hudson toward Albany. These were disputed lands. Neutral Ground. But there were no neutrals.

Loyalists burnt Rebels and the compliment was returned. Raiders were out on the land. Some called themselves cow boys, some skinners, some rangers, some scouts. For the most part their loyalties lay, in fact, with their own pockets and private feuds. Anyone who lived in the stretch between the American positions near Albany and the British-held New York area and dreamed of staying neutral would have been plundered by both sides and eventually burnt out. Or else become a wolf in his own right. Not a wolf, Emmett corrected himself. There was nothing wrong with wolves. Jackal, from what he'd read, made a better description.

From here on they must travel even more warily. Looking to be a harmless farmer and his young wife, with nothing to steal, might help. But not very much—there were men, and women, on these roads who would murder just for the sensation. The problem was telling Diana this. So far their journey was a romance any young woman of quality might read behind her prayer book. With, Emmett reminded himself, certain carnal exceptions. Now the chronicle could too easily be written by Dr. Swift or Mister Defoe.

While he considered, Diana asked, without preamble: "Would you show me how to fire your pistol?" Emmett hesitated. "The merchants who came to New Kent were always telling us of the hazards of their travels," she said. "I thought it was just to explain their terrible pricing.

"I do not want," she said carefully, "for us to meet anyone who'll intend harm, and for me to sit on this cart seat with nothing to do but scream like Miss Muffett."

There was no need for Shannon to prepare his speech. They made love again that night not from lust or romance, but to reaffirm being among the living.

The next morning he showed her how to load and aim the pistol. He planned to allow her two shots. The noise wouldn't travel far—and they would be gone before anyone could investigate. He chose a wide tree for a target, and stationed Diana ten yards from it. Emmett felt that, with care, he himself would be able to hit that tree. At least Diana would be able to place her shots in the vicinity. Diana put both pistol balls in the center of the tree. Emmett was not that surprised—it had been his discovery, years earlier, that women, if they set their minds to it, could do most things better than a man.

* * * *

They heard the yelping of dogs from the brush. Emmett checked his rifle and reined in the horse. A lean hound burst out, chased by seven more. They went across the road into the brush on the other side. The dogs were all of a breed. Emmett guessed they would have been a hunting pack, belonging to some rich fox hunter. Probably a Loyalist, and certainly no longer resident in the countryside, or possibly on this Earth. Now his dogs hunted on their own. The lead dog had been carrying something in its jaws. Something brown. Meat? Shannon was glad he had not been able to tell what kind of meat it was.

* * * *

Diana saw it first. Deep in the trees, twenty-five yards from the road, was a rude hut. Shannon swore to himself—he was becoming careless. Two children, naked except for burlap sacking worn like nightgowns, stared at them. Diana waved—and the children fled just as the kittens had in ruined Kingston.

"Squatters' kids?" she said.

"Maybe," Emmett said. "Or maybe farmers' lads. Or lasses. I couldn't tell."

"I wonder," Diana began, and stopped. She was wondering where the mother or father was. She didn't want to think on that.

* * * *

They saw other people trying to live in these outlaw lands. Raggedy men and women who ran for cover when they saw or heard the cart. Sometimes it was Emmett and Diana who fled. Twice they pulled off the road, hearing the thunder of horses. Well-mounted men rode past, with ready weapons and searching eyes. Shannon had no intention of finding out which side they were on.

Once they passed the gutted ruins of a mansion. Three brick walls reached upward, without floors or roof. The hedges and roses of a formal garden were overgrown with rank weeds. Nothing remained of barns or outbuildings.

"I shall be damned," Emmett thought aloud, "why that saddens me. Those who lived there would have been Tory-minded bas—pardon, people, who want to run this world as if God granted them the deed, who are better gone from this country. But still ..."

"That wouldn't have upset Nate Hatch," Diana said. "When he was drinking, I'd heard him mutter that the world would be better if all those original proprietors of New Kent would suddenly be bankrupt or pox'd. But when he was sober, he could not do them enough favors. When we're rich, we'll have to be very careful that we don't start sounding like that bastard."

Emmett recovered and found a smile. "With me, lass, it's most unlikely that ll be a worry."

"We'll see," she said confidently. "We shall see."

* * * *

The day would have been better suited for midsummer instead of spring. There was no breeze from the nearby Hudson. It had been hot at dawn. By midday it was boiling. Ahead, the road curved out of sight. Emmett followed habit.

Allan Cole & Chris Bunch

The cart was pulled up, and Emmett went forward, to the curve. He'd tried to convince Diana that she should stay with the cart—but had failed.

About seventy-five yards around the curve was a tiny village. One stone house—roofless—and five still-upright chimneys, two of them at either end of what had been a single structure. Perhaps a tavern. Another destroyed village. But it took Emmett a moment to realize what was different about this village. It had not been burnt. It had been taken apart. As far as he could see, there was not a scrap of wood left. Houses, fences, sheds, had been taken apart by someone.

By an army, Emmett realized. Inhabitants gone—or chased off—and then whichever side had camped here had stripped the village for cooking and heating fires. When the wood was gone—or when orders came—they would have marched on. Emmett, who had stripped his share of rail fences, felt a touch of guilt.

But all this was so much pointless moralizing, because the village was not deserted. Four saddled horses were tied outside the ruins of the stone house, and three remounts stood behind them. Their riders weren't in sight. Emmett was wishing he had an officer's spyglass when a man stepped out of the ruins. Shannon needed no telescope. At this distance he could easily see the man's long black hair, red scarf, silver spurs on booted feet, and the big, green-feathered slouch hat.

Emmett was sliding backward, pulling Diana with him, then running back to the cart. Silently he turned the animal around and they went back the way they'd come. They took the first sidetrack from the road. Shannon pulled the cart up and cut a sheaf of brush. With it he swept the turnoff and up the track itself. He could do nothing about the marks on the road, except hope McShane was moving north, with no interest in backtracking. Then he led Horse on, farther up the track, which led to yet another burnt-out farmhouse. Below it was a draw and the destroyed springhouse. They would be well-hidden.

Unhitching Horse, he suddenly realized that at no time had Diana protested, asked for an explanation, or panicked. But that wasn't what amazed him. The surprise was—that was exactly how he expected her to behave. Now how could he know that?

CHAPTER FIFTEEN

HORSE THREW A shoe three days from Albany, and although Emmett and Diana did their best to lighten his load by walking beside the dray, within a few miles he was favoring his leg. A small farmhouse beckoned just off the main road. It was gray stone and there was a well-tended kitchen garden in front, with a large stone well in the center. The farmer and his family were working in the garden when Diana and Emmett approached.

The man's name was Abraham Duval. He was in his late middle-age, and he worked the farm with his wife and two grown daughters—one of whom had a child on her hip. Except for exotic, hawklike features and long, straight black hair, they looked like any other Colonial farm family. But they were Senecas. They spoke no English—just their own language and a French/Iroquois patois that Shannon understood from his many years in the area. Diana could not make out a thing, but gathered from the initial smiles and the friendliness of Abraham's tone that he was willing to help. Then his wife, whose hair was streaked with pure white, said something sharp, and Abraham's brow furrowed and his tone became hesitant, with a touch of embarrassed sadness. Nods of welcome turned to reluctant shakes of the head.

"What's wrong?" she asked Shannon.

"I'm not sure," he said. "But I get the idea we came at an inconvenient time. He keeps telling me to go away. But then he says come back later."

Then the child's contented coos turned to a squall of anger as something fell to the ground. The squall ended abruptly when his mother scooped up the object and handed it back to him. It was a string of colorful beads—like the ropes of wampum less settled Indians favored for money. The child wrapped a strand around his pudgy fist and stuffed it into his mouth—revealing swollen gums pebbled with buttons of budding teeth.

Shannon puzzled at the beads, then his face brightened. "Now, I understand," he told Diana, but before she could ask him exactly what he understood, he was waving his hands and jabbering at the farmer.

Soon everyone was smiling broadly. One of the daughters patted at Diana's dusty clothes and made motions of washing up. Before she knew it, she was being pulled toward the house and Abraham was helping Emmett unhitch Horse. She stood on her toes, craning her neck, trying to get Shannon's attention as they led Horse toward the barn.

He spotted her bewildered expression and laughed. "It's all right, Diana," he shouted. "It's only that they're Catholic." For a while that mysterious explanation was all she got.

After a scouring with hot water and herbal soap, a change of clothing and a light meal, Diana found herself in the main room of the farmhouse, sitting in a straight-backed chair next to Emmett. The Duval family bustled around, making preparations. For what, Diana still didn't know. Emmett filled her in.

Abraham had been raised by Jesuit missionaries in Canada and had been a farmer all his life. He had grown weary of the constant and violent shifts of tide that one day made the English the enemy, the next the French, and the day after, a neighboring tribe. He'd sold his farm and bought this one six or seven years ago. Here they'd prospered, and the only sadness was that his son and his daughters' husbands had been caught up in the current conflict. Shannon hadn't asked on what side they were fighting, and Abraham hadn't volunteered. Emmett was beyond caring. An enemy was only a man pointing his rifle in the wrong direction.

"But what does this all have to do with what went on outside?" Diana asked—a little hot, because at the moment she felt that her temper was being unfairly tested.

"As I said: they're Catholic. It was a rosary the child was suckling on. Today is Sunday, and we came along as they

pg. 143

Allan Cole & Chris Bunch

were getting ready for their service. Abraham said the sheriff in these parts is a tolerant man—for a sheriff—but if we were to complain ..." An eloquent shrug of his shoulders filled in the rest. "But everything was fine when I explained that we were Catholic as well."

He lifted a questioning eyebrow at this, but Diana patted his hand. She didn't mind. The service was relaxed and, Diana thought, very sweet. She was used to thunderings from a pulpit, but here, first Abraham, and then the women, took turns reciting prayers, which gave way to gentle discussion. The only religious decoration was a cross Abraham's wife brought from another room. On it, the Christ figure was twisted and tormented in the agonized style of the French Catholic.

Emmett explained it was a "Mass in Spirit," much like the ones he remembered his mother conducting, except the Duvals mixed in a little of their ancestors' beliefs. It included, he. explained, a public confession of the sins the Duvals thought they had committed since the preceding week. And a paltry lot of sins they were; he chuckled.

There was a pause, and then Abraham broke in with a question to Emmett. Was there anything he—or Diana-felt a need to confess? Emmett started to give him a quick no, but then hesitated. He couldn't help but be moved by the service. It had brought back memories of his mother's rich voice reciting from Garden of the Soul. Words of prayer were the first he could read—thanks to his grandfather. There also was that small voice in him saying someday his soul might regret this missed opportunity.

He told them about the wagon master he had murdered. Then he told them about the other, possibly greater sin: letting the Hessian live, only because his act of mercy might wash away the murder. It was a deed of selfishness, not contrition, Abraham agreed. But under the circumstances, he said, he was sure God would understand. And forgive. Personally, Abraham said, I would have shot them both, so I must be at heart a greater sinner than you. Why don't we pray together that He forgive us both? Me for thought, you for deed. The Jesuits say both are equal, although no matter how hard I have studied and prayed, I can't understand their reasoning. Can you? Emmett, having never met a priest— much less a Jesuit—couldn't answer. So he bowed his head and prayed. A few moments later he felt hot tears on his cheeks and then Diana's soft hand wiping them away.

Later, after they had been fed again and Abraham had helped Emmett shoe Horse and treat his soreness, Shannon and Diana sat together on the porch while the Duvals went about the light work of a farm Sabbath. There was a late afternoon breeze, bringing the scent of the maple grove.

Diana held his hand quietly, thinking over the events since New Kent and wondering what lay ahead. Once again the thinking led to a question that for Shannon, at least, seemed to come from nowhere. "Tell me, Emmett. How were your father and mother wed? Was it difficult for them— as Catholics, I mean?"

"No. A little elaborate, but not difficult," he said, after thinking a moment. "My mother said they posted the banns and were wed in a legal church. They had no choice, but I recall her being a little bitter about it.

"She said she insisted on a proper Catholic wedding that same night. They got together some people of like faith and had them witness their vows. My mother said she would have felt like a harlot otherwise. As far as she was concerned, an English wedding was no wedding at all."

Shannon gave her a small, apologetic smile. "My mother had some odd ideas," he said.

"Not at all," Diana said. "I understand her meaning perfectly. Now, tell me, Emmett dear, when we get to Cherry Valley, how will we marry?"

"Oh, that's no trouble at all. We'll post the banns, and you can stay with Ruth, and I'll ask a friend to take me in until the proper time. Then we'll go to the church and . . ."

His voice trailed off as he realized what Diana was getting at.

Allan Cole & Chris Bunch

"You don't want to make a harlot of me, do you, Emmett?" she said with a little laugh.

"It's a little hard to have a Catholic wedding in Cherry Valley," Shannon said. "It's not like Boston, with all its people. I think our neighbors would give us grief over the matter. Especially in the mood they seem to be in now."

Diana kissed him on the cheek. "Why don't we ask Abraham?" she said. And so they did.

The service was performed that evening. Diana was led into the main room by Abraham's wife, who was standing in as her mother. His older daughter performed the same role for Emmett. The Duvals held to the Iroquois tradition of marriage being a maternal function, in which men had no legal standing.

With Mrs. Duval's help, Diana had done a hasty remake of one of her dresses. She had tucked it in here and there and let a few seams out, and added a sash at her waist and a small blue bow that she'd shaped like a flower in early bud. On her head she wore a bit of lace that Mrs. Duval had donated. It was old and the color of fine ivory. Emmett stood in the center of the room. He had been scrubbed a bright sunburn color, his face was clean-shaven, and his boots were shiny black with axle grease. Each of them thought they had never seen another man more handsome or a woman quite so beautiful.

Emmett asked Abraham what they were supposed to do. First you give each other a gift, he said. But Diana knew this already. She had been coached by Mrs. Duval through the universal hand signals of impending marriage. She passed Emmett a cloth containing two rounds of unleavened corn bread.

This is the proper gift for a woman to give a man, Abraham said. Now it's your turn. Shannon was embarrassed. He didn't have anything to give, he explained. Nor did he know what it should be. It should be something from the hunt, Abraham said. From the chase. A bit of meat or fish. Something to show you can provide for her. Emmett agonized. Abraham finally solved his dilemma by fishing a rifle ball from Shannon's store of ammunition. He placed it in a small pouch with a leather thong and gave it to Emmett. This should do, he said.

Emmett presented the little pouch to Diana, who blushed like it was a gift of gold, and tucked it in her bodice. Then they stood there in clumsy silence for what seemed like an eternity. "What do we do now?" he asked Diana.

"I don't know," she said. "I've never married a Catholic before." She grew flustered at her words. "I mean, I've never been married at all!"

Abraham asked him what they were waiting for. Shannon said neither one of them knew what came next. For the first time since they came to the Duval farm, Abraham showed irritation. He asked Shannon if he loved the woman and wanted to be her husband, with all the responsibilities that went with it. Or was he just trifling with Diana? If so, neither he nor his family wanted any part of this, and would Emmett leave his house as soon as possible. Shannon said of course he loved her! Of course he wanted to marry her! He just didn't know how to go about it. Then tell her, man, Abraham said. Tell her.

"I love you, Diana," Shannon blurted. "I want you to be my wife." Then he turned bright red.

"I love you, Emmett," Diana said. "And I want you for my husband."

There was a loud whoop from Abraham and squealing cheers from the other Duvals. There was no translation necessary. They were husband and wife.

* * * *

That night while the Duvals slept, Emmett and Diana took their blankets outside under the trees. Their bed was as comfortable as anyone could ask, and Abraham had given them a private room. But it seemed close in the house, and they felt shy with the others about. Besides, Diana whispered to Emmett, after all these weeks under the stars, it seemed indecent to make love with a roof over their heads. Shannon

pg. 147

warned her that if that were so, they'd get awful cold come winter.

Diana tugged him close and promised him, as long as they were wed, she would never let him feel the cold.

CHAPTER SIXTEEN

"DOES IT FEEL different," Emmett inquired, "now being a Shannon and a Papist?"

Diana giggled. "It felt good. 1 don't know about different."

"Tsk. The woman is being lecherous and obscene. Cover your ears, Horse."

Horse was concentrating on plodding, favoring his now-reshod leg. They had spent two days with the Duval family as honored guests. Abraham had given them more than enough fodder and provisions to make Albany. Elaborate protestations of eternal debt and friendship, and promises of reunions, had been made, which no one expected would ever be kept.

The day was made for traveling, sunny and breezy. Emmett, feeling most peaceful, had to force himself to load pistol and rifle. Weapons seemed a profanity for this day, this mood and this moment. With his other gear, they lay, unprimed, in the dray. Emmett and Diana walked beside Horse, hand in hand. They were about half a mile from the Indians' farm when Emmett heard the first rifle shot. A hunter—but Emmett stepped to the wagon and lifted out his rifle. Then two more thuds and the louder bang of a shotgun. Diana, startled, looked at him, knowing...

"Wait here," Emmett said, forcing steadiness. Hunting bag . . . powder horn . . . belt . . . knife . . . pistol and tomahawk. "Get the wagon off into the brush."

Diana nodded. Scared. And Emmett was running back for the Duvals in his long frontiersman's lope.

Screams. Two more shots. Emmett cut off the road and up a rise, zigzagging toward the farm, sheltered by the brush. On the crest he knelt, hand snapping frizzens back, pouring powder into pans.

A Daughter Of Liberty

The body of Abraham Duval lay in back of the house in a pool of blood. He had already been scalped. From the house's front Emmett heard a last scream—cut short. Staying low, he went down the gentle slope to the stone fence, and around to the Duvals' garden. Over the wall he saw the bodies of the three women, and that of the child. They were all dead. Pinched Face was crouched over one. He ripped the scalp free and stood, holding it up, exhibiting it to another of McShane's raiders.

Rage took Emmett and his rifle fired. The ball took Pinched Face in the stomach. He screamed and then went to his knees, guts spilling. The second man, unarmed, turned and was running for the open back door of the house as Emmett, blind in his fury as any Jacobite pikeman, went over the wall, tomahawk in hand. In three bounds he was on the man and shattered his skull.

A musket boomed out the doorway, and Emmett spun away, going down and rolling backward, behind the sheltering stone circle of the well. Movement behind a curtained window, and Emmett dropped the tomahawk, dragged the pistol from his belt and snap-fired. Glass shattered and there was a shout of pain.

His fingers fumbled ball and patch from his pouch, and the third raider ran out the door at him, musket leveled. Emmett scooped the tomahawk up, rose to his knees and threw. It hit the man just as the musket fired, and smashed through the outlaw's rib cage. Emmett heard another gun blast hard on the first—from the window—and the ball hit him in the side.

Christ, Christ, but it hurt, but there was still one of them left, and fingers poured powder and rolled a patchless ball down the rifle's muzzle, and the butt stamped on the ground to send the ball home, and powder in the pan, and Frenchy McShane, blood-bearded and half blinded, came out of the house an enraged bear, pistol aimed.

Both men fired.

And missed.

Frenchy, bawling, had his bloody scalping knife out of his belt, still attacking, and somehow Emmett was swinging the rifle by the barrel. The butt caught McShane along the jawbone.

McShane's skull crushed, and the burly man went down into the dirt. The rifle's stock was broken at the grip. Emmett dropped it. The pain crashed on him and he fell.

Not yet, Shannon. Not yet.

Emmett's numb fingers pulled his knife and drove it deep into McShane's back.

Emmett sagged back against the well's stonework.

Waiting for Diana.

There was something he needed to tell her. And then he knew nothing more.

Emmett Shannon never regained consciousness. He died just at twilight. Diana Shannon sat beside him until he died.

Allan Cole & Chris Bunch

CHAPTER SEVENTEEN

TWO MONTHS LATER Diana Shannon came to Cherry Valley.

She was still driving the dray, but it bounced on new springing; its metalwork sparkled and it had been painted bird-shell blue. Horse plodded along in his slow and steady pace.

Diana had stopped outside the town and let her traveling party continue ahead. She had freshened up at a creek and put on her best dress from Albany over petticoats so stiff that they crackled when she walked. Now she had her red hair tied up against the heat; there was a stubborn tilt to her head, and the line of her jaw was firm. Her figure had yet to thicken from the child she carried. Around her neck was the little leather pouch with the single rifle ball inside.

As she drove through the village, she saw all the landmarks that Emmett had mentioned: the inn where he told his stories and worked his charm; the church he never attended; the meeting hall, where as a man of property, he had cast his first vote.

The farm was just as he described. It was the last one at the far end of town and set at the crossroads. It was a poor farm with a thin crop, and the field was pocked with stumps that wanted pulling. The house was out of sight, but she knew it was at the end of the cart path that climbed the knoll from the main road. Emmett had said it was drafty and the roof sagged where it didn't leak; but it had a good strong chimney that drew as well as any in Cherry Valley. She was sure she would find it just so.

The rest she would tend to in good time.

Two boys burst through a hole in a hedge of wild rose and tumbled in the field. They heard her pull in Horse, and turned and stood quiet as she tied the reins and stepped off the dray.

Diana walked up to them. She didn't say a word, but just looked at first one and then the other. Lord, help me, she thought, there's not many years between us. I could be their sister. One stood at waist level, the other to her breast. She could see where their chests would broaden and their shoulders gain their breadth.

They smiled at her with Emmett's bright smile.

"Brian," she said, nodding to the taller; "Farrell," to the other. "Your father sent me."

She hesitated. How to say it? Then: "I'm Diana Shannon." Not a tremble to her voice. "I'm your new mother."

BOOK TWO:

CHERRY VALLEY
SUMMER 1778-SPRING
1788

CHAPTER EIGHTEEN

"DON'T BE AFFRIGHTED, Mrs. Shannon. We would be ogres, indeed, if the Committee of Public Safety were not allied with a widow of a Continental lines soldier."

Reverend Dunlap smiled encouragingly. The smile made him look like a quizzical sheep. For some unknown reason he wore a peruke on all occasions—including plowing his fields—as if he were still at Trinity University. Some suggested the shabby wig was the same he'd worn in Dublin thirty years earlier. Diana repressed an urge to bleat at the dominie, and retold her story, this time to a full committee hearing.

She had allies. Two of them were in the room: Reverend Dunlap and Captain Robert M'Kean, the closest thing to a professional soldier Cherry Valley had. There were others, very much offstage: the British now seemed hard-pressed to win a victory, let alone the war. The French had signed an alliance with America and declared war on Great Britain. Most importantly, the Four Horsemen were thundering very close to Cherry Valley itself: the Indians and their Tory Irregulars were burning the frontier. The hamlet of Springfield, less than a day's travel away, had been put to the torch two months ago. Cherry Valley might be next— and this was no time for fence-sitting.

Patriotism was a very convenient and easy feeling that summer of 1778, a feeling that should be demonstrated by a Noble Act, preferably one that involved no real risk nor financial sacrifice. So certainly the committee would want to help Diana now. The members were assembled in the main room of Samuel Campbell's log farmhouse. The men wore either the sober black of a Presbyterian elder—which many of them were—or any uniform they were vaguely entitled to don.

A Daughter Of Liberty

Diana had dressed for her audience. She wore a tasteful, self-designed and -sewn pastel dress—the skirt over a small hoop, and the dress sleeves short and flared to reveal the chemise underneath. In Albany or—she thought, anyway—Philadelphia, the chemise and lacing would show at the dress's plunging neckline. But this was Cherry Valley, so Diana had added a triangular kerchief to conceal her neckline. This was topped off with a very demure, very puritan-looking, close-fitting cap. She was every inch the respectable but well-to-do young matron. Her speech was as cleverly contrived as her outfit.

She explained—with only a few artful tears for punctuation—how her husband-to-be Emmett had been wounded in a skirmish and invalided home from his regiment. "I'm no doctor . . . but I think they should not have released him from the hospital." Because, she went on, he fell desperately ill in Easton, where her parents took him into their inn. "That was all we could see to do, sirs. The town is filled with poor people who have been driven off their land by the war." Her parents? No, they weren't rich. Easton had several inns more magnificent. But better in services? "It would sound as if I were boasting if I said that. But our custom grows and our guests return, year after year."

Diana heard a mutter from one of the committeemen that once again the Irish teague had fallen in love with money. It was Mister Gill—one of Cherry Valley's innkeepers—who looked too much like Nate Hatch for Diana's comfort. He added a comment that some of Easton's inns were no better than they should be. Captain M'Kean, a freight wagon of a man, growled that the Emmett Shannon he'd known since the Indian wars would have little truck with the kind of place Mister Gill seemed to be talking about. As a matter of fact, he personally found Mister Gill's statement offensive, and suggested an apology to Mrs. Shannon would be in order. Or else he'd crack Mister Gill's back for him. Mister Gill greened and stammered that apology. Captain M'Kean's nail-keg fist relaxed. Diana curtsied, flashed Mister Gill a smile she hoped was charming, and continued narrating the romance she'd created.

Sick, she had nursed the soldier, and in the natural course of things, they had fallen in love. Her parents approved of the match, but worried about Emmett taking his new bride on a perilous journey. Diana and Emmett's travels were almost over, and they had almost reached Albany, when they were hit by raiders.

"Indians?" came the sharp question from Campbell.

"No, I don't believe so. However, there were Tory renegades. White, with . . . with—" artful wail here—"scalps on their belts." She started crying. The tears were not planned. It was all Diana could do to keep from completely breaking down. Reverend Dunlap soothed her. "Emmett held them off long enough for me to flee into the woods. And then he . . . he . . ."

"I wager the raiders paid dearly for his death," Captain M'Kean rumbled.

"And . . . then I made my way to Albany. Mister van Ruysdael and his wife were kind enough to take me in. And write that letter you have before you." That letter was quite genuine, although Mister van Ruysdael had slightly modified Diana's story when she performed her dress rehearsal. He would be more acceptable to the stiff-necked committee of Cherry Valley as an old friend of Diana's parents rather than a reprobate ex-peddler of Indian potions and roistering partner of Emmett's.

"Gentlemen, I am not educated like Dr. Ruysdael," Diana continued, after each member had scanned the parchment sheet, some moving their lips noticeably in the attempt, "I am just a poor widow. Great with child. And there is no one to help me, my husband's sister, or these poor orphans." The committee looked behind Diana, at Ruth, her two children, and Brian and Farrell, all washed and wearing their best shabbies. "There is no one to help me except you gentlemen," Diana concluded.

Allan Cole & Chris Bunch

Each committeeman put on his own version of Benevolence, Patriarchy, and Civic Virtue. Then looked at Mister Campbell to make sure they were making the Correct Impartial Decision. "1 think I may speak for us all," Mister Campbell started in his Ulster brogue, "in saying there is little problem in forgiving the past-due taxes on the farm. And certainly we have no intention of seizing any of the late Mister Shannon's property. As Dominie Dunlap said, none'a us are monsters." Diana cued Ruth . . . and Emmett's sister did an appropriate babble of thanks. The children knuckled their foreheads. Very good.

"There are two other things you might help us with," Diana went on. This drew a suspicious look from Mister Campbell. An uncollected and probably uncollectible debt of a dead man is quite easy to forget. What else did this woman want? "The farm belonging to my Emmett's former father-in-law . . . Mister Hopkins? The traitor?" Growls from the committee. Some of them may have been secret Loyalists—but they remembered Springfield. "His grandchildren"—Diana indicated Brian and Farrell—"have no legacy. They will grow up knowing their grandfather was a Tory, an unhappy and unfair burden for such innocents, I'm sure you will agree. I ask you to deed them the farm. It is lying unworked but still fallow. I still have enough remaining from my dowry to purchase seed for the late planting season."

One of the committeemen looked unhappy. "I have already discussed my own plans—" and he stopped short, after getting glares. Diana figured him to be on the outskirts of power.

"A reasonable request. Granted. We will prepare the proper correspondence. Is that all?"

"One . . . very minor thing. The land . . . my husband's land is very dry. I fear our well must fail us soon. But I saw, just across the road, what looks like a tiny spring. Reverend Dunlap told me no one holds title to that land. So if I must attempt to be father and mother, farmer and cook, to my family, could you not make my task easier?"

A Daughter Of Liberty

The Reverend Dunlap said something in another language, which Diana thought might be Latin. The other members of the committee looked equally mystified. "That was Cicero," he said. "Without the highest justice, a republic cannot be governed."

Captain M'Kean was still bewildered. Obviously he didn't know any Ciceros living in Cherry Valley or serving in the army. But that seemed enough for the committeemen. The plot of land was deeded to Diana, for the sum of one shilling—which, Mister Campbell said, need not actually be paid. Just a formality.

Diana Shannon had won her first battle. Weeping thanks—as was the rest of her troupe—she managed a secret smile. Now she had land that food could be grown on, and she owned both sides of the lane at the crossroads—even though "crossroads" was a grand description for the meeting of two tracks little more than Indian trails. She glanced at Mister Gill, thinking, When this damned war is over, I am going to put up an inn that will make your own look like a flea-infested stable. Ruth was staring at her as if she were a miracle maker. From that day there was never a question among the Shannons as to who made the decisions...

* * * *

There were too many decisions, too many worries, and too few hours, Diana thought, staring down at the falls from her rocky perch. The Indian name for them, she'd learned, was Te-Ke-Ha-Ra-Wah. It was a good place to think, and close to the farm.

The blessings first: the farms were secure. There would be food that winter—not only had Ruth and the children managed to get in a crop, but they had made a meager harvest as well. That had been a relief: Diana half expected that Ruth had spent the time from sending the letter to Valley Forge and Diana's arrival doing naught but weeping and tearing her hair.

In Albany, Diana had promptly converted the state and Continental currency taken from Hatch into specie. This was

Allan Cole & Chris Bunch

very much against Mister van Ruysdael's advice—he was convinced the current depreciation of paper money was a momentary thing. Part of the future, he had told her, was paper money, secured by faith or the labor of common people instead of gold or silver. Diana noticed the good merchant owned enough land and houses to afford this romantic view. She settled for the jingle of coinage. Three wagonloads of dried or salted provisions and seed accompanied Diana on the journey to Cherry Valley, and she still had far more coinage left than she'd led the committee to believe.

Cherry Valley itself was beautiful. Emmett had not gilded anything in his stories. Its people were nowhere near as monstrous as she'd expected. Greedy, selfish, shortsighted, and opportunistic, to be sure. But that was the frontier. The town was a paradise compared to New Kent. Possibly it had been the leavening influence of Reverend Dunlap, who'd led the original settlers in 1740. Or maybe it was the casual surveying when the original patent was granted. More likely, Diana decided, the original settlers hadn't been as rich or well-connected as those who came to New Kent. Regardless, she felt she could make her way among them. For a while. For a while.

Ruth, thank heaven, was not the complete flibbertigibbet Diana had dreaded. She did make the worst of a problem— but she also made the best of a blessing. She spoke her mind to too many people—but she never lied. She hated the farm, the woods, and Cherry Valley, but that was just Ruth. If she wanted to dream of fleeing away to Boston once this awful war ended, so be it. Diana had her own dreams. Her two children had some of Ruth's faults. They would attempt too many tasks at the same time, and get none of them accomplished. But once set a single job, Samuel, fourteen, or Mary, twelve, would see it through.

Both Brian and Farrell were their father's children: bright, eager, alive to the world. She hoped they would have better luck in life than their father. To the devil with hope. Diana was determined she would make it so!

Enough of the blessings, because the problems were very large—as large as the flames that had engulfed Springfield, flames that ran wild across the frontier that summer. From Canada the great war chiefs of the Seneca and Mohawk had taken the tribes south with torch, lance, and tomahawk. Companies of white men went with them. They were called many things: Tories, traitors, rangers, "Destructors," Loyalists, or renegades. Diana, who gave not a damn for politics, thought them one and all as the monsters who had killed her Emmett. With six helpless lives to worry about, she also wished every red devil all the plagues of Egypt.

But Abraham and his family had been Indians.

She had asked Captain M'Kean about them. When home from the militia regiment, he had adopted the habit of dropping by the farm. He said he was concerned about these women and children so far from the center of the village. The captain, Diana suspected, had a bit more in mind than just the welfare of the Shannons. She would find a way to handle the problem later. There were greater matters on her mind. Why were the Indians the butchers they were?

Captain M'Kean thought a minute, and asked for another cup of the wild raspberry tea Diana was taking religiously, as part of Gramer Fahey's regime for gravid women.

"I s'pect—and since I've been against 'em since King Philip's War, there's truth to my thoughts—they ain't the heathen murtherers some would think.

"Consider. We came in. Took their land. End of the war, we'll take more of it. There's a lot more white folk than red. From the Indian's viewin', we don't fight like real warriors— and he does. We ain't willin' to take risks in battle—an' he is. We're after money, an' the Indian, he don't see no use for it except decoration. We slave on the land, and the Indian's got the forest givin' him what he needs. An' to him, we're dirty.'

"What?"

"Surely. White color's a sign of sickness. We don't have any of the ceremonies to make us pure like he does. We're drunks ... an' we turn the Indian into a drunk. We mewl when

Allan Cole & Chris Bunch

we're hungry an' scream when we're burnin' at the stake. Hard to respect a people like that. If you're thinkin' like an Indian. Not to mention we whipped 'em pretty good at Oriskany. They're lookin' for revenge. Pretty sure . . . were I Mohawk or Senecy, I'd be out with Brant, too."

"What's going to be the end of all this?"

"We're going to kill all of them ... or they'll kill all of us. Don't see any other ways."

Captain M'Kean was a soldier, Diana mused, with a soldier's simplicity. Perhaps the solution wouldn't be that brutal. She flipped a pebble down into the churning pool below her. Not that this had anything to do with her present problem. She doubted if any Indian—bursting out of a thicket with a tomahawk—would inquire as to her social feelings. The problem was keeping the six of them alive if the Indians did show up.

The Campbell farm had been fortified with a crude log-and-dirt breastworks a year earlier. During raiding season the settlers huddled behind them, working their fields in armed groups. That was not enough now. Rumors ran through the valley that thousands of Indians were out this summer. Mister Campbell had convinced General Lafayette that Cherry Valley was too important a post to be ignored. The general had agreed, and ordered the militia to build a proper fort in the village center, and for the county militia to garrison it. The fort was slightly reassuring—it was solidly built of logs, reinforced, and given a parapet. It enclosed the church and burial ground, and a blockhouse was being finished inside the walls. A regiment of regulars was on its way to garrison the post, according to Captain M'Kean.

Diana didn't think this was good enough. If she and the others huddled inside the post, how could their farms be worked? But if they stayed on their land . . . They were almost two miles from the fort. It would be a long, hard run for children and a pregnant woman. Diana determined to think on this further. She shivered. It had suddenly turned cold and dark.

A Daughter Of Liberty

She looked up through the trees and was startled to see the sun vanishing. A disk of blackness cut into it. It was an eclipse, something she had never witnessed. She didn't believe in omens. But the gray twilight was entirely too easy to see as a prediction for the future.

* * * *

The first refugees stumbled into Cherry Valley four days later. Eyes shattered, they were broken by horror. The Wyoming Valley had been obliterated. No one was sure how many Iroquois had attacked the fertile granary, nor how many of Butler's Beasts had been with them. The forts of the settlers had surrendered or been bypassed by the Indians. The militia went out to fight—and was broken and decimated. But that was not the worst. Farmers were taken captive and their children slaughtered, the story went. Their women led away or ... or worse. Farms and fields roared in flames. The valley would sell nothing to Washington's army for winter supplies. There was nothing to sell. The stories of the Wyoming Massacre that Diana heard from the broken men and women grew worse with each retelling. Diana did what she could, putting up as many people as the small farmhouse could hold. Others were quartered in the Hopkins's farmhouse and outbuildings on the property next to hers. A very poor excuse for an innkeeper's first venture, she thought. She couldn't bring herself to charge for lodgings. But the refugees could help her with her main problem.

She'd tasked a few of the abler boys and men to help build a root cellar near Emmett's house. It was a deep one. Another group, a few days later, put in cross beams, roofing, and a floor. She was surprised none of her laborers wondered why she insisted the roof of the cellar be placed well below ground level. She had another "cellar" dug and framed in a similar manner by other refugees—this one nearer to the crossroads, on the property with the spring. Eventually the refugees were collected and convoyed toward Albany by soldiers. Diana then finished her cellars. The roofs were covered with dirt and turf. Bushes were transplanted. When

Allan Cole & Chris Bunch

she was finished, it would take a very skilled eye to see there was anything except innocent land. The Shannon clan now had two hiding places.

She tried to teach Ruth to fire Emmett's rifle. It was hopeless. Ruth would aim the massive tube vaguely in the general direction of a target, squinch her eyes closed and yank the trigger. Fortunately, Emmett had a shotgun. That was kept just inside one shelter. Diana told Ruth if the Indians attacked, she and her children were to make for the hide. Don't come out, no matter what happens. If anybody opens the shelter door besides me, grab the shotgun and use it. Ruth's son and daughter proved more apt pupils in musketry. They were given other tasks—to keep the rifle and shotgun clean, and to recharge the weapons every day or so with fresh powder. Diana thought this was what Emmett would have wanted. She herself had the teamster's pistol. For the first time she realized what an awkward contrivance a weapon was, and wondered why men had such a fondness for possessing them. A better question, she pondered, was why they enjoyed using them so greatly.

Diana's fears were driven not only by the Indian raids, but by the arrival of the soldiery. Three hundred of them had marched into the valley just after the Wyoming Massacre had begun. It was the Sixth Massachusetts Regiment. Continental Regulars. The settlers of Cherry Valley felt very secure. Diana felt very insecure. Not that she was, or wanted to be, a military expert. What little she knew or cared about the army came from the stories Emmett had told her or what she'd heard at the Black Lamb. But these men didn't spend much time practicing, Diana noticed. When they did, it was marching up and down in regular lines, as if they expected British Regulars to oppose them. They were led by a fat puff of a colonel named Alden. He and the other officers dressed most finely. The men were dirty and lazy. The officers sought quarters with the better folk of the valley, while the men were left to shift for themselves in the blockhouse or to await invitations to share settlers' lodgings. Diana had asked if she could quarter a few men, but an officer said no. She lived too far from the fort. The soldiers had two shiny brass cannon, which they polished constantly but never fired.

Diana prayed the Indians wouldn't come. And, for the rest of that long, scorching summer, Cherry Valley was left in peace. Some of the more timid settlers asked Colonel Alden if they could stay in the fort. There was nothing to worry about, the colonel blustered. The time for raiding was over. A cold, windy fall was settling over the frontier. The danger was past.

* * * *

Brian and Farrell found the three bobcat kittens while playing pirate around one of the streams flowing down toward the fort. The mother was gone. Perhaps having a double estrus that year had weakened her and she'd fallen prey to a hunter. Brian had wanted to bring them back to the farm on discovery. Farrell had argued against that most vehemently. Why? Mother won't mind.

Because . . . because then we won't have a Secret, Farrell came up with. That made excellent sense to Brian. A Real Secret, not like the Pretend ones he and his brother shared that they were really Indian chiefs, or somehow related to some king somewhere, or that they were going to run away to sea one of these days. Something to exchange Knowing Looks about at mealtime, and to ask Innocent But Leading Questions to their elders. And something to giggle about when they were curled in the bed loft at night.

They'd started feeding the kittens on pap—milk-soaked bread. Now the bobcats' eyes had opened and they were exploring their den. And biting. Brian and Farrell began thinking what could be done with these three wonderful animals. Farrell wondered if they could take the cats to Philadelphia when they ran away to be sailors. Even though he was younger, many times Farrell was the Planner of an Adventure, and Brian the one who'd actually carry out that plan.

"Would they let them on our ship?" Brian asked.

Allan Cole & Chris Bunch

Farrell thought. "No," he decided. "We'd have to sell them."

"But then somebody would put them in a cage." That didn't sound right to Farrell either. But he told his brother they couldn't just turn the cats loose here in Cherry Valley when they ran away to sea. Brian understood—they probably wouldn't be able to take care of themselves.

"We could teach them how to hunt. Or ... or maybe they could hunt rats like Tabby does."

Farrell giggled. "Big rats," he said.

Then Farrell had the solution—they wouldn't just run away to be sailors, they'd start at the top and be pirates. That's what Aunt Ruth's husband had done, was it not? Nobody would tell a pirate he couldn't have a bobcat if he wanted. Brian thought that excellent.

"That's what they'll eat," Farrell decided. "People we don't like. People like . . . like ..."

He stopped. His world didn't have many enemies. Or at least ones that should be eaten alive. But there would be, later. Indians, maybe, although how Indians suddenly were encountered by Farrell's pirate ship, as clouds of sleep drifted over him, he wasn't sure. But they were. And they were eaten. And on that note of gore, the loft fell silent. ...

* * * *

It snowed all day November 9. At dusk the snow turned into sleet. Under no circumstances, Diana said firmly, could Farrell and Brian go out. The kittens would go hungry. Brian listened to his brother crying, and could stand no more. Tomorrow, he said, we'll feed them. Before anyone wakes. They'll be all right.

"Promise?"

"I promise."

Farrell looked at Brian's face in the dimness, then nodded. "You promised," he said, and promptly fell asleep. His big brother never lied. At least, not to him. . . . .

* * * *

Farrell kicked his brother, and Brian jerked up, eyes blinking. Then he ducked back under the feather comforter. The loft was chilly, and the fire down below still banked.

"Wake up," Farrell insisted. Brian growled, not emerging. Farrell kicked him again. "Let's go! Before Mother wakes up."

"She'll catch us."

"No she won't. We'll be back first."

"What're we going to feed them?"

"Milk. And some ham."

"Farrell, go back to sleep. They'll be okay."

"No they won't! It rained all night. They'll drown. Or starve dead. You promised!"

Brian said a word he didn't know the meaning of, a word Diana would be surprised he knew, took a deep breath and rolled out, the husk mattress crackling.

"Sssh!"

"Sssh yourself. Get dressed. This is your dumb idea. They'll prob'ly bite me again."

The two boys, alternately hushing each other to silence, crept down the ladder toward the door. One of the dogs woke and whined. Brian patted him back into sleep. Farrell borrowed one of the dog's pannikins from the porch and tipped milk from the pitcher into it. Brian, rather awkwardly, sawed a slab from the ham on the sideboard. He tucked an end of a bread loaf into a pocket. They pulled on their fur jackets, hats, and wool mittens, and went out into the storm.

* * * *

The boys' track led them behind the Gordons' place, toward the stream. Brian and Farrell, like every other boy in Cherry Valley, prided themselves on being able to go anywhere without being seen by an adult. These secret routes, of course, took twice as long to travel with three times the scrambling. But. who said adventure was supposed to be easy? They'd wrestled a fallen log across the creek for a footbridge, and now edged out on it. The creek was shallow—but if they came home frozen and wet, both of

Allan Cole & Chris Bunch

them would be for a switching. Farrell put the bread into the milk and started coaxing the kittens awake. Brian was rinsing the salty ham in the creek when he heard the first scream.

A woman. Then something else—it sounded like a catamount's screech. But somehow Brian knew it wasn't. The scream stopped short. Brian heard the thud of rifle shots through the sleet. And then he saw the Indian.

He was just across the creek from him, skull face leering and long lance lifted. With a bound, the Indian was at the edge of the creek. "Run! Run, Farrell!" Brian screamed, and kicked the log into the creek. Farrell found himself up the bank, over the bobcat den, fingernails ripping on the stone, and behind him the Indian's war cry, and he was going into the brush on his hands and knees and heard a loud shout from Brian.

He spun and saw the spear driving forward, down into his brother, and heard a gurgle like when they cut the pig's windpipe at slaughter, and the lance standing in Brian's body and the Indian pulling a knife from his belt, and then Farrell was gone.

* * * *

Diana was out of bed, reaching for the pistol before she realized what had awakened her. It came again. The crash of the fort's cannon.

"Get up," she shouted. "To the cellar." Her fingers needed no instructions. The pistol was cocked, powder poured from the small horn into the pan, and the weapon put down to half cock while she watched the flurry from Ruth and her two children. She turned to the loft— and saw and heard nothing. She was at the top of the ladder. Brian and Farrell were gone. As were their coats, which should have hung behind the kitchen door.

Ruth was starting to keen in panic. There wasn't time. She jerked the woman toward the door and told Samuel to get everyone into the cellar. Load the rifle and shotgun. Kill anybody who opened the trap. She pulled her coat around her shoulders and was almost out the door. No. You won't save

168

anyone if your feet freeze. She forced them into boots, then grabbed the pouch with pistol balls and powder horn. Then out the door.

She couldn't find any footprints in the muck. A thick fog hampered her search. Think, woman. The creek? It was one of their favorite playgrounds, although what they could be doing at this hour of the morning was unknown. But both of them of late had been behaving like there was some great secret. Maybe the creek. She could think of no other possibilities. The creek was nearly in the middle of Cherry Valley—in the same direction the screams and battle sounds came from.

The sleet was now coming in drifting sheets, with clear patches between. The rising wind was driving the fog out of the valley. She stumbled through the fields, deep in mire, and tore her hands and clothes pulling herself across the stone fences.

Suddenly Diana went to her knees and threw up. Damn you, woman. Damn this child in my belly. I have no time to be sick. She refused to allow her body its dictates and ran on.

* * * *

Farrell knew not to cry. But the tears came anyway. Silent tears. He'd gone back along the secret path—and seen, in a clearing ahead, more Indians. Farrell went in another direction. The fort. The soldiers would save him. The soldiers were busy. The fort was surrounded with screaming Indians. White men—Tory rangers—were crouched behind fences, wagons, and houses. Shooting at the stockaded walls.

Farrell saw one Indian holding one of the soldiers by his arm. Another soldier—Farrell thought he was fat enough to be the head soldier—ran out of a house toward the fort. The Indian ran after him. The fat soldier turned and aimed a pistol. The Indian hurled his tomahawk. The fat man's skull split and he fell. Without realizing it, Farrell moaned.

The fort's gate opened and a cannon mouth came out. The cannon blasted. Three men knotted near a wall went

Allan Cole & Chris Bunch

spinning away. Farrell saw, even at this distance, the wall painted red from an invisible brush.

* * * *

The four women walked like they were entranced. The Indians around them were laughing, joking. Diana, hidden in brush, saw a long, red scalp swinging from the belt of one Seneca. Mrs. Dickson had been very proud of her hair, the longest and reddest in Cherry Valley. The Indians passed, and Diana chanced moving along the edges of the road. She heard more happy shouts. Another party of Seneca, whooping around a farmhouse. Some of them wore women's shifts. A steady stream of goods was pitched out the door into the mud. Pots, pans, worthless tools of the white man. Diana saw one Indian replace his headdress with a sunbonnet before she passed.

The Campbells' house and barns roared in flames. Diana could see no sign of life. Nor were there any bodies. Again, in the fields beyond the Campbells' were Indians. The Campbell cattle had been herded together, and six Indians were slaughtering them. This was quite a celebration.

* * * *

Farrell looked through brush at the Mitchell farm. Mrs. Mitchell and three of her children lay dead outside the door. Mister Mitchell was holding his daughter in his arms. She wasn't moving. Mister Mitchell was talking to her. Farrell would go to him. Mister Mitchell could help him. Mister Mitchell suddenly looked up. Then put the body down and ran behind a shed.

A white man walked into the yard. He had a rifle over his shoulder. The man was dressed like an Indian. He walked to the body of the little girl, put his rifle carefully on the ground and drew a tomahawk. He lifted the little girl's body by the hair . . . and Farrell could watch no more.

He was crawling away, backward, his eyes squeezed shut. The boy had no idea where to go. Hide, in the brush. Your mother will find you. Be like Brian told you the little animals were. They kept quiet when men were around, and no one could find them. Farrell, crying for his brother and himself, crawled into the heart of a thicket and curled up like one of the bobcat kittens. His body shook with fear and cold.

* * * *

Diana would never get the chance to put the Gills out of business. The Indians had seen to that. Their mutilated bodies sprawled in the road, half hidden in a deep, dark puddle. She realized she heard no more gunshots. The fort had fallen, she thought. There were shouts from around the bend ahead of her. Diana ducked behind a rocky outcropping.

The raiders came around the curve. She didn't know how many hundreds of them there were. They were driving the valley's women and children ahead of them. Like drovers going to market, Diana thought. They disappeared into the drizzle. Shaking in fury, she continued her search. She would find Farrell and Brian. But she wanted to find an Indian. Just one. She would not miss.

After an hour she chanced calling. The raiders had gone. Soldiers came out of the fort. It had not been taken. The Tories' attack had failed. The Seneca had refused to attack the fort. They wanted loot and revenge. One sergeant chanced a boast. Diana almost shot him.

* * * *

Diana found Farrell in the late afternoon. He'd awakened, hearing her shouts, and stumbled out of the thicket. Brian! Where was Brian? Farrell could not talk. But he could lead. Brian's body lay half in, half out of the creek. His chest was torn open from the lance wound. He had been scalped. There was no sign of the bobcat kittens.

* * * *

There were still people in Cherry Valley. That night and the next morning settlers trickled out of their hiding places in the woods and into the fort. The Seneca sent halfhearted skirmishing parties back into the settlement the next day— but there was little left to loot. The Seneca wanted the white man to know this raid was in return for the butchery of their best warriors at Oriskany. And so scalps were nailed to poles,

Allan Cole & Chris Bunch

and the poles staked in the village. Finally, near midday, they were driven out of Cherry Valley by a company of Continental Regulars.

About noon there were shouts from outside the fort— and the captives came running back toward it. They had not escaped—the Indians had decided the captives would slow them down. Brant, of the Mohawks, who'd come on the raid with fifty of his warriors but refused to take part in the sacking of the village, had kept the settlers from further slaughter. But some of them—the Campbells and Mrs. John Moore—would be taken to Canada. Valuable hostages. Diana did not give a damn about any of this. She had Brian to bury.

She had failed Emmett.

CHAPTER NINETEEN

THE THIRTY-FOUR SOLDIERS, men, women, and children were buried in a common grave in the cemetery, which had been moved inside the fort's walls. Reverend Dunlap, whose wife had been slaughtered before his eyes, stammered through the ceremony. Ruth had started to say something that morning about how terrible it was, Brian being buried out of the Church. Diana almost destroyed her with a look, but relented just in time. Ruth was nearly mindless with grief over her murdered nephew. As for Diana, she had locked the horror away in the same strongbox she kept her emotions about Emmett in. Dead was dead. She had to think that way or it would be too easy to give up on the living: the child inside her. Farrell. Three other Shannons. And herself.

Ruth turned from the grave, away from the hollow thuds, as the soldiers started filling it in. "Damn this," she hissed. "Damn Cherry Valley. Damn this wilderness. Let the red bastards have it." She spoke for most of the settlers.

That night, at a town meeting in the blockhouse, there was almost complete agreement. Cherry Valley was to be abandoned. The army would escort the settlers back to Canajoharie. Only a handful of people thought otherwise. They were the stubborn; the poor with nowhere else to go; those whose relatives would be hard-pressed to take in a church mouse; or those who still had faith in the army. The Sixth Massachusetts had been ordered to remain in the valley and garrison the fort—now named after the late and rather unlamented Colonel Alden—and Diana Shannon.

She'd talked to Ruth earlier. If they fled, they would be without land. A landless man—or worse, a woman—had no rights in this country. But we would have our lives, Ruth said. But if we leave, where can we go? Diana asked. Anywhere but here, Ruth retorted. Where's anywhere?

There's nothing in Canajoharie for us. Albany? There's no work to be had. You've got money, Ruth said.

Not that much, Diana said. "Rent for a house for a few months. Food for the winter. We won't be able to carry any of the winter supplies with us. The Indians got the horses and cattle."

"What about your merchant friend?"

"My merchant friend—Emmett's friend—was closing his house. He planned to find new pastures. He told me he couldn't take Albany and the grab-fisted burghers any longer."

"What's wrong with returning to Boston?"

"Boston . . . any city . . . takes money."

"We can make it. There's no damned redmen there."

"No. But there is the workhouse." Ruth flinched. "Think, Ruth. As I said, if we run now, we will run with nothing."

"What's going to change a month from now to make us rich? Or when a year has gone?"

"We have seed. We can plant Mr. Bishop's land. There are still draft animals out there in the forest. Sooner or later they will come back to where their barns were."

There was no arguing with Ruth. Only fear of the work house—which had worn her mother down until she was an easy target for the sickness that killed her—tempered her views. "The Indians . . . they won't come back?"

"Not until spring at the earliest. And even then . . . who will be here for them to murder and rape? They won't attack the fort again."

"Until spring, then," Ruth finally said.

* * * *

Robert M'Kean also thought Diana was insane. He had little faith the soldiers were any better protection than they'd been before the massacre. She should take her entire clan and return to her parents' inn back in Easton. Diana was forced to admit she had no wealthy innkeeper parents. There was no one at all for her to turn to. If the tragedy weren't hanging close around them, M'Kean would have found the way Diana

174

had foxed the Committee of Public Safety amusing. He himself knew his only use to these landowners was as a soldier. When the Indians were gone... Cherry Valley would find him a nuisance. "I have nowhere I could put you for safety, Mrs. Shannon. Would that there was. What home I have is the army. But . . . when the war is over . . . I'll be back. I'll be needing someone beside me then. Someone named Diana Shannon."

He grabbed her and kissed her soundly. It was easier to kiss him back, theyn watch the newly promoted major mount his horse and ride off.

* * * *

Now there were many things to do. Winter was closing in and Diana worked at a frantic pace. It had always been her way of dealing with crisis. Work until your body is numb. Think only about what's at hand. You don't have the luxury to mourn Emmett or Brian. There was much to be done. She armed Samuel with the rifle and put him to combing the woods with Mary. They rounded up six horses and a dozen cattle missed by the raiders.

Six horses . . . and Horse. Somehow he had wandered into the heart of a thicket sometime during the confusion, and evidently not been able to find his way out. Mary found him after hearing what sounded a great deal like a fart coming from thick brush. The animal was still dull-witted Horse. A little thinner and a lot shabbier, otherwise unaffected by Indians, snow, or being starved for some days. And he expressed no visible affection or gratitude for being rescued, although Diana thought she saw his eyes widen when Mary unsacked oats for him back at the farm. Even though he was as useless a creature as could be imagined, Diana was very glad the animal hadn't ended up as some Indian's dinner cut or just lost in the wilderness. Horse . . . the musket ball hung around her neck . . . and the child about to be born . . . was that all the memories she would have? Diana stopped thinking of Emmett and fiercely told herself yet again there was no time for this.

pg. 175

Allan Cole & Chris Bunch

Now she and Ruth started looting their ex-neighbors' property. Almost anything was or would be of value: a plough, furniture not too charred to be usable, cooking and eating utensils. Ruth wondered why they took as many plates and flatware as they did; they had enough settings for an inn, she said. Exactly, Diana thought.

There were other treasures: books. Emmett already had a good library—five volumes, including the still-to-be-kept-hidden, badly tattered Garden of the Soul that had belonged to his mother and been brought to Cherry Valley by Ruth. Shattered by the massacre, Reverend Dunlap had abandoned most of the books from his prewar academy. Although stained by mud and water, they were a rich find. Too many of them were in Greek or Latin—languages neither Ruth nor Diana could read. They could not find a grammar that might make the books teachable. But the books were saved. The oddest find was a Douay Bible. Diana wondered what a Protestant minister, even one from Ireland, was doing with the Book of Papist Heresies. She was sorry she had not gotten the chance to know Reverend Dunlap more completely.

There were classics in translation, though, as well as Shakespeare. These could be useful. One book Diana decided could be done without: A TOKEN FOR CHILDREN, Being An Exact Account of the Conversion, Holy and Exemplary Lives and Joyful Deaths of Several Young Children. Death was something they could do without for a while. As well as the book's Puritan cant. Farrell was insisting Brian's death was his fault. There was no comforting him. The boy was eating little, and spending hours in the loft, staring at Brian's side of the bed.

In another burnt house they found two hornbooks and The New England Primer Improved. A religious alphabet book: "In ADAM'S Fall/We finned all . . . Heaven to find/ The BIBLE mind" all the way to, "While Youth do chear, DEATH may be near . . . ZACCEUS he,/Did climb the

Tree,/Our Lord to fee." Still gloomy . . . but Farrell and the soon-to-be-born child would need to be educated.

Ruth didn't realize from the book gathering that Diana had no intention of leaving come spring. The next stage of Diana's plan would have to wait. December's storms slammed down on the valley. No one went out except for necessities and to milk and fodder the livestock. And Diana's time was drawing near.

* * * *

Months ago, in Albany, Diana had planned that her first Christmas in Cherry Valley would be a special one. Back in New Kent, Christmas had been a time of snarling fights, drunkenness and greed for the Hatches, days she dreaded even if Gramer Fahey tried to make the season as loving as she could. Now Brian was dead. Farrell behaved like a wooden windup toy. Ruth and her children went about like whipped dogs, looking over their shoulders for the next beating. The few people remaining in Cherry Valley kept to themselves. The army wasn't eager to get more than pistol-shot away from the fort. When Diana encountered a roving patrol from time to time, she thought them even more terrified of this desolate valley than Ruth. At night there was little conversation between supper and the time the candles were blown out. Except for the howling of the storms outside, silence reigned. The crack of a pine knot made everyone jump.

Diana took to reading aloud. The Bible, Pilgrim's Progress. She struggled through Shakespeare, and found the sonnets far easier to cope with. No one seemed to be able to keep much in his or her mind for very long. This could not continue. She determined they were going to have a real Christmas. Even if it was only for the Shannons, there would be a feast as if the Indians had never come.

* * * *

Farrell heard Diana crying and stopped in his tracks. He was not sure what to do. Hours before, it seemed, she had gone out to the shed for some eggs. She had told him she was

Allan Cole & Chris Bunch

going to make him olykoeks. They had hog fat for the frying. This would be special, she said, and waited for a response. Farrell, raised properly, had said thanks. No more. Diana sighed, patted his cheek, pulled on a coat and went for the eggs.

After he thought she had been gone too long, Farrell went looking. He had to force himself. He knew what you found when someone didn't come back by himself. And then he heard the sobs. He covered his eyes with his hands. This would be . . . this would be something awful again. Like . . . like . . . He turned to run back for the house and Ruth. No. This was his mother. The snow came only to mid-calf, but he had to force himself to walk forward as if it were chest deep as he waded down the hill toward her.

Diana was crouched in the snow, not heeding the cold. She was beside Horse. He was lying near some boulders, as if he had curled in a summer pasture, and the blowflies were not annoying him. They would never disturb him again. Horse was quite dead.

Diana heard Farrell's footsteps. She stood up, forced a smile, scrubbed at her eyes as he walked solemnly up beside her. It was no use. She started crying again. Farrell looked away. She was not the one who was supposed to cry. Not ever.

"Sorry," Diana said. "Dumb animal. It was just that . . . we bought him . . . bought him with counterfeit, and . . ." She snuffled, took a handkerchief from her apron pocket and wiped her eyes.

"Was it Indians?" Farrell asked.

"No. I don't think so, anyway. He was . . . pretty old. I guess, I guess he just . . . just died."

"Oh . . . Why," Farrell asked carefully after a long silence, "why does anything have to die?" She started to answer him, then was silent. Farrell thought he'd said something wrong. He looked up at her. Diana was crying again. Quietly, but uncontrollably. Farrell took her hand. After a time he began weeping, too.

* * * *

The next day, Diana began teaching Farrell. Each day she took a small, smoothed oak plank and charcoal. "Farrell, today is the eleventh day before Christmas." She wrote the number 11 on the board. "Tomorrow will be the tenth day. Yesterday was . . . ?"

Farrell made only two mistakes before he began getting the numbers right. He is a bright one, Diana thought. He took to his sums as if he were born with a facility for them, gobbling up anything put before him on the subject.

* * * *

Three days before Christmas they had visitors. Samuel was the first to see them. A bright sun shone across the drifted snow. Samuel was supposedly trying to find a wild brood sow he knew had farrowed somewhere near the Hortons' place. In truth, it was an excuse to get out. He'd rather chance Indians than be cooped up inside any longer. Besides, he was carrying his Uncle Emmett's rifle—a weapon almost as big as he was.

Actually, he first heard them. It sounded like singing. Samuel crept to the edge of the bluff and peered down at the rutted, snow-covered road leading out of Cherry Valley. There were three men and a sled. Two men pulled the sled. They were blacks—young, possibly in their twenties. They wore ragged farmers' breeches and shabby hats. But they also wore, like the man in the sled, heavy, hooded, expensive blanket coats that might have been clean months and miles ago. The white man in the sled looked to be in his forties. Weather-beaten. All Samuel could see of his clothing was a large tricorner hat and high drover boots under the coat. In front of him, resting on one of the sacks that made up the rest of the sled's cargo, were two primed pistols and a curved long sword that, to Samuel, looked like what he'd read pirates carried.

What in the holy name of Jesus was this trio doing? Who were the black men? Slaves? Criminals? Renegades? Tories? And who was their guard? He puzzled even more when the

Allan Cole & Chris Bunch

white man dug a watch from under his coat, consulted it, thumped the sled's rail with the scabbarded sword and shouted: "Four bells of the dog watch! Turn out the watch below."

The two blacks gratefully dropped the rope traces. The white man jumped out of the sleigh. He picked up a canteen, uncorked it, and took a drink. Passed the canteen to the blacks, who also swallowed. Then one black clambered back into the sleigh, behind the weaponry, and the white man and the other black picked up the ropes and set off once more. Samuel realized from the zigzag track of the sled's runners that all three men were a little drunk. He checked the priming of his rifle, cocked it, and stepped out of the brush.

"Good morrow, sirs." All three men jumped. The man in the sled grabbed a pistol and the sword, then dropped the pistol in the snow and scrabbled for it. Samuel lifted his rifle—and all three of the men below became statues. "We mean no harm." From the white man.

"Where are you going?"

"Cherry Valley. But mayhap we lost our track. Navigatin' on land's a rough cob."

"May I ask your business, sirs?" Samuel had been raised as a polite young man.

"We're lookin' for the Widow Shannon's farm. If it's still manned."

Samuel blinked. "We are still there."

Now it was the white man's turn to blink. He recovered. And smiled hopefully. "Grand. Grand, indeed. Is there a Ruth Conners still living there? She, uh, might be calling herself Shannon?" Samuel took another chance— none of the three looked very threatening. He slid down the bluff to the road.

"She is, sir. Do you know her?"

Instead, another question: "Might I ask who you are?"

"I'm her son, Samuel."

The man beamed in pure joy. Then burst into tears. One of the black men patted him comfortingly. Samuel picked up the forgotten pistol from the snow and handed it to the other black. The man recovered somewhat, started to blurt, then stopped. A drunken, crafty look crept into his eyes. "Would you be willing to guide us to the farm, son?"

Samuel thought about it. Would Diana think he was being foolish? The blazes with what she'd think or do—any man who started crying with no cause was harmless. A bedlamite probably, but a harmless one. He pointed. "Follow that trail. It's about a mile." Keeping some caution, he fell in behind the sled, the rifle at half cock. He wondered why the man's voice was familiar.

* * * *

He found out quickly enough. Ruth, Diana, Mary, and Farrell boiled out the door. Diana, Samuel noted, kept one hand close to her side. Under her apron was the pistol. Ruth took one look at the white man and turned the shade of Diana's apron. The man grinned shamefacedly and began to speak. Before he could, Ruth took two steps toward him. "You bastard!" She slapped him as hard as she could. Then she burst into tears and fell against the man's chest. He put his arms around her. Ruth lifted her head.

"This . . . this is your father," she managed. Mary gaped, and started crying, too. Samuel's eyes were misty. He rubbed a sleeve across them. Farrell, seeing that tears were the order of the day, began bawling as well. Diana tried to think of something to say. The two black men were looking uncomfortable and touched.

"Inside," she finally managed. "The Prodigal Son looks to be needing a rum punch." Although she felt she herself would shortly be needing the solace of alcohol more than any of the others. Once again her plans seemed to be unraveling.

* * * *

As the Shannons trooped inside, one of the blacks tentatively smiled. "Could we take shelter, lady, in your barn?"

Diana was perplexed. Then she realized what he was getting at. "I asked everyone inside," she said firmly. "No one shelters in my barn unless the house has burnt." Two

Allan Cole & Chris Bunch

very broad smiles, and the men started for the house. "My name is Diana Shannon."

The two men also introduced themselves. They were brothers: Moses and Aaron. "Your surname?"

"We have not decided."

Diana knew what that meant. The two blacks were runaway slaves. Slaves who had been given—or rather, forced to take—the last name of their owner. The situation was becoming more and more peculiar.

* * * *

The three travelers poured down the rum/sugar/boiling water/nutmeg punch. Isaac Conners tentatively asked if there might be another such fine animal about. By that time Ruth had recovered enough to get angry again. Mary was still leaking tears. Samuel had no idea what to think or do. "It has been eight . . . no, more . . . years, Isaac," began Ruth ominously.

"Will you hear me out before you break my heart and tell me to leave?"

Ruth simmered a moment, and grudged a nod.

Isaac began his story. He had not abandoned her. Isaac maintained that he had been hopelessly stranded on foreign shores for all these years. That privateer he'd originally signed on had been wrecked off the coast of South America, "before we ever sighted a prize." The handful of sailors that survived struggled ashore to face savages. Samuel's jaw was on his breastbone. His father had been a pirate! Captured by headhunters!

Farrell had just realized that now he was the only child in the house without a father. His face started to twist. Isaac noticed. "Here lad. I'm not speakin' loudly enough." He hoisted Farrell onto his lap. The boy forgot about crying.

The sailors had been guided to a port by the savages, who turned out to be friendly. Eventually, Isaac found a small smack headed south. Then another. This one, too, sailing south. Then he was ashore, in a larger port. But not large enough for American or European ships to ever call at.

182

"I lived on the kindness of the natives. And worked in a boatyard. Buildin' what they called a . . ." Isaac gargled a word no one else in the room thought could roll off the human tongue. "... which is like what we used to see on the Charles, Ruth, my love. 'Ceptin' with twin masts. I learned a trade there. And a likin' for their food, and even learnin' their heathen language." Ruth was angry again. She didn't want to hear what was rapidly turning into a taproom sea story. Conners cut it short.

"Finally I was able to find my way to Rio. It took near a year for me to find a coaster headin' for America. Landed near the mouth of the Delaware. Hopin' against hope, Ruth darlin', that you were well and happy. But I was without a half-disme. I could not return to Boston after all the brave words I left with.

"There was another privateer signin' on. Looking to take prizes just off the coast. And we took 'em. Near half a dozen in as many weeks. Ruth, I said I was going to come home rich. And..." He took a leather bag from his coat and dropped it on the table. It had a solvent clink to it.

Ruth was not mollified.

"I made my way ashore and afoot to Boston. I was told you'd gone to join your brother near Albany. I got what provisions I could and started north. I"—he cleared his throat—"umm, encountered these two friends on the road, and we agreed to travel together for safety. In Albany my friends were, umm, forced to change their plans, and agreed that instead of continuing north, they would allow me the pleasure of their company. And here, by God's grace, I am. I do not expect you, Ruth, to allow me to return as your husband. But I ask I at least be allowed to guide you—all of you—to a place of safety." Ruth melted.

"All of us, Mr. Conners?" Diana asked.

"So I said. So I meant. And help you find lodgings and victuals with a bit of the money I took a-privateerin'." Isaac might be every bit the self-doomed dreamer she'd gathered from Emmett and Ruth's descriptions—but he also appeared

Allan Cole & Chris Bunch

to be a good man. Diana understood better why Ruth had fallen in love with him. Then Isaac frowned. Diana's advanced pregnancy had registered for the first time.

"My apologies, Mrs. Shannon. Sometimes I'm thick about seeing what's in front of me. Without bein' indelicate, might I ask ..." and he gestured. "Soon, I pray."

"Then ... if we could sleep in the bam . . . I'm sure we might be of assistance. Strong backs and weak minds and that." He glanced pointedly up at the sagging roof beams. "When you're fit to travel—I warrant the weather shall be better then, as well—we could be on the road."

Samuel and Mary were waiting for their mother's reaction. But Ruth was avoiding everyone's gaze—especially Diana's. Diana considered. A lot of assumptions were being made, up to and including whether she was for rescue, or planning to go anywhere at all. She turned to the blacks. "Does he speak for you?"

"Perhaps, lady," the younger man said, "we should keep traveling."

"Let me be open. I was once indentured. Not that different from you. I hold no man has a right to hold anyone else in bondage. I ran away. No one else in this valley knows this. I do not wish it to be spoken around. Where did you run from?"

"Outside Boston. Near Brainard."

"You were going to Canada?"

"Canada. Or the redcoat army. Whichever came first." Samuel glared. How could they admit to wanting to be Tories? "They say the British set a man free if he serves with them."

"I've heard," Diana said, "that when we win this war, slavery will be made illegal."

"We heard the same. But suppose it is not? Or suppose we . . ." Diana hid a smile at Moses's slip. ". . . don't win? We met Isaac, pardon, Mister Conners, along the Hudson. He told us he'd served with sailors in every color but green, and didn't give a . . . care about things like that. We determined to travel together. He can vote for us, lady. We're strong workers. Don't eat that much. Won't be a bother."

Diana, unconsciously, touched the pouch hung around her neck. "We'll have to think and talk about that. But . . . would the three of you be our guests for Christmas?"

Isaac smiled slowly. "I'd hoped ... to be with the ones I love for the birthday of the Christ child. Not to mention bein' glad to have a roof over my head and a fire at my feet." He smiled at his family. "And it'll be the best one I've had for more years than are worth re-memberin'."

Diana Shannon could not ever remember a good Christmas. . . .

* * * *

Diana carefully charcoaled the menu on Farrell's plank:

Haunch of Venison... Roast Chine of Pork
Roast Turkey Passenger Pigeon Pastries Roast Goose
Onions in Cream Winter Squash
Potatoes
Mincemeat Pie
Pumpkin Pie Apple Pie
Indian Pudding
Plum Pudding
Oranges
Raisins
Cider
Rum

The deer had been ambushed by Samuel. He'd decided to teach his father how to be a Wilderness Ranger—like his late uncle Emmett. Isaac said he was a man of the city or the sea—he could catch a fish, but deer were out of his province. In Boston, where he grew up, only rich people hunted. Samuel had laughed. "Huntin' is what you do for fun when you ain't worried about the table," Samuel whispered. "We're cuttin' harvest . . . Father. We're sittin' here wantin' a deer for Christmas. That's why we come out before dawn. Deer'll come down there to that spring to drink. They'll be thin. Not the best eatin'. You get them in spring. What we want is a barren doe. Best we can do."

Isaac, fascinated, whispered, "How do you know they'll be at this spring?"

"Last fall I stole me a salt lick from Mister Campbell. Wired it to a tree down there. They'll come." Six deer ghosted through the dawn mists. Samuel aimed and triggered the rifle. The ball smashed the deer's shoulders. The animal staggered a few steps and fell. "That's that," Samuel said. He took his mother's butcher knife from his belt. "Now I'll show you how to dress the animal. Not much different than cattle."

He dealt similarly with the turkeys—except Samuel wasted no powder. That spring, he'd found a glade that wild turkeys frequented. He'd baited the ground with corn mast all that summer. Now he was ready to reap his harvest. He strung out a narrow meshed twine net on twigs about a foot above the ground. The turkeys clucked their way into the clearing and pecked their way under the net. When they were correctly positioned, Samuel shouted. The turkeys jerked their heads up, through the holes in the net, and well and truly trapped themselves. Samuel staggered back lugging three gutted, plucked, twelve-pound turkeys.

The pigeons had been trapped in September. Tree limbs had been limed, awaiting the annual passage of the sky-darkening flocks. They roosted on the limbs, stuck there, and had their necks twisted. Then they were gutted, plucked, and salted down in barrels. Passenger pigeons were one of the few guaranteed meat sources the settlers had every year. The pork and geese came from the Shannons' own domestic supplies, as did the vegetables, mincemeat, cider, and fruit. Isaac still had two jugs of rum left, which he contributed. He also decided he would make the pie crusts. Diana was glad, and hopeful he knew what he was doing. She hated baking. Ruth loved it—but fretted too much at it.

Isaac also provided raisins—from the Indies. Diana had tasted them but once. He said they cost him naught. A shipmate he'd run into in Boston owed him a gift. Diana did not ask particulars. He also brought a grand present: a sack of oranges.

Diana had never seen an orange, nor had any of the other Shannons except Ruth. Aaron and Moses had seen one, once. It had been a present to their owner. About half of the sack had gone bad. Those with soft spots were discarded. But those that had dried were studded with cloves— another marvel from Isaac's pack—and handed around. "Keep these with your clothes," Isaac instructed. "Better sachet than lavender."

They ate until they could not move. Then ate more. Late in the afternoon, Diana brought presents out. She didn't know what the Christmas custom was in Cherry Valley nor with the Shannons, nor did she care. If she was part of this family, she wanted to show her gratitude. Ruth got the lace Diana had been making on the journey from New Kent—and was stunned. Only the rich owned a piece of lace, let alone a lace shawl. She cried, babbled, then sat smiling happily, holding the shawl to her cheek and occasionally sniffling.

Mary was given a sewing kit: needles, pins—all terribly expensive on the frontier—even a palm and porcelain thimble. Diana promised to show her how to use them. Samuel got a tiny compass—a blunt-ended, magnetized iron needle, floating on a bed of oil and cased in varnished hardwood. The compass had belonged to Mister van Ruysdael, who'd picked it up on his travels. Diana had offered to purchase it from him. The Dutchman had thought a moment, then had laughed and given it to her. He knew where he was going—a large city—and certainly would never find any desire to navigate the wilderness again. Isaac, Moses, and Aaron got presents—mittens that Diana had hastily and secretly knitted after their arrival. Farrell received two gifts. One was a spinning, whistling top. The other Diana explained. It was paper, a quill pen, and ink. "This was meant for Brian," she said. "But he would have wanted you to have it. Use it well." She felt a pompous ass saying that.

Allan Cole & Chris Bunch

But a few minutes later Farrell, after scribbling, announced there were only six days until New Year's, and would he get more presents then?

Christmas was food, cider, rum, the crackle of a warm fire, and the quiet drift of snow outside. Late that night, Diana heard the door latch lift. She half woke, pistol in her hand. It was Isaac slipping softly into his wife's bed. She settled back to try to sleep—aching for Emmett.

CHAPTER TWENTY

JAMES EMMETT SHANNON was born on the Second Sunday after Epiphany. Attending at his birth were Ruth Conners and the spirit of Abigail Fahey.

As Diana grew closer to term, Ruth became more and more nervous. There was no midwife in the valley. Ruth was appalled that Diana mostly ignored her advice. Her midwives in Boston had advised her to eat heavily. Diana insisted on staying close to her normal diet—but she spread her meals out over the entire day. She ate as many vegetables as possible, and trimmed most of the fat from the boiled bacon that was a winter mainstay. Ruth thought Diana was being childish . . . and not a little irrational.

Ruth threw a real tantrum when Diana refused to go into "lying in" for her final weeks, but without influencing Diana. The baby, Ruth muttered to her husband, might well be born deformed from Diana's exercise.

Diana's contractions started just after dawn that Sunday. Ruth shouted the men out of the house. Until the child was born, no man would be allowed inside. She put a knife under Diana's bed to cut through the pain, and opened all the drawers and doors to ease delivery. Then, usefully, she heated water and warmed flannel cloths. Diana was concentrating on three thoughts—that if she'd known how much it hurt, she would never have let that damned Emmett near her; to breathe as deeply as she could, like Gramer Fahey said; and finally, to imagine the old woman present in the room. Abigail had told her a woman who trusts her midwife will have an easier delivery than one who's afraid.

Diana was very afraid. Ruth offered rum. Diana wanted it to numb the pain, but she heard the voice again, Gramer Fahey: "Drink may be the Devil's curse or God's blessing. But it does not belong in the hands of midwife or birthing woman until after the child is born."

A Daughter Of Liberty

Her water burst and the contractions and pain piled closer and higher, like wind-driven snow. Diana came in and out of sweating agony to feel Ruth's hands on her, massaging, as Diana had directed.

The pain swept up, and the bloody, tiny red head pushed forth. It was a normal delivery—or so Ruth said. And an easy one, she continued later. She had done as told: washing the baby, cutting the umbilical cord, and cleaning the bed. She even went to the extent of rolling the exhausted Diana aside to put on fresh linen. Grudgingly, she'd even put the child into a loose wool garment Diana had woven, instead of binding it tightly.

Diana held the infant in her arms and looked down at the tiny, perfectly formed boy. The infant was so beautiful, she cried—but only a little, out of happiness.

* * * *

James Emmett had too many parents. Ruth fretted over him from the time he woke, squalling and filthy, until he slid off to sleep. Was the baby in a draft, or too close to the fire? Did he have too many or too few blankets when he was asleep? Were his eliminations proper and sufficient? Diana wondered how Samuel and Mary had survived at all, let alone lived through the usual childhood ailments.

The men treated the infant as something marvelous and probably quite breakable. Farrell became his caretaker. Diana had seen mastiffs around newly born children who would sit from dawn to dusk inches from the baby, as if it had been given solely into their charge. That was Farrell. Now there was less talk about Brian. Farrell and the baby had long conversations. Mostly they were about what Farrell planned to show James Emmett when he got older, or how he would teach him to do numbers. And letters.

Diana, again to Ruth's shock, insisted on getting up as soon as she could. Gramer Fahey: "I know not why, but women who stay abed are apt to be taken off with a fever. Perhaps there are fluids we do not know of that need to be eliminated and will remain inside the body if it's not stirring about."

* * * *

It may have been winter, and the fields frozen, but the Shannon farm was busy. Moses and Aaron had gone a-raiding down the valley. Any unburnt or reusable planking had been snaked back by a team of oxen to the farm. Isaac had busied himself building a second stone fireplace at the opposite end of Emmett's fine-drawing original, and replacing the sagging roof beams. Isaac planned on building an entire new wing onto the house when the weather permitted. Moses and Aaron talked about this late one night, after they'd retired to their sleeping quarters.

"So here we are, slaving—I beg your pardon, brother— away on a farm that's to be abandoned come spring. Or so the white folk keep telling us."

"Better than crawling through the wilderness with a bounty hunter behind and a scalping knife afore."

"That was not what I meant."

Aaron pulled the fat-lamp a little closer while considering how to put his words. Both men spoke in the dry, nasal accents they and their fathers had grown up hearing. "I wonder how many of them will be going back to Boston."

"Isaac for sure and certain. He's bound to let his string run out near the ocean. His wife, most likely. And their children."

"So the widow will stay. With that babe."

"She has said anyone who has not land is doomed."

"Land!" Aaron snorted. "This is the desert of Sinai. With Indians instead of locusts."

"None of this matters to us, brother. Come the summer, we will travel."

Aaron nodded agreement. Then he blew out the lamp and rolled into his blanket.

* * * *

Diana sought them out a week later. Without preamble: "I have made my mind up. I will not be going to Boston."

Allan Cole & Chris Bunch

"Your choice, Missus," Aaron said.

"What Mister Conners is to do is what he shall do. There's no place for me in Boston. What I have is here."

"That's a brave thing to say, Mrs. Shannon."

No, Diana thought to herself. No, it is not. It's just that the other devils I have yet to meet appear far larger. "I wanted to tell you two men first."

"Might I ask why?"

"Because I wanted to make you an offer. You said you would travel for Canada in the summer. That will be a dangerous road. If you're of a mind, you could stay here. In Cherry Valley."

"As runaway slaves? Waiting for the first slave taker? And you are chancing the law. There's penalties for harboring us."

"I don't think any slave takers in hot trod will come to Cherry Valley," she said.

"So we stay?" Aaron said. "To work your land? In Canada there is land for the taking and holding."

"Work my land? Yes. And the land of Mister Bishop. Or any of those who fled, if you're a mind to. The land is good. I have seed for the planting."

"Supposing the settlers return?"

"Then I will testify that you are free blacks, known to me from Easton. You sought me out at my parents' behest. Not that I expect many of them to return, at least before the war ends."

"Would you put that in writing?" Moses asked. "Although we could be fooled. Our master did not find it good that we should learn to read."

"I will do that. And ... if and when the men come back to Cherry Valley, you will be able to read those words."

Aaron spoke for them both. "I do not think things will work out that simply, Missus. People who hang a man on suspicion don't trouble themselves about a piece of paper."

Before Diana could say anything, Aaron continued: "But I am of a mind to accept. Cherry Valley we know. Canada we do not. If we are to go there, I would rather look for land to farm in the peace." He flashed a smile. Diana was relieved, especially after Aaron told her of the conversation of two weeks earlier, and the exactly opposite conclusion they had reached. Aaron shrugged when she thanked them for the change of heart.

"It probably did not matter which way the toss fell," he said with a grin. "The redmen will kill us all in our sleep before summer anyway."

Diana laughed. Now she had to tell Ruth.

* * * *

Ruth, unpredictably, took the news without surprise.

"I knew you would say that."

"How?"

"Weeks ago, when I said that once in Boston we would have to find a priest to properly christen James Emmett. And you looked at me like I'd suggested we should go to Rome to have the baby baptized. Diana ..." Ruth's tone became pleading, "understand, I cannot stay here. Every night I lie there, listening for the screams again. You are very dear to me. As are the boys. But I have two of my own I must care about."

"I know," Diana said. "And I think you're doing what is right. For you."

* * * *

By summer the house was double-storied, and the addition was framed and boarded. All that remained was shingling the new roofs and putting in the doors. Moses and Aaron were confident they could find enough unshattered glass so it wouldn't be necessary to use scraped hide for the windows. The fields were ploughed and seeded.

Fort Alden was being abandoned. The Sixth Massachusetts was under orders to join a new campaign against the Indians, to rip the heart out of the Indian nations. Five thousand men, under General John Sullivan, had been ordered to prove to the Iroquois that compared to white men, they were mewling babes when it came to burning, murder,

Allan Cole & Chris Bunch

and desolation. The campaign would be under the direct command of General George Washington.

"We go when the soldiers go," Ruth said. Isaac could find no more excuses to remain. He'd even built a steep stairway to the upper story, with rope handrails and elaborate knots that he said were like a ship's companionway.

Tears and farewells . . . and the wagon and its three people joined the middle of the military column as it marched off, on the track back toward Albany. Samuel and Mary waved until they rounded a curve and were lost to sight.

Diana sat for several hours, staring after them. She felt she had done right in staying here. But Cherry Valley felt very, very empty.

CHAPTER TWENTY-ONE

THE INDIANS—SEVENTY-NINE braves and two white renegades—came again a year later. They intended but one thing: to obliterate Cherry Valley. The frontier war had gone on too long. Atrocity begat atrocity; murder, murder. Sullivan's army had torn the guts out of the civilized Iroquois and their Susquehanna Valley granary. Forty-one Indian towns were destroyed, including the Great Seneca Castle, their citadel. Thousands of Indians fled to Canada as refugees. Hundreds more were. dead. Dripping scalps swung from the belts of American soldiers—and no one seemed to give a damn if the scalps were those of men, women, or children.

Moses was splitting logs back of the former Bishop farmhouse when four raiders came out of the brush, keening war cries. He froze—and the first Indian was on him, knife lifted. Moses reflexively hurled his heavy maul, and the Indian's chest crunched. Moses ducked a war lance and grabbed his axe. He brushed the next lance thrust aside and slashed the brave down. A pistol barked behind him and a third brave sagged. The last Indian spun and ran. Moses knew nothing of what had happened. Just that he was standing there, his brother beside him, hurriedly reloading a fired pistol. The bodies of three men lay around him. Moses saw the blood on his axe, and dropped the tool. "The springhouse," Aaron shouted, and they were both running.

Diana, Farrell, and James Emmett were already underground when the two blacks exploded down the steps. They huddled in the darkness—waiting for the hatch to open once more. It did not. At dusk they chanced out. Smoke pillared the sky. The abandoned fort, the blockhouse and church inside it, were aflame. The few buildings left un-burnt a year and a half before were crumbling ash, including the Bishop farm. But the Shannon farmhouse was unburnt. Diana thanked God for Emmett's perversity in having built over a rise. The Indians must not have seen the sprawling building. She was sure the two footprints in the yard could not have come from Indians. Otherwise, the house certainly would have been put to the torch. There could be no other explanation.

Eight settlers were killed in the attack. Twice that many were taken prisoner and driven away to Canada. History would record this as the end of Cherry Valley. The books would say that for the rest of the war the valley's ruins were tenanted only by creatures of the wild. That is not what happened.

* * * *

"You know who I am," Diana said. "I am the crazy Shannon widow." There was a slight ripple of amusement. Diana looked out from her porch at the thirty or so people in the farmyard. They were a strange group. They were the people of Cherry Valley. They did not exist—at least as far as the comfortable record books of the rich were concerned. Their names might appear on the magistrate's rolls. But probably not even there. They were the ones who squatted on unworked land; the failed redemptionists; the landless. There was a knot of French-speaking farmers: Canadian Huguenots. There were three or four Christianized Indians. There were others whose business was beyond any law. Smugglers. Criminals. Even a couple of certified hermits. They'd stayed in Cherry Valley because there was nowhere else to go.

"I guess we are all that's left of Cherry Valley," Diana went on. "That does not trouble me. I came here to stay. This land is mine. There is not an Indian, a Britisher, or a gentleman who can drive me off. I grew up in a village where there were what they called gentry. People who owned land. People who owned people. I would not," Diana said carefully, "piss on any of their beards if their faces were afire."

Diana had taken careful note of the more creative blasphemers around the Black Lamb as well as her own Emmett's ability with obscenities. Again amusement—and agreement. "Now, they are all away, fighting their war. The valley belongs to us. We can—and must—help one another."

A large rough chortled: "I'd be honored to help you, little lady." Diana leveled him with a look as lethal as grapeshot. The rough stepped back into the crowd.

"Some of us have seed. Some of us have supplies. More of us know how to do a task, and can teach others. Some of us would like to read and cipher. I can teach that. We need a marketplace. We do not need the merchants to take their share, telling us how much flax a baconer is worth, do we? I have a springhouse down at the crossroads. We could meet there two times a month."

"Cherry Valley's a day's travel away for me," a man in homespun said.

"We will build down there. Build an inn."

"Innkeepers ain't known for bein' Samaritans," came from a skeptic.

"I am not one, either," Diana agreed. "Lodgings can be paid in kind. Or by work. One day this war will end. What we have then is how the gentlemen will treat us when they crawl back."

"And mebbe they wcn't be let back."

"Believe that if you like," Diana said. "But they have the army now. I do not see why they would not have the soldiers then as well. Dream what you want. I dream as far as this winter."

"So we build again," a woman said. "What about the Indians?"

"Does any one of you have anything an Indian would want? A scalp, perhaps. But I would think that would be a pricey trinket in the getting. Ransom us to Canada? I do not have a rich relative to pay ransom. The ones I have would just spit and say glad to see the last of her. What else? Thieves do not bother poor folk like us. There is nothing to steal." She waited. No one seemed to have anything else to say. "Think on what I said. In two weeks I will have a market at the crossroads. Those who care to, may come."

Allan Cole & Chris Bunch

The crowd broke up into small groups, arguing, agreeing. Diana, Moses, and Aaron served pannikins of rum, one per person. She did not want to put the lie to being poor, and some of these people would think having more than one drink of rum still in the jar as wealth beyond comprehension.

Two weeks later there were fifteen people at the crossroads. Two cows, one heifer, six chickens, five measures of homespun, and an Indian tomahawk were traded. It was a beginning.

Diana Shannon was seventeen years old.

* * * *

The Continental Army laid the foundations for the inn. A patrol of twenty men moved through the valley, one very young, very green, very scared subaltern in the lead. Like his equally raw corporal and eighteen privates, he came from Albany. They had been ordered to scout from Cherry Valley down toward Unadilla. They were sure Indians by the thousands lurked on their route. Diana knew there were Indians out there, beyond the valley. Perhaps twenty or so.

She invited the patrol to camp for the night outside her farmyard. Over a very proper tea, she told the officer she might have a solution to his problem. In Cherry Valley lived this famous ex-ranger, she said, a very private man, badly scarred by what happened in the wars with the French. He owed her a favor.

Diana was sure she could convince the man to take the scout to Unadilla, unseen by the red barbarians.

How long would that take? Perhaps a week, Diana said. The subaltern may have been a novice soldier, but coming from Albany, he had an excellent idea that no one does anything for free.

"While you're waiting," Diana answered smoothly, "your men could be of service to me. I am building an inn down at the crossroads. I have but two males to assist me." The officer frowned. "I was once told by the commander of the garrison here," she went on, "that it was very important for soldiers to keep busy. The devil making work for idle hands and that. And Colonel Alden—of course, I am but a woman—I thought most clever."

The bargain was struck. Diana hunted down an impressively bearded old fur hunter and gave him instructions. He would get a full jug of rum for his services. "The rum beforehand."

"1 am not that much of a fool. And for the love of Jesus, don't let yourself be seen around the valley. Remember, you are supposed to be scouting in Unadilla."

By the time the old man returned, the foundations were laid, the framing up, and half the lapped wall cladding pegged in place. The subaltern started back for civilization, happy with a report that Indian forces beyond the Wyoming were scattered. His troops were equally delighted. Not only had they not marched themselves barefoot, but they'd not gotten massacred, either.

That was how the inn began. It was finished in bits by landless men wanting lodgings after market, poor travelers who preferred not to speak their reasons for being on these deadly trails, the occasional merchant's convoy, and by Moses and Aaron.

* * * *

Robert M'Kean would never return to Cherry Valley for "his" Diana. A dispatch rider told her of Major M'Kean's death, leading troops at the battle of Durlock, in the summer of 1781.

* * * *

Diana's offer to teach any interested parties how to read and write met with only limited success. Some adults showed up for a few sessions, then decided learning was too plaguey difficult. Others saw no use in the art: "If m'da and granddad before him didn't have need for ciphering, why do I?" Some wanted their children to learn—but balked when they realized learning was keeping them out of the fields and away from their daily tasks. The Huguenots were interested, until they realized Diana could not teach them to read and write in French.

pg. 199

But there were a few triumphs. Both Moses and Aaron persisted. Aaron learned fairly readily, but Moses sat for many hours, staring blankly at the primer in front of him. He could understand that the letters C, O, and W represented an animal. But how—and why—should the addition of a fourth letter looking like a snake, mean two, three, or a whole herd? Farrell would watch Moses's perplexity in frustration. To him it was perfectly obvious—the word was not, of course, the thing itself, but there was no difference. Both were equally real. Just as numbers were—six plus seven was thirteen. Thirteen cows, cats, Indians, or just thirteen, were the same. Then one day Moses got it. The squiggles on the page in front of him swam into focus—and made sense. "Whales in the Sea,/GOD's Voice obey" he suddenly shouted—making Diana jump a yard and a half. Moses could read.

* * * *

Part of Farrell's education was reading aloud to Diana each afternoon while she prepared dinner. He knew the words— or puzzled them out easily. But his pronunciation was awful. Diana made the mistake of giggling once, at Farrell's reading—". . . Children in the Midft of New-England itfelf . . ." and the boy instantly went into a sulk, refusing to read again for several days. "Why do they put an F in a book, and you are supposed to read it as an S?" Diana could not answer, other than that was the way it was done. Farrell had little appreciation for tradition. Actually, she thought, it was a good question.

Farrell would read anything. As long as it was the truth. The matter came to a head over William Shakespeare. They'd finished Romeo and Juliet without any problems, although Diana suspected Farrell was keeping his mouth shut since he saw how much his stepmother enjoyed it. Hamlet was the sticking point. He'd read the title suspiciously. "Was this man a real prince?" Diana didn't know. Farrell stopped reading within two pages.

"There's a ghost," he announced.

"So?"

"I don't believe in ghosts."

Diana erred at that point, snapping in exasperation, "It is just a story."

"Then why should we read it? If it did not happen."

"Because," Diana tried, "we can learn from it."

"How? We aren't in Denmark. And we don't have any kings or princes. Why not the Henry Vee-Eye-Eye-Eye play? He was real." Diana decided the argument wasn't worth it—for the moment—and thought it was time for Farrell to start learning Roman numerals. But the discussion wasn't over for the boy. The next day he announced he had read further into the play. "They kill somebody by pouring poison in the porch of his ears. My ears don't have porches. And I do not believe you could kill somebody like that. And even if this Hamlet was real, how did Shakespeare know how he talked? He was English, you said, so how could he know how to speak Denmarky?"

Hamlet—and any other Shakespeare play not labeled a history—went down to defeat. It was not worth the battle.

* * * *

A trapper paid for his lodging with the promise of furs that spring on his return, and a bottle of wine he'd been given. The wine was mostly vinegar—but it came packed in newspaper. Diana deciphered what she could. One paper, the New York Packet of October 25, intoned: "Be it remembered, that on the seventeenth of October, 1781, Lieutenant-General Earl Cornwallis, with above five thousand British troops, surrendered prisoners of war to his Excellency General George Washington, Commander-in-Chief of the allied forces of France and America! Laus Deo!" It sounded as if there had been a noble victory, Diana thought. Maybe the war was ending.

But the war dragged on. Raiders and Indians still struck travelers and isolated farmhouses. The man or woman who strayed more than a minute's run from a weapon or barred door was still easy prey. In spite of the times, Diana's inn prospered. Merchants occasionally traveled the roads, with

Allan Cole & Chris Bunch

heavy escorts. City folk, they were uncomfortable without a solid roof over them when night came. The bulk of Diana's clientele, however, arrived by night; deserters, runaways, hunters. These paid, most often, with labor. They were put up in a part of the inn that had a double-barred door between it and the Shannon quarters. When men like these were around, either Moses or Aaron tried to stay fairly close to the inn.

Then there were the preferred customers: men with ready carbines and tomahawks, and a brace of pistols on their saddles. The cargoes lashed to their pack animals would often be covered with canvas. Men who were taciturn about where they came from and where they were headed. Generally they arrived at night, after sending a lone rider to the inn to make sure there were no troops around. Smugglers. They paid well—either in trade goods or in money. If in goods, they were very careful to tell Diana what a fur or a bolt of cloth would be worth in Albany or Niagara, and that Diana should not take any offer below that price.

Sometimes they even paid in money. Not paper—by now it took nearly two hundred dollars in Continental paper for one dollar in specie, and a damned fool willing to make the trade. State paper was worth even less, up to 1,000:1. Diana hoped Mister van Ruysdael's idealism and faith in paper money had not included his entire fortune. When cash payment was made, it could be in a dizzying variety of coinage. Perhaps dollars. Or, just as likely, thalers, doubloons, pistoles, joes, pistareens, moidores, or Johannes. To make matters somewhat more complicated, silver coins would frequently be cut into halves or quarters to provide the exact amount. Slowly she accumulated a cache.

Farrell was the only one who knew where it was. Diana treated the boy almost as if he were an equal. It may have been a mistake. Certainly he took whatever she said quite literally. But she had to have someone to talk to, and Farrell was completely dependable. Especially at watching James Emmett.

He was quite a child. James Emmett's babyhood was a chronicle of discoveries and near disasters—fire at one and a half (minor burns); kettles at two (Farrell pushed him away as the boiling water splashed); the springhouse steps a month later (bruises); bulls that summer (dragged screaming out of the pen by Diana); deer that autumn (trying to pat a doe that had leapt into the back garden, the deer shot by Aaron before its hooves slashed James Emmett down); and so forth. Somehow they survived. But Diana could not take the next step. Not until there was peace.

* * * *

Four men brought the news. The war was over. America was free. The British army was still in New York: "Let them have the Tory stronghold and rot." But in the spring a preliminary treaty had been approved and a truce proclaimed. Congress immediately began disbanding the expensive army. Diana put the four men up, refusing payment. Not that any of the four had hard coins. "They let us go. We're what they call furloughed," one of the ex-Regulars explained.

"Did they pay you?"

That produced bitter laughter. "They say they'll come to that. But they let us keep our muskets as a bonus," one man said.

"The hell with their bonus, the hell with their pay, the hell with their army, and the hell with the whole damned Congress." This from the oldest of the four, a man wearing a corporal's epaulette. "They'll talk, and argue, and probably end by giving the officers some kind of money. Although what manner of money, is my wonderment. Continentals? I'd rather have this Brown Bess." Diana remembered what Emmett had told her about his treatment when discharged in the war with the French.

"I have all I want out of this war," another man said. "Four limbs, two eyes, and a mind that still remembers how to plant." Diana went for another round of cider, wondering if soldiers would always be forgotten the moment a war ended.

pg. 203

Allan Cole & Chris Bunch

Farrell was in the kitchen with James Emmett. "I heard them. Do you think they're lying? Is the war done with?"

"I believe them."

"So we do not have to worry about Indians? Or cow boys?"

"I don't think that will change."

"Then there is still a war. For us."

Diana couldn't argue. She could only mourn the fact that the boy had known nothing but war since he was two years old.

* * * *

In October the rider came boiling up to the inn. He was one of the French-Canadians, and had driven his horse hard through the fall storms. Diana fed him a mulled cider, and sorted through his French/Indian/English babble. General George Washington himself was coming to Cherry Valley.

Today.

He was right now coming on the road from Cana-joharie. Him, General Clinton, Old Isaac Hand, and others were visiting the frontiers.

"Why would they come to Cherry Valley?" Diana wondered skeptically. "No fort, no church, no rich society here."

The Frenchman looked a little puzzled. He hadn't bothered to wonder.

"You saw General Washington?"

No. He hadn't. But he'd run into somebody on the road who said his brother had. Diana considered, then called herself seven kinds of a damned fool and put herself and the boys in motion. Would General Washington like her inn? What did generals eat? Or drink? Aaron interrupted the scramble with some questions: "This Washington. He's rich. And comes from Virginia, eh? Rich men from down their own slaves."

"What's that got to do with anything?"

"My brother and I stay clear of slavers. Maybe it would be nice to see the General. But it sounds like a chance we'd

204

rather not take. Besides, we've got fencing to go up back of the barn."

Diana put herself and the boys into their best and struck out for where the Albany road came into Cherry Valley. She was swearing a little at being such an optimist. But supposing the General came—and she did not see him? There were thirty or more people waiting, near the ruins of the fort. They waited a very long time. An hour after dusk, even the most credulous conceded that the General was unlikely to make an appearance. Diana collected a disappointed Farrell and James Emmett and sloshed off through the rain, back toward the inn. She wondered if Washington was really at Canajoharie. Or Albany, even.

But she realized, rather suddenly and cynically, that in twenty years or so, after Cherry Valley rebuilt itself, the General would have been there. With probably every dignitary that the tale-teller could think of. Moses and Aaron, she concluded, were the only people in Cherry Valley who had the slightest intelligence—even though they thought in peculiar ways.

* * * *

"Believed you might be interested in these, missus," the man said. He dropped three things on the table. Diana having just come in from the glaring summer light outside, squinted at them in the dimness. At first she thought they were furs. They looked to be three mops, long, shiny, and black, ending in a whitish knot. Diana's stomach lurched. Scalps. She swallowed hard.

"What makes you think that?" she managed.

"They're Senecy," the man said. Even across the great tavern table, Diana could smell the reek from the man's sweat and poorly tanned leathers. "Senecy're what kilt your boy. Emmett's boy." Diana waited. "Easy takin'," the man boasted. "They come out of the forest. 'Peared like they was waitin' for me. Said they wanted to parley. Said they wanted to come an' start tradin' with us." The man guffawed. Diana realized

Allan Cole & Chris Bunch

the stink was coming from the scalps as well as the hunter. "Said they wanted to come to our market."

Diana forced her eyes away from the table. "Why?"

"Said you're a friend. Said they know how Emmett got hisself kilt. Revengin' somebody they said was Dooval or somethin'. Said that's why you didn't get burnt last time they come through." Very suddenly Diana was back, digging the graves in that desolate farmyard below Albany. She'd seen no one watching. All she had left in the farmyard were the scratched words on the wooden cross over Emmett's grave.

"They said there'd been a conference up to Fort Stanwix. Said bunch of our chiefs stood up an' told th' Iroquois they been beat. They backed the wrong horse, an' that's th' way it is. Said the Injuns gonna have to knuckle under and live by our rules. Haw! Then they tol' me Cornplanter— he's the Senecy chief—stood up in council. Said th' Six Nations gotta 'commodate with the whites. Learn to farm an' like that. Dam' fool that he is."

"What happened?"

"I tol' 'em that sounded fine with me. Said we oughter palaver. Waited till they set spears down, and kilt 'em. What the hell else you think I was gonna do? Redmen ain't nothin' but lyin' killers, anyway."

* * * *

That was the summer that Moses and Aaron left. She argued with them. No one had heard of nor seen the Loyalist Hopkins. And the committee had granted her the land. "I wonder if that was ever put in writing," Aaron said.

"How could that matter? Colonel Campbell was sitting that day. And he is a fair man."

"He is. A fair white man." Diana understood. She may have been blind to the fact that Moses and Aaron were of a different color than others. And certainly that they were runaways was a positive note to her. "All it would take," Moses continued, "is one bounty seeker. As far as we know, a slave remains a slave unless freed by his master. And that .

. . that man in Boston would never free us, nor would any of his heirs."

"You are worrying unnecessarily."

"Are we? Probably you are right. Probably Moses and I could remain on the land. Perhaps even purchase it from you, if a deed is recorded. Both of us want to marry some day. And have children. What rights will they have? Congress seems to have no concern for men of color."

"But in Canada . . . there's still lords and ladies and redcoats," Diana said.

"But no slaves," came the retort.

A week later they were packed and ready to leave. With them went two horses, a cart, and a good percentage of Diana's carefully husbanded money. "If things do not happen as you hope," Diana said, "you are always welcome here."

"We thank you. Maybe one day we shall return. Or our sons may. When America fights the rest of its war."

Diana, Farrell, and James Emmett watched the wagon until it was out of sight. James Emmett was crying. Farrell did not cry or say much until Diana was putting the boys to bed. "Why," he asked, "is everyone always leaving? And why are we staying?"

Not for much longer, Diana thought. Not for much longer.

* * * *

But it was another four years before the man of Diana's dreams arrived. By then the inn was a sprawl around the crossroads. Buildings were put up or remodeled; as times grew better, money could be spent, or there were some strong backs needing work. If Diana saw her life and her work as being Cherry Valley, it probably would have been most logical to rebuild the inn from bare ground. But she did not, of course, and never had. If Emmett had lived, they would have sold the land or possibly even abandoned it and moved west. But Emmett was gone.

Diana felt herself, at twenty-five, getting old. The world was changing, and she was not part of that change. One side

Allan Cole & Chris Bunch

of her knew this to be foolish—but lying awake in predawn darkness, when the mind sees nothing but disappointment and failure, the thought was still there. It would be the city for her. Since Farrell, at fourteen, could and did manage the inn on occasion, she was willing to travel as far as Albany. He could also keep James Emmett under some kind of control. He'd continued growing as a mischief, and probably wasn't punished enough for his troublesome adventures.

The first time she went to Albany not for business, but for pure longing. There had been a man. The head of a band of smugglers. A man of quick wit, scented hair, velvet coat, silver buckles and handworked pistols which were always primed and hung on either side of his blooded stallion's saddle. Perhaps he had a wife, at home in New York. Perhaps not. She did not ask. It was enough that he made her laugh and held her very close in the silence of the night. Laughter came not nearly often enough in Cherry Valley. Life was too much a struggle, from before the sun rose until after it set, hard work and hard thought just to stay alive, and satisfaction enough at the end of the day to fall into a dreamless sleep, belly full and scalp attached.

There had been a couple of other affairs. But always Diana was careful and kept Gramer Fahey's words that New Kent—and Cherry Valley—was "not the place to spread your knees and keep your independence. But in other places there are discreet ways a woman can leap into a man's bed as eagerly as a witch to the Devil's Sabbath, and not chance her reputation." Diana was careful indeed: "And as for getting caught out, there's little reason in these times. I have means ... so that you can have pleasure without fear— wedded or not." Pleasure, yes. Companionship once, perhaps twice. Nothing more. Not that Diana Shannon wanted more. She was too busy staying alive.

But there was more to this traveling than just the freedom of being away from the careful and moral eyes of Cherry Valley. There was the feeling that just beyond her horizon, south on the Hudson, was a world where life was more than a day-by-day scrabble for mere survival. She listened to the echoes of that world aborning in many forms. The new fabrics in the merchants' shops. Sometimes an item of luxury—pewter or silver that found its way to the frontier. An exotic silk from lands beyond her geography. Sometimes a man traveling with his wife, and the wife would describe what was worn in a city. Styles that she would carry back to Cherry Valley in her mind and then sew for herself. Sometimes the result was ludicrous—or else the Philadelphia or New York style itself was ludicrous, and Diana ripped up her own stitches in half-angry, half-amused frustration.

The feeling that now was the time grew stronger. Now was the time to move on. And finally the man she'd dreamed of arrived. Robert Bolton. He was a speculator, a man who knew he was foreordained for great riches, a man who'd convinced himself he was the natural son of Midas. Such a man—firm in the conviction that riches were one deal away—was certain he knew many things. He knew roads better than the teamster, iron better than the smith, grain better than the miller . . . and inns better than the keeper. Bolton had been in Cherry Valley for two weeks. Diana heard he was attempting to purchase Thomas Whitaker's tavern, which made her use a number of choice words culled from soldiers' language. Then the sale collapsed. Mister Whitaker was entertaining a larger offer. She began hoping.

Mister Bolton made a grand appearance the next day. His sleek horse looked like it'd come from a cavalry regiment—but it needed reshoeing. His clothes were expensive—but not what Diana heard that the men in the cities were wearing these days. She had been contemplating a litter of pigs, and planning to slaughter them before the weather got warmer. Mister Bolton dismounted and introduced himself. Then he eyed the pen.

"Three months from now, and those will be fine baconers."

Diana started to say something. Yes, in three months they might double their weight, but they also would have

pg. 209

Allan Cole & Chris Bunch

eaten several times that increase in slops. She merely smiled politely. Mister Bolton sidled into the subject. He had heard of Diana's inn, and was impressed . . . very impressed that a woman could run such a vast enterprise by herself.

"What is so impressive about that? Would a man be able to take it in his stride?" Mister Bolton backwatered. Of course that was not what was meant. But there was just her, and her two sons. A Herculean task for anyone. Diana invited him into the taproom and offered a punch. Eventually the conversation worked around to: Had she ever considered a partner? Someone who could provide financing. Someone with close connections to lenders.

Farrell had joined them. He started to bristle—and was glowered into silence by both Diana and Mister Bolton. "Partners fall out," Diana said. Then baited her own hook. No, she'd never considered a partner. But ... as the good sir could tell—the inn was quite large, and showed no sign of shrinking. Look how Cherry Valley is growing. Did you know, sir, there is even talk about us becoming another county? If Cherry Valley were the seat, which of course it would be, by the turn of the century it might rival Albany in size. Mister Bolton had not heard the talk of a new county. His eyes glistened.

"I have been thinking about returning to Easton," Diana continued. "But I would be afraid my inn would be mishandled if I sought out some local to run it for me." Mister Bolton looked around, and Diana could read what he was thinking. Certainly her prices were far too low. If they were raised—not too much—the rustics now lying around the benches would not use the taproom as if it were a meeting hall. What Mister Bolton seemed to see, just beyond the horizon, was a steady stream of rich people who would die to stay at this inn. The menu would change, she foresaw. There was no need to provide meals that left diners glutted and waste that would only go to the hogs. There should be more wines for these new, and undoubtedly gentle patrons. Diana was sure that the brilliant Mister Bolton could find some wine that would survive the roads, teamsters, and weather from Albany without becoming vinegar. The rum could be cut. As long as there was fusel oil, there would be whiskey made.

Eventually, after more politeness, Mister Bolton made a first, tentative offer to buy her out. This offer was quickly refused. Her inn was flesh and blood. The formal dance had begun. Bolton let her think on the possibilities, finished his punch, and left, promising to return on the morrow. Diana was not surprised he made no offer to pay for his drinks.

After he left, Farrell apologized. "I forgot."

Diana waved the apology off.

"Do you think he is in earnest?"

"The stablehand at Mister Whitaker's said his saddlebags were heavy as millstones," Diana said.

"What price do you think we can get?"

"I do not know," Diana said. "1 would dearly love, though, to peer inside those saddlebags. And then settle on an amount that would leave him but one copper for small beer."

* * * *

That was enough for James Emmett, who'd been listening from his hiding place behind the door that led into the kitchen. He would find out this information. His mother would be proud that her son helped in this momentous matter. He would be a spy, like . . . well, perhaps not like that Hale man someone had spoken of, back in the war. Not even if he got to make a speech first.

James Emmett blurred for Mister Whitaker's inn, making and then discarding plans as fast as his legs moved. James Emmett wanted more than anything else to be out of Cherry Valley. Anywhere would be fine. They could go on to the frontier, where he could become a famous Indian fighter like Boone or one of them. Or they could go to a seaport. Maybe that was the best. Boston was where his uncle Isaac was. Uncle Isaac would teach him how to be a pirate and a sailor, since Farrell didn't seem like he wanted to go away to sea anymore. Uncle Isaac would not hesitate, James Emmett

Allan Cole & Chris Bunch

thought. Especially when Mother said how proud she was of her son, and how he had crept into the evil Bolton's den and found out Important Secrets.

He made for the back entrance to the inn. He'd ask one of Mrs. Whitaker's smarmy daughters which room Mister Bolton was in. Then . . . then he'd do what had to be done. He never got that far. He spotted Mister Bolton, who was sitting outside in the garden, enjoying the balmy afternoon with a drink, holding forth to a man James Emmett did not recognize. And those saddlebags were close-guarded beside him. He did not see James Emmett. The boy crept close along the hedge. Maybe he could listen and hear something that would be Valuable. A chunk of meaty hand against leather, and a clink. Mister Bolton's voice: "Of course she will sell. A titty widow woman like that? She does not know what she has. Two years, no more than three, and that crossroads will be like a turnpike crossing. Way I read the map is that any crossroads anywhere is worth gold. She herself went and let on about Cherry Valley being a county on its own. That spells real riches, Farley.

"What she does not know is I have solid backers in Albany. Merchants who made theirs in the war and now have funds to put in the right places and to the right men. Like me. Like you, too, Farley, if you pay close mind. There's riches here. That inn . . . that's just the start. I have a very significant Letter of Intent here that promises much for the future." The rattle of parchment, and then Mister Bolton's laughter. "After the sale, maybe I'll celebrate with the widow, knowing she is no better than she is supposed to be. Join giblets as a sign of earnest." More laughter. "Here, Farley. It's your round."

James Emmett scuttled before Mr. Bolton's companion came around the corner and saw him. He went home, most disappointed. Not much of a spy. Maybe he wouldn't say anything about what he'd planned. Or maybe he would.

* * * *

By dinner that night James Emmett could keep his secret no longer. After all, had he not crept very close—close

212

enough to hear the gold clink in Mister Bolton's saddlebags? James Emmett had a very good memory for details and no small ability to mimic his elders. Diana and Farrell sat looking at each other after the boy had been rewarded and sent off. Farrell was still blushing and angry. Even if James Emmett did not know and could not figure what "joining giblets" meant, Farrell could. Diana paid little mind. That was, after all, how any widow was thought of. She was more interested in those backers. Farrell found another thing to be angry about: "If that Bolton had seen James Emmett—"

"He would have thought him but a boy. Besides, he was but trying to help. And help he did. I think now I know our price." She named a figure. Farrell's eyes widened.

"We'll never get that."

"Get it we shall. The man has backers, who must be as foolish as he is if they were willing to put any financial commitment in writing and give it to a speculator. Into the kitchen with you. And in your best hand, I want a letter from Albany. From a friend. The friend's name is ... is Mister Duvall. His letter is full of good news. And also to introduce two men who will be arriving in Cherry Valley next month. Men who are very interested in investments. Men from . . . from Philadelphia. Shippers, they are. Who made a great fortune on the war and now are looking for somewhere to put their money."

Farrell's solemnity dissolved. "Where will we leave this letter for Mister Bolton to snoop it?"

"Somewhere in plain sight . . . when the time is right."

"What about our books?" Farrell asked.

"When we have an offer that is close," Diana decided, "he can see them."

"But they will not show—"

"Any man who can see rich people coming to Cherry Valley will see whatever he wants to see in our ledgers, and reach whatever conclusions he has already decided on." And that was how it went. Offer . . . declined. Tentative offer . . . tentative disinterest. Offer withdrawn. No response. A

Allan Cole & Chris Bunch

suddenly panicked and increased offer—possibly drawn by the fictitious letter "accidentally" left out on a table. Finally an offer was made and accepted. Diana then played her final card. The agreed price must be in specie. Not promissory letters nor paper currency. Cash. She feared for a moment Mister Bolton would fall victim to apoplexy. He stormed out of the inn. "I was afraid of that," Farrell said. "We misspent our time."

"I do not think so. Now, I wager, he is going to consult with his backers. Or so I hope."

Two weeks later Mister Bolton returned. Strictly by chance, Diana had as guests half a dozen merchants. Their heavily laden wagons were drawn up in the yard, and the merchants, looking forward to what would be—they knew— an excellent year, were spending heavily. Mister Bolton saw them, and was sure of his acumen. It took less than a day for the papers to be drawn and Diana to receive her money. The inn, outbuildings, supplies, and goodwill now belonged to Robert Bolton. Diana wondered if he would last out more than one winter. On the whole, she thought not. But that, beyond the passing regret for a place she'd given ten years of her life to, was not important. This was the end of Cherry Valley for the Shannons. Ahead lay Philadelphia.

BOOK THREE:

PHILADELPHIA: SPRING 1788- WINTER 1810

CHAPTER TWENTY-TWO

NO ONE HAD warned Diana about boats. More precisely, no one had warned her about boats captained by an incompetent bent on drinking a New York tavern keeper's consignment of cider.

First one keg and then another was broached by "accident," and soon either the boat was running aground or the captain and his scurvy crew were cursing and poling madly away from imagined shoals. The captain swore these were uncharted menaces, thrown up by the Hudson to test a poor packet man who only wanted to scrape his way through this world of dry crusts and toil. Diana thought if Charon were as bumbling as her captain, the River Styx would be impassable from all those reefs of piled-up lost souls.

Diana's trek from Cherry Valley was routine. It didn't prepare her for what lay ahead. The passage to New York from Albany was reputed to be an easy journey. No more than four days—five at most. Instead they were nine days on the river. Even then, Diana and the other passengers had to abandon the packet and hire canoes to make complete the voyage.

Even when sober, the captain was an odd villain who seemed cobbled together by a mischievous demon. He had an amazing torso which could have served as a model for an ancient sculptor, stacked upon short legs as thick as barrels. He was as bald as a copper kettle and wore an undersized, dirty patch over a gaping hole in one cheek; the rest of his face was cider-shot with purple veins that spread like a fishnet set to catch the blemishes around them.

Other than Diana and her two boys, there were eight other passengers aboard the packet—all men. Conditions were crowded. Besides luggage, the little craft was piled with goods bound for the city. Two of the passengers pitched an awning between a bundle of hides and a stack of timber to give Diana a measure of privacy. The awning was no use against the purple language and vulgar acts of the crew, when a few hours out of Albany the first keg of cider was "dropped" and the captain ordered all hands to partake, so there would be no danger in it being wasted— "surely one of the great offenses in God's Kingdom."

Diana had heard worse in her years as an innkeeper, but it soon grew wearisome to pretend ladylike shock at every obscene utterance. But it was a pretense she dared not drop. No more than she could let her shawl fall from her shoulders to get relief from the river's midday heat, or pluck her dress away from a perspiring bosom. As a young— and, yes, beautiful, she had to grudgingly admit—widow of twenty-six, her mask of sanctity was her only means of control. Not that anyone would physically abuse her. If that happened, even the fool captain would know he'd be hanged at the wharf in New York. But her treatment aboard the packet would be rougher, and her opinion considered not a whit if anyone thought her less than a respectable woman of means.

Then they discovered that most of the food the passengers had brought had been forgotten in the confusion at the Albany docks. Along with the victuals for the captain and crew. There were no livestock aboard, only a few scrawny curs who snapped at anyone who came near them. The men held a conference with the captain, and it was decided to push on. They would rely on purchased charity from the small farms and settlements sprinkled along the river. Everyone agreed this was a routine matter, and the stops would only lengthen their journey by a day at most.

Under other circumstances this might have been true. But the captain was no better a skipper of the canoe he carried for shore excursions than he was his packet. Smoke would be sighted—a sure sign of settlement. The captain and two of his men would cast off in the canoe. Invariably they would either (a) immediately overturn, (b) be swept miles past the farm by the current, or (c) take drunken alarm at

Allan Cole & Chris Bunch

imagined Indian sign and paddle back like devils fleeing the wrath of their dark Master.

Farrell, meanwhile, remained his usual stolid self. At fourteen, he had the bearing and dignity of a middle-aged man. He had a cold look of disapproval that would pierce the conscience of the foulest villain, and a superior manner which sometimes drove Diana to distraction. Just now she thanked him for it. He was also the keeper of the family fortunes. Diana was traveling light. She had sold or traded for promissory notes everything they owned. All they possessed—mostly city clothes of latest fashion she had made for the three of them—was in three large horsehair trunks, bound with copper for strength.

The treasure chest, containing the gold from the sale of the inn and their other coin and paper money, had been Farrell's idea. It was a battered carpetbag he'd purchased for a few pennies from a wayfarer. He carried it as his own— and for anyone who knew Farrell, its raggedness was quite out of character. The leather sacks of money were at the bottom of the bag, covered with cast-off boyhood treasures. Farrell kept it near at all times, turning away the curious with his chilly look. Where money was concerned, and the future of the family, Farrell was a better guard than a squad of soldiers.

It was James Emmett who scattered her wits like ants milling about before a thunderstorm. At nine, he had a charming manner far beyond his age, and a quirky sense of adventure that drew him to the strangest people. He and the captain became fast friends. Diana wasn't sure if it was the salty stories or his tricks—like lifting the patch to expose the hole in his cheek, then smoking his pipe through it, all the while expelling fumes and foul language from his mouth.

One day the captain spotted a likely farm. Off he and his men went. To Diana's amazement, there was not a mishap all the way to the rickety landing that tilted in a crazy raking angle down to the water. The men disappeared to raucous scolding from three great swans cruising the dock-side waters. Diana went back to her sewing. A furious shout from.

Farrell snapped her head up. He was screaming for James Emmett. Diana looked about the packet. No boy. Where could he be? Then it began to dawn. Farrell was pointing frantically at the shore. Diana raced for the side of the boat.

The captain was making his way back from the farm. Perched on his shoulders was James Emmett. His shrill laughter echoed across the river, along with the mad cacklings of the two fat hens he held in either hand. The swans wearied of the noise and took flight. There was nothing Diana could do. She watched as the captain lifted the child into the craft and then clambered in with his men. Muffled, drunken arguments and fumblings with paddles and rope. They pushed off, setting an erratic course for the packet. They skimmed forward a few yards, then jerked violently to the side with shouts of fear. This scared the holy bejesus out of Diana, until she realized they were only entertaining James Emmett.

She was planning the licking she was going to give the boy and with which strap, as the canoe drew close to their boat. Another mock shout of fear. Another lurch of the canoe. Then the mock fear went out of their voices and turned real as the craft tilted slowly over, tumbling out supplies and men and boy.

After ten years on the frontier, not a scream existed in Diana, only the strangling in her throat as she watched her son disappear. Then he was bobbing up to the surface, still holding on to those damned hens and splashing and shouting in what Diana believed to be terrible fear. The current swept him agonizingly close to the packet, skimming along the side and almost gone, when one of the men got him by the breeches with a boat hook. He went under again, but came back up swiftly as the man lifted him out. The crewman held him at arm's length for a moment, shifting his grip-It was then Diana realized James wasn't frightened at all. The screams were shouts of laughter. The hens still dangled by their necks from each tiny fist. The man swung him aboard like that great clothed fish from myth, and the

Allan Cole & Chris Bunch

boy tumbled to the deck, hooting laughter and waving the poor half-drowned fowl at Diana. To James the entire incident had been one grand adventure. The fact the adventure even provided dinner made it grander still. All the men laughed and clapped him on the back and complimented him on what a game lad he was.

The next morning Diana hired a canoe and they left the packet. It was an easy thirty miles for all concerned. Except James Emmett Shannon. Who rode the whole way in silence, nursing a blistered rump.

* * * *

Diana almost wept when she saw New York. Not from joy at the promised marvels of one of the greatest cities in the new nation, but in despair. She had met travelers from this city, and knew them to be boasters. She did not expect streets paved with precious metals. Nor did she really believe every shop would be filled to overflowing with treasures the envy of the Great Mogul of China. Or that there was plenty of bread and cheese and ale for the meanest gristmill laborer. But still . . . But still. . . . The desolation spreading before her was nearly as awful as the day she and Emmett had hurried through the ruins of Kingston. Actually, it was worse, because people lived in this place by the thousands.

To begin with, if it were not for its watery boundaries, it would be difficult to tell where the city began and ended. Mostly, New York was a swampy wilderness, pocked with a few scrubby farm plots. The better houses were thinly scattered along dozens of creeks and kills that ended in swamps or meadows.

There were a few orchards and fields of buckwheat, which was a pleasant break for the dimmer view deeper into the city. Basically, the city—and it was a great stretch to call it that, compared to Albany—seemed to end at Anthony Street on the north; Harrison, the last street before the Hudson; and Rutgers, the final byway before one reached the East River.

A Daughter Of Liberty

Not many of the streets were flagstoned. On those that were, the stones had been laid so roughly a stroller had to adopt an odd kind of shuffle in his walk, or go sprawling to his death in front of a farm wagon. A few pebbles were scattered with a miser's hand on some roads, but these were only useful as missiles when the young sportsmen of the region defied the law and threat of fine by thundering along on their fancy steeds. The swagger of these dandies set Diana's teeth on edge. She was not alone in her view that their behavior was far from the Republican spirit of the times, and smacked of the bleak British class system America had overthrown.

Sanitation consisted of a few open sewers running down the middle of these streets, privy vaults to make the most hardened campaigner shudder, or simply pots of filth tossed out doors and windows. At the end of a market day the streets were strewn with the unsold spoils: animal heads and entrails, fish parts, fluttering robins with broken wings and feet scorched by the lime that captured them, grain and coffee so sour Diana just knew by the odor that a great plague must only be days or weeks away.

New York looked as if the Revolution had only ended yesterday. In fact, it had never recovered from the wrath of the king. A fire had broken out during Lord Howe's occupation, and five hundred buildings were lost to the inferno that raged for days. Even after all these years, the entire area around Washington Market was a blackened heap of charred plaster and broken brick. From the appearance of the city and its poverty-haunted inhabitants, Diana thought it was no wonder people believed the future of the state lay in Albany, which had prospered mightily after the war. From the downcast spirit of the residents, she saw no reason why it would ever change.

The letters she'd received from Ruth painted no better picture of Boston, where grass was springing up in the streets, and the once bustling shipbuilding yards were silent. The waterfront was choked with decaying wharfs and rotting

Allan Cole & Chris Bunch

wooden hulks. Emmett's assessment of Boston was as true today as it had been years ago when they wandered the country roads. He said it was an unlucky city with mean-spirited masters. The great merchants and bankers had determined there were greater fortunes to be made lending money than building ships or investing in anything that required honest toil. Diana wondered how satisfied they were in their great homes, their treasuries filled to the groaning, while the city created by their ancestors lay about them in ruin.

But she had never considered seeking her future in Boston. As for New York, if she had pinned her business hopes to this town, she would have immediately turned her back on it and—packet boat ordeal or not—returned to Cherry Valley. She could foresee no time—no matter how distant— New York would ever be a place where a person could consider opening a business with confidence. At the moment, however, all she could do was pray that things were better in Philadelphia, the city of her birth.

* * * *

Diana found lodgings in a genteelly shabby boardinghouse with a huge, tangled garden, tended by an old woman whose mind was as oddly cluttered as the grounds surrounding the home. There were countless flowers of every variety, all planted without rhyme or color scheme amid thorny weeds that were as carefully nursed as the flowers. There were no paths through the garden. One pushed through the undergrowth, taking care not to tumble over an old bed frame, or rusted stove parts, or what James insisted with great excitement was the barrel of a Brown Bess.

The woman said her name was Irene Jones, but she shuffled around in old carpet slippers mumbling what Diana was sure were Dutch curses. She heatedly denied she was even distantly related to the great Van Dam family, although Diana hadn't asked, and with a last name like Jones, didn't suspect. But when James dragged the bed frame to one corner to become a fort, Irene grew agitated and lectured the

222

boy about the evils of fornication, especially fornication with the rich, and even more especially the rich Dutch. Since James thought she was talking about "fortification," Diana didn't think it necessary to intervene.

A moment later Irene was enticing the child into her kitchen and filling him full of confections and stories of the British occupation. She pointed to the attic stairs and told the story of the long nights she spent hidden by the window, waiting with a charged rifle for the redcoats to come into view. None ever did, although she assured the boy she would have shot any of them " 'tween their lights"—a feat well within her abilities, Irene said, because of her time as a circus performer.

This brought a shower of questions from James Emmett, but the old woman drifted into reminiscing about her days as a singing and music instructor to the daughters of the rich "up by Harlem Creek." Diana wanted to hear more, but her questions were turned aside by dark comments on the handsome sons of these folk, and how they twisted their word as easy as a smith draws a sliver of white-hot steel through a screw form. This was followed by another string of cursing in Dutch and a heated denial of kinship to the Van Dams.

What all this had to do with the old lady's present circumstances, Diana could only guess. Her guesses were wild thrusts into the dark. Most of them involved a little weakness and a slight amount of recklessness on Irene's part. And a great deal of sin and even greater betrayal on someone else's. Did the boardinghouse itself offer some kind of clue? At one time it must have been worth much. Did a young man's family—the Van Dams—buy silence with it? Was there a child involved? She could never bring herself to ask, and Irene would never say.

Diana did not make the error of thinking Irene's wits were addled by age. There was information here of far more value than gossip fuel harvested from a poor old woman. If Diana was to make her way through this new wilderness

Allan Cole & Chris Bunch

called Civilization, she would have to take advantage of every scrap she could glean. She determined to start by wooing the strange old woman.

So, Diana got out her lace maker's pillow and most colorful thread, then sat quietly by the fire, laying out a pattern with her needles. Irene pretended indifference at first, but as Diana's fingers began flying and the silent room filled with the click-click-clickings of her bobbins, the old woman drew her chair close. She watched the shape take form, and grunted with satisfaction when she saw the flower emerging. It was a duplicate of the apple blossoms in her garden. Diana snipped off a loose thread with her teeth and almost absently held the lace up toward Irene's dress. Then just as absently, she nodded in satisfaction at how the colors matched. She dropped it back in her lap and began working again. Diana shot Irene a look, and saw the little smile playing on her face. The woman knew the lace was for her.

The words started flowing again. But this time they lay sharp and bright in the present. Life in New York was even worse than Diana had imagined. While most of the states generally prospered from the war, New York found itself in a limbo.

Prior to the Revolution, travel to and from New York was an easy accomplishment. Irene told of the days when stage owners could boast a trip to Philadelphia would take no more than three days. This was shortly cut to two, and on carriage springs "so soft you could place an egg on your lap and there it would remain intact until the journey's end." Now it was more of an island city than ever before. Roads in every direction were a ruin, with nothing but wilderness where once villages and hamlets had prospered. Travel by water was a nightmare—Diana could attest to the truth in this—with a journey to Philadelphia an uncertain nine days to nearly three weeks.

"Even the ferries are not to be trusted with your safety," Irene said.

New York had become nothing more than a place for goods and gold to flow through. What little money stayed, remained in the hands of the rich few. The most skilled laborer was fortunate to earn two shillings a day, and was cursed for demanding this amount. It was barely enough to keep him from debtor's jail and his family from starvation. Corn was three shillings a bushel—before it reached the miller—wheat eight and six pence, a pound of salt pork tenpence. The laborer saw fresh meat on his table about as often as he saw coal for his stove, which was never. Instead, the coarse food was cooked over a fire of collected debris: broken bits of boxes and barrels, lit by a spark from a flint, a burning ember borrowed from a neighbor.

A laborer's daughter was destined to serve the rich, if she were lucky, and besides this—since her mother almost certainly labored as many hours as her father—she was forced to run all the family errands, mend the clothing, milk the cows, if they had any, churn the butter if the cows weren't afflicted with dry udder, spin flax for the family linen, and walk ten blocks for a pail of water. Her dream would be to save a few shillings for a dowry and hope to catch the eye of a tradesman's son.

No, Irene said, New York was no place for a bright young woman like Diana. Certainly not for her sons, if she wanted any future for them. Diana couldn't agree with her more. Especially after she saw more of the town.

One expected a modicum of culture in any city. In this place, books were even more expensive than the high prices they brought in Albany. In fact, paper of any kind was so expensive, not even the tradesmen who catered to the elite would dream of wrapping their goods in the stuff. The theater—Irene hooted at the term even being used here—consisted of imports from England, playing to strangers who had the misfortune to wander down Broadway. Before she left the city, Diana saw a revival of Richard Brinsley Sheridan's School for Scandal, which she found silly and hardly scandalous except for the price of tickets, and Hamlet,

Allan Cole & Chris Bunch

which she would have liked to enjoy, except the actor was so irritatingly English, she found herself wishing the audience would rise up and tar and feather the obscene child for daring to look down his high-peaked nose at the audience across the candlelights.

Two weeks to the day from her arrival in New York, Irene came to Diana with news. She had found a means for Diana to complete their journey in safety and style.

"How much?" was Diana's first question. She was determined to make her store of cash last for as long as it would take to set them all up in style. If that meant waiting three years, or more, she was prepared.

Irene cackled at her question, held a finger to her lips in a half-remembered gesture of demure naughtiness. "Just the wisp of a smile, dear," she said. "And that given like a miser hoards his grain."

The words were as mysterious as Irene's past. But not for long.

* * * *

His manner was as big and blustery as the early winds that broke the Hudson ice packs. He was unashamedly Irish Catholic, but spoke Dutch like a son of Amsterdam. He was rich, but was committed to Republican values: admitting, while in his cups, he saw logic in the view of the Radicals, that all men should have the right to vote, not just those of property, or in kind coin.

Michael Walsh was a man who knew how to make an entrance. There was a thundering at the door as the hour of his appointment struck. Diana remained by the fire in the big main room while Irene shuffled off to answer. She heard his voice boom in greeting, then heavy footsteps. Diana watched the doors in anticipation. They came open and for a moment she thought there must be a ghost in the house, for she couldn't see a soul.

She looked down. And down. And down. Wearing his pointiest shoes with the highest heels, and carrying himself in the utmost military manner, Mister Walsh barely scraped an inch over Diana's height. He was as slender as a cabinet maker's nail, with oddly long arms, a big nose sharp enough to cut a copper hoop, and a protruding Adam's apple, which accounted for the rich timbre of his voice. Diana thought she had never seen a full-grown man so small. She rose while Irene made the introduction. It was difficult to pay attention, because she wanted badly to laugh.

Mister Walsh was a middle-aged Philadelphian, who seemed at constant war with his physical nature. He dressed in the height of Chestnut Street fashion, which meant too young by many years and too gaudy for a man his size. He carried a bright green three-cornered hat, heavily decorated with fancy lace. His hair—which included a long false queue wrapped in ribbon, dangling down his back—was thick with pomatum, and so heavily powdered the dust came off in little puffs when he moved, giving him a tendency to sneeze. He wore a light-colored cape, cut short in front—revealing the little middle-aged bulge of his belly—and long in back.

It was clasped with silver buttons engraved with his name. His small clothes were cut above knobbly knees, which his tight striped silk stockings merely accented. Then there was the green vest with enormous flap pockets—again decorated with silver buttons, and finally the pointy shoes with the silver buckles. His cuffs were so firm and perfect, Diana knew they were loaded with enough lead to stagger a Goliath. All this was set off by an ebony cane, with a sculpted silver lion's head mounted upon it.

It was almost too much for Diana. Especially when he repeated her name with a sultry murmur and bowed with a Frenchified flourish. Despite his size, he took up nearly half the room when he bowed, because here he made use of the oversize arms. His cane went in such a long, raking angle, it nearly knocked over the coal bucket by the fireplace, while his other arm stretched so far in the opposite direction his knuckles grazed an oil lamp. Diana curtsied. There was nothing else for her to do. She lowered her eyes modestly, let the scarf about her shoulders slip not so modestly, caught the

Allan Cole & Chris Bunch

hem of what she knew to be a dress of stunning brocade and dipped. The red face Mister Walsh wore when she rose again let her know the curtsy had been a great success.

A moment later they were settled in Irene's big soft chairs sipping tea and chatting nonsense. Walsh made some not-so-subtle jokes about the spicy books of Lady Julia Mandeville. Diana laughed to let him know she was a modern woman and certainly no prude. But she did it with a charming blush, hinting all of this was strictly theoretical.

He asked her if she had shopped any of the finer wares in the city. She said she had. He asked if she had been to the theater. She said yes. And he asked if she had sampled some of the tastier dishes the town was known for. She said she had done this as well. Leaving no openings.

"How unfortunate for me," Mister Walsh said. "I would have enjoyed offering myself as escort." Irene barked a knowing laugh, and Walsh turned several shades of purple.

"Perhaps you could do me that favor in Philadelphia," Diana said, then added quickly as she saw his face brighten, "You and Mrs. Walsh, that is." She could almost see the man's heart lurch in his chest as the arrow Irene had prepared struck its target.

In less time than it took for gunpowder to burn in a pan, the man was burbling about his wonderful spouse, her equally wonderful mind and spirit, a woman of such taste and gentility, she would shame the mistress of a great manor. And yes, he—that is to say, they—would be delighted to see her set right in Philadelphia, so her visit would be unspoiled by any kind of unpleasantry, so help him God, and he crossed himself, giving away his Catholic roots.

As Irene had predicted, Walsh was as disarmed by the mention of his good wife as a Hessian deserter come begging for scraps at the Patriots' cookfires. But he proved to be such a nice man, Diana couldn't help but feel a little irked with herself for the little ploy. After years as a struggling young woman of business—in a world ruled by men-she had learned to use any means to win an edge. She didn't like it, but that didn't keep her from using them.

Irene had clued her well about Walsh, although she hadn't mentioned his small size and odd appearance. Walsh was a native Philadelphian. A trader who had won a fortune by relentlessly hunting the best goods at the best prices. For more than twenty years he had stopped at Irene's boardinghouse when business took him to New York.

This trip had been a failure, he confessed, in a desperate attempt to shift the subject from his guilt. A shipload of coffee at bargain prices had proved no bargain. It was so sour, the coffeehouse had refused to allow it to be unloaded, fearing the odor would draw some dread disease. He smiled the weary smile of a businessman who has seen greater disappointments. But there would be other cargoes, with greater promise of profits and happier endings. . . . And may I have some more of those excellent tea cakes, Irene, my dear?

Mister Walsh's greatest weakness, Irene had told Diana, was his roving eye. A pretty face, a well-turned ankle, sparked the primitive in the little man. And he appears so bold about it, Irene had said. Salty talk. Leering eyebrow. If you didn't know his secret, you would show him the door the moment you met him. His secret was that Michael Walsh was an absolutely faithful husband. Irene was convinced if someday—the day, perhaps, when fish learned to crawl to the monger's stall—a woman purposely took him up on one of his hinted offers, the man would suffer a stroke. Hence the play scripted by Irene. Let the man wag his tongue freely. Ask to meet his lady. And let guilt carry the day.

Diana intended to do better. With pretended hesitancy she had asked his advice. In her ramblings about New York and her conversations with Irene and her friends, Diana had become aware of a minor scandal. Some months before, a rare wind of civic concern had swept through the town. It involved streetlights. Merchant pride had been tweaked by boasters from that dismal sister to the north—Boston. Diana

pg. 229

Allan Cole & Chris Bunch

knew even Albany had more streetlights than Boston, but there were fewer still in New York, which to the merchants was an obvious keystone for the lack of business opportunity. But there were no funds for lights. So a lottery was raised. Civic pride flagged before it reached its goal, and then the whole thing collapsed when one of the organizers absconded to the Indies with the funds. Sad story. Made sadder still, Diana learned, because a few trusting souls had bet a bundle on the success of the streetlighting program. They had bought many tons of whale oil in anticipation of the future nighttime glitter.

She had talked to a few of the captains of these ships, she told Mister Walsh, who leaned closer, knowing a good suspense story when he heard one. He knew whale oil went for twenty-eight pounds a ton all up and down the coast. Diana nodded. This was true. Twenty-eight pounds—or seventy-two dollars, Farrell had instantly translated as they stood on the docks—per ton.

But they seemed willing to sell for less. Far less.

"How much?" Abrupt, from Walsh.

"Ten pounds less." Just as abrupt from Diana. While Walsh pondered this, Diana sweetly poured more tea.

"I suppose you could introduce me to these captains?" he finally asked.

Diana said she'd be only too happy to. It was impossible for a woman of her limited means to take advantage of this opportunity. . . .

"Uh . . . perhaps a percentage . . . ?"

Which was exactly what Diana had in mind. Walsh sat back in his chair, looking at her with new interest. He knew business talent when he saw it, no matter that it wore petticoats and frilly lace. Of such things are friendships formed.

Four days later the Shannons thundered along the Lancaster road toward Philadelphia. Aboard a carriage with springing so smooth its maker called it "the flying machine."

It was built to the exacting specifications of one Michael Walsh. Merchant, trader, and perfect gentleman.

* * * *

The day had begun like every other: pounding at her door at three A.M. A mad rush from the inn. Great oil lamps picking out brutes of horses—fresh and mean at this hour, and snapping and kicking at their masters. A lurch, and the carriage surging forward, and then hour after hour plunging through darkness. The endless crack, crack, crack of the coachman's whip. Challenging curses from Walsh's outriders, springing yet another teamster's trap. A bloody face in the window, and a black form clubbing it away. But Diana felt no pity because she had seen their work—the overturned carriages, the weeping passengers, belongings strewn in the ditch or hanging from slowly turning wheels.

But then it was dawn. And a light spring rain washing to morning on the road to Philadelphia.

It became a day like no other in her lifetime, so clear, it was like looking through a lens polished by Dr. Franklin himself. Images leapt at her, crystallized in memory, and were hurled aside to be replaced by others.

On the Lancaster Road a girl and her mother bound for market. Plodding beside a farm cart in their best clothes. Shoes clutched in their hands to keep them from the dust.

A boy astride an enormous pig, switching its flanks like a horse. Trailed by half a dozen piglets just butcher's size.

A dentist's wagon, false teeth painted fore and aft. On its sides, signs boasting one hundred percent success in transplanting live teeth.

A cockfight at the Schuylkill Ferry. Men and boys shouting encouragement and wagers. The shark-faced men in red stocking caps who held the bets, passing big jugs of punch so that cups remained full to overflowing.

A wagon full of flowers! No, two. No, three. Hollyhocks and irises, and sweet primroses, begging to sit upon a fine dinner table in a Philadelphian's home.

Allan Cole & Chris Bunch

A Daughter Of Liberty

Aboard the ferry, a man with no arms, playing a fiddle with his feet. Around him, dogs dancing on their hind legs . . . whirling . . . whirling. A barker promising: "... this and more at the Southwark Fair!"

Wheelbarrow men crowding the opposite shore. Waiting to load huge piles of fresh oysters on beds of steaming seaweed.

The bell ringing them to market from far down High Street. Criers with the latest news, and people—so many people—crowding about. Heatedly debating points Diana barely knew existed. A great thundering of hooves along the Post Road and everyone making way . . . making way. More bells clanging for the entrance of the mail. And Mister Walsh gesturing at the marvels, and Diana not hearing a word. James Emmett chattering excitedly. Farrell silent in somber city clothes, but his eyes wide and his mouth open in a great big O.

Philadelphia, in the spring of 1788. A city like no other in the world. A city so wonderful, that Diana knew she would never see its equal.

She had been cast from it—the obscene child of an Irish serving wench. Now, twenty-six years later, she was returning, her purse fat with coin. Aboard a royal carriage— bearing her luggage bound up in brass like that of a noblewoman. Accompanied by two fine sons. Under the protection of one of the city's leading citizens. Yes, in triumph.

But there was no one there to know it. Except one very private person.

In the forest of her memory, hard by the glen, just at the edge of the brook, Emmett Shannon smiled . . . and blew her a kiss. ...

CHAPTER TWENTY-THREE

"WHAT A WONDER of a life you've lived, Diana dear," Mrs. Walsh said. "Perhaps my great-grandmother could equal you. Although I doubt it . . . She had a wilderness upbringing for a time. But she always had a house full of servants, so I'm sure it was not the same."

So was Diana. Servants? Hah! The fact Anne Walsh's gramer was assured a house disqualified her. But Diana didn't say this. You would have to have a heart of ice to mock a woman as sweet as Anne Walsh.

Anne was a small woman—just Diana's size—in her middle years. She had the face of a cherub, with lips like a bow that were always untying into a smile. Anne had a lovely full figure she fussed over as too fat and matronly, and wore billows for dresses to hide. Despite their difference in age and background, Mrs. Walsh and Diana became fast friends. Mrs. Walsh urged Diana to reside with her until she hired permanent lodgings. Diana refused this kind offer. She needed freedom of movement for her plans as much as she needed friendship. A lovely old boarding home was found, offering ample rcom and respectability. Meanwhile, Anne Walsh and her husband took Diana under their wings. Especially Anne.

With idle chatter and pleasantries, the woman kept hidden a mind as sharp as her husband's. But Diana noted that whenever Anne Walsh had an opinion to express, her husband listened, and always took her advice. Her kindly manner could deceive. Diana had watched her watching other people and caught the look of cool appraisal when sizing up a boaster. After weeks in her company, Diana knew that Anne Walsh passed on her views—many times unfavorable—to her husband. In short, she was a woman whose friendship was hard won, and therefore of immense value.

Still, she had many eccentricities. Like her love of nature—especially birds. The fact that Mister Peale—painter of revolutionary heroes, and keeper and owner of the city's fabled museum of American natural history—had actually raised and bred two hummingbirds, was of more import to her than the ratification progress of the Constitution. The states would either ratify it or they would not. General Washington would be president, or not. Life would go on, with or without the presence of these elements.

The high drama of the previous summer was still on everyone's lips. The meaning of General Washington's silence during the proceedings was still being debated. Madison's role as impresario and architect of the final document could still spark heated words, or worse. To Anne, the Congress had done nothing more than survive one of the hottest summers on record by drinking enormous quantities of punch.

"Every one of them was drunk," she sniffed one day when she and Diana were discussing the matter over tea. "Except possibly General Washington. Certainly not that thin-lipped little toad, Mister Madison. No wonder he carried the day. He was the only man among them sober. If the business had been turned over to women—and don't peep a word of my views to Mister Walsh—it would have been settled in a few days.

"There's talk—and money settling on that talk—that Congress will find a home here. In our city. You mark my words, Diana, if that happens, it will be our ruin."

But the matter of the hummingbirds in Mister Peak's museum . . . now that was progress of the grand scale, just as news of hunters or encroaching civilization threatening a feathered creature's existence was proof all mankind was at heart evil.

"Why, we don't even know how many species there are with any certainty," she wept, "and we've already killed off some. What if there are as many as two hundred—I believe the number to be slightly more—but by the time we learn it,

234

there are only one hundred left? What tragedy our children should not see them!"

Diana had laid siege to Anne's lack of taste and style almost on first meeting. It took time to convince her she had an excellent figure which should be displayed to its best advantage. Which meant chopping away at the material Mrs. Walsh draped about herself until a woman's form emerged. Diana then instructed her seamstress on methods of defying the dictates of bustle and hoop.

Diana would live to see a time when underwear took on scandalous connotations, but in this day it was not considered unseemly for an outfit to reveal chemise or petticoat. Anne's choice in these things was dull, but with coaxing, Diana convinced her to buy delicately made and patterned small clothes, which could nod their provocative little heads at the world through artful slits and dips and tucks.

Diana's greatest success had just come out of the seamstress's shop. It was a walking dress—a costume Mrs. Walsh had always avoided because she said on her short form it made her look dumpy. This was not the case in Diana's design. The dress fell above the top of the toe and was slightly clinging to better display her rounded form. It featured a long robin's-egg-blue kerchief that exposed Anne's lovely white shoulders, slipped under her bosom, where it was tied with a ribbon, and extended to either side, where it was secured to the dress itself, which was silver in color. The kerchief continued to the back, where it formed a tasty outside bustle. (No, Anne, dear. We'll dispense with one underneath. You don't need help in that part of your anatomy.) She helped Anne choose a hat to set the whole thing off—wide-brimmed and trimmed with gauze and ribbon. But she talked her out of the frizzy hairdo favored by the young ladies of Philadelphia and instead guided her to a softer look, which framed Anne's face in a romantic portrait

The improvements in Anne's wardrobe were greeted enthusiastically by her husband. He showered the two with compliments, Anne for her renewed beauty, Diana for her art.

Allan Cole & Chris Bunch

He needn't have said a word. Diana's ego had already been boosted by Mister Walsh's more private reactions. The couple had been going about all starry-eyed of late, with many sweet whisperings and furtive touching. It was obvious to her that although their long marriage was childless, it wasn't for lack of effort.

* * * *

Although the city Anne and Michael Walsh introduced Diana to would grow enormously during her lifetime, it would always retain its heart and basic form. Her first impressions of Philadelphia—no matter how romantically tinged—proved correct. This was the place to make her stand. But it wasn't until fall that Diana became confident enough to trust her business instincts.

Meanwhile, she had a city to investigate, a future life to ferret out. Mister Walsh had a carriage waiting outside the boardinghouse each day for Diana and her sons. She began the morning full of enthusiasm and ideas; by night they had all drifted into vagueness, like the reverse side of bad embroidery.

The first physical feature that struck Diana about Philadelphia was how flat it was. Flat and swampy, except for a slight rising tilt in the lands to the south. The city consisted of a few square miles between the Schuylkill and the Delaware, and owed its prosperity to the natural sheltered port the Delaware provided—the Schuylkill was useless for anything but small craft—plus the great road that led out beyond its western boundaries to Lancaster County, Chester, and beyond. Within a few years of her arrival, the road became the Lancaster Pike, the finest paved highway in America, connecting Philadelphia with the headwaters of the Ohio River.

There were a few foundries in the Schuylkill Valley that smelted iron with native hardwoods. It was a region that would soon see countless foundries, forges, and ironworks up and down the valley. From the Middle Ferry at the Schuylkill until just beyond Broad Street, there wasn't much to the city.

Although the streets in this area were broad and straight and crisscrossed with alleys and courts, they were sparsely populated by the poor. Their homes ranged from Irish thatch-and-wattle straight from the Old Country, to pine shacks, to roofed-over holes.

One thing of note: even in the poor section, the city was as clean as a Dutch housewife's kitchen. Every morning and every evening the women and their unwilling children were out scrubbing steps, holystoning the board sidewalks— brick, or even white marble in the nicer areas—and actually washing down the flagstone streets on their hands and knees. It would be five years before Diana learned there was more behind this cleanliness than a charming Quaker-influenced custom.

No one visited Philadelphia in those times without being stunned by the main market area, and Diana was no exception. Philadelphians bragged the High Market was the largest of its kind in all the states. There was no exaggeration. It ran a full mile—eight squares—down the High. More remarkably, the whole thing was entirely roofed over. On main market days all but foot traffic was barred by the chain men, who also hustled a fistful of pennies parking and minding carriages for their owners.

The official market days were Tuesdays and Fridays, but actually every day was Market Day in Philadelphia— including Sunday, when an enlightened ordinance allowed the delivery of fresh milk. In a letter to Ruth, Diana told how she saw the milk being brought to market in churns. But not ordinary churns. These were "white as curd and bound with copper hoops, and as bright as hands and clean sand can make them."

There were also spontaneous market days when a fresh boatload of provisions arrived from the West Indies or France and the whole city would be turned out by the great market bell. A bell alerted people to the arrival of mail, and they'd rush to the central delivery area with their shillings— or even empty-handed—to loiter about and hear other

Allan Cole & Chris Bunch

people's news. Another event was the arrival of the stage, and the folk would hurry to the Indian Queen Hotel to see what famous person was arriving.

The High Market was exceptionally clean, with all the benches and stalls scrubbed white. Even the meat was clean, well-cut and laid out on tables covered with constantly changed white cloth. The butchers presided over their stalls, nodding and smiling at the crowds, looking like brawny, red-faced angels in the white linen frocks that covered their clothes. There were vegetables of every variety, and also fruit, which included oranges from the Indies; fish and shellfish—especially the oysters; game right from the hunter's pocket; butter and cheese; and spices and herbs from far afield, "fit to flavor any dish or cure any ailment."

She was also struck by the orderliness, especially after the confused squalor of New York. "Everyone has a place assigned to them" she wrote to Ruth in Boston. "The butcher his table, the woman her stall . . . and there is no one moving about except the public, who come and go throughout the day from nine o'clock of the morning till nine that night . . . and all in great order, with only a little prompting from the chain men. ..."

There were other markets in the city, but the one on High Street would remain her favorite. With one exception: the Southwark Market by the Delaware. But only on what was known locally as Jersey Market Day. Anne tried to describe it to her, but kept succumbing, lapsing into honks of laughter. Finally, she gave up and took her friend to see for herself.

Diana met the ladies from Jersey that day. They were overgrown, shapeless businesswomen who were accomplished bargainers in the morning, but grew friendlier and less tight-fisted as the day progressed. This was because, as Anne said, they had a "fondness for the comfortable, which you can spy for yourself as that great jug of jack they keep under their stools. Mark my word, dear, they'll nip at that jug until they're well corned and fast asleep where they sit. Then watch the fun begin."

A hefty snore fluttering the lips of a face as round as a melon and purple as a plum. The first snore brought the plunderers. The second the thieves. The third the saucy children who plagued the area. Diana watched as two of them sauntered up to a cake stall. Behind it, Mrs. Plum Face, arms folded on a vast bosom, chins tucked under her shawl, lips in a dainty quiver of sleep. One child snatched, then the other. They would have gone undetected, but a neighbor of Mrs. Plum Face raised a howl. This brought Plum Face to her feet, sputtering and wailing as the boys took to their heels. And off she went after them, like a Spanish galleon, sailing into first one stall then another, until the boys were gone and she collapsed in weeping self-pity on the ground. But another Jersey woman—you could make them out, Anne said, because they are thicker than they are long, and their faces are like the Lady Moon at the full—brought her a jug of comfort. Soon the incident was forgotten in a big boozy embrace.

Now to the shops, Anne sang, and off they went to the district sprawling along Chestnut. A profusion of merchandise filled the long, low windows that projected into the street. Dry goods were strewn along the brick sidewalks. Flannels, cloths, muslins, silks, and calicoes hung over doors in whole pieces, or draped down on either side of the pavement. Other materials were stacked in rolls all down the street, pure heaven for a seamstress. There were barrels of sugar and raisins and coffee and dried fruit, intermingled with shoe shops, jewelers, saddlers; china, tin, iron, and copperware; and grocers with goods from every hill and creek in the land.

Anne giggled and pointed to the fine young men lined up to see the daily parade of beauties, who vied with hoop, bustle, and big flowered hat for their attention. Diana couldn't help but imagine how she would nip here, tuck there, and

Allan Cole & Chris Bunch

blouse out there, and tsk, tsk, don't you think the color a touch drab and matronly, Madame?

To James Emmett, the best time was night, when the little man went around with his small can of oil, bag of tools, and a short ladder over his shoulder. James never tired of watching the man. The lamplighter would clean the glass of each streetlight, trim its wick, top it off with oil, and light it with his long match. This went on for street after street, until the whole town glowed. Now the shops gave off a magic gleam. Especially those filled with silver, or worked glass, or the medicinal stores with their beautifully colored potions in even more beautifully colored bottles of every shape and style, filling row after gleaming row until the whole window throbbed with light.

The ever practical Farrell most admired the homes. He noted that the best residences—including the Walshes', who lived a few houses down from the eminent Dr. Benjamin Rush—were near the city center, especially in the Walnut area between Third and Fourth streets. Farrell loved to stroll down these avenues. The homes were of elegantly handcrafted brick, shaded by beautiful buttonwoods and willows and other native trees. Farther west, toward the Schuylkill, were the less elegant, but comfortable homes of the tradesmen. Like those of the rich, these residences were also tree-shaded against the city's stifling summers.

Through all this Farrell remained his humorless, but dependable self. His lack of humor made conversation dullish, but when Diana thought about James Emmett, she supposed this was a blessing. Now there was a boy who had humor stuffed into him like a great bag of pudding that kept swelling and swelling until it burst in every direction. The child was curious about anything not good for him. She'd already caught him experimenting with tobacco, spirits, gaming, and even a girl—his breeches down to his knees and his bony behind sticking out, and him brandishing his little thing as if he knew what to do with it.

Yes, she punished him. Sometimes she feared she was too strict. But then just as she was considering some other approach, off he would go again, committing a transgression whose only answer was a licking. But it never seemed to do any good. No matter how much he was punished, James Emmett never relented. Never said he was sorry. Not that he was sullen, or resentful. Oh, no, not James Emmett Shannon. The boy would bide his time, then come up to you with a great soft smile on his lips. love in his eyes and an embrace to melt a snow witch. It was as if you were being forgiven for not realizing all he did was as necessary as breath itself. And he pitied you for not understanding.

Only Farrell had some control over James Emmett, although who actually was doing the controlling could be debated. Regardless, Farrell's protectiveness of his half brother was one of the few things that made him human. He was stern with the child, but seemed to know his fears and needs more than Diana. Although the two were nothing alike, Farrell usually anticipated his brother. If he didn't, and the error threatened disaster, James would throw himself on Farrell's mercy. This would result in a stern lecture, which the child listened to in all apparent seriousness. Then would come the inevitable rescue. Sometimes this would mean intercession with Diana. Most likely, Farrell would cover up the trail James Emmett left.

It was the only time Farrell would lie. Diana had never chastised him for this, or even told Farrell she knew he was lying. Because if she did—if she confronted him, broke him—she wasn't sure what, or who, would be left.

One day after the Jersey Market, Diana and Anne had taken the boys for an outing on Front Street. A lovely stroll on a riverfront packed with ships and people and bargains from everywhere. Suddenly Diana noted a Great Absence of James Emmett. Fortunately, so did Farrell. He looked about with a start, then noticed Diana doing the same. More eye-darting, and then a sigh of relief. "There he is, Mother," he

Allan Cole & Chris Bunch

said, pointing vaguely at a crowd of people. "You go on. I'll fetch him."

Go on, they did. Fetch him, he did not. For a long time. Just past the point of worry, as Diana was trying to turn Anne about without alerting her, she spied Farrell. And James Emmett, coming from quite another direction. She saw Farrell shaking a finger at the child, James Emmett hanging his head in shame. More lecturing. More head hanging. Then James fumbled in his pocket and handed an object to Farrell, who looked nervously about before stuffing it away. Then Farrell hustled James down a side street and out of sight. A moment later they'd both appeared, this time walking from the correct direction. James's face was as innocent as an angel's as he joined her on the stroll.

That night she searched Farrell's clothing. A small, wooden object fell out. It was a carving of a man and a woman, in naked embrace, and carved in such stark detail that Diana flushed in shame. And then the flush disappeared as she marveled at the craftsmanship. And their features, not rutting rictus grins. She saw, or imagined, tenderness . . . brought to life by soft burnishing. She thought of the hand that had brought out such emotion with each stroke of emery. And in a slip of a dream it became Emmett's sweet stroking. . . . She shuddered, suddenly cold, and replaced the figurine.

* * * *

The priest was a fiery old man in purple vestments. His name was Father Coogan and he held the congregation spellbound as he led the faithful through the mysteries of the mass.

St. Joseph's Church at Fourth and Walnut was a plain building, a square, drab edifice with only a tower and bell to prove it a church; no different from any built by the Protestant faiths. Ostentation was distrusted in these days of Republicanism, and there was nothing about the church to test this view. It sat upon land owned by the lay members of the congregation—also like the Protestants.

Inside there was no elaborate statuary, only hard pews, and a cross above a thin, pine tabernacle without even a simple carving to show it held the Sacred Host. The drabness of the church, however, gave way to a mystical hue the moment the priest entered and the mass began. The atmosphere was heavy with incense, the silence thick as fog; so that each Latin phrase falling from the priest's lips had a romantic, ghostly tone. During the blessing of the Sacrament, small bells chimed, chalices rang like larger bells, and the leaves of the great book the priest read from rustled—all with unnatural loudness.

Diana sat quietly in her pew, feeling as out of place as if she were attending the Presbyterian church in Cherry Valley. She knew she was witnessing a rare thing. Few people outside this city had ever seen a simple mass, much less a full-blown ceremony with lovely vestments for the priest, laymen to attend him, and a worshipful congregation that knew every step of the way—with enough churchly Latin at hand to decipher the holy words the priest spoke.

St. Joseph's was one of two Catholic churches in Philadelphia. It was nearly fifty-five years old when Mister and Mrs. Walsh took the Shannon family to the services. Before that Catholics in Philadelphia gathered at the home of Elizabeth McGauley on Nicetown Road for the plain, communal services and shared reading of prayers that Emmett had described to her.

Elsewhere, as Mister Walsh had said, intolerance kept the choices for Catholics slim. After all, there were perhaps no more than thirty priests in the whole country. In all of America there were 35,000 of the faith, Mister Walsh had said, and of that number, possibly 7,000 resided in Pennsylvania.

The mass was well-attended, but Diana's friends had reserved places ahead of time, so with a bit of squeezing she, Farrell, and James Emmett were made at home.

Prior to the service the first thing they noticed was a long line going up the far aisle. It stopped at a small door. Anne

Allan Cole & Chris Bunch

said it was people for confession. Diana saw Farrell raise his brows at that. He whispered a question to Anne, and she explained that Catholics confessed even their most dire sins to the priest in private, that the priest was sworn never to reveal the shame, and that a penance was set afterward. Once it was performed, absolution for the sin was assured.

From the look on Farrell's face, Diana could see he was impressed with this system, although she didn't know why. What possible sin could Farrell imagine was marring his young soul? Now, if it were James Emmett—she looked at her youngest son. As usual, he was squirming and paying little attention to anything. Ah, well. At least he was quiet.

Finally the mass began and Diana lost her direction in the dead language liturgy. She could see there was a rhythm to it that everyone else could follow, but it made no sense to her.

Later she asked Mister Walsh why they just didn't use plain English. Knowledge of Latin, he said, was the boast of noble, lettered men. This she thought pretentious, and a danger as well, because it hinted at a class system. This was a new nation, with theoretical equality. The language of the common folk—the vernacular—would be better. Mister Walsh agreed and said many others felt the same way. This included Father John Carroll of Maryland—one of the signers of the Declaration of Independence—whom everyone said was sure to be named by the Pope as the first bishop in America.

"They want no one to have the notion," Mister Walsh said, "that we do the bidding of a foreign monarch. But it's a battle I fear has been lost, once and for all. Some say— and I mean the common folk you spoke of—that Latin makes them feel special, that great secrets are being divulged to them, and them only. Personally, I believe they love the ceremony more than the Lord."

Little bells called the freshly innocent—Anne and Michael among them—to the altar, where they partook of the Host. This was followed by the gospel. Then a sermon in

English. It was a thundering good one, too, Diana observed. Sinners were warned, hellfires were pumped up with scriptural bellows, and the repenters were praised. After that there were more odd mutterings by the priest, the big book and the chalices changed places for some reason, and the mass came to its conclusion.

Diana thought it was all very refreshing, but mainly because it was a new experience. Now that she had seen it, however, she had no desire for repetition. This was an attitude of hers she would have to watch. If she was too disdainful in front of her sons, she would be hard-pressed to keep her promise to Emmett that they would be raised in his faith.

James Emmett burst away as soon as the service ended. For a change, Farrell was not right on his heels, dragging him away from potential mischief. She saw Farrell had hung back. He was gazing at the tabernacle, his eyes wide, and there were tears welling up. Diana tugged at him to go, but he pulled away before he realized it was her plucking at his shirt.

He looked up at her, so full of emotion he seemed about to burst. "Didn't you feel it, Mother?" he asked. He rushed on before she could answer. "At first, I was a little bored, to tell the truth. Then, when the priest began speaking, I got interested in the Latin. I was trying to make out some of the words—it's not that hard, you know. A lot of them seem the same as English. I got so interested, I lost the time until communion.

"The priest was praying over the bread and wine for communion when I started thinking about what was really going on. That wine was becoming the blood of Jesus Christ . . . our Savior. And the bread became his flesh ... I thought, how could that be?"

Diana frowned, thinking of Farrell's trouble with all fictions, no matter how well meant. To this day he mocked Hamlet for its ghost. What was happening here, with her hard-headed practical son?

Allan Cole & Chris Bunch

"Then it—I don't know—it suddenly made sense. No. Not sense." He stumbled for words, his face flushed with effort. Then: "He forgives you, Mother. He really does."

Farrell lapsed into silence, but she could see the thoughts swirling, swirling.

"What, Farrell? Forgives you what?"

"Brian," was all he said.

"But you don't need forgiveness for that, Farrell, dear," Diana said as gently as she could. "You weren't responsible for what happened to poor Brian."

Farrell looked up again, his eyes a tempest. He started to speak, but emotion overcame him and he just shook his head. "I'd like to come again," was all he said.

There was no reason for Diana to say no. She should be happy at this turn of events. Wasn't a church an important ritual in raising a child? Why did she distrust this so?

How could she deny him? And for what reasons? Diana said he could.

From that day forward, Farrell became the most devout member of the congregation. He went at religion as he did everything—at full force. In not many years he was as knowledgeable as the priest, if not more. Church became the center of him. Even James Emmett came second.

The oddest thing in his behavior was that as the mystical part of him rose, the practical side grew as well. In business he was still all facts and double totted-up figures.

Ah, well, Diana thought. If it comforts him, what can be the harm?

* * * *

In matters of finance, Mister Walsh was a disciple of patience. He constantly counseled and supported Diana to take her time in setting a future course. Just as he had counseled others since the end of the Revolution.

"Anyone could see difficult times were ahead and hurry would court disaster," he said one night. "It cost sixty million dollars to rout the king. All of it debt with no means to pay.

"Who was responsible? Congress? How were they to raise the funds? No law required it, and without a law, no one has yet volunteered to be the first to make the gesture. The small authority we granted gave us Shay and his rebellion.

"The states? Bah! They can't get funds for a bridge, much less a road of any length. No, the war debt will not be assumed by the states. That's why we must suffer these infernal lotteries. We have no other means of launching a civic program."

Diana listened intently, soaking up every bit of information. Mister Walsh smiled at her gently through his pipe fumes—seeing real talent in the young, pretty face, thinking what a fine son she would have made Anne and himself.

A cough from Anne brought him back to his point.

"But where we bought uncertainty for our sixty million, we also purchased opportunity," he said. "A little care. A little reason. And unless God smites thee, a profit will result."

Mister Walsh had kept his own counsel all those years. Especially the last four, when hard times had settled over the land as each state struggled to make sense of its own highly individual economy.

Alone, he believed, the task was nearly impossible. "You saw the result," he said, "when talk grew serious that we must all unite under one banner. To act in concert. Just talk of unity stirred the fires of hope . . . happy times, again. Just from talk, if I may repeat myself. Now, with ratification fever upon all the states, let us see what real action can do!"

"You present a lovely view," Diana said. "And I pray that it is real, and not the product of the fever you mentioned."

Mister Walsh sighed. Diana was correct in thinking he painted too glowing a picture. "Damned ignorant fools," he muttered. "Money is at the root of it. Just as money is the way out."

"I don't see the connection, if you please, Mister Walsh," Diana said.

Allan Cole & Chris Bunch

"No, of course you don't, my dear," Anne broke in. "Michael prides himself in obscurity in matters of philosophy. This is because he has a notion that in the laws of finance, all things can be explained."

"Well, not all," Diana said. She knew some mysteries of life had nothing to do with money. But with a few tragic exceptions, she couldn't think of any. In a flash she eliminated one of those exceptions. It was money—or the lack of it—that killed Emmett. Just as sure as Frenchy McShane.

"Go on, then," she said to Mister Walsh.

"I said we must act in concert," he resumed on cue. "But we have a host of laws that prevent this. And the laws are different state by state. Why, in some of the places I travel, if my religion were revealed, I could be cast out, or worse. They fear because our spiritual leader is in Rome, that we Catholics are under the influence of some foreign devil of a monarch. Never mind how many of us took up arms and stood side by side with other Patriots. Our mettle somehow remains unproven, our Republican ideals and loyalty in question.

"In other towns, they would tax me at twice the rate of other citizens. Should I deny my Savior? Or withhold my business? Must Michael Walsh suffer the thrice-crowing cock? But I am a fortunate man. I have money to choose the countenance of saint or sinner, and let God be the judge when I'm done."

"At least you can afford that luxury," Diana said.

She did not mean this archly. To her the lesson of the Apostle Peter had always seemed incomplete. What of the two Marys? Whore and mother. No cock crowed for them. And it was they who rolled the stone from the grave. But Peter was rewarded in this world for his cowardice. The two Marys had to await the hereafter. But that had always been her trouble with religion. Gentle words, but muddled thinking. Of course she believed in and feared a higher power. But in her experience it always came with tomahawk or gun. Or was simply represented by a body of men who could change her life with a nod and a quill scratch on paper.

So that was what she meant by her comment. Mister Walsh was as secure in his home as he was in his beliefs. To Diana, the two went together. The afterlife was for the rich, or hopeless.

Mister Walsh plunged on, warming up to his favorite topic, the plight of the Average Man. "If you are poor, you can be compelled to take a master, who may use you and pay you as he wishes. If you are in debt, you can be placed in prison, or condemned to be chained to a barrow to collect the offal from the streets. On the land, the practice of tenancy can require you to toil for another's profit.

"And then there is the keeping of slaves. Illegal by the laws of God and man in all the civilized world. Which by definition does not include many of our sister states. Why, it was only outlawed two years past in New York! And here we are, the most modern people since the days of Athens, in the waning days of the eighteenth century, eighteen hundred years since the birth of our Lord and Savior."

Ah. Finally. Mister Walsh was nearing his goal.

"I submit to you, Diana Shannon, that in all those years since He died for our sins, we have made less than an inch of progress in matters of humanity. And most of that is recent. And most of that when we told the king to go to hell!

"So, yes, I see hope in unity. Despite the ills I mentioned. For in this land a pact was made for Freedom. The rich were the architects of the Revolution, true. But they could not accomplish it without striking a bargain with the poor. And now the rich have no choice but to see that bargain is kept."

It had not been kept in Cherry Valley, Diana thought. Or in Boston, where Ruth struggled to keep her optimism. Not even here, in Philadelphia. The City of the Enlightened, where the beggars swarmed behind the carts and gobbled the raw grain that fell in the filth. Or the Irish teagues who stayed eternally drunk at the waterfront taverns. The king was gone,

Allan Cole & Chris Bunch

but the order remained. And Diana believed her only hope was to build a wall so high and thick that not even Joshua's horn could bring it down.

Mister Walsh's views were pretty thoughts, in keeping with the times, if Diana was to judge from the free-spirited conversations she had heard during her journey. Here they all were, a few desperate souls abandoned on a narrow coastline with a great unexplored and dreaded wilderness at their backs. And if they could all put aside their narrow interests, that elusive and magical Grail of Freedom would be theirs.

But who was to define this Freedom? To Mister Walsh, it was the happy pursuit of fair profit. The farmer Shay agreed with that principle, and federal troops were sent against him. The printers in Philadelphia defined it as six dollars per week. They got it. But the next time they struck—especially if the commodity were more precious than the production of broadsides—would the fates smile so sweetly? For the desperately poor, a full plate would suffice. And a bit of fire. For the indentured and the enslaved, Mister Walsh's definition might take on philosophical tones again: Dignity. Ah, but fire and food were easier to win.

Some pursued this elusive freedom in distant forests and field. But it still had to be won at someone else's expense—the Indians. Or even the poor pigeons of passage that Anne mourned, shot from the rooftops by the hundreds of thousands as they soared to their winter homes.

Diana gave no hint of these thoughts as she looked at her mentor and smiled. He was quick to respond. "Do you see my point?" he said anxiously. "Do you agree?"

She didn't. She also wanted to ask how far her enlightened friend would take this business of equality. He said he was with the Radicals, or near to it. That all men—not just the propertied—should have a say in the nation's affairs. Did that mean in his Utopia, the freed man of color would have that right? Possibly. But what about her own sex? She doubted it. What if Diana married? Would Mister Walsh agree all her worldly goods were hers and hers alone, to be shared with her husband as she saw fit? Or would he agree with the law, that it would all belong to that man, as if he had earned it himself?

She looked over at Anne, who was watching her husband with loving eyes. Diana decided not to ask.

"I suppose you're right," she said.

Allan Cole & Chris Bunch

CHAPTER TWENTY-FOUR

ALL THAT SPRING and all that summer she searched. She visited the textile mills in Kensington, weighing the quality and cost of the cloth produced there. She noted there were few deficiencies in grade and color. She also discovered a shortage of hand looms. What looms there were belonged to immigrant weavers who had transported them at great sacrifice when they fled Ireland. The dankness of their shops should have been oppressive, but the lively talk of the men and women—their brogue soft and musical, but barely decipherable—seemed to lift the gloom.

She pored over the newspapers, delighting in their freshness and number, charting prices of goods and services so numerous her mind was a constant swim of figures. Shopkeepers grew accustomed to her bursting into their store, turning over objects, fingering the quality, asking the cost and then departing with only a smile for their reward. And who could object to the time spent with such a lovely young widow?

Diana went on excursions to far-flung farms and saw how cheaply things could be had there, and how the costs leapt as the distances and roughness of the roads grew. Even after so short a time in the city, the slow pace of things in the hinterlands irritated her and she was always anxious to return to the city. She noted in these distant places that the post was carried by rough boys on big farm horses, or by old men who didn't care a shaved shilling for their duty. On the way to one place she saw an old post carrier astride his horse, knitting mittens. The horse had stopped to munch tender shoots by the roadside, and the man didn't seem to notice. Hours later she returned, and the two had only made a few miles— although one of the mittens was nearly done.

All the farms in these areas were prosperous, with earth as rich as dark pudding, and large broods of children she doubted ever took ill. Although she had nothing to sell, she took a lesson from Emmett and befriended the farm women. Exchanging gossip, she casually explained how great their profit would be if they eliminated the teamster middlemen and took their goods to market themselves. When that time came, she said, be sure and stop with me for supper.

Back in the city, with the newness wiped from her eyes, she noticed the underlying tension among the poorer class. The weavers casting dark looks at their masters, the coal loaders on the Schuylkill muttering and flexing their muscles when the ships came in and the wages offered were the same no matter how burdensome the task. The misery of the homes along Water Street, where the riverbanks came up to the shanty porches and the stink grew near unbearable in the dry summer. The immigrant families sold into indenture right off the boat. The hot talk issuing from taverns, like The Jolly Irishman at Race and Water, or The Lamb at Second and Lombard, and especially at Isabella Barry's Faithful Irishman.

She knew the people's wages were too low and set out of greed and stubbornness. She was sure this could not last long in a city brimming with money. But at least in Philadelphia there was some outlet in that a home—no matter how squalid—could be purchased by any man—or woman. By law, land could be leased for a lifetime at low cost, and any sort of structure put upon it.

Diana had taken advantage of this early on. She'd purchased the old, comfortable boardinghouse she'd been staying at. With Mister Walsh's assistance, she leased the lots on each side. The home was at the end of a court, just off Tenth Street and near the High. The area was shabby, quite unlike the luxurious sections the Walshes had steered her toward at first. When she'd reminded him of his own investment in the Lancaster Pike, and pointed out all traffic would have to come down the High—right past her home—to reach the market, he saw the wisdom. And leased some parcels himself in the same court.

Allan Cole & Chris Bunch

What she was going to do with the home, besides refurbishing it and setting aside some apartments for herself and the boys, she'd yet to decide. It would be no boarding home. She was through with innkeeping. But there was space enough for a shop of some sort, with room to spare.

Remembering those farm women she'd visited and her own advice on eliminating the middleman, Diana advertised for some adventurous young men. From her own dreary experience in Cherry Valley, she outfitted them with small necessities and baubles sure to bring a few moments of pleasure, and sent them off on long selling trips. Most of them returned with empty packs and fat pockets. As for those who didn't—the cost was so little, it didn't matter. More important, she had means of communicating with those women that didn't depend on old men knitting mittens on spavined horses.

She loved the docks. Ships from all over the world put in here, brimming with goods that teased the imagination or begged to be tasted or worn. She renewed acquaintance with the oil-ship captains she had introduced to Mister Walsh in New York. Other skippers were recommended to her by Ruth's husband up in Boston (the poor dear was good for some things). She would sit in the coffeehouse with them, savoring the brew that came from the big sacks of beans stacked to the ceiling, and listen to their adventures; they, bristling with charm; she, nodding, oohing, smiling, and picking their brains empty.

Sometimes she was accompanied by Anne, sometimes by Mister Walsh. But always there was Farrell, walking quietly behind, or sitting nearby, scratching in his notebook with a smaller and smaller hand, until the book was full and she had to press him to let her buy another.

Mister Walsh watched all this with amusement, figuring she would eventually settle on some small business that wouldn't be too taxing, but would allow her enough profit to live easily. But he noticed it was Diana who could always snoop out the best prospect, then bargain it down to a fair price. He began asking her advice, which she gave freely. If he took it, the result was certain to make him smile.

One day when she was visiting Anne, he asked her into his study. She sat in the big leather chair across from his writing desk, and they chatted easily about minor business matters. The atmosphere grew so relaxed, for a moment she swore Mister Walsh forgot her sex and almost pushed over a humidor for her to enjoy a cigar. Then he got to the point. He asked if she'd chosen a trade, and then, quite bluntly, asked how much money she had. She told him without hesitation.

His eyes widened—in all his life he'd never met a woman with so much who had not inherited from husband or family. He knew he had only an inkling of what she had suffered to win it. He brushed at his brow, as if wiping away all previous conceptions about this woman, realizing that all the ideas he had in mind to assist her were too small.

He began laughing, in that great booming voice of his that defied its tiny frame. He laughed so hard Anne came in to ask the jest, but he just waved at her helplessly. Finally, he sputtered to a stop, filled a glass to the brim with brandy and drank it in one long swallow. Then he wiped his chin and settled back in his chair.

"Diana, dear," he said. "When you settle on your life's work, let me know. And I'll be with you all the way."

* * * *

It was coming on to fall when she made her discovery. And it was all on account of James Emmett. The boy's behavior had been better of late. Diana hoped he was exiting a difficult age and settling into the business of growing up. He still went about like a tightly wound ball of thread, always threatening to unravel. But his misadventures had been relatively minor. And so, when James Emmett begged her to take him to the docks to see the ship from China, she agreed.

They could smell the cinnamon and sandalwood drifting in the breeze long before they reached the wharf. It was one of several small ships that had been regularly following the

Allan Cole & Chris Bunch

route of the Grand Turk for several years now, daring Drake's Passage for the riches on the other side of the Pacific.

And riches they had aplenty: Nankeen Chinese silk, blue Canton plate, sparrows from Java, mangoes and coconuts, Malacca cane and monkeys. All guaranteed to fire a boy's imagination. But Diana was only mildly interested. The goods were exotic, but so was the means of supply; she saw no permanent business possibilities. But James Emmett begged and begged until she had a whisper with the captain, who let him come aboard in the company of Farrell.

Diana wandered on, planning to spend a pleasant hour or so on the docks, seeing what she could see. Mister and Mrs. Cogley ran an emporium near the Shepherd's Crook. It was a tidy building with gay trim and tasteful advertisements for all manner of exhibits and goods. On this day they were featuring a wondrous clockworks just down from Boston. It was purportedly an exact duplicate of the Boston Harbor, complete with the Long Wharf and several ships and many small boats that churned through miniature waterways for many minutes before their springs needed rewinding.

There was also a fashion exhibit, boasting examples of the Latest In Ladies' Wear Direct From The Royal Court In England. The costumes were displayed on several beautiful hand-painted dolls, with delicate features and tender limbs that could be twisted this way and that to better show off each dress.

crowd of wealthy women were gathered about the dolls, commenting on the long trains festooned with loops of bobbin, and small covered buttons the same color as the dresses.

"How simply marvelous," a woman was saying. "One isn't even confined by the number of festoons. You can put on as many as you fancy ..."

"... and look at the shape of the hats," another was saying, "there's no slope in the crown, hardly a rim . . . and see how the bonnets are open at the top so one can pass her hair through any which way she pleases ..."

"... this one over here ... no such thing as long sleeves! Why, they're halfway to the elbow..."

"... don't you adore how they have colored ribbon pinned round the bare arm—see, it goes here . . . between the elbow and the sleeve ..."

The dolls were completely outfitted, down to slippers made of colored kid or morocco, with small silver clasps artfully sewn on. But it wasn't the fashions that caught Diana's attention. It was the dolls themselves. They brought the costumes to life—showing how each item was worn by women just like these, but far away in "more civilized surroundings," as one woman put it.

She realized from the conversation about her that these women would return with their seamstresses to copy the dresses on the dolls. Diana thought of all the fashion ideas she had, scribbled on paper or—more often—worked out in her head. Many of them, she believed, were far better than what was displayed in front of her. Just showing one of these women a drawing was no good. In her experience, people had too little imagination to translate a picture—no matter how cunningly drawn—into what would look good on them. Especially if it involved the expense of the fine materials these fashions dictated. Just as it would be poor business for her to turn her ideas into life-size costumes. How much money would be wasted before her reputation warranted purchase?

She sought out Mrs. Cogley, a cheery little woman who taught dancing to young girls on the side, and with her husband sponsored one of the assemblies that were just coming into fashion with the unmarried folk.

"How much for the dolls?" she asked.

The woman puzzled at her. "If it's one of the little dresses you like, madam," she said, "you can bring your seamstress along on the morrow. There's plenty of time. This exhibit doesn't close until—"

Allan Cole & Chris Bunch

"I don't care about the dresses," Diana said, shocking the woman even further. "It's the dolls I want. And not just those. Perhaps a hundred more to start. And then ..."

It took time to explain. Even then, Diana had to wait until Mrs. Cogley fetched her husband so she could go through the same thing again. She wanted to order dolls. Naked dolls! By the crateload, if she could get them. She needed a lot of them just to get started; until she could find artisans in town of sufficient talent and speed to make her own.

Mister Cogley was no genius—and he was stubborn about it. If she wanted toy dolls, that could be arranged. But these dolls were constructed to serve the purpose that Diana could see with her own eyes. They were too delicate for children. No, no. He wouldn't take Mrs. Shannon's money for something so foolish . . . she was sure to blame him when it all went wrong . . . and besides ...

Diana bribed James Emmett off the ship from China and sent him and Farrell to fetch Mister Walsh "as quick as if there were Indians about!

It took only a few minutes to explain the idea to her mentor. The dolls would be her calling card. She would deck them in riding habits, wedding dresses, gowns for the assembly, slippers and hats and shawls and chemises. Her ideas poured out like a great tide rushing up the river. She could adjust the costume to taste, right on the doll, before the astonished lady's eyes, take a tuck in here, let out a little there, here a flounce, there a flounce . . . and bows and lace . . . and . . .

Mister Walsh smiled at her, nodding, nodding, nodding ... all the way back to his house and all through dinner with Anne.

Diana's house had plenty of room for workshops, and she could put in an elegant waiting room for her clients and a private trying-on area where her seamstresses could measure and pamper and gossip. She'd start with bolts of material she could buy on the street or off the ships. With the two leased lots next to the house, there was plenty of room to expand. Have her own cloth made and dyed to order . . . And she'd just heard of a lace-making machine which she estimated—given enough orders to warrant its high price—could cut the cost of lace by at least sixty percent or more. . . .

Diana's face was flushed with excitement. She looked even younger than twenty-six. A bit like a bride contemplating her wedding day. Her two friends smiled at one another as the plans came tumbling out in ever-growing detail.

Their fledgling bird was ready to take wing.

Allan Cole & Chris Bunch

CHAPTER TWENTY-FIVE

IT WAS A year people would look back on and swear they saw the dark times coming. Diana had to admit the signs were plentiful for those who wished to claim them. For the superstitious, the scientific, or religious, there was a host of cause and apparent effect to fuel any side of any argument. The winter of '93 was unusually mild: there was no snow, the frosts were moderate, and the creeks and streams hadn't frozen. In January the weather was so warm, people lay on their backs, shielding their eyes from a dazzling sun, to watch Monsieur Blanchard—the famed French balloonist—ascend from the prison yard and float over the city and across the Delaware.

In early April the fruit trees were blooming, and Mrs. Walsh commented excitedly that the birds had returned from their winter homes two weeks early. Even the old people couldn't recall a time when the passenger pigeons were so numerous; the carts in the marketplace were so overflowing with them—a dozen went for less than a penny. Much later, some said the presence of so many pigeons was a sure mark that the air was stagnant and foul.

May was very wet, and day after day a dismal driving rain from the northeast turned roads into a thick muck. Residents kept their fires burning later than usual. The streams overflowed their banks, creating marshes and swamps where none had been before. Alleys in the low areas were awash in filth.

June was suddenly hot. It was followed by the hottest, driest summer in memory. Rivers sank to rivulets. Marshes became stagnant pools when the creeks dried up. Drainage of streets and the less than adequate sewer system ceased. Firemen were called out to flush the gutters, and pits were dug at Fourth and High to receive the runoff, leaving thick scummy ponds. Fish entrails and animal corpses putrefied in the marketplace. On the Delaware, retreating tides left a stinking mass on the muddy banks. A horrible odor oozed up from the docks and all along High Street.

The dry spell became a drought. The drought a disaster. Out on the farms, Diana's women friends sent word the pastures had dried up, the grain shriveled. And their men were being overcome by the heat in the fields. Closer to town Diana saw men walking along dry creek beds usually waist-deep with water. All around them hung clouds of mosquitoes, buzzing and leaving streams of blood on naked flesh as the men slapped at them.

There were other foreboding signs. Dr. Rittenhouse had seen a comet in the constellation of Cepheus. Oysters were watery and inedible. Lightning shattered an ancient and noble oak in Kensington. In Ipswich, a midsummer hailstorm smashed windows, stripped the fields of their grain, and denuded whole orchards of fruit, while a few miles away all was calm and sunny. Animals were stricken with strange diseases, like the "yellow water," which afflicted horses in Jersey and cows in Virginia. For the human residents of Philadelphia, there had been outbreaks of mumps, flux, and scarlet fever.

For those who read the entrails of the political body, there was the presence of the Congress, which had taken up temporary quarters in Philadelphia until land speculators— including President Washington—had completed a new capital on the Potomac. Or that a federal bank had been created amid great controversy and settled in Lord Penn's city. Or that the Anti-Federalist—Democratic-Republican, sniffed Mister Walsh—party had been formed and quickly gained the upper hand in both houses of Congress.

More omens came in July when Philadelphia had some unexpected guests. First one ship, then another descended upon the city. They were filled with refugees from the West Indies. Sick, and gaunt and hungry, they were mostly from the French island of Santo Domingo. They told terrible stories of three years of warfare. There was a great revolution in the Sugar Islands. Carnage and slaughter. Whole towns were destroyed and great merchant houses brought to ruin.

There were tales of a pestilent fever ravaging other islands—also in revolt. Grenada, Dominica, Hispaniola, Jamaica, and even Barbados were stricken. As were Antigua and all the Leewards. They told of how the great port of Cap Francois had burned against the sky as they sailed to their escape. But that wasn't the end of their ordeal. There were agonizing voyages on ships stalked by fever. People were packed into cabins by the droves during the night, while during the day they sat on the decks under the hot sun until their skin blistered and peeled and blistered again. So quick was their haste to flee, they had little clothing, or food or drink aboard.

Mrs. Leclerc, a mulatto seamstress whom Diana recruited—more out of pity than need—told her it was then the English privateers struck. They gathered like sharks off a whaling ship, armed with the legal fiction that they had the right to search and confiscate contraband from the French ships. On Mrs. Leclerc's ship, a group of pirates had robbed everyone of what little they had managed to carry away. They found a cargo of wine, bound for America, and seized that. Finally they had taken off five black girls— "barely children," Mrs. Leclerc wept—for their pleasure and eventual profit. Two days later another privateer descended on them. They were angry because there was nothing left. And so they took the clothing and belts from their bodies. In final revenge they took off the water casks and sank them in the sea.

Mrs. Leclerc counted herself passing lucky. Other ships, and their passengers, simply vanished. In storms? On an uncharted reef? Or at the hands of "privateers" whose pillaging had been so monstrous they could afford no witnesses?

This stirred many a patriot's breast in Philadelphia, especially those opposed to Lord Washington's policy of neutrality, who sought war against the British for all the bloody Indian raids they were encouraging along the frontiers. The people of Philadelphia fed and housed these refugees. A thousand or more settled there—sorely testing a city already bursting the seams with a population of 55,000. Fund-raisings were staged. Fifteen thousand dollars alone was brought in by Mister Ricketts, who had built a wondrous circus just up from Diana's place. It was his last event of the year, and everyone who was anyone attended, including Diana and her friend Dolly Todd.

Yes, there was a great outpouring of charity. And no little sympathy. But Philadelphians didn't quite take these refugees into their heart of hearts, Diana noticed. No one was quite sure what to make of them. The exiles were mostly white and (formerly) rich. They professed Republican ideals and support of the revolutionaries in France and hatred for the British king. But the good folk of Philadelphia could not ignore the basis for their great misfortune. They were slaveholders, one and all. Their wealth had been founded and maintained on the ownership of other human beings. Which put in doubt their Republican fervor.

Not that black citizens of Philadelphia were looked at as being equal. Bigotry was a condition as common as all those pigeon bodies in the High Market. It was an ideal that was being tested here. A high principle. Slavery was a despised practice the civilized world condemned. Not to be confused with the reality that a man or woman of tropical hue had best step aside when encountering a fair-skinned better.

The generous, but frosty welcome of these refugees was eased somewhat by the fact that anything to do with the French was the current rage in the United States. Newspapers were already beginning to publish some items in that language. Salons and fencing studios were opened. Assemblies and balls were French-themed. And, to Diana's delight, so were the fashions. Waistlines were being pinched in, chemises spouting expensive lace froth, bodices a-dropping, and earrings a-dangling.

The refugees did their best to fit in. They were a little edgy in this strange new city with its frightening windows

Allan Cole & Chris Bunch

that opened up and down like a guillotine. But they mostly made the best of it. Still, the sudden presence of these foreigners was called the final and most compelling sign by the latter-day prophets of doom.

Yes, there was evidence enough for any who chose to be wise. After the fact. It was a wisdom Diana never claimed. Actually, she said, as far as she was concerned, 1793 had been one of the best years on record.

Women of means flocked to her house on Elm Court.

They came with fat purses and left with leaner ones, but glowing with pride in her colorful costumes. There wasn't an assembly or event that didn't see at least one person wearing a dress of Diana's design. The sewing and fitting rooms she'd built were soon outgrown, and she'd leased several other buildings in the court to expand. She now employed spinners, weavers, and seamstresses by the score all over the city.

It wasn't only for the rich that she designed. Just as Mister Walsh had predicted, the Lancaster Pike was bringing people to market who had once rarely left their farm. Tempted by the patterns Diana sent along with the young peddlers she financed, and remembering her own constantly repeated invitations, the farm women cozened their husbands into stopping at her shop on the way to market. They were flattered because Diana treated them as importantly as any grand city woman. She gave them coffee and tea and nourishment. Worried with them over their needs for church, or wedding, or christening. Taught them how to disguise ample waistlines, or smooth callused hands with gentle balms and lotions. Remembering the woman and daughter she had seen plodding along that dusty road into Philadelphia, she even had made up as gifts bright little sacks decorated with flowers to carry their shoes.

Situated as she was on High Street, well above the main market, Diana saw these women before they had turned their raw goods into coin, which was quickly snapped up by the hawkers and thieves who preyed on their kind. She and Farrell set up a barter system: so many birds, or a pig, or bushels of grain, for such and such item or items of clothing. This led to a profitable resale business. She and Mister Walsh had even invested in a stable and saddlery shop at the end of the court to care for the farmers' animals and harness. Now they were building a warehouse to hold the goods their joint enterprises were bringing in.

Much more was possible. She could see a time when a blacksmith and carpenter would be necessary. A bakery might also bring more profit if she turned the grain into flour and then bread instead of just selling it straight out.

Yes, it had been a most rewarding year. And it was all because of the dolls.

It was a once-in-a-lifetime idea. And like ideas that plunge forward like a cockerel let loose among a new flock of shapely hens, it came not piecemeal, but as a whole vision.

She saw the dolls fully dressed in her designs. She saw them carried to her spacious and well-appointed salon by ladies as anxious as those hens when they spied the cockerel. She saw those ladies fingering expensive cloth and buying without thought of price. She saw her spinners at their spindles, the weavers at their treadles, the needle makers extruding the fine flawless wire they would pierce so exactly and burnish so smoothly that her seamstresses would smile and nod and blush when complimented on how well they kept their hands. And the fabrics, oh, the fabrics! Cottons and linens as soft as silk. Silks so light a bolt would weigh less than a pound. Dyed with colors only dreamed of in the gods' royal courts.

But she went at it with characteristic caution, spending the best part of a year on her plan. She ordered dolls in a number that had the Cogleys gasping and barely objecting to her bulk-rate offer. She hunted close and far afield for the cloth, sending back any goods that didn't meet her standards. She sought out the best men and women in the crafts for her purposes. A few came to live with her. Others took her coin to hold themselves in readiness when her orders came. They would work in their own homes, paid by the piece, but so handsomely that no upstart competitor would find it possible to cozen them away.

The entire process to Diana's success took the better part of five years. She spent an enormous sum getting her surroundings ready for the carriage trade she knew would come. The old boardinghouse was remade like new. Cracked brick and aging mortar fell before her workmen, old wood replaced and fresh paint applied, a grand front door added, along with brass work and expensive iron all about. The inside was gutted from the cellar to the attic eaves. There was a spacious and well-lit salon to receive her customers; fireplaces and chimneys installed so that not a cold draught could spoil the most isolated corner. For the homier touch, she had an enormous kitchen built out over the back gardens, which she landscaped with plants and herbs and spices that would draw comment in the dullest conversation. At first only the farm women gathered in the kitchen, but soon even some of the grandest ladies found themselves basking in its cheery glow, shoes off, feet up, gossiping freely with their country cousins.

She befriended her neighbors on Elm Court, and at her expense had the whole thing repaved with new drains and gutters so there was no chance of filthy water spattering her customers' shoes or dresses. She tore out the latrines near the well and had new ones built in a far corner. She kept them sweet with lime, and connected them to the house with an arbored walkway. She had deepened and covered the well, so she was one of the few people in town with fresh water at all times of the year. She put in another garden around the well and sprinkled the area with tables and chairs for people to take their ease. She hired servants to tend her customers' needs—housing them in apartments she'd refitted in a small building on one of her leased lots. She helped Farrell draw up a set of books so exacting it would take no more than a moment to trace the fate of a penny.

She also had James Emmett enrolled in a school with a notorious taskmaster, who guaranteed to cram his head with learning and empty his heart of its wilder stirrings. It seemed to be working. James Emmett was soon going about the house spouting Greek and Roman quotations, and the scrapes he got into were of such a minor nature, she hesitated to chastise him too severely, because there was such improvement. When he reached his teens, the scrapes seemed to stop altogether, which made her suspect the boy was only growing cannier with age. But overwhelmed by her business ventures, she adopted a "what I don't know won't harm me" attitude.

Farrell had been so taken by the Church since that first mass, he spent all his spare time studying his catechism, or helping in church affairs. He was talking about becoming a priest himself, which disturbed Diana. Besides believing it a waste, she couldn't see such a passionless young man taking up the life of the Book. Perhaps if she didn't comment beyond a "that's nice, dear," he'd grow out of it, take a wife and raise a family. Although argument number two in the matter of the priesthood also seemed to fit the situation of Farrell and marriage. What kind of a woman would have him? She imagined her son would see the marital bed as a duty to be performed as quickly and as efficiently as he did his sums.

In the months preceding her opening for business, she asked the Walshes to introduce her to society. It took no coaxing. She began attending the dances and assemblies they recommended. She became acquainted with Dr. Benjamin Rush and his family, as well as half a dozen of his colleagues. She was on social terms with the mayor, Matthew Clarkson, and especially his wife, Lydia. She met Israel Israel, the prominent tavern keeper—not Jewish, she learned to her surprise, although she soon became friendly with a host of people from the Holy Congregation Mikveh Israel Assembly. Also in her circle were the wives and daughters who had followed their husbands to Congress, although this was a transient trade and not to be depended on.

Allan Cole & Chris Bunch

Finally, all was ready. There was not another drop of paint to spread, or errant thread to snip. So she sent out the dolls.

Their arrival at the homes of the wealthy women of Philadelphia was not a total surprise. People knew she was an expert on fashions. They had already begun to ask her advice, which she gave for free, and a few had even urged her to open a shop they could frequent. She had more than just a shop in mind, but widened her eyes in interest when the subject came up. Mrs. Walsh had been letting out broad hints about some stunning notion in the making from her lovely, young, and oh so respectable widow friend.

What was a great surprise was the costumes the dolls wore. Each was different, designed especially for the woman who received it—from color and material, to the shoes and jewelry. Each costume was familiar enough to make its potential owner feel safe, but looked at as a whole, was startlingly unique. Each doll bore a card: Diana Shannon will begin receiving at two o'clock on Monday. Below the print was a carefully inked personal message asking her "friend, Mrs. Such-and-such, to please attend, for I fear this will not be a great success, and your comforting presence would be a welcoming cure to the malady of the lonely failure sure to afflict me."

Not one woman failed to attend. Not one woman failed to buy. And not one woman was not back in the company of her friends and daughters for each fitting. Diana's success was instant. So quickly did her business bloom, she was forced to expand, then to call on Mister Walsh to accept his offer to invest, so she could expand again. Her circle of friends and acquaintances grew, although she felt more at ease in the plain company of the ladies from the farms. Their problems and complaints seemed more real to her, their victories much larger because they were hard won. Still, it was nice to walk down any street and never fail to meet at least one person who would smile and nod their greetings. It was very nice indeed to be Diana Shannon.

There was one well-born young woman, however, she became quite close to, whose company she enjoyed more each time they met. The woman in question was not a customer. She was a Quaker. And when they first met, she was called Dolly Payne.

She came to the shop in the company of a few non-Quaker friends. She was dressed entirely in white, including her little cap with pitch-black curls peeking out, and her eyes were wide and blue in amazement at wonders all around her. Wonders that her religion's custom discouraged. Yet she didn't seem envious of her friends' purchases, but instead clapped in delight as each was guided to her discovery by Diana.

Dolly returned many times. To Diana's initial amazement, she was knowledgeable in the realm of fashion. And curious. She asked Diana a thousand questions, and posed as many problems for theoretical solution. It wasn't just dresses and dressmaking she knew about. Her head was filled with facts and information rare for a woman of these times. All of which she was anxious to discuss. Although, as time went by, Diana realized that Dolly had rarely expressed an opinion of her own. Actually, she went out of her way to avoid such a situation, throwing back a generality, or leading the conversation to safer ground. Still, Diana liked her. And although they were only a few years apart, Diana thought of her as the kind of little sister she would have liked to have.

She also felt sorry for her. Dolly was from an important family that was in decline. Her father, John Payne, had once owned a great plantation and many slaves in Virginia. After the Revolution he returned home marked by the blood he had seen and the Republican spirit it had let loose. He brooded for several years. One day he suddenly came to life. He sold his plantation and freed his slaves, packed up his family and their belongings and made the perilous journey to Philadelphia, where they had permanently settled.

It was a courageous act Diana wished had been appropriately rewarded. John Payne may have been noble,

Allan Cole & Chris Bunch

but he was no businessman. He put his money in
Revolutionary dollars. What was left over he invested in the
starch-manufacturing industry. The dollars were worthless.
The factory bankrupt. His wife Mary was forced to open their
house to boarders. There was no shame in this, as far as
Diana was concerned; the Paynes were vastly connected, and
their boarders consisted of some of the most famous men of
her time. People like Thomas Jefferson, Aaron Burr, and
many other prominent members of Congress.

But Mister Payne didn't see it that way. He retreated to
his room and his bed for the rest of his life. Yet he still ruled
his family with an iron hand. He would call them up and
issue his orders from behind closed doors. No one would
ever think to disobey them. There was no resentment in this
from Dolly. She was a good Quaker girl who would never
question her father. She also loved him deeply, and confessed
to Diana she was constantly in fear for his health. The love
was returned. And so was the concern. John Payne doted on
his oldest daughter. What father wouldn't? Diana thought.
There were few women she had met who were so beautiful.
Black hair, blue eyes, a face that was a perfect oval. She was
so lovely, men would gather at corners where they knew she
would pass just to get a glimpse of this Quaker maiden in her
white dress and modest cap.

But Dolly wasn't all she appeared. She was capable of
temper. When they knew one another well enough to confide,
Diana related her own history: Emmett. The journey from
New Kent. Their marriage. Emmett's death. Dolly wept, then
swore a surprising oath at Frenchy McShane and said she
wished she were a man so she could wipe out his kind. An
amazing admission from a Quaker.

Dolly also yearned for a life that was forbidden to her—
witness her interest in Diana's wares. She confessed to Diana
that when she was a child her grandmother used to give her
little gifts of jewelry. This was all done in secret, because her
parents frowned on such things. She kept the jewelry in a
little bag which she wore on a string about her neck and

tucked out of sight. One day, on the way to school, she lost the bag in the woods. It was never found, because she couldn't alert anyone and get help in her search. She said she knew it wasn't very important. Especially considering the terrible things people suffer in their lives. But just the same, she said, catch her in a weak moment, with no one around to see her, and she still wept at the memory of her grandmother's lost gifts.

Then Dolly married. To a young and handsome Quaker attorney named John Todd. Although the marriage was arranged by her father, Dolly said she loved John more than life itself. Diana guessed she believed her. Or, at least, hoped it was so for Dolly's sake. Her first child was a son they named James Payne Todd. Then, in that wonderfully mild and sunny January of 1793—the year everyone later said was so full of foreboding—she became pregnant with her second. Dolly brought all of her clothing to Diana, who helped her let them out, then coaxed her into allowing her best seamstress to make alterations so the dresses didn't look like they'd just had their seams ripped open and resewn to allow for a swelling belly. Dolly was easily convinced.

The year continued. From mild, to storm, to drought. Then the people came from the Sugar Islands. Diana and Dolly went to Mister Ricketts's marvelous circus in the great wooden-domed building he had built. They cheered with all the others as Mister Ricketts rode his horse about the ring. Standing on its back. Performing unbelievable acrobatic feats, such as leaping over ten horses. He even went through the complete manual of arms with a musket while riding a horse, then fired it and hit a target so true that people gasped in astonishment.

The weeks went on and Dolly grew in size. Then gloomy news arrived from Boston. Should she have added this to the list of the signs of doom? Diana wondered later. Ruth was frantic. The chandlery was in danger because of her husband's generosity to all his sailor friends who came to visit, and sup, and drink, and borrow. She desperately needed a loan or Isaac was for debtor's prison. Diana dispatched Farrell with the money. She sent James Emmett with him, because she knew they would be tempting Satan or worse if he stayed in Philadelphia without his brother's supervision. She instructed Farrell not to turn the money over directly, but to pay the debts, take over the business until it was sturdy again, and then—when the time was right—to leave it in the far more capable hands of young Samuel. Farrell wasn't to return until this was accomplished, and yes she would be fine, thank you very much, and could do without his assistance for a few months.

Then there was the tempest in Ipswich and all that hail in so small an area. And the great Kensington oak was blasted into twelve pieces by lightning.

No one knows when the first person died. But on August 19, Dr. Benjamin Rush lost a patient on Water Street.

The diagnosis was yellow fever.

CHAPTER TWENTY-SIX

IT WAS JUST after midday on Wednesday, August 21, that Diana received a message from Mister Walsh urgently requesting her presence. She put on a heavy walking dress and high boots for the short journey. She drew on long gloves and pinned a heavy veil to her hat, so not an inch of flesh was exposed. She loaded a cotton swath with penny royal and dabbed every possible gateway with the strong-smelling oil.

Diana knew what lay outside. It wasn't the stifling heat she was guarding against. Some said Philadelphia was the hottest port town in the nation, even hotter and more humid than Savannah. Diana didn't doubt this, but she saw the weather as just a condition no one could change, so there was no sense in complaining. Besides, she noted the most vocal of the complainers seemed to be the rich. They could spend the summer in one of the cool luxury homes along the Schuylkill, or even flee to kinder climes. Diana had to stay. She had a business to run. More importantly, she had many people who depended on her. What would they do if she left? How would they eat? Provide for their families? No, for the working class there could be no escape, no matter how unpleasant or intense the season.

There was one thing about this summer she detested. She knew it was silly and leftover childhood nonsense fear. But it was there just the same.

Mosquitoes disgusted her. The thought of one of them piercing her flesh and sucking her blood almost made her violently ill. It was because of Nate Hatch, and one of his favorite summer jests. In the long, sultry afternoons after a storm, he would sit on the stoop drinking with his friends, slapping at the mosquitoes that prized this weather. He would drink and talk until he became bleary, flushed, and full of that touchy kind of humor that borders quick anger. When he was ready for his little joke, he would hush everyone to silence and demand loudly that they sit quite still. Then he would bare a fat, hairy arm to the buzzing insects. They would alight by the scores. Then he'd suddenly tense, trapping their beaks in his flesh. He'd laugh, waving his arm about like a great prize. Then he would smash all but a few. His arm would run with blood, trickling through the thick black hairs and mingling with the beads of sweat. The others he would let escape. There would be greater laughter as the insects bumped about, stunned from the alcoholic brew they'd sucked in along with his blood.

The first time Diana witnessed this jest, she'd been quite small. He had spied her at some menial task, shushed his companions, and called her over to see. When he began slapping at the beasts and the blood ran, she had screamed and ran to Gramer Fahey, where she was sick all over the floor. The old woman tried to tell her it was just Nate Hatch being a fool. But little Diana was inconsolable. She couldn't get the blood and the mosquitoes and Mister Hatch's mocking laugh from her head. It was a joke he'd terrorized her with ever since that day.

Now that she was the mistress of her own home and business, she saw no reason for torment. When the sultry season came, she ordered the windows covered with muslin doused with penny royal. She even went so far as to use a trick that Gramer Fahey had taught her. The wrigglers that became mosquitoes, the old woman pointed out, lived in standing pools of water. A little oil applied to the water would cover the surface with a thin scum, and the wrigglers would smother. It was a remedy Diana had carried out with a passion. If she spotted the smallest little puddle in the court or her gardens, or if she saw the little wrigglers swimming about in a rain barrel, Diana would run to fetch the oil. And she would gleefully murder every one of them.

Her friends' house was a twitter of servants when she arrived. All was in disorder, with small groups huddled about, whispering and casting dark looks at the staircase. Diana was met by Beth, Mrs. Walsh's personal maid. The woman's eyes were red-rimmed from weeping. She quickly led her up the stairs and tapped softly on Anne's bedroom door, which was flung open with such haste that Diana jumped back, startled. It was Mister Walsh. His face was drawn and gray, bare spots on his face stubbled from a too quick shave. His dress was uncharacteristically disheveled. His eyes were as red as the maid's.

He tried to speak, but his voice came out a croak. He shook his head, and Diana realized he was fearful he would break down if he tried to speak further. He wavered in front of her, struggling, then drew her into an embrace so desperate she could barely breathe. Diana didn't draw back. She let him hold her until he recovered and drew away.

"She's sick," was all he said. In such a trembling voice that Diana needed no other description.

"How long?"

"Three days. But it might as well be weeks for the toll it's taken. I wanted to send for a doctor, but she refused. She . . . Please, Diana . . . She asked for you."

She pushed past him into the room. Anne had aged twenty years. She lay unconscious in her bed, twisting and turning, uttering low moans. Diana touched her, the skin feverish. Anne's eyes opened at the touch. They were glazed and yellow at the edges. Then they sharpened as she recognized her friend. A hand moved toward Diana's slowly, as if it were a painful weight the arm could hardly bear. Fingers touched, then squeezed. She took a breath to speak, but all that issued from her lips was: "Diana ..." Then she was still. Her eyes closed again. So soft was the whisper, and so sudden the stillness, that for a second Diana feared her friend had died and her soul had taken flight.

She looked at Mister Walsh, who seemed as if he were about to rush headlong from the room, screaming wildly for help. And so, with a confidence she did not feel, she rose from the bed and began issuing a stream of orders. ". . .Go to the apothecary on Seventh Street . . . I'll need the bark . . . only the freshest will do . . . laudanum . . . the same . . . tell

Allan Cole & Chris Bunch

the cook . . . the very best broth ... I want it hearty . . . and
fruit . . . again, fresh . . . boiled to a soup and chilled..."

Soon staff and Mister Walsh were running about to do
her bidding. She turned back to Anne to start thinking what
she really needed to do. First, it was plain Mister Walsh was
not happy with this arrangement. He wanted a doctor. And he
wanted him now! Specifically, he wanted Dr. Alexander, to
whom he paid thirty dollars a year insurance to treat his
family. Diana knew the man to be a disciple of Dr. Rush, a
confirmed believer in massive bleeding and purging. Anne
and Diana had talked about Michael Walsh's faith in modern
science and medicine. It was a faith both felt unjustified,
especially Diana. She had witnessed more people killed or
injured by doctors' cures than made whole. Anne had made
her promise if she ever really fell ill, to dissuade "dear
Michael from summoning a powder wig who will lay me in
an early grave with his remedies."

The trouble was, although Diana knew much about
country medicine, and had been forced to depend solely on
her knowledge most of her life for the good of her family and
friends, she felt herself far from expert. The great problem
she had right now was if she tried to call in someone with
more expertise, Mister Walsh would overrule her. Dr.
Alexander would come, with his purges and his emetics and
plasters so hot, the skin would blister and scar.

At this moment it was Diana, or . . . Ah, but you're here,
Diana Shannon. And you must act. So, displaying a
confidence that she didn't feel, she set about her task. She had
the maids haul in a tub and fill it with icy water. She
undressed Anne herself and helped lift her into the bath.
There was only a sigh from her friend and she remained
unconscious. Diana had Beth bring in pans of hot water, and
she washed Anne's hair and dried it tenderly.

She had the sheets and bedding changed and the mattress
turned. They lifted Anne from the bath, dried her and placed
her on the bed. Diana sent for spirits and rubbed Anne's poor,
frail body. Almost immediately the fever broke and the chills

and sweats set in. Diana had her wrapped tightly in a sheet. When her supplies came, she had a soothing tea made up with a camomile base, which she dribbled through Anne's parted lips. She also sent for Madeira and mixed in a little laudanum. This she coaxed Mister Walsh into drinking. A preventative, she said. Actually she just wanted him out of her way.

As the hours progressed, she got some broth down her friend. Then the cold fruit soup to ease her constricted bowels. And water. So much water Anne groaned with the effort. But in time the padding she had placed beneath her was soiled and changed and soiled again. Diana stayed all night and most of the morning. By the time the midday sun pressed through the open windows, Anne's eyes were open. And she was weakly alert.

In the parlor, Mister Walsh thanked Diana profusely, calling it a miracle. She told him flatly not to talk nonsense. Anne was strong, she said. She would heal herself.

Diana left directions for her treatment. The fever would return, she was sure of that; but in theory it should be milder. And if treated properly, should finally disappear.

"It's the way of the flux," she said. "It has to run its course before it can be coaxed out." She gave stern orders she was to be sent for if Anne's condition took a turn for the worse.

A weary Diana dragged herself back the few blocks to Elm Court. Nothing was changed outside. The air was still stifling. The dust still billowed up from cartwheels. The mosquitoes buzzed about in clouds thicker and blacker than that dust. People sat on their porches, or on the curbs in front of their shops, hardly moving in the intense heat. Halfheartedly brushing away insects that fed on them. Panting like dogs. But, after many weeks of drought, this was all quite normal.

What was making her uneasy? There was nothing remarkable about Anne's flux. Midwives and barbers and healers were always kept busy this time of year. Although

pg. 277

she'd heard this summer was more severe than most. What was so different? So ominous?

When she reached her court, she realized what it was. A bell was tolling. For a funeral. Were there more funeral bells ringing of late, or was it her imagination?

* * * *

Diana was exhausted. All she wanted was to float away the filth from the streets in a hot bath, then fall into her bed to sleep. But the uneasy feeling persisted. She called her staff together.

There was Mrs. Leclerc, the head seamstress, high-strung and nervous, but sound, in Diana's judgment. The burly, aged Mister Park was her driver, loader, and general handyman, along with his two not too quick, but strong and willing sons. There was real strength in her housekeeper, Miss Graham, a rangy, middle-aged spinster who took no nonsense from anyone, especially James Emmett.

Finally, there was her cook, Mrs. Kenrick, a tubby, salty little widow of a ship's carpenter.

"What is the trouble, missus? Is it your friend, the dear Mrs. Walsh? Is she still unwell?" This from Miss Graham.

"She's doing better, thank you," Diana said. "And it's not about her. And I'm not sure if there's trouble or not. . . ." Her voice trailed off, uncertain. Her people looked at one another, worried. They'd never seen Diana uncertain.

"It's probably nothing," Diana said. "I'm being a child and letting my imagination go spooking in the forest. But . . . when I was returning home, I heard funeral bells ..."

" 'Twas only Paul Read. The old man who owned the Drunken Squab down Water Street way," said Mister Park, a man who knew his tavern keepers. "Died of the flux, I believe. No one will miss him, I suspect. He was a surly sort. And mean-spirited. He'd only buy a round when we threatened to take our business elsewhere." He gave a brisk nod at this, as if it was only to be expected that such a man was the special mark for the Reaper.

278

"But haven't there been more funerals of late?" Diana asked.

"No, missus, I don't believe it so," said her housekeeper. "Four or five a day at most, I should think. No more than usual. Especially in this heat. Which, as any thinking person knows, is nearly as hard on the old as a harsh winter." Miss Graham sniffed at Mister Park. She was of the opinion he lacked this natural talent. Although not as much as his sons.

So it wasn't the funeral bells. Still, with no letup in sight for the drought, Diana decided it was time to take a few extra precautions she'd had in mind for some weeks now. She explained what she wanted done and her reasons for it, so as not to unduly alarm her staff. The longer the drought, she said, the higher the market prices. She wanted to be prepared for as long a spell of harsh weather as possible. Also, Mrs. Walsh's illness reminded her of how many afflictions could strike the unwary during especially hot summers. Even so, the shopping list she laid out had them all raising startled eyebrows. There were so many supplies required that several trips would be needed.

The water level was falling in the well, she noted, so she also set Mister Park the task of deepening it. This was to be done immediately. She also wanted a good supply of those medicinals her garden didn't provide. If there was flux about to trouble her staff, she wanted to be prepared. She was too tired to hear them all out after she was done. She left them at the kitchen table, rattling on about their tasks and what assistance would be required from one another.

Her room was upstairs and overlooking the garden. An ancient elm shaded the room, so that even in the stillness it felt remarkably cool. All she wanted was sleep. The bath would wait. She stripped off her clothing, doused a soft cloth with scented spirits and dabbed herself all over. It brought instant relief. Coolness. She even imagined a touch of a chill. She pulled down the covers and crawled into bed, pulled a sheet over herself and fell into a deep sleep.

Allan Cole & Chris Bunch

She awoke with a start just before dawn. Her heart was hammering as if she had just had a bad dream. Her throat was sore and raspy. Her limbs were aching and heavy, her skin dry and hot. She wanted badly to get up for a glass of water, but for some reason she found it impossible to move. For a moment she was frightened. Her senses seemed to be warning her. But of what? Was there something just beyond the door? She struggled to get up again. But then a great feeling of lethargy overtook her. Almost against her will, she was swept back to sleep.

But this time she dreamed constantly. Snatches of dreams, each one oddly troubling. Bits of innocuous conversation. But all of them loaded with peril just beneath the surface. Once she thought Miss Graham was trying to awaken her. Diana protested. But the woman kept tugging at her. Trying to tell her something. Something urgent.

"Is it Mrs. Walsh?" Diana thought she asked. But Miss Graham shook her head. Mumbled to her. Mumble. Mumble. Tug some more. Then the tugging became the sheet being pulled back around her and tucked in.

"What is it, Miss Graham?"

"Yellow fever," she said. At least that's what she thought she said.

"No it's not," Diana said, matter-of-factly. "Just a chill. A summer chill. Let me sleep."

"Yellow fever," Miss Graham said once again.

Would the woman never stop! Then a cold cloth was draped over her eyes and everything was comforting darkness again. The last thing she heard was the buzzing mosquitoes outside her window. The buzz grew louder and louder, until she could hear no more. The next time she awoke, there was a heavy thundering outside. The crack of lightning. The sound of a heavy downpour. She opened her eyes briefly. The curtains were closed, but she could hear the rain battering against the sill. The sill. The one that needed caulking. She must get up to see. Call Mister Park if it wanted fixing.

Miss Graham was asleep in a chair near the bed. What was she doing here? Why wasn't she in her own room? Then Diana realized it was the middle of the day. But which day? She knew she had been asleep for . . . well, a long time. Since she came back from Anne's house. She wondered how her friend was. On the table next to her bed, she saw a cup of tea. Was it for her? Of course it was. She touched the cup. Cold. But she was so thirsty, she didn't care. She lifted the cup to her lips and sniffed. Lemon tea. That's good. And something else. Brandy. Better. She drank it down, and was surprised there was no resistance from her sore throat. Then she realized her throat was fine now. In fact, she felt well all over. Except for this confounded sleepy feeling she couldn't shake.

She thought about waking Miss Graham. But the woman seemed so tired, poor dear. No, let her sleep. And in just one minute, I'll get up myself. Come on, woman!

You have a business to oversee. Get up and get about it. Yes. But just a small nap first. And then I'll . . .

* * * *

She didn't come fully awake again until Monday. It was August 26. Diana's diagnosis had been correct. She had only suffered a severe case of the summer chill. The storm was no dream. It had rained heavily for two days, but the drought had instantly seized the city in its hot grip again.

The incident involving Miss Graham had also been no dream. Her housekeeper had come to awaken her with urgent news. But then she had found her mistress desperately ill, and had nursed her and coaxed her back to sleep.

But what was the news, Miss Graham? What was so urgent? Farrell sick? James Emmett in trouble? A ship in port with goods at bargain prices?

"No, missus. It was in the papers. Everyone's dying! Yellow fever, missus. Yellow fever."

It began with chills, a desperate headache, and a rapidly climbing temperature. The bowels and bladder refused to work and so the chamber pot remained empty. This condition

Allan Cole & Chris Bunch

lasted several days, then the patient usually made a rapid recovery. In other words, yellow fever began as no more than a mild case of the summer flux.

Herbalists and wandering quacks did a brisk business in purgatives, restorers and tonics. But they were soon overwhelmed by what followed. The fever came back full force. The patient began vomiting black blood from internal hemorrhages. The skin turned bright yellow. Then came the typhoid state: stupor, deep depression, dry brown tongue, incontinence, a pulse rapid but weak, a sudden and frightening wasting. The stink of the sickroom was overpowering. Then the body turned a purplish hue. Death came within twelve hours. One symptom the doctors noted accompanying the disease was tiny, angry eruptions on the skin. They were usually inflamed, sore, and they itched. They looked like small bites, and no one could account for their presence.

* * * *

Diana's imagination hadn't regressed to childhood. She had heard more funeral bells than usual. On Thursday twelve had died. Thirteen on Friday. Saturday seventeen. Miss Graham wasn't sure about Sunday. Besides the weekend storm, the city had been put into a panic by the plague.

The storm had turned the dusty streets into a sea of mud. Despite this, hundreds of people had fled the fever. Entire wagonloads of personal belongings were left stranded in the muck as the well-off or unattached poured out of Philadelphia. As the weeks went on, the flood grew to even greater proportions. Employees and servants were abandoned without funds or means of getting any. And even if they had the money, there was little to buy. The market stalls were empty. Rotted fruit, vegetables, and animal carcasses were left lying in the gutters. Water was getting scarcer by the hour, since the countryside had also panicked and no water carts dared to cross the Schuylkill.

Meanwhile, the death toll was growing. Even as she and Miss Graham spoke, Diana could hear the church bells ringing. As soon as one stopped, presumably as the dead were lowered into their grave, another bell took up the mournful tolling. Miss Graham said people had become so fearful, the city fathers were considering banning the bells. As if that would hold back death itself. She said when coffins passed, people were slamming their doors and windows to shut out the plague.

"What else are they doing?" Diana asked.

Old public health laws were dusted off and put into action. Houses were ordered thoroughly cleaned and whitewashed, gutters flushed with precious water, sidewalks and streets scoured. The scavengers had been ordered to make daily pickups of garbage to reduce the number of breeding spots for the fever. Bonfires were also being lit. Tobacco and gunpowder burned on every street corner. Diana thought all this made good sense. Clean the city. Purge the air.

There was a sudden rolling crash, as if the storm had come back with three or four times the fury. All over her household, Diana heard shrieks of alarm. But she knew it wasn't thunder. It was a terrible sound she knew too well. For a moment she had an almost uncontrollable urge to flee to the safety of her root cellar. But this wasn't Cherry Valley. There was no threat of war or Indians.

She rushed out of the house, Miss Graham in her wake, and sprinted across the cobbled court street to the entrance. As she reached the corner, she saw the uniforms. It was a squad of soldiers, hauling a cannon. They would march in unison for ten or twenty yards, fire the cannon into the sky, reload, march on, stop, fire another volley. With each volley, windows shattered and old brickwork rattled loose and showered to the ground. Up and down the street people were shouting and screaming. The heavy scent of gunpowder was laden with the sickly, overpowering smell of tobacco from a roaring bonfire down the street.

A voice came from a few feet away. Diana turned to see a man sitting astride his horse. A gentleman. From his dress,

Allan Cole & Chris Bunch

he had just returned from a long journey. He was bewildered, asking what was going on. Before Diana could answer, shutters flew open overhead. She looked up to see a wild figure. A middle-aged man in his nightdress, his hair standing straight up on his head.

"Is that you, Mister Niven?" he shouted.

The man on the horse said he was.

"Why in God's name have you come back?" the man screamed. "It's the plague! Flee, man, flee!"

Without a word, Mister Niven swung his horse about and fled. At the corner he had to pull up fast, his horse pawing air and wheeling to the side. Another kick and the horse squeezed frantically past a hearse bearing a load of fever victims, and then was gone.

The coach was black. The driver in rags. A starveling no doubt, so hungry that he was willing to dare a nightmare to ease the one he was living. As the coach approached the soldiers, a young officer shouted for the driver to stop. The coach came on. The officer shouted again. Still it came on. Closer. The squad wavered. Now the officer was shouting at his men. But the coach still came, creaking forward with its fearful burden. The squad broke and ran. The officer stood there helpless beside the cannon. The coach passed. After a moment the officer walked away. There was nothing else to be done.

Diana turned back into the court. She would put her household in order and then see about Anne.

* * * *

The Walsh house was barred and shuttered. No one answered to the bell. Diana knocked next door. She spoke to a woman through shuttered windows. The woman didn't know anything. She thought Anne had died. Down the street, another conversation through barred windows. No, Anne had recovered, this person said. It was Mister Walsh who had died. Still another said both were well and had fled the city, taking all their servants. This made more sense, but not fully. If they had left, either Anne or Michael would have stopped to see her. Diana went home again, sure, at least, both were alive.

* * * *

Once again Diana called her staff together. The atmosphere was entirely different. No easy, but respectful jollity, or casual sniping at one another. And they were all dressed in their best clothes. Bathed. Coiffed. In Mister Park's case a few lonely strands of gray hair were slicked to his bare skull with water. Their faces were frightened. Eyes bruised from lack of sleep. All were silent. Waiting for what she would say.

Diana was surprised when she had learned that almost her entire household was intact. Few had bolted the city. At first she thought it was out of loyalty to her. This was only partly the case. As she looked at them, she realized they had no place else to go. No gardened farmhouse in the country. No summer place by a cool stream. No faraway relations with provisions to share beyond the immediate family. Now they fully expected Diana to issue final orders, then close up the house and go. Mrs. Leclerc sobbed softly, was patted to stillness by Miss Graham.

Diana asked if her orders had been carried out, the previsions bought and stored, the well deepened, the medicines stocked. Yes, all this had been done, Miss Graham assured her.

"I am schooled in keeping accounts, madam," Mrs. Leclerc said, voice rasping from crying, her skin an unhealthy pallor beneath its lovely light chocolate hue. "To which address should I post them?"

Diana pretended surprise. "Why, nowhere," she said. "I'm not going anywhere."

There was instant relief all around the table. A chorus of stage-whispered "I told you so's." Diana waited until they were quiet again, Miss Graham sweeping the small gathering with hot eyes that said she doubted least of all.

"I didn't flee the Indians in Cherry Valley," Diana said. "Nor the soldiers. None of them drove me out. I stayed. I

pg. 285

prospered. And everyone with me prospered as well." She paused for effect. "If the Indians couldn't roust me," she said, "I'll be damned if I'll be put to flight by the fever. At least you die with your hair on."

There were only four people in the room besides herself. But the shouts and cheers of joy sounded like a crowd coming to its feet at Mister Ricketts's circus. Diana had a bottle and glasses brought in, and they sat about the table, talking and joking like old tavern chums.

Diana joined in, laughing and jesting. But it was a sham. Not everyone had prospered at Cherry Valley. Far from it. She looked about the table and wondered how many faces would still be there when it was all over. And wasn't even that thought selfish on the face of it? Foolishly so. When it was over, would she even be here to see?

CHAPTER TWENTY-SEVEN

THE DEATH TOLL mounted daily as the crisis worsened. Residents were stunned the great storm from the northeast brought no relief from the fever. Some thought it was the stagnant air, trapped over the city since winter, now replaced by equally foul solids from the inland ether. A few blamed it on the shipload of spoiled coffee that had been dumped on the docks. The city ordered this removed, but weeks went by with no action because there was no one to carry out the orders. Others said the infection was carried by the refugees from the French islands. Others held this to be nonsense. Yellow fever could not be transmitted by one person to another.

Dr. Benjamin Rush said the cause was the climate. His theory was listened to as intently as were his prescriptions. He was America's most prominent doctor, educated at Edinburgh University, published author, signer of the Declaration of Independence, and a noted educator and reformer. As far back as Hippocrates, Rush noted, doctors had said mild winters followed by drought brought great illness. It was an observation borne out by previous outbreaks of the yellow fever in Philadelphia; although it had been many decades since the last, and that had been far less deadly. Also, that epidemic had ended after a large storm. Why not this time?

Diana and her people huddled in Elm Court watching the city's social structure collapse.

Most members of the Congress were already on summer holiday. But the heart seemed to go completely out of the residents when President Washington reluctantly agreed to return to the safety of his home in Virginia. Thomas Jefferson left the city for a home along the Schuylkill, and then spent most of his time writing cynical letters deploring the discomfort of the house that had been made available to him. One by one the few other great national leaders took flight.

Soon the courthouses were nearly empty. City offices closed. Only the mayor, Matthew Clarkson, and a few other council members dared death by remaining in town to fight the plague. But all efforts seemed so puny.

Daily, Diana walked down empty streets to the offices of the Federal Gazette. Andrew Brown was the only publisher to remain in the city. The Gazette was the sole source of news. Diana knew she looked like a specter on those daily walks, draped head to toe and heavily veiled, reeking of penny royal, drifting through dust which stood as deep as two feet in some places. No one ever spoke to her. The few people on the streets would go to great extremes to avoid another human being. No handshakes. No greetings. When a person saw another, he would make a wide berth.

At the Gazette she heard deplorable tales. Husbands abandoning stricken wives of many years. Mothers deserting ailing children. Helpless old people left to starve. Stranded servants too frightened to fetch water from the street. Diana, a close and cynical student of human nature, did not doubt these stories.

Although the cannon fire had ceased, the eerie silence that had enveloped Philadelphia was occasionally broken by crashing musket fire when frightened householders tried to purify the atmosphere with their guns. Everywhere there was the smell of smoke and rotting trash. Corpses of cats littered the alleys; killed by the foul air, it was said. Businesses were shuttered. The entire harbor out to the sea was choked with ships filled with cargo no one would unload. The captains had no other markets for their goods.

More refugees arrived. But this time they were denied entry and quarantined on the Delaware pesthole known as Mud Island. Hospitals barred victims with fever symptoms. The city was forced to take over Mister Ricketts's empty amphitheater for the ailing paupers and their orphaned children.

Doctors argued heatedly on methods of treatment. Sometimes, Diana thought, there were as many theories as victims.

Dr. Young and his adherents insisted the only course was massive purges and blistering on the wrists and back of the necks. Others added dust baths to this remedy, and injections of wine. Or chewing garlic. Or constant doses of vinegar and tobacco. Camphor was also considered a preventive, and the city was filled with people—especially children—whose throats were raw from breathing noxious fumes.

But mainly it was Dr. Rush's method of treatment that prevailed: intensive purging followed by equally intensive bleedings. As week folded into horrible week, he increased his purging and bleeding and urged his colleagues to follow suit in impassioned letters to the Gazette. He assured all he was seeing success by taking a quart of blood at a time, repeated several times a day. Diana remembered the late Dr. Franklin had mocked that the great fevers plaguing the Sugar Islands hadn't ceased until the last physician had fled or died. In her view, it was no jest.

But no matter what anyone did, people kept dying. Two hundred or more burials a week. Hundreds more lay decaying in their homes because no one would come to fetch their corpses.

On Saturday, September 7, a bonfire set to ward off the fever was left unattended. It spread to Mister Kennedy's soap factory, which burned to the ground, taking an adjacent stable and warehouse with it. A few brave souls came out to fight the blaze, blankets soaked in vinegar draped over their heads. But it was no use. The incident spurred orders from Mayor Clarkson to end the bonfires. The orders were ignored. The fire was the major event in the city that day. The plague toll was a by now commonplace twenty-five dead. For the Jews in the community, the day had special bleak significance. It was Rosh Hashanah, the new year of 5544 on their ancient calendar. It was mentioned in the

Allan Cole & Chris Bunch

Gazette that only a handful were left to celebrate the day with Rabbi Jacob Cohen.

Diana would remember that Saturday for a different reason. For her it was the day of an unusual request. Mrs. Leclerc wanted time off from her duties. A silly request, since there were no duties for a seamstress to perform. Then she told Diana why. It had been noted by the African Society's leaders, Absalom Jones and Richard Allen, that no person with black skin had been infected. The word was spreading through the city that men and women of color were immune. Mister Jones and Mister Allen were urgently asking for volunteers to tend the sick and bury the dead. Black volunteers.

Mrs. Leclerc wanted to be one of those volunteers. "Everyone has been so kind," she said. "I lost everything. Family. Friends. My possessions, which I care nothing for. But here ... I have found a new life. I feel I must do something to repay—"

She burst into tears. She was terrified of what she was about to do. Especially since Diana's court seemed a haven. Not one person who lived under her roof had taken sick, although no one could say why. To leave such apparent safety would take great courage. More, Diana feared, than poor Mrs. Leclerc could provide. So she told her no. Firmly.

She thought of Moses and Aaron. God—whoever, or whatever that might be—certainly never granted them any immunities to compensate for their exile among people of fair skin. They caught all of the common diseases, including the childhood illnesses of Farrell and James Emmett, Diana told Mrs. Leclerc. In her experience, tropical skin offered no special protection.

The woman greeted this with visible relief. Strange. Diana had just informed her that she was as vulnerable as the rest of them. Still, she was no longer the victim of her conscience. Mrs. Leclerc could die along with the rest of them. For one week the black residents of Philadelphia rallied to their white employers and neighbors. They eased the desperately ill to their graves. Nursed people in conditions of unbelievable filth and squalor. Cared for their orphaned young. Fed them from dwindling supplies in their own kitchens. Drove the funeral coaches. Tenderly lifted rotting corpses into coffins. Wielded the shovels in the graveyards. And commended their souls to their Maker.

On Saturday, September 14, forty-eight people died. Among them were six blacks. The occasion was marked by a meteorite which fell in Third Street.

* * * *

From September sixteenth through the twenty-third, sixty or more people were buried each day. Some saw hope in this. The plague had to get worse before it ebbed. Now it was almost over, these optimists said. The following day was horror. Ninety-six people died. As month end neared, the toll was edging two thousand—already far more than the yellow fever outbreak of 1762.

That terrible day created a panic upon a panic. Hundreds more fled the city. The roads out, it was said, were jammed from edge to edge with wagons and livestock and foot traffic. There were stories in the Gazette of whole communities turning their backs on these people. Damning them to starvation or death by illnesses caused by exhaustion and exposure to the intense heat of the drought. Diana took bitter note of the worst of these heartless communities: Bethlehem, Nazareth, Easton, and Reading. Emmett had told her about these cruel folk. Could even he have imagined just how cruel?

On the twenty-sixth a note came from Dolly Todd. It had taken nearly two weeks to reach Diana, although the letter only had to travel a short distance from the Gray's Ferry home in which Dolly's husband had installed her and her family. Diana read it with relief. She had feared for her Quaker friend, whose pregnancy was near full term when they last spoke. The note contained the cheerful news that she had borne the child, her second son, William Todd. Dolly would be safe out of the filth of the city. The note urged

Allan Cole & Chris Bunch

Diana to join her on the cool banks of the river. It was an invitation Diana would have ignored even if she were not determined to see the disaster out. If she were going to flee, she would pick a place farther from Philadelphia than the far bank of the Schuylkill. But she took comfort her friend was out of this horror. It would be more than a month before she learned Dolly's true fate.

Her handsome young lawyer husband, John Todd, saw her to the safety of the old farmhouse and then turned back into the city. His own parents were too ill to move. They died several days later. John himself was afflicted. Delirious from the fever, he made his way across the river. And fainted on the doorstep. Dolly's mother helped her carry him into the house and placed him on a couch. A few hours later Dolly was stricken. She lapsed into a coma for several days, then recovered to learn that her husband and infant child were dead. But at least her first son, Payne Todd, survived. Years later Diana would wonder if his survival was as great a tragedy as his brother's and father's death.

For the moment, however, Diana believed the note to be good news. She saw it as a leavening to the tragic news that came the following day. A minuscule leavening, as small as the little animals that lived in the ether and somehow entered people's bodies to kill them.

It was another letter. From Mister Walsh. Diana was wrong in her belief that neither Anne nor Michael would leave without first telling her. The letter was even longer delayed than Dolly's. It was from Baltimore, where Mister Walsh had taken refuge with a cousin. Anne was dead.

The letter was rambling and hysterical. Full of guilt. Anne had seemed to recover. Then came the relapse. Exactly what followed was difficult to make out, so frantic the prose, so tear-smudged the ink. In desperation, Mister Walsh had chosen not to ask Diana for help. Although how could she have aided, sick and helpless herself from the summer flux?

In letters to the Gazette, Father Fleming had been urging his Catholic parishioners to follow the course of treatment prescribed by Dr. Rush. Only this would save them, he wrote, commenting that he himself had undergone the bleeding and it had prevented him from falling ill. Mister Walsh had sought out the good doctor. He almost turned back when he saw the scene in front of the famed physician's home. The front yard, sidewalk, and street were packed with people begging for help. Exhausted, Rush and his assistants strode through the crowd, ministering to the sick and the merely frightened as they stood. Purges were given. People vomited in the street. And always there were the lancets, plunging into vein after vein. Until the gutters ran with all the spilled blood. The blood dried in thick scabs upon the street, drawing huge clouds of mosquitoes.

But Mister Walsh had taken courage. He would have to be brave if he was to save his Anne. Dr. Rush had agreed to come. He purged her, then purged her again, until Anne's stomach constantly and involuntarily heaved and she screamed with pain from the cramps. And he bled her. Fifty ounces the first day, seventy-two the second. But he took only a pint the third day. He couldn't take more. Because Anne was dead.

The letter went on and on. Mister Walsh had become hysterical in his grief. He had left the city with only a horse and a barely packed saddlebag. But he couldn't escape what he had done. Diana could see him, weeping and beating his Catholic breast, praying, over and over: "To my fault ... to my fault ... to my most grievous fault."

"I killed her," Mister Walsh wrote in one clear, almost sane sentence. "I killed her as sure as if I had wielded the lancet myself. Oh, my darling, darling Anne . . ."

Diana knew when she saw Michael again it would be difficult to comfort him, because in one thing he was correct: he had killed her. Although he would have to share the blame with Father Fleming. But it was only his memory the two of them could blame together. Father Fleming had died of the fever as well.

But Diana would never have to face this task. In the fall, Mister Walsh's cousin would write to her. Michael became suicidal. The family had him committed to a home for the insane. He was dead before Christmas.

* * * *

Tragedy comes in threes, the folktales say. But this year they came three times three times so many more threes, it would take a mathematician of Euclid's like to count all the woes that piled up at everyone's doorstep.

For Diana, the next bleak incident came from her own household. It was her stalwart housekeeper, Miss Graham. This time there was no letter. The spinster failed to show up after four days. A little over a week into the plague, Miss Graham had informed her she could no longer in good conscience stay overnight at the Elm Court house. She had a sister fifteen years her junior, a widow with five children. They lived packed into two small rooms in a Water Street tenement. Miss Graham said—and she was firm about this— it would be necessary for her to go to her sister's home each night to help care for the children.

At the time, Water Street was the most notorious pesthole in the city. In the course of eleven days, forty people had died on Water Street, eleven in one family. Diana warned Miss Graham of this.

"If I'm to die," the housekeeper said matter-of-factly, "I'd soon it be with my own."

"Then have them come live here," Diana urged.

Miss Graham gave a sharp shake of her head. This was impossible, she said. She could not permit it.

"But why?" Diana asked.

The woman wouldn't answer. It was the way things would be, and she refused to offer a reason. So there was nothing Diana could do but grant her request.

For weeks Miss Graham arrived early every morning to work, and left for Water Street before dusk. Then, no Miss Graham. Another day passed; still nothing. On the fourth day, Diana determined to investigate. She wanted to go alone, but Mister Park wouldn't allow it. He said even in the best of times the section along Water Street where Miss Graham's sister lived was no place for a lady like Diana to dare alone. She could fire him for insubordination if she chose, but he would go just the same.

He carried his stoutest cudgel and wore his fiercest look for the journey. But Diana could tell that beneath the gnarly surface was a man as frightened as a small child. She pretended female weakness, and gripped one of his thick arms for reassurance. Soon as she laid a small hand on his forearm, she could feel his spine stiffen. His walk took on a bow-legged swagger. He growled fiercely at the few who dared to walk into their path.

It was late afternoon. The heat hung as close to the city as the swarms of mosquitoes that skimmed just past the fumes of penny royal that Diana had daubed heavily on her veil, gloves, and outer clothing. She tried to get Mister Park to follow her example, but he insisted the little biters affected him not at all. He said there was something in his blood that turned them away, and it was rare the insects made a meal on him. But within a few squares of the oasis that was Elm Court, he was already cursing under his breath and slapping at his exposed neck and face and hands.

The city was silent. It was a silence no one could grow accustomed to. Blocks away someone hammered on a door with its big brass knocker, and Diana could hear the hammering echo all along Race Street. Almost no one was about, especially children. She knew from the Gazette and the stories from her staff that the fever had been especially cruel to children. The young died faster and in greater numbers than their elders. It was one of the many oddities of the plague—equally as odd as how few old people had been afflicted. Or that not as many women had died as men.

They found the building just past Alum Court. It sat at a crazy angle on the bank, half buried in muck and rubble. The river stink was so thick, Mister Park accepted a handkerchief soaked in vinegar from Diana. When she saw the place,

Allan Cole & Chris Bunch

Diana began to get an inkling of why Miss Graham had insisted she not meet her sister. It was set amongst a nest of dirty yellow buildings, notorious in the city as a breeding ground for whores. She entered the building pitying Miss Graham, whose sister was a whore.

Everyone was mad in this place. Mad or dead. She could smell the rotting flesh as she entered. Mister Park tried to go in front of her, but she brushed past him into the dank warren. Silence. Except for the creaking of timbers. Or the cracks of steps as she ascended the stairs. She moved by instinct, hesitating at first, then quietly opening doors and looking inside. Most of the rooms were empty. Horribly, some were not. Skeletal remains swarming with maggots. Corpses fully dressed. Others gruesomely naked. One of the rooms held a coffin set upon a pallet. It was made of expensive wood and lined with soft cloth. In it lay a woman in a revealing dress of bold red. She wore flashing beads at her throat and wrists. The woman had doused herself with what seemed like gallons of cheap perfume. A whore at final rest. Was it Miss Graham's sister?

Diana stepped in to see. And the woman rose up. Mister Park shouted a warning and leapt forward with his cudgel raised to strike. Diana jumped in between, then saw something gleam at her and ducked aside just in time to avoid a knife so sharp that, although it barely brushed her, it sliced through her dress like a whisper. Mister Park swung around to strike again, then stopped. The knife cut seemed to have taken everything out of the whore. She sagged back on the satin pillow. But her eyes were still open and angry red. Her skin was yellow with oozing sores.

Diana asked her name. She got an obscene curse for an answer. She asked for Miss Graham. Another curse. And then the children. Five, weren't there? A short silence. She asked again. More silence. The woman began babbling. Meaningless babble. Except for a few obscenities, Diana couldn't make out a word. For a moment she thought wildly of that child Emmett had tended. The child with the pox. The only one alive in a community of corpses. What was her name? Emmett was insistent she remember. It was important to the child, he said. As were the other names in the commune. As she faced the dying whore, the names escaped her. Every single one of them that she had committed to memory. Ah, well, perhaps the shock. When this was over, she would recall. Yes, she certainly would. But she never did.

"Ricketts," the whore was muttering. "Ricketts. They took 'em off to Ricketts's."

Diana knew to enter that amphitheater requisitioned for the poor was to be sentenced to death. Although, hadn't she heard it had been abandoned, the dying moved to the great, dilapidated mansion Andrew Hamilton had built many years ago on Bush Hill? In either case, she feared for the children and Miss Graham—if, indeed, the whore was Miss Graham's sister. Diana had no other options but to assume she was. She left the woman to die in peace in the final resting place she had so carefully prepared.

They retraced their steps back down Water Street, up Race, and then cut across to the High. Then past Diana's house to the circus. There were no bands to greet them this time. No crowds of eager people with shillings in their hands to press on the ticket takers. No one about at all, except a great crow sprawled noisily in a heap of dust by the entrance. It squawked at them as they entered, and Mister Park brandished his cudgel, but it paid him no mind. Inside the place was dark. The stands empty, the ring littered with garbage, bed ticking, and mounds of moldy blankets.

The last time she was here with Dolly Todd, the seats were packed until they were groaning. The wooden roof strained with the huzzahs, Mister Ricketts amazing one and all with his feats. The colors of the audience's dress flashed, colors to make a rainbow envious. But now no one could imagine there had ever been anything like a circus here. The only smell was the cloying, musty scent of stale blood and human waste.

They searched among the heaps of greasy blankets. They found two corpses, neither of them Miss Graham. Several more were lying in the stands, the fresh wounds of the lancet marking their arms. A few pitiful dribbles of blood stained the ground next to them, all that was left. Someone screamed from a side room off the stands. A woman. Mister Park and Diana rushed off.

Two black women were trying to load a middle-aged white woman on a stretcher, her skin the telltale yellow of the fever. She was begging them not to take her. Not to Bush Hill. She had survived this place, she pleaded. Let her stay. In an hour or so she would be well enough to make her own way home. As she wept and pleaded, tears streamed down their own faces as they pleaded in return: be calm, missus. They have doctors there. And medicine. Even food and drink. Help us, missus. No, no, please, missus. Don't fight us so. Finally she went limp. The black women noticed Diana and Mister Park. Not a word was exchanged. No need to. The woman had won. She was dead.

Diana and Mister Park set off for Bush Hill. They found Miss Graham. She was lying on the clumps of dead vegetation that had once been a lawn and garden. Around her were fifty others, some dead, others moaning and weeping bitterly in their misery. There was no remorse so great as that brought on by the yellow fever, it was said, and Diana knew it now to be true and no hoary folktale. Miss Graham was alive but unconscious, waiting to be carried inside to join the hundreds there for treatment. A young doctor paused over a man on the lawn to watch as Diana helped Mister Park lift Miss Graham up and over his heavy shoulders. The doctor didn't protest as they walked away. In fact, Diana thought for a moment that he looked relieved. Then he went back to work with his bloody lancet.

They carried her to Elm Court and laid her in her own bed. Diana nursed her for a week. Slowly she regained her health. Mister Park died three days later. His death was unusually swift. But it was the fever just the same.

As for the five children, Diana never found out whether they were real or part of the fiction Miss Graham had invented to hide her sister's seamy business. She tried to ask, but Miss Graham would always just stubbornly shake her head and go about her tasks in that firm, bustling manner she had.

Miss Graham stayed with Diana for another ten years, until her death by natural causes. And she never, ever was heard to speak again.

Allan Cole & Chris Bunch

CHAPTER TWENTY-EIGHT

THEY BURIED MISTER Park in the Lutheran cemetery. He was a Methodist. But it was the only cemetery open. Just as Reverend Helmuth was one of the few ministers to stay with his flock to the last.

Diana quite liked the little minister. The man confessed that for a time he went through much soul searching. It seemed as if so many more Lutherans were dying than Quakers, or Catholics, or Methodists. Each day the boy he kept at the gate issuing tickets for burial saw scores of people arrive. The poor brave grave digger, a Mister Martin Brown, toiled all day burying corpses no one else would touch. The Lutheran driver was one of the few men who would lift a corpse into its box.

At first the good reverend assumed there were so many Lutherans dying because the people of his flock were relatively poor. He prayed it wasn't also because his people were greater sinners than the others. Then he realized there was no place else for people of other faiths to be buried. There was nothing else to be done but have the corpses convert to Lutheran. When he finally understood this, Reverend Helmuth ended the small charge required for burial.

Before the fever ended, one thousand would be buried in the tiny cemetery.

* * * *

The city was coming apart. The clocks had all stopped because there was no one to tend them. Sometimes the watch called the wrong hour the whole night because they were given the wrong time. The stories grew worse. Nurses looted patients. Hearses were sent for, and living bodies placed in coffins to avoid the bother of waiting until they were properly dead. Even heroes fell. Captain Sharp, of local Revolutionary War fame, hid himself in his room for days while his wife lay dying. The only people on the streets seemed to be doctors, nurses, bleeders, or the servants of the dead. The true heroes were the small people, many of them black. Sarah Bass, a widow Diana knew, went from home to home, nursing the sick far into the night. Another woman, Mary Scott—also black—nursed for fifty cents a day. Barely enough to keep herself alive. Many times she charged nothing. When one poor old woman insisted she name a price, Mrs. Scott answered: "... a meal, missus, on some cold winter's day." Caesar Cranchal, a friend of Mrs. Leclerc, refused all offers of pay for his help. He said it would be wrong. He couldn't sell life for money. Even if he should die himself. Which he did.

Meanwhile, misery heaped upon misery. The living starved and went about in rags, and the dead were to be envied. At least it was over. No more awful suspense. Diana finally had enough. She went to see Lydia Clarkson, the mayor's wife. Diana wasn't the only one who had decided to seize the reins if she could. There were other men and women like her who seemed to have come to the same conclusion at the same time, all of them middle-class or less. Merchants and carpenters and brick layers, salt makers and butchers; and shopkeepers like herself. Somehow order must be returned. Later, Diana thought the simultaneous decisions came because the rich and landed had fled. Ordinary people finally realized they held their fate in their own hands. Not unlike Dr. Franklin's jest about the plague ending in the Sugar Islands, she thought, when the last of the medical men had gone.

Lydia told her that scores of people had been to see the mayor. An organization was already beginning: the city had been divided into ten districts, and brave volunteers had come forward to police the area and see to the needs of the healthy as well as the sick. Streets were starting to be cleaned, the garbage carried away by scavengers—at musket point if necessary. Word had gone out all over the land for food, clothing, drink, anything at all that could be spared. No

Allan Cole & Chris Bunch

one knew if the cry would be answered. Even the greediest traders had stopped coming into the city.

A dark bit of plague humor summed it up for Diana. It seemed there were two Germantown farmers who had heard of the plague, but also had heard of the incredible prices being offered at market. They could not resist. The farmers found the city yellow as a pumpkin patch and filled with terrible odors. A breeze came up. The smell wafted over a crowd and ten fell instantly dead. The deadly wind shifted for the farmers. They ran screaming, but it overtook them. Both fell to the ground, one dead, the other senseless. The surviving farmer came to several hours later. Instantly he rushed to market, where he received five and nine for butter and four shillings for eggs. He returned home with fat pockets and sorrowful tales. The next day he loaded up his wagon again to return to Philadelphia. His wife wept and pleaded with him. How could he dare the plague again? "Be quiet, woman," he thundered back. "At four shillings an egg, I'd dare the Devil himself!"

The problem with supplies is what Diana wanted to see Lydia about. She had a plan, but she required wagons and drivers to carry it out. Lydia agreed. There was no need to consult her husband. He would support her in whatever she decided.

* * * *

Diana sent for Mister Park's sons, Bob and Little Tom. They were brutes in size and intelligence, but not in demeanor. They always had such sweet smiles on their faces that you had to forgive them their stupidities. She carefully explained what she wanted, watching closely for signs of fear. She saw nothing except dumb smiles and nods. Off they went, leaving her to feel a bit like she was sending them to the hangman. They scoured the city for Diana's lads—the peddlers. A dozen or more remained. She had packs waiting, filled to the brim with little baubles and trinkets for the farm women. All gifts.

She also sent the dolls, dressed in her finest. To each one was pinned a letter. A letter begging for help.

* * * *

On October 1, seventy died. On the fifth, Father Fleming was buried. On the seventh, the toll was eighty-two. Ninety on the eighth. More than a hundred on the ninth. The same on the tenth. And on the eleventh of October, Black Friday, 120 people breathed their last.

The weekend of the twelfth, another storm broke. It rained steadily for two days. The following two days the weather was brisk. The death toll was lighter. People began hoping the end of the plague was in sight. Then sixty died. Then eighty. And then eighty-one. At any one time, Lydia Clarkson said, at least six thousand people were ill.

Little Tom took sick and died. Diana knew it was she who had killed him. She ordered the house scoured and painted. The court itself she had flushed out with precious water. She did her best not to shiver at the mosquito swarms the water attracted. She had more oil poured on the worst of the standing pools to murder the wrigglers. But the luck that had been with her from the start seemed to end with Little Tom's death. The stable man followed. Then his assistant. Her cook, Mrs. Kenrick, became ill. But she rallied, with no apparent danger of relapse. Diana and the rest huddled in the house. Waiting. Who was next?

The first wagon crossed the river on October 21. It was from the Widow Grubb of Chester, who clutched one of Diana's dolls in her hand. The wagon was heaped with supplies. Diana wept as the lad helped the driver unload the wagon into the city's warehouse. She prayed it wasn't the last. More wagons came, and livestock, and blankets and medicines and clothing. And not just from Diana's farm women. The city's pleas were finally being heard. Within three days, 36,000 pounds of goods had arrived, and there were more crossing the river; so many that the ferrymen were shamed out of hiding at last and the long wait on the far banks of the rivers ceased.

A Daughter Of Liberty

Like magic, it rained again on October 21. The temperature dropped to the mid-fifties and a brisk wind blew in from the seas, sweeping away the smell of smoke and the enormous insect swarms. The death toll dropped to fifty-four, then thirty-eight, then twenty-five. On Sunday, October 27, only twelve people died. The plague was over.

On October 28—again like magic—the first packets returned. People poured back into Philadelphia. Boards came off the windows of shops and houses. The heavers went back to work at the docks. The ships came in to unload their goods. Within a week all seemed normal.

The people who returned found a place different from what they had left. The streets were sparkling, the marketplace cleaner than anyone had ever seen it. The crowds of beggars had dwindled to nearly nil. The same with the poor, and the orphaned. It was no wonder, Diana thought, because most of them had died.

Some said it was human spirit that conquered the plague—people like Diana, or Absalom Jones, or Lydia and Matthew Clarkson, who finally forced their will upon the fever. Others said it was the last storm that cleared the air and ended the drought. A few said it was proof of the power of prayer—even though most of the ministers had fled their flocks.

But Diana always believed the end came for different reasons. A little over a week prior to the arrival of the Widow Grubb's wagon, Dr. Rush had been publicly branded a fool. Already his colleagues were turning their backs on his drastic cure, and had adopted far milder methods of treatment. Methods that at least allowed the body to heal itself if the fever gave it the chance. The number of deaths, she noted, plummeted from that time.

The plague's final toll was never counted. Gravestones held no clues. It was the rare person's grave that had a mark. And what of all the corpses that had no name? And never would? Some said the death toll was over ten thousand. Others mocked this, charging this figure only counted people of means. Twenty thousand was the number they favored. Diana would live to see even this eclipsed by scholars who said it was more like thirty thousand. From a city of 55,000.

Whatever the number. Diana only knew this: there was one murderer in this piece. The man who slew her friends. And thousands of others. He was a famous man. One of the signers of the Declaration of Independence. A hero. A man of science, renowned even abroad.

Before the plague, Diana didn't believe in Hell. She thought the notion superstitious. Now she believed, prayed, even, that the hell-fires burned as eternally and painfully as promised. For it, she had some fuel. A great villain she was sure would make a lovely flame.

His name was Dr. Benjamin Rush.

CHAPTER TWENTY-NINE

FARRELL HAD DECEIVED her. For weeks he'd been
sending bleak progress reports from Boston. The chandlery
was in worse shape than Ruth had portrayed. He complained
it was near impossible to keep Isaac's generous fingers out of
the till. Each time he'd won agreement, Isaac would find a
charming way to circumvent him. But then he would assure
Diana he only required a bit more time. The potential for the
business was great, he said. He only needed a means to
exploit it more fully, then leave the day-to-day operation in
Samuel's capable hands.

At first Diana was sympathetic. She could imagine dear,
dumb Isaac, wrinkling his brow as Farrell spoke. Nodding at
the wisdom falling from his nephew's mouth. And he would
agree. Oh, Lord, would he agree. Yes, I see it now, he would
mourn. You've shown me the way. Ah, if only I had a bright
lad like you at my side all these years, we would have
whipped the world, nephew. Whipped the world.

There would be no flummoxing in this. For that moment
as he feverishly paced the room, brimming with newfound
energy, Isaac would believe. A moment later he would
forget. And it would be business—all bad—as usual. Ruth
would be no help. Diana'd met few people of either sex who
were as big flibbertigibbets. She was the most amiable
woman in the world, but she had this way of drifting through
life, closing her eyes when there was some obstruction, and
trusting to God that somehow she would avoid it. Diana
loved them both and knew they were as well-matched a
couple as any two people could be.

In a way, Isaac was Ruth's strength. If she could get his
attention for only a moment, Isaac would do anything Ruth
required. And unlike most men, Isaac would never dream of
ordering his wife around. If Ruth held a view that he or
others opposed, then be damned to all of us, love. Do it your

way. If it turns out wrong, well, bless you, at least your conscience will be clear.

Their daughter Mary had wed a shipping clerk who took to drink whenever there was a downturn at the harbor. The word drifted back that Joe O'Donnel was laying hands on Mary. Isaac showed up at the clerk's door and horsewhipped him so badly the man was abed for a week. It was said by the neighbors that from that point on, the fellow would jump from his skin whenever a passing coachman cracked his whip.

It was true there were few things to admire in Isaac. But what few there were, Diana admired vastly. So she was tolerant of the many delays. And she didn't catch Farrell's deception. Perhaps it was because of her affection for Isaac and Ruth. Or perhaps because she was still in shock from the summer of terror.

It was Farrell himself who revealed the deception. A letter came so thick, it cost five dollars to retrieve. The first part was page after page of black confessions, Farrell beating his breast, donning a hair shirt, flogging himself for his lies. Could she ever forgive him? And he could never blame her if she refused.

The situation boiled down to this: the business was hopeless. He'd known it from the beginning. The chandlery wasn't even worth selling. Far better to close it and make a settlement on Isaac and Ruth. It wasn't all Isaac's fault. People liked him, trusted him. He was good at drawing new trade. No, the real fault lay with Boston. The city was constantly depressed. Even when the money flowed elsewhere like a great river, in Boston it was less than a trickle down a creek.

Very well. But Diana had a better solution. She had been thinking of starting a chandlery in Philadelphia. And she realized her own far-flung affairs were nearing the bursting point. She would soon need much help. Loyal help. Which meant family. As she read Farrell's confession, she resolved to pluck the entire Shannon clan out of Boston.

Then she turned the page to see why Farrell had been lying to her. It seems there was this girl . . .

. . . Her name was Constance O'Hara, and she was the most wonderful girl Farrell believed ever existed. So pure, so admirable in every human trait, Farrell wanted to shout her name from the mountaintops. Diana found herself giggling. Constance? Constance? She could imagine the echo. She could also imagine the woman her Farrell would love. Some hawk-faced spinster. Diana knew the woman would drive her mad, disapproving of everyone's views except her own. Butter wouldn't melt in her mouth. She wouldn't lift a finger at the smallest chore; as helpless as any female who had existed since the time of Eve.

It was all very un-Farrell-like. Especially the remaining part, which begged for her quick permission to marry. If it were anyone else but Farrell, Diana would assume from the frantic tone that there had been some heavy dallying in the meadow. Well, maybe she was wrong. Maybe . . . But Farrell? Impossible!

Diana was wrong. She met Constance at the wedding a few weeks later. All her preconceived notions went out the window. She was a pretty, dark-haired little bundle that approached her and offered a hand in greeting.

And the first words out of her mouth were to call her Connie. "I hate Constance," she said, "and Connie isn't much better. But at least with Connie you know I might have a glass of ale with you if asked. It might also give you an inkling of my views ... A Constance would never allow the word 'obedience' to be removed from the marriage ceremony. But someone named Connie would agree with the modern view. You'd have to hit me over the head to get me to say it."

Diana burst out laughing. Constance O'Hara— correction—Connie O'Hara, was incredible. Flashing eyes. Sparkling wit. Even in repose there was a smile on her face. She found humor in any situation. Just before the ceremony she sidled up and gave Diana a grin and turned in profile to pat the flat little stomach beneath the white wedding gown. "I don't show too much yet, do I?" she said. But it was with a giggle. Not real concern.

Things grew odder as Diana got to know Connie. Little comments about the courtship. How Farrell had overwhelmed her with passion. She never had a chance to keep her knees together, she said. Diana was incredulous. Farrell? Tripping a girl into the hay? Overcoming Connie's maidenly fears? She had to keep looking at him to make sure they were talking about the same young man. Yes, there he was. Farrell. As tight-lipped as ever. But then Connie would slip up behind him on some small pretext. And from the yelps Farrell would give, Diana was sure she had just pinched him ... or worse.

Connie proved to be no opportunist looking to snare a man for his money. Or, more correctly, Diana's money. She was the only child of Tom O'Hara, a tavern keeper who owned The Coachman, one of the finer establishments of its kind in Boston, always alive with young men and women attending the many fashionable levees and assemblies. This gave Connie a keen business mind—obviously one of the first things that had attracted Farrell. Diana saw her trim little figure, heard the saucy laugh, and corrected herself. No. Not the first thing.

At the reception, where she met Connie's mother and father—and they were just as genuine and light-spirited as their daughter—she pulled James Emmett aside. He was fifteen, towering over her, gangly, neck crooked, elbows askew—and he seemed to be getting handsomer with each passing month. But he was still just as full of mischief, and his lips twitched in amusement as his mother searched for the correct words. "How did they, uh . . ."

"Meet? At an assembly. The O'Haras had a dance a week or two after we arrived."

"Oh. That's nice. Then, uh . . ."

"It was amazing, Mother. They spoke for the first time at the punch bowl. I was standing right there with Farrell, and then she walked up. Suddenly, it was as if I never existed.

Allan Cole & Chris Bunch

They only had eyes for each other. It was like that the whole night. Then Connie invited him to dinner with her father and mother. One thing led to another. They had a picnic."

"A picnic? Oh, I see." As if that explained anything. But she didn't know how to go on. Trust James Emmett to take the initiative.

"Farrell rented a carriage and they went for a ride in the country. Then there was a big storm. And they were, uh . . . forced to take shelter. Honest, Mother. You can ask Mr. and Mrs. O'Hara."

"Oh, I believe it," Diana lied.

"It was an old farmhouse. The people wouldn't let them in. But they got leave to use the barn. I guess it was comfortable. They were gone two days."

Diana gave James a sharp look. He was amusing himself with her. But he was keeping it hidden, except for the light in his eyes. James Emmett was growing up. Just as, apparently, had Farrell.

The wedding was in early January. Diana left alone for Philadelphia shortly after, with the understanding the entire clan would join her in two months. She hurried home to make plans. The new chandlery. A few business ideas she could investigate now that she would have more dependable people to operate them. And room for everyone to live. Diana thought the first thing she'd do was buy a house for Farrell and Connie. A big house. With a nursery. If her instincts were correct, the nursery would be sorely needed.

This time Diana was right. Seven children followed. In eight years.

* * * *

Jack Reilly was his name and he was a master weaver from Donegal. He had fled Ireland two years before, and his only possession besides the clothes on his back was an ancient two-bar treadle loom. For a time it was the most famous loom in the city.

She'd been introduced to him by Mrs. Kenrick, also from Donegal, who said Reilly was the greatest weaver in a region where mere excellence was considered mediocre. But she warned Diana that Reilly was an artist, given to black moods and absolutes. The yellow fever had cut so heavily through the city's textile force that Diana had no hesitation in seeking him out. She needed another weaver. Artistic temperament be damned.

He lived and worked in a one-room basement apartment near Tenth and Lombard, just down from the alms house. There was snow on the ground, and a brisk wind stabbed through her heavy cloak as she made her way down the steep set of stairs. Despite the cold, the door stood ajar and Diana leaned into the gloom, a hesitant hand raised to knock on the jamb. Deep inside she could hear the creak of a treadle and the whiskering back-and-forth rasp of the shuttle as someone smoothly passed it through the warp. Then another creak and a dull thud as the batten fell and then rose again for another pass.

Gradually, she made things out. There was a great fire in the far corner of the room. Mounds of coal stood on either side, with a shovel propped against the mantel, and Diana swiftly totaled the cost of such warmth and wondered how a weaver—especially a moody, difficult one—could afford such comfort.

Vaguely she made out the loom—polished like a chalice and gleaming in the fire. On the other wall she saw the shadow of the weighted warp hanging in its harness, like the web of a marvelous spider. She could see the progress of the weaver in the shadow. The hand holding the shuttle getting ready, the sound of the treadle pushing threads forward, the shadowy hand hurling the shuttle through the warp to be grabbed by the other hand. Treadle down. Treadle up. And the shuttle flew back again.

The outline of a head appeared in the shadow. The weaver. Without speaking, she edged deeper into the room. She could make him out now, the firelight shading his features into dark hollows. His hair was thick and curly and black. His eyebrows were heavy and met nearly in the middle, over a strong nose that was once perfect, but now lightly crooked at the bridge. The chin was square and firm and smooth. The weaver worked naked to the waist. Thick muscles played at his chest and back as heavy arms directed the hands to their delicate task. Sweat rolled freely down his skin, and he glistened as if coated in oil like some ancient wrestler. But his skin was fair. As fair as a maiden's. She had never in her life seen so beautiful a man.

Another step forward. Her foot scraped against a discarded shuttle. She froze, heart hammering. Fear? No. Something else. The movement stopped. The huge head lifted up. She saw his eyes now. Black. Under long dark eyelashes a woman would sell her soul for.

"Mrs. Shannon." Flat. And that was all.

"Would you be Mr. Reilly?"

He nodded. A little impatient. Absently fingering the warp for imperfections, tying off a broken thread. No embarrassment at his naked torso. Waiting for her to speak her piece and leave so he could get back to work.

"Mrs. Kenrick said you might be wanting employment. I pay well. By the piece. And I expect I can provide you more work than you have time."

He nodded again. Absently. As if he were only vaguely interested. He pulled an oily rag from his back pocket and began polishing the loom, smoothing here and there and into secret places where the dust might gather and foul the action. Then out came a bit of beeswax. Stroking and caressing. So tender. As if the wood were his lover . . . and suddenly Diana wanted to be under those stroking hands. The room closed in on her. She could barely draw a breath, and felt hot and confused. The look of him. And all the silence . . .

Then she was angry. What a rude man! To barely acknowledge her. She had come all this way to offer him work. Well, if he didn't care, why should she? "I'll come back some other time," she said. "When you're not so busy."

Diana turned for the door. She heard a small sigh from him, then the treadle creaked and the shuttle began to fly

312

again. As if she had never come. This was too much. She whirled in the doorway. "If you were so busy," she snapped, "why did you ask me to come?"

"What?" The hands had stopped moving again. The brow was furrowed. Puzzled.

"I said, if you were so busy—if you had work enough—why did you tell Mrs. Kenrick to have me come by?"

"Busy? No . . . I'm not so busy. This"—he waved vaguely at the loom—"is for my rent. Mister Beadle said I could make some cloth for his wife. For the rent."

He stared at her. Eyes glowing in the fire. For a moment Diana thought some secret was passing between them. The head lowered and he went back to his task.

"So you do need work. Do you weave twill?"

"Aye. Twill. Nice and tight, and it falls without a crease when I'm done with it. And satins. We like to do a satin weave."

He caressed his loom—one part of the "we."

"I work my own hours," he said. "And I won't put up with poor quality thread. Give it to another weaver. Or send it back to the spinners. Okay, missus?"

She was too bewildered by his manner to get angry again. "Don't you want to know the pay?" she asked.

"It'll be fair," he said. He went back to his loom, shutting her out as if he had closed the door.

The wind was brisker when she left. She shuddered and pulled her coat tight . . . but not against the wind.

* * * *

Diana had often remarked that widowhood produced a strange effect on men. When she was still a girl, she thought it was because men assumed that once a woman had been introduced to regular sex, she couldn't do without, and the death of her husband would leave her panting like a bitch in heat, with no will of her own when there was a fat cock about to pleasure her.

Widows, therefore, became fair game for any man. And that same man was doing the woman the favor of her life by stealing a kiss, pinch, or even throwing her on her back and taking the whole slice whether she agreed or not. When a widow said no, she really meant take the decision from my poor confused hands. Do me as you will! Now Diana also believed this thinking concealed a larger arrogance: most men couldn't bear the thought that any woman could live independently. Rule her own life. Make her own way. Somehow, widowhood—particularly if it involved a widow with looks, or money, or both—was a black mark on all manhood. A threat to the greatest degree to sacred masculinity.

Having experienced this attitude for half her own life, it was with no surprise at all that she saw all the men scramble around the widowed Dolly Todd like bears going silly at a lightning-blasted honey tree. In many ways it was harder on Dolly than it had been on Diana. Beyond her own strong will, circumstances had protected the young Widow Shannon. There really weren't that many eligible men about when she was at her most vulnerable. Secondly, Diana had almost no friends—and certainly no family—to pressure her. Lastly, it was difficult for a man to maintain the posture of the great protector in the wasteland that was Cherry Valley. That same man couldn't assure his own scalp's safety, let alone a woman's.

Like Diana, Dolly was beautiful. Perhaps more so. But she was also well-born. And her husband had left her rich. Although he had been a struggling young lawyer when he died, his parents' death had left a large estate. Solely owned by Dolly. This was a far greater enticement than just a suddenly accessible honey tree. This was a whole forest of such trees. Marriage to Dolly would provide her lovely body for the bed, wealth for investment or leisure, and the powerful influence of her family's name.

The men laid siege to Dolly's mother's house. Not just the young and well-formed and single. Lifelong bachelors, their legs wrapped against the swelling of the gout, were handed down from carriages by their servants or slaves. Bankrupt cripples.

Even the Turkish ambassador pursued her for his harem—which already held eleven wives. He was turned aside by the sight of one of Dolly's cooks, a woman who easily weighed three hundred pounds. When he spied her, he left off his wooing of Dolly. "My God," he breathed, "she's as beautiful as my first wife. A burden fit to stagger a camel." Only some skilled quick talk from Mister Burr kept the diplomat from chasing the cook all through the house.

The siege went on for months. Outwardly, Dolly appeared to be flattered by all the attention. Invitations to dinner and theater and dances flooded her doorstep.

"What do I do, Diana?"

"Refuse them."

"Yes. I know that's what you would do. And have done. But . . . I'm not so strong. I must think what John would have me do. I have our son to raise. John would want to see us both protected, wouldn't he? And . . . forgive me, Diana, but isn't it going against the nature of things? Being without a man?"

"I suppose it is," Diana said. "At least I thought so for any number of years. I would awaken in the night, from some terrible dream. I couldn't remember the dream, but I knew it was . . . about Emmett. Besides a stray child, there was no one in bed with me during those moments. No one to tell my doubts, or to console me. I would lie awake for hours mourning my fate. Wondering . . . No, not wonder. At those times I was sure all I was doing was in error.

" 'Foolish woman,' I would admonish myself. 'A man could take care of all of this. A strong man could lift the burden. Or would know instantly from his vast and superior knowledge exactly what must be done and how to go about it.' Whereas I always had to work from ignorance. Each task and decision was made with difficulty. And I was usually wrong the first time. Sometimes the second. Or the third. It

Allan Cole & Chris Bunch

was so grueling, and humiliating. To get it wrong so many times, before I could get it right."

She stopped, memories of those long nights flooding back. Memories as recent as . . . the night before last. She picked up the teapot with shaking hands, then set it down again, quickly, as she realized that Dolly was silently weeping.

The death of her husband was difficult enough for Dolly to bear. But the same stroke that cut the life from her husband had also taken her infant son. Diana found it remarkable Dolly was even able to speak. To do something so sensible as to seek advice—whether she took it or not. Diana knew women who had gone mad and shut themselves into a room for life after the death of a child. Or even gone after the rest of their children with an axe.

She did her best to ignore the weeping. She pushed aside the tea and poured two glasses of wine. When Dolly was done with tears, Diana had her drink the wine. And then poured her more and went to fetch a scented kerchief to wipe away the tears. Diana waited until all was calm again.

"Do you really want my advice, Dolly, dear? Or just a sympathetic ear? I'm quite willing to provide either, or both. You are a dear friend and it pains me to see you this way."

"Your advice, Diana," Dolly answered. Quite firm. But Diana knew it a lie. She gave it anyway.

"Do nothing," she said. "There is no need to make any kind of decision just now, pro or con. Of the many choices you have, the one that can harm you not at all is to wait. And that is my advice."

Dolly agreed this was the wisest course, indeed. She could see now that no course could be simpler. Dolly would wait and rest and smother young Payne Todd, her surviving son, with love. She would politely accept a few invitations, and politely spurn the rest.

Dolly was back within the month. A man had been introduced to her. No, introduced was not the correct word. Aaron Burr had personally carried this man's request that he be permitted to call on Dolly. He was an important man. A rich man. Older by seventeen years. And one of the greatest heroes of the Revolution.

"And you didn't refuse," Diana said. A statement, not a question.

Dolly hadn't. They had met. And he was courting her now with a passion so furious, all the other men had been frightened away. Despite his age, he was a bachelor. A condition, he said, he was anxious to end now that he had met the beautiful Dolly Payne Todd.

"Do you love him?"

Dolly didn't answer. It was a stupid question anyway. This woman was in no condition to define the term, much less apply it to herself.

"You don't have to marry anyone, Dolly. You're one of the most intelligent women I've ever met. I've never known you to forget a face or a name, and all the little particulars about the smallest person, no matter how briefly met. And this is only one of many talents. You have funds to do as you wish. Become an artist, a poet, or writer. Start a business. Come into business with me. You can do anything you wish, Dolly, dear. Anything."

Dolly thought about this for a long time. They shared another glass of wine while she thought. Then: "You're probably right, Diana. Except . . . it's different for you. As different as flax and silk.'

"In what way is it different?" Diana asked, exasperated. "If I could do it, why can't you? In fact, it should be easier. Considering who you are."

"Exactly why it is harder," Dolly said. "You see, the greatest difference between us is this: you had no choice, Diana. Really. Think about it. What else could you have done?"

Diana had no answer. Dolly left no wiser than when she came. She agreed on one course, at least. To continue to wait. To avoid a decision as long as she possibly could.

Allan Cole & Chris Bunch

But Diana had her doubts how long she could delay. She wouldn't have believed it, but according to the gossip, James Madison made a very ardent beau.

* * * *

The debt collectors put Jack Reilly in prison. He was the Master Weaver of Donegal, but with no head for money. He bought food when hungry, drink when dry, and fuel when cold. It didn't matter a whit that his pockets might be empty, he put what he wanted on account with any merchant who would let him.

The weaver was as easy with his meager funds to his neighbors as he was with the merchants and stall keepers. On those rare days when he had a few coins to click together to thin a debt, the first person he met who seemed in need was as likely to be graced with his silver as his debtor. He ignored threats or cajoling, and it was only a matter of time before the piper would come to collect his final due.

His debtors got together and totaled the sum he owed. It equaled the price of his loom. Give us the loom, they said, and we'll call it square. It was my father's loom, he answered. And before that, his father's. The loom is as dear to me as life itself. And so he refused. Give them the loom, the judge said, and the matter will be settled. Again the weaver refused, and he hid the loom where no one could find it.

Their implorings turned to anger. Especially since the news of his refusal spread among the working folk. He became a minor hero: the great Irish weaver who dared the law for the sake of his ancient loom. This could not go on. The System was being jeopardized. So they put him in prison. A stone cell eight by eight. With no one for company but the jailer. Only bread and thin stew for nourishment. He would be let out, they said, when he released the loom.

Then I'll stay till I die, Jack Reilly said. But he did not mean he would sit in this cell for forty years or more. The instant he said it, he began to refuse food. Days became a week. Then another. If no one intervened soon, he would be dead. Diana knew the creditors. They would not relent.

More than anyone, Diana understood why he would never part with his loom. She'd not gone to his shop since that first time. She employed him, but sent someone else with the order and the materials. She paid the same way. The work was marvelous. He was quick, but his quickness did not harm his art in any way. Diana had never seen such cloth come from any loom. It was almost magical in its feel. Her seamstresses said the needle and thread slipped through it. In any joining there was barely a seam. When the scissors approached it, the cloth seemed to part at a touch, like Moses commanding the sea. But she never personally congratulated him. Or even sent a note. He wouldn't care or appreciate it, she told herself. Which was the truth. But it wasn't the reason she never went to that dark cave with its great fire that he called a shop.

She knew the real reason. Jack Reilly was too dangerous. They had not spoken more than a dozen words or so, and yet Diana knew that if he'd asked at that moment, she would have stripped off her dress and petticoats and laid down for him on the rough ticking of his bed on the floor. Since that meeting, she'd spent too many nights aching for his touch. Dreamed of it. Even during the day—in a quiet moment—desire would suddenly flash. It would vanish just as quickly, but she was left shaking and drained from the violence of her emotions. No, she would keep away from this weaver. It was the wisest course.

It wasn't as if after Emmett she'd never had another lover. She was too practical a person not to realize that the itch sometimes had to be scratched. But they were always, hasty affairs. Rarely more than a night with a handsome stranger passing through the inn. She was the soul of discretion when these affairs occurred, and she had the knowledge—thanks to Abigail Fahey's tutoring—never to get caught out with a swollen belly.

But the weaver was different. This wasn't an itch. It was an obsession, one she was determined to deny herself. When Jack Reilly went to prison, she knew she had lost. But Diana

Allan Cole & Chris Bunch

held firm. Then she learned he was starving himself, and it became more than a battle of wills—although it was her will alone doing the fighting. She was sure the weaver had never given her a thought.

Diana sent funds to pay off his debts, and Reilly was released and went back to his loom. She waited then for him to send some word of thanks. Or an acknowledgment of any kind for what she had done. All this was without reason, because the last thing Diana told herself she wanted was contact of any kind with the man. It was better this way. He would ignore her, and she would become so angry at his selfish soul that she would be done with him once and for all.

Then she could bear it no more. She used the excuse of an important but urgent order for a wealthy customer.

She waited until dusk, gathered up the materials and marched to his shop off Lombard Street. She would present the order, all the while never mentioning the debt of his freedom. She would be cold and aloof, and when done, would march out again as quickly as she had come. It was a test, she told herself. An important test she was sure she would pass. And once passed, she would never have to face it again. But under her dress she wore silk. And in her bag she carried the little sponges and vials of unguents Abigail had taught her to prepare.

Reilly was at work at his loom just as before, the fire roaring and the great shadow of the loom's harness cast on the opposite wall. Once again he didn't notice her until she stood before him. But this time he didn't ask her business. In fact, he didn't speak a word. He just stared at her with his dark and glowing eyes. His torso was as bare as before, but now the fair skin pinched at his bones from his self-imposed starvation. She could smell the scented oil he used to wipe his loom.

She spoke his name, and he flinched like a bee had stung him. "What do you want with me?" he asked.

Now it was Diana who didn't answer. For the first time she felt in command. She took him by the hand and led him to the pallet on the floor. He gave her no resistance as she pulled him down to it, and then tugged off what he wore. She didn't make love to him, she consumed him. As if it were she who had sat without nourishment all that time in the prison cell. When they were done, she fetched a pail of steaming water from the fire. She washed his body from head to toe. And the whole time he uttered not a word, nor made a motion to either help or resist.

She made love to him again. But there was no real satisfaction in it. She lay under him, willing him to speak her name, give any sign of tenderness or awareness that it was she who was there for him. Not just any woman, but she alone. The orgasm was violent. But she bit her lip until it bled to keep from calling out his name. Diana crept home just before dawn, swearing it was over. The itch had been scratched, and she would go back to that place no more.

It was useless. She returned. And returned again. The affair was humiliating, but there didn't seem to be anything she could do to stop. The opposite seemed to be true. The more she had him, the more she wanted. And he treated her no better. Rarely speaking. Staring that stare of his. Forcing her to make the first move. She did everything she could to please him. Fetched food from the marketplace and prepared it with her own hands. He ate without comment. She cleaned the room, built the fire when it grew cold, gave him money so he would never want. Nothing she did seemed to touch the man.

The situation was getting dangerous. She was too well known to keep up such a long affair. Especially since the fever. She was the brave Widow Shannon who had stayed with her staff until the end, taking her chances with everyone else. And wasn't it Mrs. Shannon who had brought in the wagons from the farms to ease their misery? People she had never met would smile at her now when she passed, almost tugging at their forelocks in respect—which angered her Republican soul. She was Diana Shannon, no better or worse than any other man or woman. Wasn't she?

Allan Cole & Chris Bunch

Then one day she was granted her greatest wish. Jack Reilly acknowledged her.

They were lying on the pallet after making love. The weaver was puffing on a cigar she had brought him and sipping at a glass of fine brandy. He turned on his side to speak. "This can't go on," he said. "Not this way. It's no good."

Her heart jammed against her breast. Was he sending her away?

"I think we'll marry," he said. "Yes, that would be best."

Diana was stunned into silence. Marriage? Was this the next step? She hadn't taken it that far. But . . . she had never even said she loved him. And he had certainly never given her a sign that he felt anything at all.

"The dress shop is a good business," the master weaver said. "I'll keep it going. But the rest ... no time, woman. I'll sell it off. Should make a tidy sum. How much do you think it would fetch?" It was the longest speech Jack Reilly had ever made to her. And it was the last.

Without another word, Diana got out of the bed and put on her clothes. She went home—it was early for a change, not long after the eight o'clock watch. She drew a long hot bath, spiced it with perfume and soft oils, and immersed herself. She lay in it for a long time, going over her feelings bit by little bit. Like a person who had just taken a frightening fall, and was now gingerly testing her bones for damage. There was none. She was tired. And regretful that she had been a fool. But it was over.

And be damned to the Master Weaver of Donegal!

* * * *

The course of lust, Diana thought, was far easier than love— at least love as it was meant in this romantic age of fluttering and flirting and long letters protesting undying affection until the end of time.

Dolly held fast to her strategy of delay. She told Diana Mister Madison had begged for her hand in marriage. Swore to her she was the moon and the stars to him. That he had never loved and would never love another, and that to be denied would doom him to a life of despair. Dolly had yet to answer.

She had made one great change. Mister Madison had been encouraging her to be more of a creature of fashion. She should be a modern woman and exchange her white Quaker costumes for all the glorious things she spied daily in shop windows.

Dolly took to high fashion like a peacock denied its feathers since it first cracked the egg. She became one of Diana's best customers, putting all the knowledge she had won by pressing her nose to the window into practice. In a few short weeks she was one of the best-dressed women in Philadelphia. Her only regret was that it had taken so long for her to see it.

Diana knew it was over then. Besides, the pressure had increased to the bursting. Mrs. Martha Washington, wife of the great George, had called Dolly to the President's House only a few days before. Dolly was a frequent visitor there— her sister, Lucy, was married to George Steptoe Washington, the president's favorite nephew. Lucy lived now at Harwood Estate in Jefferson County, Virginia.

Dolly told Diana that Mrs. Washington had pressed her on the matter of her engagement to James Madison, and implied strongly that she and the president would look favorably on the match.

"What did you tell her?" Diana asked.

"That I wasn't sure. But she just said to never mind. There was no hurry. And that she and the president were certain that in the end I would make the proper decision."

"And what is that decision, Dolly? Do you have a clue?"

"No, I don't," Dolly said. "But I can't wait much longer."

She didn't. In September she and a party of gay celebrants rode their carriages to Harwood. Riding beside hers was Mister Madison, and people said he cut a dashing figure on horseback. They were married at her sister's home. The president and his wife were in attendance.

Allan Cole & Chris Bunch

A Daughter Of Liberty

Diana made Dolly's wedding gown.

CHAPTER THIRTY

FAMILY TRADITION HAD it that "golden times" dawned for the Shannons after Diana gathered the clan under one roof. With "Elm Court as her engine and the family at her back"—as Isaac liked to tell it—she "built a glorious machine I ain't seen the likes of in all my years of wander." Elm Court prospered. She not only bought the remaining leases on the court, but her enterprises spilled down Tenth Street to the High, backed up all the way to Chestnut and then filled the little alleys and courts in between.

What she didn't buy and rebuild, she encouraged others to snap up. Especially if the endeavor were complementary to her own. She loaned people money to get started, or became a silent partner. She lost money so rarely that she waxed philosophical when she did and called it just "the cost of doing business." Diana encouraged her employees to take cheap long-term leases in the area and then helped them build homes. She saw it as a means to provide comfort and stability for her workforce, and also improve the value of her own holdings with small investment.

As time passed, some of her people started their own businesses—sometimes even in competition with her. Once again Diana was philosophical. She saw no betrayal in this— "all they owed me was a decent day's work, and they gave me that, so the ledger is clear"—but as the natural order of things. The more competition, she believed, the more new markets would be opened. Gradually the dressmaking side of her business became less the core. Its earnings were credible and continued to grow, but they were overshadowed by Diana's other efforts.

There was the chandlery on the waterfront, where she installed Samuel and his family. A much mellowed Isaac was encouraged to make use of his considerable charm, and with careful management the store became a success. Enough so that Samuel soon found himself running her blossoming riverside trade, ranging from warehouses to a fancy tavern. If she hadn't been pregnant most of the time, Connie would have been perfect to put in charge of the tavern. Mary proved adept at this, but only after Diana had driven off her husband.

Joe O'Donnel had given a great speech of weeping repentance to the entire family, and was allowed to join Mary and the children in Philadelphia. Joe was quiet for months, then Diana learned from a courthouse friend he'd been inquiring among the greedier lawyers in town about forcing his husbandly rights of possession. It was sheer coincidence that shortly afterward he was arrested outside a whorehouse—on a Sunday morning. Mary's husband was given the choice of the stocks and then prison, or the stocks and making himself scarce from the city. O'Donnel wisely chose to leave, clinking some of Diana's coins in his purse as he went.

Mary opened up considerably after his departure. She appeared ten years younger—her look of constant gloom turned to unrelieved cheer—and proved so adept at the tavern business, it became hers to run. Not all went well with the Conners: Samuel lost his first wife to childbirth, a second to the flux—only months after the wedding—and remarried a third time to a woman who seemed too mean not to have a long life.

Connie proved to be one of those rare women whose health and beauty seemed to grow with each pregnancy. It didn't hurt that Diana hovered over her like she was a daughter. Connie benefited from everything Diana had learned from Gramer Fahey on. Although she refused any methods of preventing pregnancy, Connie followed Diana's advice on diet and personal care, and her complexion and figure remained the envy of her friends.

Her first child with Farrell was a son. True to her broad hint to Diana, Luke Shannon was born a little over six months after the wedding. She bore a succession of daughters, naming them after the months they were born in:

April, then February, then January, followed by September, July, and finally another boy. She and Farrell named him David.

Their last child was a girl again. Also born in April. Farrell worried at this like it was an old bone a dog couldn't let go. Two Aprils in a family was an impossibility. But all the girls had been named for the months! What were they to do? Connie went along with this for a while, frowning and pretending that it preyed on her mind at least as much as Farrell's. Came the christening, Connie laughed and named the child Susan.

"But, why Susan?" asked an alarmed Farrell.

"It reminded me of April," she shot back.

"April? April? What does April have to do with Susan?" Farrell whined.

"Simple," Connie answered. "Susan is April's sister." It was one of those legendary Connie answers to which only a fool would respond. When it came to humor, Farrell may have been dim. But not so dim that he didn't know when to put a pin through his lips.

Where Farrell was concerned, Isaac would see no wrong. Despite Farrell's frustration as he struggled with the chandlery in Boston, the two men took a great liking to each other. Oddly, Farrell was the father figure in the match. Isaac weighed every word he said as if it were gold. And Farrell was as protective of his uncle as of his half brother, James Emmett.

"He's a hard man to get to know, our Farrell," Isaac would say. "But it's well worth the wait. And look at him now that he's married Connie! I'm not saying he's gone so far as to master the jig. But I've spied him tapping his feet to the tune! That's a marked difference in the lad, if nothing is!

The "marked difference" lasted about three years. For a time, Farrell beamed under Connie's influence. He grew fat and jovial, with a broad Irish face, cheery eyes, and a dimple in his chin that Connie teased him about and he denied mightily despite the evidence for all to see. But he blushed

pg. 327

the whole time he was denying it, and everyone knew he was secretly pleased.

It was during this period that Farrell and Connie got the habit of stopping by the chandlery in the evening, when the doors were closed, the fire warm, and Isaac and Ruth held forth until the dockside watch called the warning for decent folk to be getting on home. While there was still room on his lap, Isaac would dandle his grandchildren and grandnephews and nieces, and spin tales of distant places and dangerous events. But even when the children became too many and spilled off his lap and all around the floor, Luke Shannon always had the place of honor on Isaac's gnarly right knee.

Farrell always smiled to himself when he saw that, remembering a boy many years ago who'd lost his father. How low he had felt—as cursed as any of God's most miserable creatures—until the sailor spied his plight and made a small excuse to place him on that same knee. It was a secret he shared with Isaac. A secret they'd never spoken of. Later, when Farrell had lost himself forever in a bleak search for his soul, Isaac was the only person besides Connie who could cheer him, make him laugh at himself. It was only during those evenings at the chandlery that he would let down his guard, suspend judgment and listen to Isaac spin his wild tales with Luke perched on his knee.

Luke Shannon was enthralled with his uncle's stories. There was Cherry Valley. Isaac would tell how he wandered far across the snows to find his wife and children.

How he met Diana and begged her to come back with him to safety.

"But your grandmother would have none of it," he said. "She just coolly fired her musket over my shoulder, killing a savage as he was about to lift my hair. And calm as you please—charging her musket as she spoke—she said, 'Thank you for your kind offer just the same, Mister Conners, but I think I'll tarry a bit whilst the Indians are still tame.'

"I recall looking down the road after we left and seeing her mournful figure there. With that brave head of tempting red hair. I thought I'd never see her again. ... I was wrong, and the rest is history. Perhaps we ought to have stayed. What would things be like? Maybe the Conners would be as rich as the Shannons. Sure we would. As sure as the sun comes up at midnight, and the summer winds off the Sugar Islands tame the sea."

Like any fine tale-teller, Isaac was also a good listener. He'd set the stage for Cherry Valley, then throw the floor open to others who'd lived there. If the teller was too humble, Isaac would break in with exclamations at their brilliance or bravery, or sheer luck. Isaac always made another's luck sound like genius on his or her part. His own he described as dumb, or blind. But then Isaac always made himself the butt of his own stories.

It was at the chandlery that Luke and the other children were first introduced to their long-dead grandfather, Emmett Shannon. "It was my misfortune not to know him," Isaac said. "But you should understand this: he was a hero, your grandfather was. And heroes are born to die young. It's the tears in the blessings the Lord gives us. And Emmett was a hero, no doubt of it. Even his enemies would say so. Bastards that they are . . . excuse the language, dear."

"My grandfather had enemies?" Luke would ask. It was always the same question, but it always led to something new.

"Oh, yes, indeed he did. Tell him, Ruth. And that brute who apprenticed him. And what young Emmett did about it." And Ruth would tell the story about her brother's trick on the sawpit master.

"The Hessian," Isaac would remember. "The great weasel of a Hessian who tried to turn a kindness into his own dirty tricks. Tell them about the Hessian, Diana!"

Diana was a good storyteller as well. If Emmett was larger than life in the telling of these stories, what was the harm? To the children he was a saint, a genial rogue, a sinner, a loving husband, a man of peace, a hero who threw away his life without a thought. Emmett was none of those

pg. 329

Allan Cole & Chris Bunch

things. But then it would come to the moment in the tale when Diana would draw out the old leather pouch she wore about her neck. And lay the rifle ball that was her wedding ring upon a grubby little palm for inspection. For that moment, Diana would believe.

Luke soaked this in. And yes, he thought his grandfather was a great hero of long ago. But he was dead. Before him he saw his grandmother. An Indian fighter in the flesh. He hoped all the Indians wouldn't be gone before he grew up. This worried him. It must have been a hundred years ago or more. Finally, he asked Diana the crucial question: "Uh . . . Grandmother, please?"

"Yes, Luke, dear?"

"How . . . old are you?"

"Forty-one," Diana said without hesitation. She had an idea what was going on inside the boy's head. Swirling fantasies of high adventure.

But Luke still wasn't sure. "Is forty-one more than a hundred, Grandmother?"

Diana laughed and tousled his hair. "Don't worry yourself, young Luke," she said, "there'll be plenty of adventure left when you're of age. Indians and pirates aplenty. Ask your Uncle Isaac. He went a-pirating once."

Luke didn't need to be prodded. Nor did Isaac, because there was no topic of conversation more pleasing than the sea. For Luke, the fact that Isaac Conners had been a pirate put his great-uncle into the realm of the gods and ancient warrior kings. Luke soon became equally enamored with the sea. First it was the stories and his endless questioning for detail. In the early days it was asking what it was like to board a ship. Did the cutlass hurt when you held it between your teeth? How many cannonballs did it take to sink a ship? And when the ship sank, could you get it back? Later, the questioning grew more sophisticated, even expert. Luke would finger items in the chandlery and ask their names and their intention. Or he would pose a problem in navigation, or geography. This alone was enough to endear the boy to Isaac.

But he was also such a bright, ingenuous lad that Isaac had to love him.

"He'll be into mischief, that one," Isaac would laugh. "He's more like his grandfather. The great rogue. Or his uncle, James Emmett. You don't mind my saying so, do you, Jim? No, I thought not. Teach your nephew cards, James. It's a talent I think this boy will have sore need of."

James Emmett was another Isaac would speak no ill of. In this, he was far worse than his protector, Farrell. Any misadventure would immediately draw a comment, like: "The lad must have had his reasons. We should try and see it his way." Perhaps it was James Emmett's natural charm. More likely, the old man lived vicariously in his adventures.

James Shannon never actually left home, he drifted away. He had no interest in business or money, except as a marker in his play or a tool to get him what he wanted. At sixteen his skill at cards and connivance cut him from the need for Diana's purse. Farrell became so busy with his own life—and later his absorption with self-pity—that he lost all control over his half brother. But sometimes James would still come creeping to Farrell's house, his clothing torn and bloody, his pockets empty, and Farrell would go to his aid just as in the old days. But those times became fewer and fewer as James roamed farther afield, then almost dropped from sight. The last time he returned, it was not for assistance. And the meeting ended in a fight—an Irish feud with the bitterness lasting until both men were dead.

The fight was over Luke. He was the first and greatest victim of the change that overtook his father. In the early days Diana blamed it on the demon that was stalking the land. A demon bearing book and cross.

It started in the hinterlands. Her peddlers brought her tales of a great religious upwelling. Frontier orators shook the sky with their voices, crying out against the materialism of the cities. They saw Satan roaming the cobblestone streets. A Satan who had set his sights on the common folk and was now marching off into the forests and plains to recruit them.

This demonic evil was personified by men like Thomas Jefferson—a disbeliever and a great devil to many of these people. Evidence of the threat was the growing power of the Democratic-Republicans.

A preacher would pitch his tent in a distant valley. The word would go out and entire families would travel hundreds of miles to hear him scald sin with his boiling rhetoric. Thirty thousand or more would come. Wagons and tents, or just campfires, spread out to the edge of the forest. At night, one peddler said, when darkness was as thick as a new quilt, you could see all the fires with their red, flickering eyes. And the spirit would come on the people like a thunderclap, voices weeping and shrieking with remorse, people collapsing on the ground, speaking in tongues. Or a sudden wave of hilarity would sweep across the crowd until the hillsides rang with all the mad laughter.

Diana was too young to know much about the "Great Awakenings" that had come before this time, although she would live long enough to understand that revivalism and national self-loathing were cyclical. As inexplicable but as certain as the killing fevers that descended upon Philadelphia every so many Summers. Regardless, when it first began, she blamed this for the troubles that had overtaken Farrell.

There was no single event or cause one could put a finger to. One moment Farrell was the comparatively jovial man Connie was nurturing into being. The next, he was austere, passing dark judgment on trifles. He attended mass with heightened fervor. He became a figure of power in the parish. However, so harsh was his view on matters of sin that even the priest grew alarmed that Farrell and his faction would drive away the common folk.

Farrell shed weight like a man being consumed from within by a ravenous worm. He stopped short of skeletal, but added to the specter of his appearance by taking to wearing black. His business judgment was the first noticeable thing to suffer. Always a cautious man, Farrell became so conservative, so critical of every detail, Diana lost faith in him. After all those years of depending on Farrell for his understanding of what she was about, this was a difficult loss to Diana. As was the realization that although she loved him, she no longer liked Farrell very much. This dislike came not from business, however, but from his treatment of Luke, and eventually, David.

The daughters—from April to Susan—Farrell left for Connie to raise as she saw fit. But he would allow no interference when it came to his view on how to deal with his sons. Connie was such a wonderfully warm and patient woman that she managed to slightly balance the effects of the harsh treatment of the boys. And it was to her credit alone they managed to emerge somewhat whole. Farrell believed in an iron hand with his sons and a sharp switch to make his points.

Luke would never forget the time he and a friend "borrowed" a skiff from the docks. It was an old and useless thing, so shot with wormholes the two small boys spent as much time bailing as sailing. Still, he thought it a wonderful adventure. They spent the afternoon playing pirate, spying out rich merchant ships suitable for plunder. With only a scrap of canvas for a sail, Luke scooted among the great ships, calling out greetings to the crews. He was hailed once by a grand captain, who shouted out an offer to join him as first mate. The day ended without incident. Oh, there were a few obscene words from the drunk who owned the wreck of a skiff when they returned it to its proper place. But Luke had left a few coppers on the bench to soothe the man's temper. It wasn't enough.

Farrell's face was black fury when he returned home. "I'm raising a thief, God forgive me," he shouted.

"We didn't steal it, Father," Luke tried to explain. "We only borrowed it. I paid him as well, sir."

"Don't lie, sir," his father thundered. "Don't add that abominable sin to your soul. You are a thief. But I see you are blind to the meaning of the word. Well, I shall teach you, Luke. It will be a lesson you will never forget."

Allan Cole & Chris Bunch

A Daughter Of Liberty

Farrell whipped Luke until his shirt and breeches were soaked with blood. Luke learned the lesson well. The difference between borrowing and thieving. He also learned to become a skillful liar where his father was concerned.

Diana worried about Farrell's treatment of his oldest son. Luke was mischievous, although not as much as James Emmett. But small scrapes were built by his father into offenses against God and society. Although she would never openly criticize her husband, Connie was helpless in this matter. Perhaps she feared she would lose her freedom to deal with her daughters. Diana couldn't say, and she hesitated for a long time to even hint at criticism. When it came to parenting, Diana knew she stood on shifting ground. Look at her success with James Emmett, for example. Or the other child she had reared. Farrell. Diana believed herself a failure as a parent and saw this failure as fatally weakening any objection or advice she might have.

For a time only Isaac seemed to have some power over Farrell's grim moods. Even after his reconversion to Catholicism, Farrell went along with the rest of the family to those evenings at the chandlery. And Isaac could still manage a smile from him. Or an agreement to temper his punishments of Luke. Then one morning Ruth awoke to find Isaac cold beside her. He'd died in his sleep with no illness to warn anyone. The family mourned him deeply. But no one—except possibly Ruth—mourned him more than Farrell.

If he were iron with Luke before, now he was steel. As the child entered his teens, Farrell would rage for hours about the growing villainy of the young in the city. The lapse of family values. The questioning of institutions by the public. A morality that somehow had gone so astray, people were not paying their rightful debts. In proof of his point, the prisons were filled to the overflowing with debtors. So full, that people were being released after a short time with just their word to pay as bond. So there would be room in the cells for others. This, he said, was the reasoning for his firm hand with Luke and David. Someday they would thank him for it.

Diana saw no breakdown, or even a pinhole in the fabric. For some time now, she believed, the money situation had strayed off any sensible path. With few exceptions, the great cities were barely gaining in population. People were swarming to the frontiers and there were few to replace them—not since the British caused the price of passage for Irish emigrants to rise four hundred fold. There was a shortage of labor, especially skilled labor. But all along the coastline, merchants and bankers joined with the failing Federalists to keep wages at a minimum. Which required a great pool of unemployed. The docks and tenements and streets of Philadelphia were swarming with them, fighting without seeming reason, stealing at will, committing arson so they could loot freely when they were called out to quell the fire. Conditions had so deteriorated, it seemed there were more rum shops, pawnbrokers, and soup societies than people.

In Diana's view, the causes of all this were unnecessary.

But what could she do about it? She paid her own employees an enlightened wage. But this was nothing compared to the overall problem. She argued her view heatedly with other business people. But as a woman, her thoughts were dismissed. Despite her successes, most men saw Diana's abilities as a freak of nature, like the armless fiddler she saw on the river many years ago who played his tunes with his feet. So they paid her no mind.

Then Luke ran away. The first time, he was thirteen. He was big for his age, so he soon found himself aboard a coaster. Luke had a vague goal in mind: Jamestown. The last place James Emmett had written from. Luck was with the boy, and he quickly found his uncle. James Emmett was at the card tables in a tavern playing for high stakes with planters whose judgment had been impaired by inbreeding, alcohol, and sudden wealth from cotton.

It was at a crucial point in the game, but James made no complaint or gave no hint of bother when he saw Luke standing there so many miles from home. Luke knew this because he watched him carefully when greeted, and would have taken to his heels if impatience had crossed his uncle's features. Instead, James Emmett folded his hand on the spot and threw his arms around Luke, thumping him mightily and joyfully on the back. Then he swept them both out of the tavern without a look behind him as the planters raked in his silver. Some months later that same group would lose it all back to James Emmett—with a plantation thrown in for good measure.

James listened intently to his nephew's troubles. When Luke said it was his plan to join him or to seek his fortune elsewhere, he made no objection. But he asked the boy to swear a promise first. They would return to Philadelphia. Both of them would confront Farrell. James would reason with his brother, urge him to give Luke a chance. "He won't," Luke said.

"I'm not saying your father will change. I'd be lying if I even suggested that as a possibility. You just need some breathing room, Luke. And a few more years of seasoning. Then you can join me anyplace or anytime you like, and I'd be proud to call you partner!"

James accompanied Luke home. Connie collapsed in tears when she saw her son. But Farrell went to cut a stick. James stopped him and asked for a word in private. No one in the family ever learned what passed between them. There were only shouts from the closed study to give a sign. Luke sat next to the door listening. At first there were comfortable-sounding mutters from inside. But then the mutters were broken by a great shout:

"You'll not tell me how to raise my own son!" Followed by: "You! Of all people!" And then: "I've protected you your whole life and this is how I'm repaid!"

Then Luke heard Farrell shout something about, "... if our father were alive ..."

James shouted back: "... he would agree with me! You're nothing like our father ... no right to use his name ... if anyone is like Father, it's me!"

The voices dropped again. Luke could hear his uncle's tone change. Forced reasonableness. Apologies for saying things the wrong way. All the things he knew would work with his half brother, a man he had always been able to win over to his side. Farrell cursed him. A mild oath, but shocking from his lips. And Luke knew all was lost.

His uncle's voice rose in a desperate, pleading wail: "My God, Farrell! It's Brian, I'm telling you! All because of Brian. That's all. Can't you see it?'

His father screamed something unintelligible at the mention of the name.

"Don't do this, Farrell," his uncle pleaded. "Don't send me away with those words as fresh as new blood on your lips. I'll not be able to return. Ever."

Silence swelled, then a chair was flung back. Boot steps sounded to the door. It came open. James Emmett stood there for a long moment, his face as pale as if an artery had been pierced by a surgeon. He looked down at Luke, small in his chair by the door. He didn't say he was sorry. It would have done no good. He just patted his nephew gently on the shoulder and stalked out of the house. James and Farrell never came into one another's company again. Luke ran for good a short time later. This time he didn't make the mistake of looking up his uncle. Instead, he went to sea. And remained there.

The blade Farrell used on his brother was double-edged. If anything, Farrell suffered a deeper cut, from which he would not or could not recover. With his remaining son, David, he swung from even greater harshness than his rule over Luke to confused, weak pleadings. It also left him useless to Diana in a particularly difficult time.

Diana saw bleak prospects for her business so long as it relied on shipping. The constant European wars had created great volatility in the market. As the British king and French

Allan Cole & Chris Bunch

emperor flailed at one another, embargoes and seizure were
the rule, not the exception. Already difficult conditions
worsened. Diana looked elsewhere for ideas. And set her
sights on the western trade.

She'd dabbled in it from the very beginning. But twenty
years ago the West was only a few score miles from the far
banks of the Schuylkill River, close enough so that
immediate gain was realized when they opened the pike from
Lancaster. Now the distances were so vast as to be
unimaginable. Forget about the great tract opened by Mister
Jefferson in his contract with the French emperor. Just over
yon mountains might as well have been the moon. The costs
of transport were so great, men on both sides of the
wilderness were beggared even contemplating them.

What roads that existed were awful, the tolls charged
immense. Even near the seaboard at least four horses were
required to haul two tons over the roads. The tolls charged
ranged from two and a half cents every two miles in the New
England region to twenty-five cents per twelve in Virginia.
Everywhere there were goods for sale, they either languished
without buyers or—in the case of the far north— were traded
to smugglers to be carried across the Canadian border. Diana
knew firsthand how many generations those smugglers went
back.

There was a renewed call to solve the situation with
massive highway and canal programs. Lotteries were all the
rage again. There was pressure on the Congress to provide
support from its new capital in Washington. A system was
proposed that would cost upward of twenty million dollars.
Diana thought the program not enough. But she supported it
just the same. As she hunted for a means to escape the
economic mudbanks of the docks, she became skilled in the
ways of river traffic and what goods were best to move along
what roads existed, and how to shelter merchandise along the
way. Or what distant industries might be encouraged to
lighten the load of raw goods by reducing them through
manufacture.

A Daughter Of Liberty

It was in the middle of this—sometime in May of 1809— that she got a letter:

My dearest friend, Diana,

I pray this finds you and your family prospering and in good health. I am anxious to hear all your news, and I promise another letter will soon follow this with a list of questions whose answers I eagerly await. I would hope we are friends of such long and deep affection that the brevity of this will in no way cause offense. The truth is, I need you desperately, Diana dear, as the president and I are overwhelmed by our new duties. I seek your understanding and assistance...

The letter went on from there. And was signed by Dolly Madison.

In the fifteen years since she'd married, Dolly had gone from a small, bright planetary object to a constant stellar presence. She was considered the most knowledgeable woman of the land in matters of fashion, and acclaimed as a skilled hostess who rescued Mister Madison's widower friend, Thomas Jefferson, from shaming the office of president by neglecting the small things that kill diplomacy faster than a cannon fired in error.

She and Diana had kept in touch during those eight years, although Diana had not troubled her with anything more than a congratulatory note since her husband announced for president, an office he'd won the previous December and assumed that March. The letter gave no firm clue on what Dolly wanted. Diana doubted that it was for her dressmaking abilities. Dolly had only to ask advice—as she had in the past—and Diana would give it freely for Dolly's own seamstresses to make up.

All the letter clearly said was the new—unspecified-duties were immense, particularly in the rough-and-tumble town that was Washington. From the descriptions Diana had heard, it sounded more like a frontier outpost than the capital of a brave new nation. She'd have to find a gentle way to respond. She had no time during these difficult days to

Allan Cole & Chris Bunch

devote herself to "dove parties"—as Dolly's little get-togethers with the wives of congressmen and diplomats were called. What on earth could Dolly be thinking? Diana serving tea to some simpering brain of soapsuds? Smelling salts at ready for those who staged a faint attack? Long, empty correspondence with pen clubs, purporting to weigh the great issues of the day?

Diana could tell them what they were. The price of wheat at its source and bread from the oven. The safety of a person's scalp in some lonely wilderness cabin. Or—failing all that—if there was no help, please, then, no interference. The government should get about its own business and leave us to ours. But she didn't think those fine people would want to hear that. And now that she was nearing her middle age, Diana had no intention of keeping her mouth shut.

As delicately as possible she would turn Dolly down. She drew out her writing tools to respond, and puzzled over the opening lines. The delicacy would have to be heavily laced with firmness if the rejection were to be permanent. One thing she had always admired about Dolly: she was a damned persistent woman.

BOOK FOUR:

VIRGINIA - JUNE 1814

CHAPTER THIRTY-ONE

SHE WAS THREE days out of Manassas on the road to
Richmond when the river burst its banks and flooded the
highway. It was no surprise. Though the weather had been
delightfully clear all morning, Diana and Kitty had watched
distant storms rage across the Appalachians, lightning
crashing continuously on the black peaks. She was sure the
storms were more than the little Pamunkey River could bear.
Certainly the poorly maintained dikes thrown up where the
river's banks curved in to kiss the road were no match for the
unusually wet spring and summer of 1814. From where she
sat in the carriage, she could see raw marks of many other
breaks.

The driver cursed, said something in the unintelligible
English of a lower-class white southerner, then clambered off
the coach to oversee the unhitching of the horses. By the time
he'd harangued the two sullen slaves into turning the coach
on the narrow dirt track, it was late afternoon. Diana hid her
amusement as the blacks pretended puzzlement over the
simplest directions, then invariably got them wrong. When
the job was done and the red-faced driver had bustled over to
her with great importance, Diana saw the slaves whispering
animatedly in obvious satisfaction at the distress they'd
caused the boss. She caught the eye of one of the men and
gave him a grin of sympathy. He flickered, then she saw the
flicker turn to a great blank look that she was already
becoming familiar with, although she had been in the South
less than a week.

The driver was muttering to her, and she forced herself
to ignore the foul waves of whiskey rising from him and pay
attention. Jamestown she recognized. It was her destination.
He was saying something about another road. It apparently
bypassed Richmond, which was a disappointment, but it
eventually hooked up with the main thoroughfare to
Williamsburg and then Jamestown.

Kitty whined about the uncomfortable delay, but Diana gently hushed her. Poor child. She was the granddaughter of her cook, Mrs. Kenrick. In looks she was a lush, ripe twenty. But she'd only just turned fifteen, and even this age seemed beyond her. She was a pleasant child, but a bit of a scatterbrain, and Diana had only taken her on as a favor to Mrs. Kenrick.

Kitty seemed to have few defenses. Recently she'd been "discovered" by a group of apprentices, who swarmed about her like a pack of wasps invading a sweet shop. They praised her and flattered her until her head was spinning. It was obvious all they wanted was to get her skirts over her head. To rescue her reputation, Mrs. Kenrick had begged Diana to take the child with her to Virginia until matters cooled in the city. Kitty would act as her maid, if Diana could bear her clumsiness. Perhaps the journey would mature her. So, Diana reminded herself to be patient with the child. Mostly Kitty's natural, cheery good nature had been a plus. Now, however, her youthful complaints about the fate luck had handed them were beginning to grate. On this long road— which had been empty of traffic for nearly two days—there weren't any other obvious choices.

Diana soothed the girl, then nodded agreement to the coachman. She settled back as the coach jolted and slowly creaked forward on its rickety axles and wheels. And they were off, more or less, to Jamestown. Where James Emmett was to be wed.

* * * *

The letter announcing her son's betrothal had struck Diana like the lightning on those Appalachian peaks. He was marrying Eliza Hope Beecham. Of the Five Forks Beechams. The woman brought a dowry of 1,001 acres, planted mostly in cotton and some tobacco, with one acre reserved for a family graveyard. God's Acre, they called it down here. James Emmett boasted the cotton was of the finest and whitest variety: Nankin Boll.

Allan Cole & Chris Bunch

It was what he'd left unsaid that troubled her. Her son hadn't mentioned whether the dowry also included slaves. First Diana had wept. The tears were followed by a rage so great, no one could remember a time when the Widow Shannon had been so angry. The rage was followed by intense self-loathing.

It was her fault she'd failed him, Diana thought, and failed the memory of his long dead father. On and on she berated herself, endless torment, until Connie could bear no more and told her if she wanted to wear a hair shirt, could she be doing it in private so everyone else could have some peace. Let Farrell take on all the guilt of the Shannons, she had said. He'd consider it a favor, I'm sure.

Diana had sat down with Connie for a long heart-to-heart. Her first instinct had been to avoid the wedding at all costs.

"What if there are no slaves?" Connie asked. "And you didn't attend the wedding of your own flesh and blood? You would never forgive yourself."

Diana grabbed at this as if her life depended on it. Connie was right. Besides, how could James Emmett contemplate such an action? Of all her failings with her son, the issue of slavery certainly couldn't be one of them. Could it? It was settled then. She should go.

As soon as she said it, she knew she was lying to herself. James was an ardent sportsman, risking life and broken limbs to ride with the hounds after some bloody stump of fox fur. Hunting and fishing and gambling were his sole passion. At thirty-five, he lived the life of a young buck. It was a life idealized in the South. Temptation would outweigh his conscience. On this she was positive. Diana Shannon had always had trouble not speaking her mind. At age fifty-two it wasn't getting any easier. If James proved a slaveholder, she would rip his heart out, ruining the wedding and the memory of that wedding for as long as he and his new wife lived. Therefore, she shouldn't go.

"Then no one from his family will be there to support him," Connie argued. "In the circumstances, I fear for his future marriage. I've watched events unfold like this at my father's tavern," she said. "Decisions are made that can never be taken back once put into effect. And in every case, the tragedy that resulted far outweighed the momentary victory of pride.

"I urge you to go, Diana. If his situation is as you fear, then he has doomed himself. But by his own hands, not yours. In other words, I think you should make the selfish choice. Hoist the flag for the family, as Isaac would have put it. Run out the guns and sail up their damned river. In the long run, the tears you shed on your pillow may not be quite so bitter."

It was this flawless logic that had set her upon a desolate highway across an equally desolate land.

* * * *

The moment Diana crossed the Potomac, she entered a country so foreign to her that all notions were been turned upside down. They'd traveled for miles without seeing a single active hamlet or village or farm. There were no ruts in the roads from the big four-axle wagons that carried trade goods in other parts of the nation. And almost no travelers. Diana knew this hadn't always been so. Before the cotton boom here'd been life where now she saw none. But all that life had been devoured by the big plantations and their masters. All that easy money, fortunes as vast as those of any European noble family, to be squandered or put to some decent use. The men of the South chose the former.

During her journey, they sometimes passed the fields of one of those great plantations. She saw no ploughs or any other farm implements, just row upon row of slaves working the ground, using clumsy hoes with unpeeled sapling handles that must have made the hardiest hands bleed after only a few minutes. Once, they paused at a crossroads to let traffic pass. The traffic was twenty slaves taking their master's tobacco to market, with no wagons or beasts of burden to aid them. The

Allan Cole & Chris Bunch

tobacco leaves had been packed in large wooden hogsheads. Makeshift axles were attached to the hogsheads, so the slaves could roll them to market. Eighty miles or more.

There were certain things Diana also knew from her traders. A long time ago someone had described the beautiful port at Savannah. The shipyards were among the finest in the land, the man had said. And the docks were a picture for a palace wall. They were faced by palmetto logs with oyster shells and white sand. Seven ships at a time would sail up the Medway, loaded with lumber and indigo and rice. Now, she was told, the docks had rotted and fallen into decay. There were few ships sailing into Savannah . . . and this had been true even before the war started and the British blockaded American ports.

Elsewhere, decent roads had collapsed and gone unrepaired. Plans for new ones were abandoned, canals ignored, bridges built and maintained only under threat of heavy penalties. There were almost no schools. Even at the plantations, education for the owners' sons and certainly the daughters was as great a fiction as any of Washington Irving's New York tales, although certainly not so humorous. Money—real cash—was nearly nonexistent. The great fortunes of the South were mostly on paper, and mostly encumbered by debt. Money was so scarce, they'd taken to cutting silver coins into four parts or bits so there could be a little more cash to go around. There was no business as she knew it in this place, no manufacture. How could there be when everything the planters enjoyed was purchased from abroad with cotton money or foreign debt: from brooms to linen, from shoes to the smallest item of furniture. Even with foreign trade strangling from the British blockade, small ships from the South were daring the king's guns to slip across the Atlantic—not to resupply desperately needed goods, but to bring in more of those luxuries, at dearer prices, for the self-declared American aristocracy.

A mile from the sea, however, and the most gifted leather apron went begging for work. No one would hire a smith or a mason. There was no need for these crafts. Nor hooper or cooper, or even a miller. She was told they threshed the wheat by driving horses across the fields. And the slaves ground it by hand in huge hollowed-out stones with eight-foot pestles. Most of the whites seemed not much better off than the slaves. She saw their cabins made of clapboard or rotted logs. From what she could make out, these poor folk spent all their time drinking themselves into oblivion at the unmarked grogshops that appeared now and then right in the middle of all this wilderness.

When they were forced to stop at these places for water or to rest the horses, no one seemed curious. No anxious requests for the latest news of the war, which had raged now for two years with no sign that any end was in sight. If it weren't for the worsening poverty of these people, one could scarcely guess there was any war on at all. Yet wasn't it the South that had pressed so mightily for this war? She looked at the stupor in their eyes and the barely disguised hatred behind that stupor and despaired for the future. What had they done to this place? And why? Could slavery alone explain it? Or was it the nature of the people? That couldn't be, she thought. One way or another, we all came from the same stock. She was beginning to think she'd been a fool to leave Philadelphia. Although as the miles clicked away under the rickety wheels of the coach—and the cares of her business faded with distance—she saw that perhaps it was only the purpose of the journey that was the fool's errand, not the act of leaving. From the moment the stage reached the far side of the Schuylkill, she'd felt as if a great weight had been lifted. Freer now, half-formed thoughts had come into focus.

For some years she had fought against a feeling of dissatisfaction. It was as stifling and stagnant as the worst Philadelphia summer. She had marked it off as merely the heavy burdens of maintaining the family. Diana reacted in her usual manner: she worked harder, constantly rebuilding and adding to the structure of safety. Now it seemed that all her recent efforts were a fiction. All she'd been doing was

Allan Cole & Chris Bunch

deepening and improving that root cellar she had dug in
Cherry Valley to hide from the Indians. But the greatest
fiction of all, she thought, was she was doing it all for the
family. For Emmett. No, Diana, she told herself, I won't
allow you that. Perhaps it was that way at first, but later it
was all for you. For the glorification of the Widow Shannon
who defied social tradition to make her own indelible mark.
She'd set goals and achieved them. Replaced those goals with
new ones. These, too, she'd achieved. On and on at a frantic
pace, as if her goals were perishable possessions, until the act
itself had become as empty as the cold transactions of the
Boston bankers she so despised.

The restlessness she felt had intensified during the two
years of warfare. She believed it a stupid war—if any war
had any sense to it—and knew it was beyond her control.
Young men were dying again, and this tormented her,
although she worried that from the safety of Philadelphia the
torment was more intellectual than heartfelt. She'd always
hated influence peddlers, but hadn't she used her own
friendship with Dolly Madison to help David, one of her
grandsons?

Oh, come now, Diana, she thought, you've put on that
hair shirt again that Connie was mocking. Don't question all
of it. You might as well regret the lies you told Nate Hatch to
keep your legs beneath you. Or the gold you stole from him.
It was rightfully yours, but that's a quibble. And that farmer
just beyond New Kent—you helped Emmett cheat. Take that
back. And die in the road when the troops catch up. Or,
worse, be found out by Nate and carried back to be branded
and forced into servitude.

Like his brother Luke, David was for the sea. Farrell had
failed to learn his lesson. David became desperate for escape.
And so two years ago Diana had written Dolly asking
assistance. David had been granted a midshipman's post
aboard the Essex under Commander Porter. She had no idea
where David might be, but she hoped he was safer, or at least

better off, than if he had just run away to sea. He was only fourteen years old.

And what about Luke? He would be twenty now. The last she heard, he was aboard a merchantman out of the Sugar Islands. This would place him far out of harm's way. But what if he weren't? She didn't want to imagine the cannonball crushing out his life, or the great splinter piercing his breast. What would she do if it were necessary to protect him? Would she lie? Certainly. Steal? Without hesitation. Kill? She knew she would.

Diana drew back from what she saw as self-pity at its worst, and pointlessness at its best. She took stock. It was an accounting that was far overdue. As the war had progressed from minor victories to failure to defeat to empty talk of suing for peace, Diana had reduced her business risk. She'd shifted her emphasis from the sea to the western trade: the new lands opened by Jefferson.

She'd also dabbled in the manufacturing boom created by the war, although she refused to put any money in Eli Whitney's guns. Diana was told his process of building identical guns with interchangeable parts was a marvel of the age. Each part was the duty of a single worker. The weapon would be passed from him to the next man or woman until the thing was complete in a matter of a few days instead of weeks. Diana preferred the little inventor who had been using the same system to make cheap clocks for the mantelpiece. Priced so they could be afforded by almost any household or farm, he sold the clocks by sending men out on the road, like her young peddlers of long ago. He expanded on this by creating territories and selling them to eager buyers. Diana was a silent partner in a few of those territories.

She had a host of other ventures, most of them beyond the mountains: steel mills near Fort Pitt, salt works in the Lakes region, furs, goods of all kinds moving up and down the Mississippi and Ohio rivers. But just small pieces of them. No great shaking of the dice and a single roll to win or lose at a toss—like the dolls that began it all. She laughed at

Allan Cole & Chris Bunch

this thought. Of her whole family, only James Emmett would really understand. So maybe he wasn't such an odd creature to burst from her womb after all.

Diana pulled herself up and put all of it aside. She was nearing the point, no sense shying from it: What do you want, Diana Shannon? It doesn't matter, she told herself. They won't let me have it. Evasion again. Who are they? Answer: the same people as always. The ones who keep me from my task.

It had always been difficult for a woman alone in business. She had to be twice as good as any man who meant to cross the same ground for the same ends. And no mishap of the most minor sort was allowed. For some reason it had seemed to grow harder each year into the new century. It didn't have a name at first. Business dealings became more awkward. To begin with, her money was accepted, but less and less her advice. Which to Diana meant she would be a fool to invest. Then, as her success had grown, they stopped even seeking her investment. It was as if some secret council had met—which she knew was certainly not so—and decided there was to be a ceiling placed over her possibilities. This, more than the war, had forced her hand.

As her business had shifted to the frontiers, so had her spirit. All about her, common folk were being squeezed. Harsh words were being put into laws. Outbursts from working people were quickly quelled. And so people were beginning to trickle away once more. As the lands opened up, the wilderness beckoned; with new dangers, but also with new possibilities.

So that's it, then, she thought. You want out. As badly as your grandsons, David and Luke. Escape from this thing the magazines were calling "The Cult Of True Womanhood." Her sex was to hold itself above the fray. Business, politics, and opinions on matters of the world were for men. Women must be kept as spiritually intact as a maidenhead. Otherwise, the reasoning went, the American family was doomed. But if she were to escape, where would she go and to what purpose?

Once again, Diana, you come to the question: What do you want? I want Emmett. That is foolishness to the extreme; he's been dead for thirty-seven years. I know it's foolish, but you asked the question. And that is my honest answer. She knew that Emmett was a girlhood fantasy, and that over the decades, the few months she had spent with him had taken on mystical qualities. In reality, how would it have all come out? Would Emmett have allowed her the freedom of her mind? Or would he have been like most other men of his time? Who could say? It was an unfair question based on a faulty premise. He died. And she had been free to make her own choices. And she had made them.

The crucial decision had been to remain alone, in control. And now, thirty-seven years later, it had come back to haunt her. She had built this marvelous edifice, and as she stepped back to survey it, she found it empty of purpose and therefore pleasure. In her groping, a candle winked to life. Deep within her, Diana believed that what she had accomplished was what both of them would have wanted, with minor variations here and there. Such things that had escaped her grasp—Farrell, James Emmett, David and Luke, and so on—might not have gotten past both of them.

As she thought it through, she realized just how wrong this assumption could be. But it did not remove the belief. And as long as she was afflicted with this lingering malady, she would never be happy. Should she purge Emmett from her system? No. After all these years it wasn't possible, and certainly not desirable. Although he was only a memory, she loved him still. She couldn't bring herself to kill that. Besides, she was no longer certain where Diana left off and Emmett began. They seemed to be as inseparable as any of those joined calf twins that were pickled in brine and placed on display at Mister Peale's museum.

Fine, then. There was no immediate answer. She determined to think harder. When she returned to

Allan Cole & Chris Bunch

Philadelphia, she would act. She knew what course that action would most probably be. The family would have to learn to fend for itself. She would go to Pittsburgh, the same place Emmett had in mind during that spring of mutual daydreams. What she would do there, she wasn't sure. It didn't much matter. If there was no cure for this disease, setting new goals under fresh circumstances should at least mask the symptoms. For a time.

While she was in this dark mood, the coach gave a frightening lurch, and she simultaneously heard the crack of an ancient and badly maintained axle. Kitty shrieked as the coach swayed back and forth. There was more cracking all along its length. Then, defying total disaster, the coach settled to the ground. The door opened to her touch, and Diana pulled Kitty kicking and screaming out with her. The coachman hurled curses like foul lightning bolts. The two slaves cowered in fear, although how the accident was their fault, Diana couldn't tell.

Then, as she tried to calm her hysterical young maid, an apparition rose from the side of the road and hailed her. He was old and the color of blasted oak. He hopped about on bare feet, splayed half again the size of a normal man's from so many years treading furrows. What clothes he wore hung in rags that flapped about as he danced and shouted his greeting.

At least Diana thought it was a greeting, because she couldn't understand a word he said. He was quite mad, poor man. And a slave. Chanting, he danced forward a few steps, beckoning with flapping arms and hands. Then he danced back again like a wary bird. What did he want? Gradually, she made it out. He was leaving to fetch someone, and he wanted her to stay where she was until he returned. Diana looked at the disabled coach and shrugged. She would wait whether through his bidding or not. The slave took her shrug as agreement, turned on his heel and lit out across the fields, disappearing into the tree line.

"What did he want of us, missus?" Kitty asked.

"I think he went to get help."

Kitty looked about the overgrown fields, and brush-choked woods. It was a very lonely place to be. She shuddered. "Are you sure he won't be bringing back some devil, missus?"

Diana ignored this and got Kitty busy pulling a few things from the coach to make them comfortable while the men attempted repair. But once or twice she glanced over her shoulder to the spot where the old slave had disappeared. Diana wasn't superstitious, but she half expected to see the Devil.

The coach was hopeless. The driver said it would take four days to fetch a new one. The only lodgings were a half a day back, and they were reputed to be even meaner than the inn they'd left at three that morning. That had been a shack with infested beds and only a tattered handbill on the sagging door to announce its purpose. All of the inns she had seen or stayed at had been like that. No sashes on the windows. Roofs that let in the rain. Three shillings for lodgings, six pence more for clean sheets, if they had them. Six shillings for breakfast, and no supper available at any price.

The innkeepers laughed when someone complained, and blamed it on the custom of the land.

What food they offered was exceedingly poor. Even the region's highly praised pig flesh was inedible in those inns, putting to lie the famous observation that north of the Potomac there was only good beef and bad bacon, while south of the river there was only good bacon and bad beef. So much for the vaunted southern hospitality.

* * * *

The man who came to fetch her was no devil. He was about her age, and handsome in the way men become if they take care of themselves. He was tall, his waist as narrow as a boy's, and his shoulders stretched the material of his riding jacket. His face was tanned and smooth—except for a silver moustache and the smile creases near his eyes and lips. His hair was dark with heavy streaks of silver and curled a touch

Allan Cole & Chris Bunch

carelessly just above the ears and the back of his neck. His eyes were as blue as the Virginia skies. He said his name was John Maguire. Later, she heard someone call him "Major," and was impressed that he had been content to introduce himself without the airs of rank.

As they stood next to his carriage, he only told her his name and that he was not from this plantation—which was owned by Mister Adam Carter—but one farther down the road. He was visiting, he said, and told her news of her misfortune had excited the entire household. Guests, especially guests from distant locales, she gathered, were exceedingly rare. Maguire said that while the master and mistress of the plantation made themselves presentable for her welcome, he had been sent out to fetch her.

"It would be most impolite to reject them, Mrs. Shannon," he said in a soft, civilized voice only just tinted with a drawl.

But he didn't press the point. Instead he inspected the broken-down coach and conferred with the driver while Diana made up her mind. He had a quiet conversation with the two slaves. She was surprised at the unforced animation in their faces as they confirmed the driver's tale. They know this man, she thought. But what was more remarkable was that they seemed to like him.

She found herself idly wondering how this could be. Perhaps she'd misheard him. Perhaps the neighboring plantation he spoke of wasn't his, but belonged to a family member, and he was visiting from the North after many years' absence. Yes, that must be it. Despite his age, his legs were slender and well-formed under the tight riding breeches. Diana was sure he was married.

Maguire turned back to her. "I would offer you the hospitality of my own house," he said, "but the Carters would never forgive me for stealing you." That answered the first question, and she was disappointed in her error.

"Besides," he said, "I live alone, and it would be unseemly." Error number two, but no matter. The answer to the first question canceled out any satisfaction in the second.

Still, he put her so much at ease that she accepted the Carters' offer of rescue and soon found herself being helped into the carriage. Kitty followed. Diana noticed his glance didn't linger on Kitty's young and well-rounded form, not the way he looked at Diana when he handed her aboard. This pleased her. She knew her figure still drew admiring gazes from men much less her age, but it had been a long time since she welcomed them.

Perhaps it was the confusion in her own mind that caused this. When she was unsettled, she had no patience for any kind of distraction. It wasn't that Diana disliked men. Far from it. She enjoyed their company, and if the circumstances were right, relished their lovemaking. But too often, she thought, men drew the most alarming conclusions from the scantiest evidence. In matters of business or love, they sometimes saw signals where none existed, mistook kindness or attempts at fair play for weakness. And so, more than most women, Diana chose caution as the best defense. Otherwise she feared she would soon have an empty purse and bankrupt reputation. But as she grew older, Diana had grown more and more weary of the game. For once she would like to simply relax and let the moment carry itself.

She studied Maguire's handsome profile beside her. He had a cheery, intelligent look about him. Yes, and admit it, sensuous as well. She wondered what he would be like in bed. The quick flush she felt partially answered her question. Diana let the feeling linger a few seconds, enjoying it. It had been so long since she had let a man hold her, she sometimes jested that revirgination was becoming a real possibility.

Beneath the cheeriness, there was something a bit sad about John Maguire. No, not sad, but apart. As if he didn't quite belong because of some secret and treasured difference between himself and others. Diana knew the feeling well. His hands were strong and sure on the reins, and he guided the

pg. 355

Allan Cole & Chris Bunch

horse with a gentle touch. Diana let the moment pass. These hands are also slave-branding hands, she thought. Like the people she'd seen along the roads and in those inhospitable taverns, she knew him to be as fatally flawed as Cain himself. No, John Maguire, if you're contemplating what I think you are, cut it from your mind with as sharp a knife as you can find.

Except for occasional outbursts of excited chatter from Kitty, they moved along the narrow carriage track in silence for a while. Diana didn't know if the trail was the main road to the plantation. The road was pinched in closely by untended trees of such wide variety, Diana couldn't tell which had been brought here and which were native. They were choked by thick brush with large, fleshy leaves that were so green, they appeared somehow unhealthy. She heard no birds singing or movements of small animals, only the dry buzz of locusts in the trees and the abrupt rat-a-tat of a woodpecker. The brush was broken here and there by what seemed to be thin Indian paths that snaked through the vegetation and disappeared. Once in a while she thought she heard rustling—as if a large body was moving along one of the trails—and snatches of what seemed to be whispering. Her skin prickled and the small hairs on the back of her neck rose. Diana knew she was being watched by many eyes.

She shivered and turned to Maguire. A little conversation might mask her edginess. "It was fortunate for us," she said, "that the old man happened to be out on the road to see our dilemma. Otherwise Kitty and I would be making poor beds tonight. You must point him out to me when we arrive, so I can thank him."

Maguire flinched when she said this. Instead of starting a conversation, her remarks seemed to make the silence deepen. What had she said to give offense? She saw him struggle to find words to answer. "You won't find him there," he finally said. "It was no accident that he saw you. The roadside is his post. His duty."

Oh, now she could see. He didn't want her speaking to the old man. A slave. A chill descended on her as quickly as a squall in one of Isaac's stories of the sea. How in hell was she to survive the next few weeks among these people?

"We get so few visitors out here," Maguire continued, not noticing her reaction, "that each one is a prize. Some of the planters—like Mister Carter—set men upon the road to watch. They have standing orders to waylay any and all travelers and to bring them to the master's house. So you see, the accident to the carriage had nothing to do with the invitation. You would have been pressed to stay in any event."

Maguire chuckled at this. But Diana thought she caught a forced edge to the laugh, and she realized he was just as unsettled. For what reason, she couldn't make out. Another long silence followed. Then: "I gather you haven't visited a plantation before," he said.

"No." She said it flatly.

"…Then, perhaps I should . . ." His voice trailed off. Although he tried to hide it, she could see the mental struggle resume. What was the man finding so difficult to say? His look became a little grim as a decision was reached. He forced a smile and continued, but Diana knew the words that followed were not what he originally meant to say.

"Perhaps I should explain about your hosts ..."

He said Adam Carter was middle-aged and, like Maguire, had been a widower for a number of years. But not before his wife had produced six sons and as many daughters. All of them were grown now, and Carter had recently remarried.

"Sarah—that's Mrs. Carter—is with child. But she's been having difficulty. So her sisters and two of her aunts are here to help. Counting them and Adam's great brood, you'll find quite a crowd to welcome you."

"I hope they find me worthy of the trouble," Diana snapped. She couldn't bear the blather any longer.

Allan Cole & Chris Bunch

A Daughter Of Liberty

Diana didn't care a whit about the Carters, and dreaded the prospect of forced politeness in her near future. But as soon as she snapped at Maguire, she regretted it. He had been about to say something more, but lapsed back into silence, pretending to concentrate on his driving. And so she had no warning of the strange sight that greeted her as the carriage track suddenly broadened and then curved into a broad avenue of yellow Virginia sand, lined with graceful, well-cared-for trees.

At the end of the avenue was the Carter house: a mansion dropped from the skies into the middle of the wilderness, more than a hundred feet long and three stories high. Diana learned later the top story was entirely devoted to a ballroom, where hundreds of guests could be entertained by a full orchestra of costumed slaves. The house was the color of the sand, with green sashes and trim and an enormous front door that appeared to be faced with copper or brass.

Everything about the house and its grounds was bizarre. There was a sprawling garden—aping the style of the British magazines. To the side of the garden Diana could see black figures erecting a false arbor thirty feet high. Behind the arbor another slave was pursuing a litter of pigs with a sack and an axe. An open fire was being built, and a grate readied for the fire. Pig and fire and grate equaled barbecue. I'll have supper, at least, Diana thought dryly. A crowd was gathering, and in all her life Diana had never seen anything quite so strange. Twenty or more slaves were hastily lining up. They wore stunning green and gold livery, as if they were the servants of European royalty. A few carried the marks of their posts: a silver tray was held by a butler; a whip by a coachman; there was even what proved to be a cup bearer. As the coach drew closer, Diana saw how great a mockery it all was. The slaves' faces were pocked with disease, their hair tinged orange from lack of nourishment. Rags peeked out from the livery as the clothing was hastily drawn together and buttoned or hooked to a frog. Footwear ranged from boots to old shoes sliced along the side for a better fit. Some had no shoes at all. One man to the rear of the group was turned away, his back to the road, pulling a jacket over his naked torso. The man's back was livid with ancient scars.

It was only then that Diana saw the white masters. They had been standing there all along. A group of about a dozen of them, men and women, as expensively dressed as any grand assembly in Philadelphia. Except the clothing was all ten years or more out of date. A big, dull-faced man stepped out in front. Beside him was a wisp of a girl, no more than fifteen, but she looked even more a child in her blue frock with little bunches of ribbons spotted about like posies in a garden. Her hair was pale yellow and her skin a ghastly white.

Diana did not need an introduction. It was Adam Carter and his new wife.

CHAPTER THIRTY-TWO

DIANA STAYED WITH the Carters for two nights and three days. She was welcomed with such enthusiasm that under different circumstances she would have felt guilty for disliking her host. Mister Carter was so courtly and deferential that he drove Diana to distraction. If she took one sip from her glass, he was glowering at a slave to refill it. He was so intense, Diana was in a terror that if the slave did not move quickly enough, Mister Carter would have him whipped.

The moment he spoke, even his oldest son would fall silent. The silence would last until everyone was sure Father was done. His method of entering a conversation was to abruptly ask a question. No matter his audience was discussing something else. He would wait impatiently until he felt the answerer had enough time to get out whatever was to be said, then veer sharply to the topic Adam Carter had really been bent on discussing—hunting, gambling, and horseflesh.

For instance, at the barbecue that commenced shortly after Diana's arrival, his wife had been shyly pressing her on fashions. Diana had been delicately trying to get across that waistlines were no longer gathered just under the bosom, without mocking Sarah's own costume, and that oiled Grecian curls were definitely out, when Adam Carter broke in.

"If you please, my dear Mrs. Shannon," he'd said in his heavy drawl, "I would treasure your opinion of this ham." He cut a thick slice with his own hands, and had a slave pass it to her.

She had dutifully tasted it and remarked on its goodness. It was true: the ham was delicious. Adam had nodded proudly around the table. Then, as Diana had tried to resume her conversation with his wife, Mister Carter had addressed John Maguire: "How's that speckled foal of yours getting along, Major?" It was the first time Diana heard Maguire addressed by rank.

"Over the colic now," was all Maguire had said.

Evidently, from long practice this was the most he had attempted. It was sufficient for Mister Carter's purpose. He had then launched into a lengthy discussion on animal husbandry according to Adam Carter.

The man reminded her of Nate Hatch. It was an unsettling connection. She found herself watching Adam Carter more closely. The accent was different but the attitudes were similar. Like the New Kent innkeeper, Mister Carter was a bloated monarch in a minuscule society. In his extreme isolation, the power the planter wielded increased proportionally. It was like one of those mathematical games invented by the ancient geometers, where a small sum quickly grows to the size of mountains. Remove his dependence on his fellow citizens for profit, allow him greater freedom to manipulate the law—in fact, give him vastly greater power over his fellow man—and Nate Hatch would have behaved exactly the same as Adam Carter.

What made the situation intolerable was that the power of the planters had been confirmed on the highest level. First Jefferson and then Madison—both slaveholders—had forged a Democratic-Republican coalition of southern planter and northern merchant and tradesman to make their party supreme for fourteen years. Diana realized only a hopeless optimist could imagine anything changing in this lifetime. Or the next. But here she was, a lowly woman by Adam Carter's lights, being treated with a respect far beyond her role as guest. There was condescension, to be sure. Diana was used to that. Still, even in this place where the "Cult of True Womanhood" reigned supreme, she was listened to in greater detail than most other people of her sex. Money and presumed influence was the answer. Perhaps all that achieving hadn't been wasted. Perhaps it wasn't so empty. And her current frustration was that she was growing tired fighting alone all this time, and felt she was falling behind.

Allan Cole & Chris Bunch

Then her head had come up as she realized she had drifted into a long reverie. No one had noticed. But the conversation had taken several turns since her attention had lapsed. John Maguire was holding forth. He was talking about the war. Actually, it was more of an impassioned plea than mere talk. The major was describing the desperate plight of the army, telling of his fears that the war would be lost if desperately needed troops were not continuously supplied.

She noticed Mister Carter and his sons listened respectfully, but with small smiles playing at their lips. Diana also saw that the rank conferred on Maguire was no empty title. Whispers among the women confirmed he had fought long and valiantly during the Revolution when most men from these parts were only peripherally—if at all—involved. Plainly, the major was making a pitch. A recruitment pitch. He was pressing Adam Carter for his sons; he was raising a militia to fight the king.

As soon as she caught the drift of what he was attempting to sell, she could see from the faces of the Carter men that they would never enlist. Still, she thought it a brave effort and was disappointed on his behalf when he came to the end. Mister Carter waxed long and eloquently on his great poverty and how—although Maguire must be aware of his ardent belief in such a patriotic cause—such a sacrifice would be his ruin. With regret he was forced to deny this favor to his neighbor and dearest friend.

Oddly, she had caught no sense of loss on the major's features. He seemed to have expected the answer. In fact, he was shaking his head, sympathizing with his host and encouraging Adam Carter to describe his difficulties in great detail. He has more in mind, she'd thought.

Sarah Carter rose, a signal for the other women to withdraw and leave the men to their business. Diana had nearly snapped at the woman. She wanted to see how the game between Maguire and Carter came out. But custom and dreaded tradition ruled otherwise. As she withdrew, John Maguire had looked her way, disappointment on his face.

Then he turned back to focus all of his attention on Adam Carter. The more she saw of Major Maguire, the more she found favor in him. What a pity.

They were only a few steps into the garden—on the way back to the house—when Sarah gave a gasp of pain. She stood frozen and what little color she had drained from her face, until she was ghastly white. She sagged, and her sisters and aunts had descended on her. Propping her up, spewing orders to the slaves who always followed as if they were living shadows, they had fled through the garden with their burden. Leaving Diana forgotten in their wake. She'd wondered what the trouble was with the poor child. It didn't seem to her that a difficult pregnancy could be the sole cause. But it was none of her business, she had told herself. Besides...

Diana slipped back to the edge of the garden. A thorny hedge, covered with tasseled red flowers, hid her from the view of the men.

". . . How can I refuse you, John?" Mister Carter was saying. "If it's that nigger wench you want, then you shall have her. And at a fair price as well ..."

It was as if the sun had been blown out by a mighty breath. Chilled by these words—delivered as casually as if they were discussing a prized hunting bitch—Diana had fallen back from the hedge, so stunned at witnessing the sale of another human being, she had almost fled to her room like a maiden.

Reason had returned with the sound of footsteps coming down the garden path: Kitty. Before her maid could speak and alert the men of Diana's presence, she shushed her with a raised finger. Another wave had brought the girl to her side, and Diana had resumed her spying.

". . . Then it's settled, and I thank you," the major was saying. "When I return home in a day or so, I'll send my headman, Paul, to fetch her."

From Carter's reaction, Diana could see the bargain was not as settled as the major was saying. For some reason, the

Allan Cole & Chris Bunch

planter seemed about to object to the timing, or some other matter that Diana could not make out. But Maguire had seemed prepared for this.

"Now, as to my first request, Adam," the major went on, "all I'm asking is for one of your boys. And only for a month or so. It would have a powerful effect on my recruiting efforts, for a man such as yourself to stand with me in this matter. And volunteer his son to his country's call."

Mister Carter had blustered. But still the major pressed. Then he suddenly relented with good grace. He let the planter steer the conversation back to the bargain involving the woman slave. There would be no delay in delivery. Then the major had shifted the conversation to an idle discussion on the prospects for the hunting season. Silently, Diana had ghosted away, pulling Kitty with her. It was plain what Maguire's real mission was: the purchase of a "nigger wench." But why would this be more important than recruiting soldiers for his militia? It didn't make sense. Later, Kitty had enlightened her.

The girl was so young and naive that she had quickly shed her shyness in the company of the other children running about the Carter plantation. Diana had watched them at play: the boys, young ruffians like their fathers and uncles, stalking each other and small unwary animals with pointed sticks for rifles; the girls, sunbonnets the size of bassinets to protect their skin, dresses hiked up so that all one could see of them as they ran about was the floppy hat and long, coltish legs. So wild was their play, that trees seemed no bar to their path. Even the girls ran right up them like squirrels.

Kitty had fit right in. Soon she was spending all her time with them, playing and gossiping. "... They're all odd ones here, missus," she had said, "but they don't see it that way. They're so used to the way they're living, they think we're the ones that lost the bell rope. Us and the major."

"Us, I understand, but why the major, Kitty, dear?"

"I think it's because he's more like us. At least that's what they say. He doesn't whip his black fellahs, missus. And he feeds them well. And it's said he spends all his money putting clothes on their backs, and good roofs over their heads."

"It's still slavery, Kitty. And he's a master, whether kind or foul."

"I know that, missus. But they don't see it the same. They say he's weak in the head. And that he's gonna ruin his fortune until there's nothing left for his sons to inherit. . . . It's like that girl he came to buy."

Diana's interest perked. "Yes? What about her?"

"The children say he didn't want her for himself. They said the girl belonged to one of his sons, who gave her to Mister Carter to settle a gambling debt. The trouble was, Major Maguire has this black fellah, named Paul. The girl is the black fellah's wife. That's why the major wanted her back. They all think he's crazy for that. But I think it is just grand, missus. And very brave of him. They could make a lot of trouble."

"I wonder why they haven't?" Diana mused, not expecting an answer.

"Oh, because he's a great hero, missus. He came back from the Revolution with everyone singing his praises and giving him honors. Now, he's the only real soldier in these parts. They're all ashamed because they don't want to fight. Cowards. I'd fight if they let me. But I'm just a girl. So they won't."

Diana saw the major in a different light. But so sudden and bright was the glare, she couldn't quite make out the details from the size of the shadow it cast.

"But I still don't understand why once Mister Carter agreed to let the major have the girl, he resisted doing it right away. What does it matter if it's the day after tomorrow or a week from tomorrow? Can you answer that?"

Kitty turned scarlet. She ducked her head and muttered.

"Speak up, Kitty, dear. I can't hear you."

More mumbling. Then she had reached up with a hand to brush away a tear. Diana gentled the girl, smoothing her hair,

Allan Cole & Chris Bunch

straightening the folds in her frock. When the girl was calm, she had repeated the question.

Again Kitty flushed. But she looked Diana straight in the eye and got it out: "He hadn't had her yet!"

"What?" Diana was aghast.

"She's said to be very pretty, but Mister Carter hadn't had his chances with her yet. With all of Missus Carter's family about, I guess he was ashamed to. And now I don't think he'll have that chance, missus. He was mad at first, but then they said he thought it was an awfully good joke on him. ..."

Kitty had lapsed into silence. From the shudder she gave, Diana knew she was putting herself in the slave girl's place, and thinking of Adam Carter crawling into her bed. "I don't think it's very funny, missus."

"Nor do I," Diana said.

She went riding the next day with John Maguire. They packed a picnic lunch in the saddlebags of his big blaze-faced chestnut, Balthazar. Some cold meats and fruit and a little wine. She rode a sturdy bay mare.

Maguire took her on a long, circuitous route, avoiding the shacks where the slaves lived and the fields where they worked. She knew this because she felt no eyes on her for the first time since she'd left the broken-down coach. Diana was not surprised at his sensitivity to her unspoken feelings. For a man she had only known a short time, he seemed amazingly natural with her, talking lightly of this and that, searching out common ground.

They moved through pure Virginia countryside, dressed in its best green and floral print. Little trails took them across small brooks and around leafy bowers through the woods. They broke out of the treeline and into a large, overgrown meadow. A stream rushed down the hills and emptied into a wide pond in the middle of the meadow. At the edge of the pond was a long-abandoned mill, a relic from a time of individual enterprise. The roof was caved in and the mill wheel stopped by tumbling rocks. Maguire found a soft, grassy place near the wheel. While she spread the blanket and laid out the food, he freed the horses to graze in the meadow. Maguire said Balthazar would come when he called, and the bay would follow. They made a lazy meal in the early afternoon sun.

He asked about her, and Diana gave him a much edited version of her life. At least she attempted to. But Maguire had a way of asking a quiet question that meant no harm and was easily evaded if privacy were threatened. But it made a person want to answer. Because John Maguire was sure to understand and be supportive. She had not met a man since Emmett with whom it was so easy to talk. Maguire seemed honestly in awe of her success.

Unlike most planters, he was not disdainful of business. "I wish I were better at it," he said. "Otherwise I might be much farther along in my plans."

"Which are . . . ?"

He hesitated for so long a time that Diana was first a little hurt, then angry that her confidences in him—edited though they might be—were not to be returned.

But when he finally spoke, she immediately relented. "Part of the blame is the war," he said. "At least that's the excuse I make to myself. But ... to be absolutely honest with you, Mrs. Shannon—"

"Diana, please. A rescue from that dreaded coach deserves at the very least first names between us, don't you think?"

He laughed at this, nodding vigorously, taking heart. She liked his laugh. "For some time now," he continued, a little firmer than before, "I've had a mind to give up everything. Make an early settlement on my sons and daughters, sell what 1 can, and go. Of course, my family thinks I'm mad. And if my neighbors knew, they would believe worse."

"Where would you go?"

"I have some land on the river in Mississippi Territory. I was thinking of a farm. A real farm. Vegetables and meat. And perhaps a little shipping business on the side. I think the traffic is enough so that it would be profitable."

Allan Cole & Chris Bunch

"What's to stop you?"

He turned his blue eyes on her with a look so mournful she almost lost her heart. "I'm fifty-seven years old," he said in a harsh whisper. "And I don't know how I came to be in this place."

He looked around, brooding. Diana knew it wasn't the lovely meadow he was seeing. Then: "Sometimes I think a great trick was played on the Maguires. But there's no humor attached to this trick, only a curse. And I call that curse the fifty human beings I own body and soul. Besides that fifty, there are thirty more. Men and women: the property of my sons. They inherited them from their mother, but I've kept them in trust far past the legal limit ... a source of great controversy in my family, as you can imagine." The last was delivered a bit dryly, with a hint of a cynical smile.

Diana hesitated to answer. To her it seemed simple: free them. But if it was so simple, why was this otherwise intelligent man suffering so? She needed to know more. Diana determined to make it her business to find out. Not so much for John Maguire, but for the eighty men and women in his power.

Feeling a bit like a young, guilt-stricken sailor quizzing a harlot, she asked him how a nice Irish boy came to be in such foul company. John told her that his grandfather had been transported early in the last century. His crime was lost to family history, but was said to be quite minor. The fact that he was Irish made things much worse for him. More telling, however, was that the crime was committed in an age when even slight offenses were considered great threats to the social order.

After months of living in the squalor of the old prison ships at the London docks, he was transported to the colonies. The first American Maguire landed in Connecticut and was sold into indenture. For seven years, it was said, he labored for a cruel farmer. But when the term of his service came to an end, the farmer used lies and influence to have another seven added as a penalty. He fled and made his way to Virginia. He was twenty-seven.

John Maguire's grandfather was noted for his thrift and hard work. He labored at menial jobs, but studied late into the night. He taught himself to read and write, and finally came to the attention of a judge, who employed him as a clerk and tutored him on the law. Eventually he became a judge himself. He married well, the daughter of a prominent family with land but no money. The first American Maguire had money, but no land. It was said to be a great match. The dowry included one hundred slaves.

"But how could he?" Diana interrupted. "I'm sorry if this offends you, but after hearing that tale, I think your grandfather must have been . . ." She hesitated to use so impolite a word.

"A great hypocrite?" Maguire helped.

"Yes," Diana said. "Where was his sympathy? He knew the evil firsthand, had lived under a master's hand, or worse. I see no excuses or hope for him, and I'm sorry once again for maligning your family. But I can't help but speak the truth."

"I agree with all of it and more," Maguire said, surprising her more than a little. "But my grandfather is the minor villain in this piece. My father was much worse. He doubled my grandfather's fortune ... in the slaving trade."

Maguire attempted no verbal tricks to soften the statement. Instead, he watched her steadily as she reacted in shock to the news, judged him, and found the Maguires guilty.

"There's more," he finally said. "But I won't torment you with it. I'm sure you can see that I have come to my current confusion by a long and tortuous route."

With that, he stood up abruptly, strode to the mill wheel, and began kicking away the rock barrier that kept the wheel motionless. Not another word passed between them for a full hour as he worked steadily at this odd task. A shriek like a banshee rent the silence. The great wheel jumped forward six feet or more. Then it hung there, swaying back and forth.

Allan Cole & Chris Bunch

Maguire kicked loose a remaining rock. The wheel sprang into full life. And the meadow was filled once again with the peaceful sound of the millstream at work. For a long time they watched it spin. Then Diana patted the grass beside her and John came to sit.

Without taking her eyes from the wheel, Diana said: "I think you must be a very kind man. But kindness, you see, is of no consequence under the circumstances. The Greeks, I understand, wrote that the moral scale can only be balanced if an ethic is set against another ethic of equal weight. But they were ardent slavers themselves, so might think your moral exchange sufficient."

"There isn't enough coin in the world," Maguire said.

Diana turned to him with a smile. "That's the other thing I was going to say. That I think you are greatly exaggerating your confusion. I believe you have made up your mind, John Maguire."

He nodded. Diana was right.

"When?" Flat. Demanding.

Maguire struggled with his answer. "It's not so easy as that," he said.

"When?" Insistent.

"I'm not sure how to go about it. No, that's not true. I know how to accomplish it. But I fear for their future. How will they make their way? They would be in danger of starving."

"If that occurs, I agree," Diana said. "It would be a terrible tragedy. But they would be free. It's not for you to say or judge or rule."

"Yes, I know," Maguire said. Anguish in his voice. "I've thought about giving them a choice: travel with me to Mississippi as free men and women, or take their chances with freedom here. I can provide them with some money to make it easier."

"Then do it," Diana said. "But don't tie it to a new beginning elsewhere. That is another and quite personal decision. The issues are separate. And these unfortunate people should not have to wait out one second of your own crisis."

"I've thought that already." Maguire sighed. "Although you make the point far stronger. But there's also the matter of the thirty or more people owned by my sons. ... I don't have the legal right to free them."

"Buy them," Diana said. "Then act."

"It would bankrupt me," Maguire said.

Diana just stared at him. He had no answer. "I'll loan you the money," she said.

He shook his head: no.

"You are a soldier," Diana said, "and from what I hear, a very brave one . . . who has risked his life, and is willing to do so again. What's a fortune against a life? Answer me that, John Maguire!"

He had none. Because there was none to give.

Their words were strained and a little forced on the ride back. Even so, they both somehow felt closer: a bond had been established. But it was as fragile as a web spun across a garden path.

* * * *

To Diana, the rhythms of plantation life were all a-kilter. Carter and his sons slept in until ten most mornings. They would be greeted with a toddy or a sangaree in a chilled glass fetched by their personal slaves from the icehouse. A leisurely breakfast was made on a veranda, then they would retire to loll upon a cool pallet. There they would remain most of the day with endless drinks and tidbits fetched for them, fanned and cozened by their slaves like Oriental pashas. Dinner was at two, followed by more relaxation, or hunting or fishing. Or endless talk of sporting feats.

Gambling seemed their greatest passion. She heard tales of enormous wagers on the most trivial events. Adam Carter said his doctor had wagered an entire year's medical practice against a gallon of rum in a dispute over how a viper delivered its venom. The doctor lost and was impoverished along with his family—who had never been consulted in the

Allan Cole & Chris Bunch

matter. Men would travel for days to witness a cockfight. More tobacco notes would be bet on a blood feud between two chickens than there was cured product to support them. A man with the pedigree of a southern aristocrat would think nothing of sucking a clot from a favored rooster's wounded throat so it could continue the battle.

But this was nothing against their favorite pastime: racing. In the South, Diana reflected, horseflesh and horsemanship defined manhood. The bloods—young men like Carter's sons—deigned to wear only one spur upon their boot. They said it was to lessen the risk of being hung up on a stirrup during a racing heat. Which didn't explain why they wore that single spur all day, even if no race was contemplated. John Maguire said the crops of entire plantations were bet at these races. The crops were often redeemed by money borrowed at enormous rates of interest.

But if the men lived their whole lives in idle games, they did it not only at the expense of their slaves, but also of their wives. The women were in the kitchen at five in the morning to oversee the cooking. Anything of value was kept under lock and key to guard against theft. They carried bunches of keys at their waists and were always doling out portions of food and drink and even soap to wash their husbands' clothes. Every task was done by hand by the slaves, but it was up to the mistress of the house to check each detail.

From talking to one of Sarah's aunts, Diana realized few wives of northern farmers would envy her lot. A plantation mistress was raised to believe that a woman's most priceless possession was her "magic spell," defined as some mystical power her sex had to subtly bend men to her will. The reality was that the men paid little attention to their wives at all. And that was even if they had been coaxed out of bachelorhood by a handsome dowry. Then, with no previous education or training, the new mistress of the house would be expected to be an expert housekeeper whether she wanted to or not.

Of course all sewing, spinning, weaving, and knitting was to be done by her. She was also expected to be doctor to her family and household slaves, as expert at poultry breeding as she was at making cider, candles, or soap. In the fall she oversaw the hog butchering; in the winter, drying the fruit.

Where and when she was supposed to learn to perform these feats, Diana couldn't tell. Sarah was certainly unprepared. Even at fifteen, Diana had seldom met so ignorant a woman. She could barely read or write. But she struggled desperately just the same, in constant fear of her husband's displeasure. So much for the mistress.

From what Diana could see, the life of a slave was far worse than anything even she had imagined. The plantation—which she later learned was typical—was blotched with their cabins every thirty rods or so. These were built of rough timbers, crossed and then interlocked at the corners like a cob house. A very few had outside chimneys constructed of stone. The floor inside was hard earth. Diana quizzed Sarah, who was proud to say her husband allowed his field hands a cap, shirt, and a pair of drawers—paid for out of his own pocket. They also got a blanket, but only in the winter. The household servants lived with their master and mistress and slept on the floor in front of the fire. She noticed they all had classical names, like Plato or Pompey, or Flora or Lily. With so much human labor, there was no thought of any kind of convenience. The main well was a long way from the house, and all day long the slave women trooped back and forth, carrying big stone jugs on their heads. The kitchen was so far from the house, it was impossible to deliver hot food to the table. At mealtimes the path between kitchen and house was one long line of women fetching and toting.

She watched them make cider one day. There was not even the cheapest apple press available. Instead, the slave women wielded big logs, crushing the pomace in a big wooden trough and singing to the rhythm of the work. One of the women was larger and appeared stronger than the rest. But from the odd way her cotton shift hung from her body,

Allan Cole & Chris Bunch

she appeared deformed. When she turned, Diana could see that one breast was missing, and the side of her face was a large, white blotch. As if someone had placed a hot blister pack on her cheek. Why this would be done, Diana couldn't say. The woman's voice, however, was a marvel.

It soared above the others, as sweet as a bell at Eventide. Her song was so beautiful, Diana closed her eyes for a moment, shutting out the terrible view—not of the woman's deformities, but her plight. The singing abruptly stopped. Diana opened her eyes to see the women working silently at the cider trough. But now there was no pleasure in the work. The big woman dared to glance in Diana's direction. It was a look that branded her a thief of songs. Ashamed, Diana stumbled away. When she was well beyond sight, she heard the wonderful voice lift again, soaring free in the sky. Diana walked quickly out of hearing. She had no right to the music.

* * * *

On the final day, Adam Carter's wife came to her for advice. She was so shy and fearful of coming to the point, that more than an hour passed in silence, with only occasional one-word answers to Diana's questions to break it. Diana could see Sarah was not only shy, but in pain. And her face—already a sickly white—was heavily powdered in an attempt to hide the tiny red eruptions on her skin. Whether this was a symptom of the pain or adolescent blemishes, Diana didn't know.

The longer she spent with the child, however, the more difficult Sarah's mysterious errand seemed to get, until Diana could see she was about to depart without speaking up. She almost let her, as some sort of vague revenge for the part she played as mistress of the plantation. Diana thought it was as if cruelty were an affliction caused by some small organism that bred in southern air. Like the pox. And now maybe she had been infected. So she took pity and asked her hostess why she had come.

"I have been feeling . . . unwell for some time," Sarah said. "I thought it was the pregnancy at first. But my aunts . . ." Her voice failed along with her courage.

Diana now understood the nature of the visit. How it came about was obvious: her medical prowess had been vastly exaggerated by young Kitty. Still, from what she had seen of the region, it was likely any doctor would be even more ignorant. Especially if it involved a female complaint. She coaxed Sarah into describing the symptoms. They were delivered haltingly, with long lapses between each descriptive fact. And the whole time the girl spoke, she never once looked Diana in the eye. But Diana knew the answer before more than a few words were out.

At first the little red spots had only appeared on her palms and the soles of her feet. Then they spread to the rest of her body. Then her private parts had become sore and greatly inflamed. Not just her vagina, but in the anal region as well. This was followed by a painful and embarrassing discharge. More recently, she had suffered from nausea and intermittent fevers. And her entire body ached as if from the flux. But this was a torment she was willing to bear, compared to the awful cramps she had been suffering. It was as if a clawed hand were reaching straight into her gut to rip at her.

As Sarah spoke, Diana realized she knew the answer as well, but she was fearful of admitting it. It was a disease few had ever cared to name, much less admit its cause. A hundred years before it was said to have been transmitted in the air, or by a giant lizard. Some modern quacks even blamed it exclusively on women. They said all females carried the organism and denied they even suffered from it, but only passed it on to innocent men, who caught it from engaging in excessive sex. These doctors also had an odd notion for its cure.

Diana gently steered the conversation to Sarah's relations with her husband. Normally, she would never have questioned Carter's reasons for marrying so young a bride.

Allan Cole & Chris Bunch

But he was too rich to need the dowry, and he was so cold to his wife that she knew it wasn't lust or an old man's pride of possession.

Sarah had the clap. And there was only one person who could have given it to her: Adam Carter. If Diana was right, his marriage to Sarah was part of his doctor's recommended cure. What a lovely present for a marriage bed.

Now Sarah was not only infected, but three months pregnant. If the child survived the womb and delivery, it too would be infected. If she told the girl all this, the only comfort she could offer was that it was unlikely Sarah would live to see the child weaned, much less the pain and deformities of its later life. So all she told her was that she had the clap, that she and her unborn child were possibly in grave danger, and that there could be no other source for her misery but her husband.

For a time the girl fought so hard to keep her head that Diana almost burst into tears herself out of sympathy. Sarah asked her for the cure. Diana carefully explained there really was only one, but that it failed more often than it succeeded. She would have to take a pill every day, containing fifteen grains of calomel and ten grains of mercury. It's a poison, she said, and it will make you miserable. But you dare not weaken, even if your teeth get so loose they rattle in your head. The doctor will also want to bleed and purge you. If you let him convince you of this course of treatment, I doubt if you can survive. I know your child won't.

Diana desperately wanted to leave the girl more hope. But she knew if she lied to her, or put a sugar teat on the facts, Sarah Carter and her baby were doomed. The only thing else she could tell her was that at all costs to keep her husband from her bed, at least until Diana returned home and could send her a supply of "British Overcoats." She told her these devices were simple to use, but she would enclose instructions just in case.

Invented by a Col. Cundum, these devices were made of lamb intestines, and should not only protect her from further infection, but any unwanted pregnancy as well.

"What if ... he won't ... use them?"

Her faltering whisper was torment. Diana just stared at her. There was nothing else to say. From this moment on, what happened to Sarah was entirely up to her. The silence was broken by the sound of two young slave girls giggling as they worked outside the door. Sarah flew into a blinding rage. She flung open the door and shouted hysterically for silence. Then she slammed it on the shocked faces and whirled back to Diana.

"I live in a harem," she screamed. "Full of nigger whores. I see them after my husband. I know how they entice him. Sluts and whores and—" She collapsed on the floor sobbing so fitfully she could barely breathe.

There came a tap on the door. But Sarah was so overcome, she didn't notice. Diana slipped it open and saw it was one of the girls Sarah had ordered away. She was frightened, but had forced herself to return to see if she could help. Sarah saw her and screamed an obscenity. She tore a large pin from her hair and rushed the door like an animal in a panic attack. The pin was six inches long and as sharp as a shoemaker's awl. She thrust it at the girl, but Diana closed the door just in time. The force of the thrust was so hard that more than an inch of pin was buried into the wood before it snapped off.

Sarah came to her senses for a moment. She stood there motionless, staring at the pin. Realizing what she had almost done. She looked up at Diana, her eyes brimming. Pleading. Then her face became quite cold and stern. She apologized to Diana for troubling her. And left without another word.

Diana found John Maguire alone in the stable, tending his blaze-faced chestnut. She was sick to her stomach, and her hands were shaking from tension.

"I must leave here," she said.

Allan Cole & Chris Bunch

Maguire was startled. "It shouldn't be much more than another two days or so, Diana," he said. "Plenty of time to make the wedding."

"Please," she said, "I can't bear this any longer. If you are my friend ..."

Diana stayed that night at Maguire's house, in a room he had hastily made ready. But she didn't sleep. Instead, she sat on the hard window seat, staring out into the darkness, brooding on the madness in this sad land. She spent the whole next day in her room. John sent for Kitty and their baggage, and the wife he had bought back for his headman. He didn't trouble Diana, but only had food and drink sent up to her room. Which she didn't touch.

That night he coaxed her down to his library, where he built up a fire against a sudden, sharp spring wind. He plied her with a little brandy, but didn't speak or in any way intrude on her thoughts until she was ready. After a while Diana told him the story of Sarah Carter and her complete despair. She also told him of the woman's final outburst, and how she almost slew the little black child who had come to her aid.

Maguire listened without comment until she was done. Then he poured them both another drop and turned down the lamp until only the fire lit the room. Then he told her a story of his own. It was about his mother. Her name was Angelina and she was from a very old family that predated even the institutions of the king. She was intelligent and literate and John thought her quite beautiful, although this memory was dim. He was not quite thirteen when she died.

"I remember her as the most talented woman who ever lived," he said. "And not just in those skills which are said to be the sole province of women. My father was hopeless as a manager. He would have lost everything he had gained from his evil business if my mother had not overseen the plantation. She tended the crops and the money and the slaves who tilled our land. For a long time this worked well. Especially since my father was usually away in the trade.

"But several years before she died, he came home to stay. We had an orchard then. With a few figs and almonds, and some fruit trees. There was even a brook and a small path with flowers growing along the lane. Quite lovely. My father had a small, white house built out in this orchard. He made it his permanent home. He rarely came to the main house, except for holidays or visitors. He filled this house with slave women. And I don't mean just young, pretty women. But women of every shape and age and variety. And as far as I know, he never came to my mother's bed again."

"How could she bear it?" Diana asked.

"I can't say. In the same circumstances, I know I couldn't."

"Did she ever speak of it?"

"Only indirectly. But I'll tell you this—she had great sympathy for these women. As much sympathy as she had hate for my father. I think she saw them as doubly enslaved. In fact, she used to say all women are slaves. And that even queens were forced to sell themselves into marriage."

Diana understood exactly what Angelina Maguire had meant by this. She also understood her reaction to her husband's massive infidelities. Some women—like Sarah Carter—refused to blame the betrayal on their husbands. To them the villain was the victim. She was a slut and a whore, with morals so loose and compelling that no man could resist. Even if it was rape. Angelina Maguire reacted the second way: she placed the blame squarely on the cause and pitied the victim. Diana was sorry she had died so long ago. Angelina sounded like a woman she would have liked to have known.

"The next thing you may find odd," John said, "was her attitude on slavery."

"She opposed it," Diana said, firmly. She knew this without a flicker of thought.

"My mother was quite outspoken in her views," John said. "Of course, it was safer then. Although, if it weren't, I doubt that it would have stilled her tongue."

Allan Cole & Chris Bunch

Diana nodded: absolutely!

"She said her grandmother had been opposed as well. The two of them used to pray together the thing would be outlawed. I remember her arguing with a doctor's wife. She said this: 'If they don't end it soon, my headwoman and I will die from exhaustion.' She was right. I believe it killed them both."

Diana wanted to ask him why—if this was his background—he had not divested himself of this manner of life many years before. But she hadn't the strength to manage it now.

She was not surprised, however, that Maguire's mind was on the same path. "When I was young," he said after a while, "I was stupid and filled with conceit." He smiled at her. A shy, little boy smile. "I think, after all these years," he said in an aside, "I have at least shed some of the conceit.

"I was not much different than my own sons, or even Adam Carter's. I was a young blood up for the game. I can't say when things exactly began to change. After the war, I suppose. All of it seemed so pointless and alien to me when I returned home. I began to read. I know that affected my views.

"Then I married. She was a good wife. I was a faithful husband. And I believe we loved one another. At least, later we did. She had a cancer. It took her some years to die. Terrible years for her. And then . . . when she was gone ..."

Maguire didn't go on from there. He didn't need to for Diana to fill in the rest. He had suffered the kind of wound from which many people take years to recover, if at all. The silence lingered. Maguire stared into his glass.

Diana thought about his tale for some time. She didn't remember falling asleep. But when she awakened in the morning, John was gone, and she was curled up by the still glowing fire. A blanket drawn over her. And a pillow under her head.

CHAPTER THIRTY-THREE

SHE DIDN'T WAIT for the return of the hired coach. Instead, John Maguire took her to Jamestown in his own carriage. It was an old vehicle, but well-maintained. The paint was sparkling red and the interior was of soft, dark leather. There was enough room for her, Maguire, and Kitty, and more to spare.

John's headman, Paul, drove. He was all smiling and proud with his lady perched beside him. Her name was Adele, and she was a small, lovely woman with skin as black as the heart of a rare tree from a distant forest, and smooth and clear as an infant's. She had dark flashing eyes with curling lashes like a fine Spanish fan. Her voice was low and unintentionally sultry, and she was afflicted with a nervous giggle that would sound like a schoolgirl's even when she grew old. As Diana saw Paul and Adele cuddling and cooing, she thought of the old wagon—hauled by Horse—that was once her honeymoon chariot. Seeing the couple rejoined and happy lightened her mood immensely.

It was an easy journey, made more enjoyable because John had brought his chestnut along and a black gelding for Diana. They spent most of the trip riding beside the coach, dashing off whenever they liked to view some marvel seen from the road.

She asked John about his family. He said he had three sons and all were grown men with wives and families of their own. As each one had wed, John had parceled off his land and helped them build and furnish their houses. His response was so brief, Diana surmised that Maguire and his three sons were not on speaking terms—because of his radical views. John's face grew grave when he spoke of his children, but then he gave a cynical laugh and said, weren't children a source of great comfort and joy to their parents' dotage?

Diana thought of Farrell and James, and for the first time in many years laughed at her own dilemma.

They made camp each night in three small pavilions of gaily painted canvas he'd had packed on the coach. The nights were as cheerful as the days, and the only time Diana thought of what lay ahead of her was just before sleep. How would she find her son? More difficult: How would she deal with it? Then she'd hear Adele's musical giggle and the soft sounds of lovemaking. She'd smile and the dark thoughts would vanish as she fell into peaceful sleep.

Once they heard singing deep in the woods—it sounded like a choir. John said it was most probably a slave congregation gathered in illegal worship far from the eyes of their masters. Paul called Maguire aside and they had a brief conversation. Paul smiled and thanked John, and he and Adele disappeared in the direction of the singing. John said they were off to be married.

"He just asked your permission?"

Maguire laughed. "Not exactly," he said. "Actually, they wanted to be remarried. A second ceremony to celebrate Adele's return. He wanted to know if it would be convenient right now. I not only said yes, but I gave him his wife's freedom for a second wedding present."

He looked at her expectantly, for her approval. "What about Paul?" she said instead. "Why not free him as well?"

Maguire was astonished. "Paul? But he is free. He's been with me since he was a boy. I freed him when he was old enough not to blather it about and draw my neighbors' wrath."

"And he stays with you?" Now Diana was astonished.

"He has thus far. Although, if I delay much longer in those plans I revealed to you, I don't know if he will continue. If not, I told him long ago that I would get him north and assist him in any way I could. I'm not sure if he would have stayed this long on any account if it hadn't been for Adele. And the war."

An hour or so later the couple returned. They were like children in love, arms about each other, finding humor in the smallest things. John shook Paul's hand and lightly kissed the bride. Diana kissed them both and promised them a lovely present when they reached Jamestown. Kitty said, Wasn't it romantic, and she cried like it was her sister who had just left the altar. All in all, Diana thought it a wonderful wedding.

The last night of the journey, Diana retired early. She said she had many letters to write and they must be posted when they reached Jamestown, else her family would be in terror for her, and her bankers distressed at her long and silent absence. She lied. Actually, the night was so bright with moon and stars, and the warm air so heavy with the sweet scent of flowers, that memories of more precious nights were flooding back. Sitting next to John Maguire with those nights on her mind made her feel like an adulteress. She retired early to avoid spoiling his evening. She lay on the pallet with a cool scented kerchief across her eyes. But once again, instead of brooding, she fell asleep.

Diana came awake to a voice whispering her name. She looked about, bewildered, not sure where she was for a moment. The carriage lamp she used for light still burned brightly at its post on a peg. The voice called her name again. It was John. She asked him in, surprising herself that she, too, had whispered.

"I saw the light . . . still burning," he said. "Is everything ... all right?"

Why he spoke so hesitantly, she didn't know. She told him everything was fine. She had fallen asleep, she said, but thank you for looking in. Silence, the kind that meant he should go. He almost did. Maguire even took a step away. Then he stopped. But he stared at the ground as if he didn't dare meet her eyes.

Diana asked what was amiss. He didn't answer . . . only stood there, trembling. His body was leaning toward her, but he seemed to be held back by some long invisible line, as if braced against a great storm. He was wearing a loose, silk

Allan Cole & Chris Bunch

drawstring shirt, open at the throat. The hair on his chest was fine and gray. She could see the muscles tensed and cabling along his neck. But the skin was so tender, it begged to be kissed and nibbled and caressed. Maguire looked at her, his blue eyes a storm under the gray brows. He tried to speak, but the words strangled in his throat. Diana felt the tinder catch spark. She resisted, but the heat was so intense, she was overwhelmed. Every move was slow in this heat, at odd counterpoint to the quickening pace of her heart. Almost against her will, a hand rose like an ascending balloon . . . beckoning. . . . He came to her pallet in a rush.

It was like coming home after many years in exile. His caressing hands did not seem a stranger's, the motions of his lovemaking tantalizingly familiar. All night long they whispered each other's names excitedly, as if they were glorious words only recently discovered. At daybreak he said he had never met such a woman as she or known such sweet comfort, and would she be his wife, Diana, please? She looked him up and down to see if she could spy the master weaver in him. All she saw was Emmett in the woods. She did not spring back.

Diana thought at some length. This alone surprised her: that she should even contemplate his offer. Then she sighed and shook her head. She did not have to list the reasons for him. Although there were many, perhaps he could sweep them away if she let him. All but one: the light that would die in Paul and Adele's eyes when this journey was done.

Maguire started to speak, but she silenced him with a soft hand at his lips. He had been about to pledge the earth, the sky, and what lay beyond. This was not what Diana wanted to hear. She believed promises under such circumstances soon proved flaccid. More important, she viewed the gulf between them as so vast, no bridgework ever conceived could be hurled across it.

"I want nothing from you, John," she said. "There is no coin to be paid for my hand, just as I have nothing to sell. Act as you will on your own account, not mine. Meantime ... if it pleases you, I'll be your lover. For a while. But not your wife."

Maguire didn't argue. He listened closely, nodding as he took in her meaning. She could see the conflict in his face, that he saw she spoke the truth. He only wanted to know one thing: "Will it anger you ... if I ask again?"

Diana hesitated, then saw the hurt in his face at her hesitation. Still, she couldn't lie. "I don't know, John," she said. "It might. I'll not forbid you . . . but . . . please know . . . my answer will always be the same." He smiled at this. As if he had achieved a small victory.

He did not bring up the matter again until they were just outside Jamestown. The closer they got, the more distracted she became. Until the circumstances of James Emmett's marriage entirely filled her mind. Maguire said he understood and did not plan to press his intentions until she was done. He asked her if she wanted to go on alone to her son's place, or if it would be easier for her if he were by her side. Alone, she said, but started to change her mind and laughed at her own confusion.

"I have business in town," John said, "and friends to stay with nearby. I can be engaged in these affairs as long or as short as you like. I'll wait until you're done. Or come the instant you send for me."

She tried to tell him this was senseless, that he should go on about his own life and pay no mind to her. He said she was right. This was the course for any sensible man to follow. "Meanwhile, madam," he said, "your fool awaits."

He helped her hire a coach and a trustworthy driver to take her the rest of the way. And kissed her thoroughly farewell.

* * * *

Eliza Hope Beecham was as beautiful as any bridegroom's fantasy. She was tall and slender and her hair was a crown of thick black curls. Her eyes were dark smudges under classic brows. She fell on Diana's breast when she met her and wept and called her "Mother, dear."

Allan Cole & Chris Bunch

James Emmett looked on with amusement on his lips, but Diana could see no humor in his eyes. He was . . . afraid? This was a surprise. But of what? Her opinion of him? It never seemed to matter before. After she'd gently shed Eliza's sticky embrace, James bent to give her a kiss.

He was hesitant, as if expecting his mother to push him away. She wanted to, but didn't. She met Eliza's parents. They were warm and hospitable and seemed amiable enough people—for unrepentant slavers intent on ruining her son. She despised them almost as much as she despised their beautiful, empty-headed daughter. But after her experiences with the Carters, there were few surprises lying in ambush in the brush of idle conversation.

The Beecham holdings—even compared to Carter's— were vast, consisting of so many thousands of acres and hundreds of slaves to hoe the pristine white Nankin Boll that Diana was reminded of the legendary estates of the French king whose head was taken off by his subjects. They had cattle and pigs and fowl of all kinds, several smokehouses to hold all that flesh, cellars brimming with tubers and dried fruits and nuts, an icehouse Mister Beecham boasted he kept full even in the hottest summers, and enough imported wines and spirits to float a British fleet. It was Diana's professional opinion that despite the display, Mister Beecham did not have two coppers to squeak together. This was also usually the state of James Emmett's fortunes, so she wasn't sure why the Beecham family was so intent on the marriage.

For two weeks the wedding guests arrived. The slaves were worked to exhaustion tending their needs, then were worked some more. It was torment, but Diana held her tongue. She kept young Kitty close to her, so no conversation could dare beyond the casual. She even held her son distant, although James constantly hinted at a private talk. Diana evaded him with light jests and bewildering shifts in chatter, so the boy must have thought his mother had lost her wits. Although she was certainly fooling herself about this—few things had ever escaped James Emmett's attentions. From the looks he gave, Diana could see he was gradually understanding her plan.

By inviting her, he'd asked her to play a role. She was here in her official capacity as head of the Shannon family, not as his mother. A mother would weep and tear her hair. She would curse the moment she first let him suck. Then all those cloying memories would come back, thoughts of the cord that once had bound them, and might bind them still. The bottom she had wiped. The tears kissed away. Motherhood was perilous terrain. She would lose her footing and sink into sentimental mire. No one knew better how to play those strings than James Emmett Shannon. So although she didn't deny it when he called her "Mother," any attempt at affection or delving at mutual memory she brushed away with a casual laugh. Diana could see she was hurting him. She took no pleasure in it.

* * * *

The wedding was a great success. The bride was beautiful, the groom handsome. Mrs. Beecham wept, and her husband was moist-eyed as well. For different reasons, Diana felt like crying herself. The guests danced and partied for more than a week, with the blushing couple holding court. It was easy for Diana to stay aloof during this silliness. She only had to be still a little longer, then she could take her leave. She thought of John waiting for her, and the question he would ask again. Then she put it from her mind as well as she could. It was not fair to judge his proposal under the cloud of her current misery. Her answer would be the same, she was sure. But she wanted the rejection based on reason.

With all the drinking and sporting, the young bucks sniffed around Kitty in small packs Diana kept driving away. She caught one young man cozying up to her in an empty hallway, turning her head with his compliments, urging her into a nearby room for "just one chaste kiss from your sweet lips." Diana ran him off and confronted Kitty.

Allan Cole & Chris Bunch

The girl was upset and for a change spoke up about it. "They don't mean no harm, missus," she said. "I'm grown enough to look after myself. Besides, they think I'm pretty."

"You are pretty," Diana said. "This is a fact of nature, not flattery. The difficulty, Kitty, dear, is these young men think they are quite safe in pressing their attentions on you beyond what would be seemly with their sisters' friends."

"Because I am a servant?" Kitty asked, sullen.

"Yes, child. They have no fear or care of ruining you because of your current station. Now, keep your wits about you, and your skirts down. When we return home, we'll see what we can do about improving matters. . . . Do I have your promise?"

Kitty promised, a bit resentful, but Diana thought she'd keep her word. How she would keep her own, she wasn't sure. Perhaps Kitty was only a little tardy in her mental growth. Her mind hadn't caught up to her body. Diana vowed to seek a solution. Schooling, if that seemed the avenue. If not, the least she could do was to advise Kitty how to keep her reputation intact, and tell her this didn't necessarily have anything to do with keeping her knees together, as long as it involved men who had a bit more thought for her than these careless young fools.

Despite this difficulty, Kitty once again proved a sound source of intelligence. Kitty said the young men were all talking about Mister Beecham's grand plans now that Emmett had joined their clan. The plans seemed to consist of many improvements and additions to their property, as well as a wish list of luxuries that would founder a Boston merchant house.

"Where do they expect to find the money?" Diana asked. The longer she stayed with these people, the more she could see everything about her was a paper and glue facade.

Kitty's response astounded her. "From young Mister Shannon, missus."

She gaped at the girl, almost sputtering. "James Emmett? And where do they expect him to find it?"

"From you, missus."

This was more than Diana could bear. The people she'd met seemed worth less to her than the sewage gouting into the Schuylkill. That such foul people were making plans involving her participation was worse than any sin contemplated by Farrell. She stormed about until she could waylay her son. Diana demanded to know what this business was about. She smashed away all his protests and excuses and insisted he say if he'd used her name with these villainous folk.

"I admit I've taken a few liberties, Mother," he said. "But I have made no promises of your involvement. Truthfully, I haven't."

She wanted to strike him. Instead, she took back some control over her anger. "Don't the Beechams know what kind of a son-in-law they've won? A gambler and a rakehell, and a minor one to boot."

James didn't argue, instead he said it was an accurate portrait of many young men from these parts. "If anything, they think I'm more settled than most. I've boasted of your success wherever I have gone, Mother. If some people believe I also own a few of your talents, why should I dissuade them?"

"How have you said I would help? Don't deny you said it."

"I only spoke of your knowledge of many markets. I suppose this has led them to think you would help me win investors."

The situation was this: like most planters, the war had brought commerce for the Beechams to a near halt. While prices soared abroad, blockaded crops languished at the docks or warehouses. The Beechams feared bankruptcy. James had pledged to find investors to keep the Beechams afloat, in return for a share in profits sure to follow once the war was done.

The rest was also plain to her. James had taken a great gamble in inviting her. If he could keep his mother from

Allan Cole & Chris Bunch

speaking her mind to the Beechams and their ilk, her business assistance would be presumed. "How do you hope to accomplish your aims?" She had to ask it. Curiosity was getting the better of outrage.

"Alone, you mean?"

"Yes."

"You may not believe this, Mother, but I really am not that poor a businessman. People like me. Respect my opinion. And I can usually coax them into what I want. I don't think you can see it, however, because I have always lived in your shadow. Like Farrell. Except I was not so content."

"You blame me?"

"I did. For a time. Later I saw you had no choice. We all survived, Mother, because you slew dragons. If you had set your sights on smaller game, I doubt we would be alive to speak together now. Still, I learned much from you. And although I will never be as skilled, I think I can succeed better than most."

Diana sighed. There was some truth in what her son said. She also saw a breath of a chance she might salvage him. She knew the cost to herself would be great. The plans she'd contemplated since she'd left home would have to be abandoned. Then her heart gave a wrench as she realized her lover would have to be so harshly rejected that he would leave and never return. So your mind was not so firmly made up as you supposed, was it, you great liar Diana Shannon?

But she gave no hint of the sacrifice. If anything, it made her plea all the harder. She begged James to see the evil in these people. She warned him that no matter how much he struggled, their disease would become his as well. James said he understood her fears, but he was made of better stuff. He was only going to play their game for a short time, make use of their markers and then cash them in with impunity.

"What of the slaves?"

"I'll do my best for them, Mother. No matter what my course, they will be slaves just the same. I can free some of them when it is convenient. I've promised myself I'll do that, I really have . . . and you must admit that if they are to have a master, it is better if they have me."

It almost killed her to have him say this, that he should take refuge in woods so thin they wouldn't hide the smallest shrew. She wanted to run weeping from the room. Instead she asked him to please come back to Philadelphia with her, to bring his new wife, whom she promised to welcome and love as if she were her own daughter. She would make a fine place for them, and find a business for her son he could be proud of.

"Please stop, Mother. I can't do that. I am James Emmett Shannon. My father's son. I must find my own path."

"Your father was not so ashamed to ask a woman's assistance," she said.

James had trouble with what he had to say next, which was that he knew Eliza could not be happy any place except here. That Philadelphia would be hell for her, a gentle southern lady. "I love her, Mother," is what he finally said.

Poor James Emmett. He really believed love conquers all, that it drives back armies and defeats oppression—or makes oppression easier to bear, that it would redeem all the lies he told himself. James Loves Eliza: a bold truth carved upon a tree. Ah, well, he was right in one thing: it had defeated her. The last road was blocked. She could travel no further.

Diana kissed her son and wished him well, although she wasn't sure how she meant this. She tarried a few more days, then made her excuses and took leave of the Five Forks Beechams. As her carriage rolled along, she saw James Emmett kick his horse away from the farewell party and head for a distant knoll. He stopped there and watched her pass. She almost raised a hand to the window to wave goodbye. Instead she turned away.

* * * *

John listened to her account . . . absorbing it all and much more besides. Then he held her close so she could weep if she chose to. But she didn't. Instead she drew away and prepared herself for what she had to say next. She said what had happened was a warning sign both should heed instead of curse. For strength she fingered the little pouch with its bullet which lay hidden in her bodice. It seemed to burn at her touch. She pulled the hand away. John begged her not to speak further, because if she did, they both might regret it the rest of their lives. All this talk of lifetime regrets. Connie had said that . . . and Diana had listened. What had it gotten her?

"Only let a little time pass," he pleaded. "Then let me come to you. And if you still reject me, I promise I'll go away. Will you do this for me, Diana? Is it so much to ask?"

She almost said yes, it was; but then thought, no it wasn't. So she gave him her pledge.

"Where will you go now?" he asked. "Home?"

"I suppose so," she said. "First I have to stop and see an old friend. I made her a promise some months ago that I now regret. But if I renege, she will never forgive me."

"And where might this old friend of yours be?"

"Washington," Diana said.

"Ah well, then, I should see you sooner than I thought," John Maguire said. "I'll be in Washington myself before the summer is out."

BOOK FIVE:

WASHINGTON - AUGUST 1814

CHAPTER THIRTY-FOUR

"YOU'RE LUCKY TO be away," the sweep oar muttered to Luke Shannon.

"Quiet in the boat, there," was the shrill order from the fourteen-year-old midshipman in the boat's bows. Luke made no reply. He sat near the stern, hunched next to his sea chest, staring across Chesapeake Bay at America. Luck and Luke Shannon were strangers on this August day of 1814, and had been for more than two years. Probably, he thought, Laurence Sterne, Pope, or Voltaire would find his situation risible. The idea of an Irish-American sailor serving in the forces of the enemy, once again a British enemy, especially in a fleet about to invade the hapless teague's own country, might also have amused Luke Shannon if he'd heard the story during a rope yarn or cozy in some Philadelphia groggery when the winter wind blasted. But not when the poor sailor was the one Luke saw in his shaving glass.

Luke sat morose amid a pile of supplies and dispatches as the Weser's boat crept toward the hulking HMS Albion, a seventy-four-gun ship of the line. Adding to his misery was the intense summer heat. The bay was dotted with ships. There were more than fifty of them—all British men of war. Plus thirty troop launches to carry the landing forces from the transports. These forces included four regiments of England's finest combat soldiers, fresh from forcing Napoleon's abdication.

From the Albion's mizzen hung the white ensign of Admiral Sir George Cockburn. His name was pronounced Co-burn, and he was the most hated British sailor off America, Boatswain Henderson had told Shannon. "I was told," Henderson had said, "that you Americans have a price on his head. Damn if that wouldn't happen from a nation of bastards and red Indians. Do your soldiers still scalp women and children?"

Luke managed not to say anything. He was in more than enough trouble already, because Bos'n Henderson had just told him he was detailed on special service, to the admiral himself. Shannon scoffed in complete disbelief. "Aye," he said. "The admiral's a rare good friend of mine."

"It's the mouth that does it," Henderson warned. "He did not ask for you by name, shit sack. A signal from the Albion required a reader who wrote a fair round hand. It was a stroke that Purser Evans thought of you. The captain found it a dam' great plan.

"They say," Henderson continued, "this admiral is a rare sort. Believes in leading by example. From the front, they say. Amid shot and shell, as one of those poets you're fond of readin' might put it." Henderson let that sink in. "Hell of an experience to tell your gran'children of. 'Course, war bein' what it is, 'specially at the sharp end, there ain't many live to the point of thinkin' of children, let alone gran'children. Pusser Evans said to remind you of Uriah the Hittite. Now below with you! I want you and your dunnage on deck in ten minutes."

It took less than five for Shannon to secure his belongings. That left time to enrich his scanty knowledge of the Bible. One of the more religious topmen enlightened him. So he was not supposed to return to the Albion, but go over the side, a shroud of sailcloth and a cannonball at his feet. Or, more likely, be a rotting corpse somewhere in a thicket.

In Shannon's case "Bathsheba" would be the covering of a tidy little fiddle he had discovered and, most unwisely, talked about.

The Albion's shadow bulked over the small boat. Shannon went up the battens and through the gangway Bristol fashion, like the skilled sailor he was. His chest was swayed up with the supplies. He was told to clean himself and stand by for orders. The call didn't come for hours. Shannon could feel the Albion up-anchor and begin tacking up the bay, gliding slowly in the light winds. He continued pondering his predicament and its origins. A different man

Allan Cole & Chris Bunch

might have found three central causes. As Henderson said, one was the mouth. Luke had a tendency to blurt—blurt the truth or blurt an opinion. His second greatest problem was his making and then standing by spur-of-the-moment decisions. He was very much his mother's son, but considerably lacking Connie's common sense. Luke had an explanation for all of his actions. Which was his third failing: when things went wrong, it somehow was not his fault.

Naturally, then, when Luke ran away a second time, he signed aboard the first ship that would take a boy with an unconvincingly forged letter from his parents. His first blue-water voyage was on a hellship. But somehow Luke kept to the sea. By 1810 he was an upper yardman, the young elite of the sailors; skilled, strong, and bright enough to swarm up to the topgallant and royal yards of a ship while the mast swung through thirty or more degrees, the canvas whipcracked in a full gale, and the ship plunged and reared, green water over her deck. But in the winter of 1812, Luke was forcibly drafted—pressed—into the Royal Navy.

Pressing was an age-old right of the Royal Navy. The right was carefully if confusingly defined by Act of Parliament, saying the only men liable for forced conscription were men who "used the sea." There were limitations on just which sailors could be grabbed by the press gang. For example, no foreigners could be taken against their will. However, when it came to foreign sailors, the British took the not entirely unreasonable view that anyone who spoke English was a British citizen, even on an American ship. They felt anyone born before 1776 was British, and let's hear no nonsense about a revolution. There was a certain amount of logic to their thinking—about 2,500 British seamen deserted to American ships each year. So British warships fell into the habit of stopping American ships and impressing Americans along with the British deserters. That was one of the issues—at least for speech makers—that had caused this war.

Free Trade and Sailors Rights, Luke thought. Damn that and damn the bag of wind who shouted it. Luke had been pressed by Americans—by one of his own officers, in fact. Again it had been the mouth. Luke had signed on another deathship—this one, quite literally. Three days out of New York, a yard let go when rotten cordage gave way and two men died. A week later an old sailor died. Of exhaustion, Luke thought. Rotten food, insufficient crew, incompetent officers—Luke told the mate and captain that, once landed in Le Havre, he would have them roasted by the American charge d'affairs. Which was when the Royal Navy showed up. The lieutenant in charge of the boarding party first asked for volunteers. Four men decided to change "loyalties"— about average for a pressing. Then the lieutenant passed down the ranks, spoke to and seized two other sailors who were British deserters.

At that point the mate suggested to the lieutenant he'd overlooked one man: Luke Shannon. The mate vowed he'd gone overside from a British frigate. Shannon screamed an oath and dove for the mate. He woke up aboard the British ship.

Given Luke's skills, he could have quickly been favored and even promoted to petty officer in time. The Royal Navy paid less than he was used to, but the food was better, the ship far cleaner and better found, and the rules and regulations far more fairly served.

But Luke was Irish, Luke was American, and Luke automatically objected to blind authority. And he was still mouthy. He had heard from his grandmother the tales of Emmett and Emmett's grandfather, and had nothing but contempt for England and her servants. So he was pressed from ship to ship, until he ended on the Weser—no longer as a topman, but demoted to lowly waister, a common laborer of the sea. Then they found he could read and write, and made him pusser's steward. That was when he stumbled onto the "tidy little fiddle." A ship's purser—or pusser, as he was commonly called—was technically an officer, but in reality

Allan Cole & Chris Bunch

was a contract civilian working for the Admiralty under license. He bought the ship's supplies out of pocket and made his profit on the "purser's pound," a deliberate underweighing that meant, among other things, twelve ounces of butter equaled one pound. With this legal short measure, the tight-fisted Admiralty kept from actually having to buy their brave seaman food or drink.

Pusser Evans had improved the situation by deliberately marking quite edible supplies as SPOILED on the cask. When the Weser returned to London, Evans would be able to sell these supplies for a handsome profit. Shannon assumed, though he had no knowledge this was the truth, the captain was in on the swindle. Certainly the boatswain was. Luke didn't give a damn if the Royal Navy was crooked to the seams. But from either pure meanness or maybe a love of the truth, he let slip he'd figured out the accounting. So here he was, in training to become Uriah the Hittite and dead.

At the first bell of the first watch—eight-fifteen in the evening by landsmen's calculations—the summons came. A bosun's mate sought him out and gave very explicit sailing orders. He was to speak only when spoken to. He was to answer all questions honestly, with a yes sir or a no sir. He was to remove his hat when he approached the quarterdeck. The mate advised that if Luke erred, he would be "lord of the head" until the Albion paid off or they pitched him to the sharks—whichever came first.

Shannon thought of asking to whom he was being summoned. At the very least he expected Saint Peter. But he thought better of it. This was a wise thing, because, waiting at the foot of the companionway leading down from the poopdeck was more gold braid than Luke had seen beyond a museum collection of the portraits of revolutionary heroes. Christ have mercy, the admiral was among them. Cockburn was in his forties. He was sunburned, tall and confident-looking, but Shannon was slightly disappointed. He saw no filed teeth or evil facial scars to mark him as the Hellhound of the Chesapeake. He was just an average British admiral with life and death authority over a fleet and several thousand men.

Cockburn stood to one side, watching him closely. The lieutenant began: "Shannon. You're Irish?" Answer that one with a single word, Luke thought, and repressed a scowl.

"Yessir. And nossir."

"Either you are or you are not."

"Family is Irish, sir. I am American."

"That is not how you were entered on the ship's log."

"A mistake, sir."

"Who made it?" A complete explanation would have probably put Luke on the grating for wasting the time of important men. The simple one—that the Royal Navy was at fault—did not seem advisable.

"Not sure, sir."

"You read and write?" Evidently the subject was not worth pursuing.

"Yessir."

The lieutenant indicated a small field desk. "There is pen and ink. Copy what I tell you." Shannon obeyed. "Umm . . . this being the seventeenth of August, permission is granted—"

"Could you spell that, sir?"

"G-R-"

"Nossir. Permission, sir."

"P-U-R-M-I-S-S-I-O-N."

"Thank you, sir.' It was all he could do not to laugh.

"... authorized for the following ..." There was little sound but the scratch of Luke's pen, the creak of the ship, the wind, and the wash of the waves overside. He finished, and the lieutenant examined his work. "Very fair. You will need write a smaller hand in the future. But you will do."

Cockburn suddenly spoke—and Luke discovered one of his distinguishing characteristics. Unfortunately, it was not something one usually thought of admirals as having. The man had a rather high voice, not unlike a castrato Luke had once encountered in Italy. "My aide, Lieutenant Scott, is of a

Allan Cole & Chris Bunch

mind that a journal of our expedition would be profitable reading in London. He therefore requires a secretary, to assist in keeping a log of our landing. But not for the military reader.

"You—Shannon, it was? You will be responsible for the keeping of this journal. Lieutenant Scott will dictate possible items of interest. Your station will be with the lieutenant. He will ensure the journal is kept properly, as well as assign you to other duties as he deems proper. Is that understood?"

Expedition. Shit. It would be an invasion. "Yessir."

"You said there had been a mistake as to your service. You were pressed, I warrant."

"Yessir."

"Pressed—unjustly if you are really an American—for being a deserter."

"That is what the muster book says, sir." An officer growled at Shannon's barely civil answer. Cockburn seemed to ignore it.

"That is as it may be. I have nothing in particular against the odd race that calls itself Irish, nor against Americans. Although I have heard that one of your countrymen has offered a reward of one thousand dollars for my head or five hundred dollars apiece for my ears. Tsk. Serve well, and you could end this campaign as a petty officer. Serve badly ... or run again ... I am not fond of the cat, but these are parlous times.

"We gave a man a hundred lashes for attempted desertion but a month ago. From this day forward, the punishment will be one thousand. Or even . . ." Cockburn looked up significantly at the mainmast's yardarm. Then: "Do your duty, however, and you have nothing to fear."

Luke Shannon's interview with God was over. That night, lying in his hammock, with barely a foot between the snorer on one side and the groaner on the other, Luke Shannon sweltered and tried to plan. It would be romantic, but impossible, to try to get word ashore of Cockburn's plans. And he really didn't know exactly what the hell they were.

Not that there weren't rumors. Luke had heard several around the scuttlebutt. He had been told this expedition was a mere feint. The fleet would sail out of the bay, up the Delaware, and sack Philadelphia. He almost dropped the musket barrel that was used as a drinking tube. Christ. His family could be caught up in this damned war. If the British burned Philadelphia like the Americans had burnt York, the capital of Upper Canada, four months earlier . . . everything could be lost. The family left destitute—or worse. His incipient panic was stopped by a carpenter's mate, a breed generally credited with better-quality rumors than most.

This was a feint—but the real invasion would be on Long Island, followed by the bombardment of New York City. Then he heard yet another tale. This was no ruse— the attack would be on Baltimore. An addition came from somewhere else. Before sacking Baltimore, the fleet—now just off the mouth of the Patuxent—would sail upriver. The target was the American warships Cockburn had bottled up months ago. Sink them, then sail for Baltimore. Luke thought that highly unlikely—he could not imagine an entire fleet of seventy-four-gunners moving up a river that looked, to his eye, less than a mile wide at its mouth.

He realized no one really knew anything. So how could anyone except Cockburn himself alert the Americans? Besides, the fleet had been in the Chesapeake for two days now. Surely they knew in Washington, and surely they had armies marching out, waiting to trap the British like they did at Yorktown. The British would be cut to pieces. Which brought up another consideration. Luke Shannon had no intention of being part of the massacre-to-come. The question was, how to escape? He would have but one chance.

He finally decided he would have to wait until the proper moment. Perhaps when the British landed, into the mouths of the waiting American artillery, he could find in the confusion a path to freedom. That being the best plan he could devise, Luke closed his eyes for sleep.

Allan Cole & Chris Bunch

CHAPTER THIRTY-FIVE

THE THREE MEN before her were as menacing as any
Diana had ever encountered. The sergeant was toothless, and
a red scar cutting from crown to chin lit his face in a ghastly
glow. The two privates gripped rusty muskets; the homemade
knives, sharp and gleaming, winked in odd contrast through
their rags. Her breathing was difficult in the swelter of a
Washington summer afternoon.

The young lieutenant had the men drawn up at unruly
attention. He was issuing orders in a voice as uncertain as the
authority he presented. "You will accompany Mrs. Shannon
to the Tanner Warehouse in the vicinity of North Carolina
and Virginia avenues," he squeaked. "There, you will assist
her in determining the ownership of the goods stored within.
If they are innocently acquired, you are to withdraw and
report back. If, however, they belong to the government"—he
indicated the three rickety farm carts, their drivers and
loaders—"you will seize them forthwith and assist in their
speedy delivery to wherever Mrs. Shannon desires. ... Is that
understood, Sergeant?'.'

The sergeant shifted the wad in his mouth and spat, then
flashed tobacco-stained gums. "Yes . . . sir. We'll do that
little thing for you."

The young lieutenant waited, expecting a slice more
larding on the respect. None was forthcoming. He blushed,
squirmed, then gave it up before false dignity failed.
Embarrassed, he addressed Diana. "If you have any troubles,
Mrs. Shannon," he squeaked, "alert me at once." Diana
thanked him and bid him adieu. He fled in humiliation.

She turned to her slouch-backed command. If the men
were surly before, they were worse with the child lieutenant
gone. They shifted and leered and made their contempt plain.
The sergeant spat again, as disdainful as his command. The
only thing Diana knew about soldiering was the toy militia of

New Kent and the slaughter she'd witnessed at the fort in Cherry Valley. Even she knew this lack of discipline was not only wrong, but deadly. So much for the oft self-quoted theories of Secretary Armstrong, who claimed that drilling and training doused a militia man's spirit. Armstrong also was continually laying farfetched plans for the invasion and occupation of Canada, which had produced results as sweet-smelling as the three men who stood before her. Not that it mattered. Diana was sure she had medicine in plenty to cure their affliction.

She dipped into her purse and drew out jingling silver. The men's eyes glowed, and she gave them a mother's loving smile. She had a whole tool kit of these smiles at ready: mother, daughter, sister, flirt, and any number of other mythical feminine beasts. "Gentlemen," she said, "if you serve me well, you will be rewarded." She clinked the coins under their noses, then they vanished in her purse. For a moment she thought the sergeant was going to leap in after them. Then she blessed them with what Connie had dubbed "the Voice." It wasn't loud, but firm and as imperious as a queen who wanted heads for posies to decorate her palace gates.

"However . . . if you fail me," she said, "I will personally see you are provided with three fresh horses." Even the sergeant was stumped by this. What kind of punishment was the gift of a horse? "And you will sit upon those horses facing their tails and your nature. Your hands will be tied behind you. You will be tarred and feathered . . . and then flogged from the ranks for the amusement of your fellows. Do we understand each other?"

She'd picked up the punishment described from Emmett's tales. Whether such things were still done to men, she didn't know. From the reactions of her trio, they certainly thought so. Even the sergeant paled. He tried to cover by sucking on a hole in his gum, but it didn't fool anyone. "Yes, missus!" one of the privates blurted. He was not admonished for speaking out of turn. The sergeant's voice cracked and his

Allan Cole & Chris Bunch

men became better imitations of soldiers. They waited respectfully until she climbed into her low-slung black coach. She signaled through the window, and they marched off, followed by Diana and her wagons.

It was August 18. Diana had been in Washington since James Emmett's wedding.

* * * *

The capital was mired in premonitions of defeat, thick and deep as one of President Madison's moods, with no sweet-natured Dolly to coax it away.

Washington had always been a leeward refuge for wild rumor, a dank place for harpies to wait out the storm. But this was a late-summer blizzard: slave revolts in bordering states; betrayal in the territories; armies tempted with Pope, whores, and rum; foreign plots as twisted as the alleys of Old Jerusalem; intrigue as deadly as the shot that slew Mister Hamilton. And Aaron Burr, the man who slew him, had returned from exile and would finally be king of Louisiana for his troubles. Northern states threatened to quit the Union, and southern states pledged armies to drag them back. All of the rumors were mostly lies. But there was just enough truth for leavening to make a lovely cake.

The war had seemed an insanity from afar. Up close it was plain to Diana insanity was too simple a plea. Insanity requires a single intelligence. Washington hadn't lost its wits, for it had none to lose. Two years ago war had been declared with such panoply and loud boastings, the voices of dissent had all but been drowned out. Never mind the narrow vote in Congress. America would beard the British Lion—heavily engaged in a death match with France—and prove to the world it was a nation to be reckoned with. To accomplish this, the president and his cronies said, there were troops and money aplenty. Thirty-five thousand regulars and 50,000 militia would easily overwhelm weak resistance in Canada. The British side could only claim 6,000 regulars, perhaps 2,000 militia, plus 3,000 Indian warriors. Actually, there were fewer than 7,000 Americans under arms. The navy had been all but dismantled by President Jefferson. As for money, the Treasury was now broke and fortunes were being made on specie issued to mount the war.

These were the facts, and they were generally known to everyone involved from the very beginning. As near as Diana could make out, Madison and his men had simply wished the opposite to be true and had acted on those wishes. Now the British had smashed Napoleon and turned yellow eyes on America. Sometimes it seemed that only the great distance of these shores and the desperate weariness of their own populace seemed to prevent America's complete humiliation. There were other factors, of course. Such as equal incompetence. But how long that could be relied on, no one could say.

If politics were business, Diana concluded, then most politicians—up to and including the president of the United States—would have been put in debtors' prison. For Diana, the most startling revelation was that no one was in charge. As near as she could tell, this had been the case from the moment Dolly's once ardent beau had taken office. The president didn't govern—he witnessed, then complained about the poor outcome of events. He seemed determined to rule by political manipulation. Men were named general because they appeared to be important in their home state, not because of any military abilities.

A man like Henry Dearborn, for instance, was made a major general and briefly put in charge of the Canadian campaign. The appointment was won solely because of Mister Dearborn's position as collector of customs at the Port of Boston. Boston bitterly opposed the war, and there had been serious talk of Massachusetts quitting the Union. The same rules applied to the president's Cabinet, which he was constantly shifting and naming and renaming as the fortunes of war altered the political landscape. Maryland might provide some militia, therefore boost the fortunes of the governor's nephew.

Allan Cole & Chris Bunch

What could one expect in a city that produced nothing but government, and that mostly bad? It seemed to Diana that everybody she met was here to serve his own purposes. There certainly was no real emotion for the "People" whose causes were supposedly represented. This was no surprise. Diana well knew that no one without property or money had any power in this land. Even those requirements were not enough if one were of the wrong religion, race, or sex. Power was mysterious and slippery to the grasp. You could have it one moment and lose it the next. Seven years before, the women of New Jersey won the right to vote. A few months later the right was withdrawn. What happened? There were weak reasons given, but none satisfactory. Now the whole thing was merely viewed as a silly, failed experiment no one would try again. It reminded her of a woman she'd once known who had been a maid in an eccentric household. All the servants were required to dose themselves daily with salts. Half the morning was then spent in a line to the privy. It all would have been very funny, the woman had said, if only one didn't have to live in that house.

This morning, before Diana had set out on her errand, she had received a letter from Connie. Her daughter-in-law said David had just returned home. After harrying British whalers and merchants in the Pacific, the Essex had been caught and sunk. David and most of his shipmates—including Commander Porter—had managed to escape. Now the boy was back, unharmed and strutting about the city with his young male pride swollen to the bursting. Diana could picture the child and was almost amused. Humor died when the thought crept in of what could have been another, as likely, outcome to events. The whereabouts of Diana's other grandson, Luke, were unknown, Connie wrote. But she presumed that all was well, since there was no reason to believe otherwise. Diana took some comfort in this.

Considering her own feelings, Diana was amazed she'd remained in Washington. Sometimes she blamed it on the confusion she had yet to shake, sometimes on Dolly's earnest urgings and flattering tongue. Mostly, she realized, it was because the choices seemed meager. She did not like the system. She deplored the war. Now that it was not only being fought, but was in grave danger of being lost, the alternative—life anew under the king of England—was unthinkable. It was like the concepts of Purgatory and Hell that Farrell was always going on about. Both burned, but one burned forever. Diana doubted things would change in her lifetime, or even her sons' lifetime. But she had hope-however faint—for her grandchildren. Perhaps this is why she stayed when Dolly asked. Or maybe it was her own nature. When something was wrong due to incompetence, or lack of effort, Diana was drawn to the problem as sure as lightning was drawn to Ben Franklin's jar. She had an irresistible urge to tinker with such matters, to be at least a part of the solution. So, maybe she had stayed for purely selfish reasons.

She had come to Washington with her resolve starched and pinned back with stays of solid bone. Not one word of her dilemma would escape this feminine armor when she greeted Dolly. She would attend her friend's famous teas and musical recitals. A few days—even a week—should suffice. Then home to Philadelphia. The instant they were alone, the starch melted in Dolly's warm embrace. Even then Diana did her best to hold back. But Dolly fixed her with those great searching blue eyes that found the pain with an aim as true as a frontier bullet.

Dolly had asked her what was the matter, and Diana had burst into tears. "Oh, Dolly," she moaned, "I am a most unhappy woman."

It had all flowed out so fast, she could barely edit to spare her friend's feelings. She marveled later that Dolly— a slaveholder herself—hadn't flickered when she described her emotions during the journey to Jamestown, how the foreboding grew and was confirmed and grew again to even greater proportions, until her final confrontation with her son. Dolly Madison had a remarkable ability to sympathize, even

Allan Cole & Chris Bunch

when that sympathy was directed at a view opposite to hers, if one could determine her views at all. As Diana spoke, Dolly peppered the pauses with: "And you were quite right ..." Or, "I would have done the same myself . . ." Or, "What barbarians!" She was particularly moved by Diana's portrayal of the bed James Emmett had made for himself. More than anything, this seemed to strike home. Dolly's only child— Payne Todd—was a notorious rakehell himself, a constant source of pain and humiliation for his mother.

Dolly said Diana had done all she could. What followed was in the hands of God. She smiled when she said this, knowing her friend's doubts regarding heavenly assistance. Then she asked the question Diana feared the most: "What of your beau? How will you deal with your gallant Major Maguire?"

Diana said the romance was hopeless. The differences were too many. She felt like a young fool to have her head turned so easily, and was looking forward to an old age blessed with peaceful solitude. Dolly laughed. It was jolting to hear the music of her humor echoing along the corridors of the President's House. If Diana were not so upset, she might have pinched herself at being in such famous quarters.

"There is no woman or man alive too old for romance, Diana, dear," she said. "I won't accuse you of lying, for that would be too rude. But I will accuse you of something else . . . Don't you think you are behaving like a flighty maiden? A handsome man woos you. You fall in love. I won't allow you to deny it. It's plain to see. From what you say, the major is a good man, determined to overcome any differences or obstacles you put before him. . . . Still, you say you won't have him. Yet you refuse to finally tell him no, and instead flee like a breathless girl who wants to play the game of coy pursuit. ... If you want to end this game, look him in the eye and tell him you don't love him. And send him away. Or ... do what your nature tells you, Diana. I think you know what that is."

Yes, she did. She also remembered the advice she'd given Dolly many years ago, which urged a different outcome. Dolly had ignored her advice. Just as Diana believed she would ignore Dolly's. Still, it was comforting to discuss these things with such a sympathetic friend; the problems didn't seem quite so fierce. She wondered if Dolly had thought the same that day in Diana's house, when she had advised Dolly to discourage the attentions of the future president of the United States.

Wouldn't it be interesting if that were so?

* * * *

The small procession moved along dusty streets, spined with ruts sharp enough to break a wheel. When it stormed, she was told, the mud was so deep in places it could swallow a wagon whole. One of the boasts of Washington was to be the first capital city in history designed from birth to be the center of a government. To this end the avenues were broad and laid out so all of the main streets regularly bisected traffic circles, meant to manage the congestion foreseen by the city's designers. Diana had heard the real intent of the circles was to protect all future governments from the anger of an unruly mob. The traffic circles would make it easier for troops to control dissident citizens. The designer was a Frenchman—a people notorious for their vacillating democratic principles—so Diana tended to give some faith to this explanation.

At one time all of the land for miles around belonged to farmers. Some of the farms lay in Maryland, some in Virginia. Their sovereignty over this land was donated to the federal government to build a capital city. The farms were broken up into lots for speculators—one of whom had been George Washington himself. Many of those farms still remained. Homes were clustered in pockets, and the population was so slight that in many places Washington looked more like a series of villages than a city. There were government buildings peppered about, but most seemed to be in a permanent state of construction, with small hope of

Allan Cole & Chris Bunch

funds or will to complete them. The President's House, for example, seemed less a home than a barn built to stable cold drafts. On one side of the mansion there was a lovely wide creek lined with sycamore and oak, and deep enough for small pleasure boats. That same creek was a source of frustration for Dolly, who was engaged in a constant fight with the rats swarming up from those idyllic banks.

When the city was founded, the speculators had wonderful names for their work. Such as the "City of Magnificent Distances." George Washington himself favored the "Emporium of the West." Not much later it drew more cynical—although accurate—descriptions:"Wilderness City," or, the "Capital of Miserable Huts." Diana's favorite was: "A Mud Hole Equal to the Great Serbonian Bog." Mostly the city was a tawdry place of low taverns, pawnshops, and sporting houses, with enough whores to fit any taste or pocketbook. If a stranger were to count the places where politicians and officials could take their pleasure, they would be stunned to learn so many existed in a city with a population of less than six thousand.

Washington drew scoundrels and liars like dung drew flies. Some scoundrels were there in official capacities won by corrupt appointment or ballots cast under the eye of a local militia. Many were foreigners who had fled crimes committed in their own land, but who loudly claimed it was tyranny that was the source of their misfortune. Scattered about the city were the poor, who seemed to be the only permanent population. They were a constant source of cheap labor. Many were black, both free and enslaved. Others were Irish peasants seized or lured from northern ports and set to dig the great ditch that was bisecting the whole city and led nearly to the door of the President's House. The ditch was twenty feet deep in places, and even in the summer heat there were pools of stagnant water lying on the bottom to breed Diana's mortal enemy, the mosquito. Some months from now the ditch was scheduled to be turned into a marvelous canal that would carry goods from distant regions to the Potomac.

The project was funded by private lottery, meaning, once again, the poor.

The remaining population was entirely new: refugees from the war. Most were poor and without a roof over their heads. Even those with a few coins sewed into their rags had to do without. What goods existed tended to be stores looted from the troops by their officers, or farm produce brought to the capital at spiraling wartime prices. It was this last group—the refugees—that had drawn Diana's attentions.

The carriage bumped over broken pavement and came to a halt. She parted the curtains to peer out. They were at the warehouse, and she didn't want to be seen just yet. The raid she was carrying out was only the latest in many other successful encounters. From experience, she knew some of what would follow. First, a few loaders would laze out to see what the commotion was about. Waiting would be the sergeant and his raggedy little army. Not much of an impression in that. But the long, low black coach was a different matter. The coach was on loan from the owner of a theater, recently closed for the summer. With her own funds she'd dressed the driver in the most expensive and foreboding outfit she could find. The entire assemblage presented a wonderfully menacing picture: black coach, evil-appearing driver, tightly drawn black curtains, empty farm wagons with toughs at the reins, the sergeant and his privates with their knives and muskets. The loaders would see this and rush off to find whomever was in charge. The final appearance might take some time as messages flew by fast runner about town. Eventually, someone would come. Diana was content to wait.

* * * *

Dolly had pleaded with Diana to stay and help. She'd made the same request by letter many times over the years. Diana had always politely demurred. It was more difficult to refuse Dolly in person. Especially now, with the situation so desperate. Diana had at first persisted. What could she possibly do? Wrap bandages? Sew blankets into leaky tents? Help like this she was already providing to a degree in

Allan Cole & Chris Bunch

Philadelphia, except there she commanded a small legion to carry out these efforts.

Dolly had not been swayed by her logic. "Stay with me awhile, Diana," she'd said. "Spy out the ground for yourself. You were always wonderfully talented at that. Then if you come to me and repeat the same thing, I will release you from your promise." Dolly's final argument had ended all resistance. She'd pointed out that Diana's present mood would only worsen at home. Family and business obligations would overwhelm her, endangering any possible solution to her personal troubles.

"At the very least," she'd said, "you will be so busy with new troubles—and not your own—that you may find a little peace."

"Diana stayed, but refused to let Dolly find housing for her in one of the homes of her wealthy friends, such as the well-meaning but, frankly, boring Mathilda Lee Love. Diana would do everything Dolly asked, except give up her privacy. She was weary of the road and doubly weary of strangers. Lovely, comfortable rooms were found at the old Tomlinson's Hotel. It was off Maryland Avenue down the hill from the Capitol, and boasted modern amenities such as water closets and a bath in selected rooms. Diana had written to Connie and Farrell to explain her plans and issue instructions. Another flurry of business letters had followed, including one to her bankers so she would have a ready source of funds. Then, with little optimism, she'd set out to see what needed doing.

The first few weeks were taken up by the usual roundelay of social obligations. Parties at the homes of foreign diplomats—or diplomatic pretenders. Teas and recitals. Dull salon conversation aping French social pretensions. An enormous amount of talk about fashion. The last was a waste of everyone's time, since so little had happened for nearly eight years. The French Revolution, it was said, had given women back their figures. Then Napoleon had distorted them by drawing the waist clear up to

412

the neck. Mostly, things were back to the old pre-Napoleon norms, with some differences. Dresses were cut higher so the material would flow more naturally over a woman's curves.

There was much daring talk of transparent materials and bosoms cut so low that exposed nipples were rouged. As far as Diana could tell, such things were fictions even in France. Perhaps some great temptress—the favorite of a nobleman—could toy with such fashions. But not for long. In America, the facts of fashion were that transparent material was merely flesh-colored. Bosoms did their tantalizing under wraps—frilly, to be sure, but wraps just the same.

With so little happening in this realm, even Dolly, who had surpassed her teacher, was easily bored. "I think we mostly talk of such things," Dolly said, "because it is expected of us. Also, there is nothing so fearful in any gathering than silence. So even babblings are seized on as if they were pearls."

Diana could not imagine how Dolly had borne up for all those years. Mister Jefferson, a tragic man and committed bachelor since the death of his only wife, had persuaded her to preside as hostess of the President's House for eight years. There was no occasion that did not have Dolly's hand in it. Jefferson became so dependent on her—and her sister, Anna—it never occurred to him a request might be a bother. A message would come from the President's House saying there was to be a luncheon, or a "dove party." The guests might be a hundred or more, the affair scheduled on the morrow. No matter. It would be accomplished, and so successfully, few would suspect any trouble had been taken. When her sister wed Richard Cutts, the congressman from New York, Dolly had carried on alone. By now she was so sure at her tasks and so knowledgeable a hostess, few believed her match could be met in any capital of the world.

This assistance carried on into her husband's presidency. The more Diana saw of Madison, the more she was convinced if it were not for Dolly, he might not have been such a great success. Diana had met few men so good at brooding as the president. It was an affliction as well as a weapon. A small slight could trigger it, or nothing might have occurred at all. Suddenly he would rise from his chair and stalk into a chamber. He'd have the drapes drawn and would sit for hours or days in dark contemplation. Only Dolly could speak to him during these moods.

She would do everything she could to draw him out: tempting food and drink, artful jests, salty gossip. Finally, when she had elicited at least a grunt for a response, she would gather a group of her most delightful friends. Musicians would be invited to play. Dolly would place them in a nearby room so that the echoes of the music or the laughter of her friends would reach the brooding Madison. Eventually he would deign a smile. It was a system Dolly had developed that worked without fail, until the last two years, as the news of the war worsened. Now the moods were longer and bleaker, the period of enthusiasm for life that followed shorter. It was Diana's opinion that Mister Madison and Dolly's long-dead father—that other master of emotional tyranny—were twins of the same bleak spirit. Despite her fame and position, Dolly had gotten the worst of the marriage bargain.

Diana kept her own counsel, attended the functions and wandered about to see what she could see. The heat of summer cleared the ground for easier hunting. Despite the war, the capital was nearly empty of all but a few of the major players. Diana had heard the same practice was kept in London, where summer sent the rich into the country to seek relief. No matter how urgent the crisis, the estates outside of London were filled with the elite taking their ease, just as the rich in Washington sought out the hot springs in nearby Virginia or Maryland. Diana had the thought that if summer were eternally year-round, all wars might collapse from the absence of the very men who started them.

Gradually, she had seen there was just a bit of caulking that kept the ship from foundering. It was an oakum composed of the rare woods of sincerity and sacrifice. There were a few young men and women who were determined a happy ending be written on the sad tale. They held minor positions, or were the wives or sisters or daughters of men with far less funds than spirit. Some came from familiar places, such as the cities of the North, and a few from the desolate South. Mostly they were frontier people, so used to adversity that the greatest crisis was seen as nothing more than a tricky problem whose solution would just take a little more work and thought than usual. It was these people who rushed to fill the gaps left by their superiors. Failing that, they worked steadily at their tasks as best they could, reasoning that if everyone else did the same, things eventually would turn out for the best. Diana felt an instant kinship. It was her educated opinion these folk were more representative of America than all the self-important men about Washington with their purchased offices, ranks, and honors. It was also her totally uneducated opinion that the British were no more able to conquer now than they had been nearly forty years before. If only America hung on long enough, she thought, the British will to fight would eventually collapse. But no one sought her counsel in these things, so she kept her views to herself and watched the painful fumbling that was the summer of 1814.

The network of wives, daughters, and sisters who propped up the ambition of the important men in the capital was a rich source of information for Diana. Through them, she became acquainted with some of the most powerful men of her generation. There was Elizabeth Monroe, for instance, a lovely woman a few years younger than Diana with two grown daughters. She was an astute player of hostess politics. It was a quality her husband badly needed. James Monroe, the Secretary of State, seemed to be an intelligent man who learned from his mistakes, which were many. Before the war, a string of lucky successes ended when he bungled a treaty with the British so badly that President Jefferson was forced to send it back to London for adjustments. Remarkably, he recognized his error and made himself an expert in the carrot

Allan Cole & Chris Bunch

and stick diplomacy of the European nations. Monroe was a handsome man of fifty-six with hawklike features and a dimple in his chin that pleased the ladies, especially his wife. His nature was also of a far younger man, which seemed to be a weakness as well. Monroe was always discovering new enthusiasms and rushing about in a state of great excitement that tended to leave his underlings scurrying in his wake.

Then there was Armstrong, the Secretary of War. Like Monroe, he laid claim to youthful deeds during the Revolution. He was also about Monroe's age. For Diana, the similarities ended there. From intelligence to abilities of all kinds, he was the equal of few men. His background consisted mostly of failure, from politics in New York to diplomacy in Paris.

A lovely, brassy woman from her native Philadelphia gave Diana insight into the Secretary of the Navy, William Jones. She had reputedly been Jones's mistress, a charge she heatedly denied. Not that she was unwilling to take on such a role, just not with that man. His main talent, outside of drink, seemed to be his reputation with the ladies. He had a marked eye for the leg, and would sniff at and pursue any woman who came into his presence. "He'd bed a lizard if only someone would hold her tail," the woman said. "The very idea that I'd take up with such a person ... I rather enjoy a man's attentions, but only if I'm interested in the man. Otherwise, I'm filled with disgust at the picture in my mind of dogs sniffing around a bitch who means nothing to them at all except as a sturdy mount." So much for Will Jones.

Diana thought one of the greatest fools of the city, however, was a person who had nothing to do with the federal administration. Mayor James Blake was not only an incompetent, but seemed the kind who would scream fire when there was none. He was a prickly man of intense dislikes, particularly of people with tropical skin. He was not appointed by the president to his post, as had been the practice of the past. Blake was chosen by the members of the City Council, who were themselves elected at large. Diana thought Blake ought to be hidden far from the sight of any visiting tyrant. The mayor was a walking argument for any failures democracy was deemed to possess. It was another, much greater incompetent and rogue, who'd indirectly helped Diana make up her mind. General James Wilkinson was a man with few friends, but those he had were ardent in their support. For seventeen years Wilkinson had headed the army, but despite this vast experience, his supporters said, he was continually passed over for any important post in the Madison administration. In this case, "Little Jemmy" had managed to get something right. The quip was that Wilkinson had never won a battle nor lost a court-martial. Diana had not met him, but his reputation among people she respected was as a slippery individual with a traitor's conscience, a Judas's loyalty, and a sutler's thieving soul.

The specifics of his alleged crimes, she'd learned in the streets. That Washington was a city of a few rich men and thousands of poor, with very little in between, was underscored in the summer's heat. To not see a starving beggar or a crippled veteran on any single street would be an event remarked on for days. Now there was a flood of these people and others equally poor and desperate. The fact that there was little to eat and few facilities for these people, Diana had already noted. There were some soup houses about, but they only opened for an hour or so and then closed immediately, since there were so few charitable supplies. She'd visited the kitchens to find the reason why. Some drove her off with rudeness. Others were nervous when she quizzed them, and so vague in their responses, she was sure they were selling for a handsome profit what goods had been provided.

It was a weary churchwoman who'd been donating her time to a soup society who had finally explained to her there was no food to feed the people and no rags to offer as clothing, because there was none to be had at almost any price. All goods entering the city were funneled to middlemen who sold them at prices that must have made them believe they had died and gone to wholesalers' heaven.

Allan Cole & Chris Bunch

The woman said this even included the stores meant for the military. She'd gone on to comment that officers looting their own men was so common that rumor had it General Wilkinson himself was involved.

Diana had not been shocked. Profiteers were a fact of life in any war. But it had still made her angry. She remembered Emmett's troubled conscience over the teamster he'd slain for ruining supplies meant for the starving soldiers at Valley Forge. Diana shared the original anger that made him fire the shot. But not his guilt. She checked further. If soldiers' stores were being looted, where might the loot be held? You could not sell all those goods very quickly—not at a price that greater patience would bring, in any event. And what of this rumor regarding General Wilkinson? The man had not only been a confederate of Aaron Burr's, who survived by betraying his master, but had already survived three courts-martial. Such a man must be very canny. Diana decided to leave the general to the dubious justice of his Maker, and set her sights on easier game.

There was a theory Diana had established early on: superior business practice drew superior thieves, and poor business methods attracted a poorer class of thieves. In Washington, with so much legal incompetence about, she was willing to bet a purse of gold against a tub of turnips her theory would soon be proven an axiom.

With Dolly's powerful support, she launched a two-pronged program. The first was to reestablish the soup kitchens. Diana called them evacuee centers, since she planned more than soup to be available. She sought out every able woman she'd met, and had no difficulty convincing them of the soundness of her idea. Wasn't she putting a great deal of her own money down to help finance it? Once convinced, she urged them to seek out others. Key committees were formed and the first centers were opened. Some were in rented cellars, or once boarded-up shops. A few inns whose business practices wouldn't bear investigation grudgingly provided space. Makeshift commissary wagons were set up on the street corners. It was Diana's intention to fill the city with these centers and stock them with all the food, drink, clothing, and medicine she could purchase with money or threats of jail.

Then came the second part of her program: the getting of the goods. Diana and her little legion had some success with the direct approach. They simply sought out legitimate suppliers and appealed to their better natures to sell at fairer prices. If this failed, all these women had important men in their families who could appeal to other tangibles, such as licensing, or continued business health. Some of the centers opened, and the refugees swarmed to them. Diana was far from satisfied. Much more was needed than what she could win with gentle persuasion.

But now her spies were reporting back and she was getting news of stolen government goods hidden in abandoned barns, infested cellars, warehouses, and any other number of places the thieves imagined safe. She had also kept hearing more about General Wilkinson; but where he kept his loot, she didn't know, only that it made an impressive pile. Armed with official documents, only a little authority, and much bluff, she launched a series of raids that had come up with all sorts of wonderful and useful things. The supplies for the centers had mounted slowly, but she was just beginning to see a future for them not quite so grim. And today the grimness was lighter still. Wilkinson had been ferreted out.

She heard the sergeant's rough voice, then a cursing bluster of a reply. It was time. She signaled the driver. She heard a creak and the weight of the carriage shifting as the driver dismounted. He rounded the carriage and flung open the door. Diana waited a breath to add drama to the moment, then let the man hand her from the carriage. She pretended to ignore the flush-faced fellow standing before the sergeant and his men. "What is the difficulty, Sergeant?"

The sergeant started to speak, but Flush Face broke in. "She wants to look inside," the man said in horrified tones.

"And she has no right to do it. This is private property." He said it as if she were about to invade the sanctity of a church.

Diana chilled him with a look and continued to address the sergeant. "I am shortly expected at the President's House," she said, "so if you will be so good as to get on with our business ..."

Flush Face drew himself up and crossed fat arms across an egg-stained waistcoat as if his presence were enough to bar entry into the warehouse. His men were no help in this charade. The menacing carriage and the mention of the President's House had them quaking and looking for a place to hide.

"I am the landlord here," Flush Face said. "It is my responsibility to protect the possessions of my tenant."

"And who might that be, sir?"

Flush Face grew redder. "I'll not say. I'm not required to. And I'll not let you in."

Diana shrugged. "Arrest him, Sergeant," she snapped. The sergeant bared stained gums and stepped forward to do her bidding. His men seemed as delighted as he.

"By what authority?" Flush Face's sudden shrillness gave his fear away.

Diana pulled an official-appearing document from her purse. It was from Brigadier William Winder, Madison's commander of the local military district. The document she bore was merely a "To Whom It May Concern" introductory letter, urging anyone who read it to assist Diana if it were convenient. Diana tapped it with a fingernail, as if it were a Letter of Cachet condemning anyone whose name she inserted to have his head taken off. Flush Face jumped back, perhaps seeing in his mind the gory blade. From that moment on, he was hers.

She swept into the warehouse like a queen with a royal guard instead of three ragged soldiers. The warehouse was heaped to the ceiling. There was no attempt at disguise here. She saw blankets and uniforms and tents and great bags of grain and rice. There were chests of medicines and hogsheads of meat.

"You can tell General Wilkinson that Mrs. Shannon sends her respects. And thank him for his thoughtful donation to our cause."

She didn't bother listening to Flush Face's heated denials of her identification of his mysterious tenant. Instead she motioned to the sergeant to get busy, and went outside to issue the same orders to the teamsters and loaders manning the wagons. The three soldiers were so angry at the sight of stores looted from common men like themselves, they would have slain Flush Face on the spot if he made many more protests. He wisely moved down the street, no doubt to alert the general of his business reversal. It took most of the day to haul away the supplies and disperse them to the evacuee centers. Her fellow volunteers were as delighted as she at these new riches. They all felt as if they had participated in a great military victory over their lobsterback enemy.

Diana returned to her hotel late that night. The streets were nearly empty as she alighted from her coach. Outside she was met by a message runner—who traded her an envelope for a coin. Diana looked at it and drew back in shock. It was a letter from John Maguire. She held it in trembling hands. Another shock struck as she realized her error. This was no letter, but a note freshly written and freshly delivered by hand. John was in Washington. And he'd want to see her. She tucked it in her pocket to read in the privacy of her room and went inside.

Diana expected to find the public rooms dark and empty at this time of night. Instead they were blazing with light and packed with men and women in advanced stages of panic. There was pushing and shoving and hoisting about of luggage and the spilling of hastily packed contents. Shouts were mingled with weeping and angry blustering threats. The confusion was so fierce that it took Diana a few minutes to find out what all the madness was about. The answer was a heavy blow.

Allan Cole & Chris Bunch

A Daughter Of Liberty

News had come that a great British fleet was moving up the Chesapeake. No one knew its ultimate target with any certainty. But Washington was easily within reach.

CHAPTER THIRTY-SIX

DAWN. AUGUST 22. Luke went on deck when the lower watch was roused. He had slept poorly. The heat continued to blast—only just now lessened by a strong wind blowing downriver. The "Little Grenadier" posted at the scuttle looked sidelong at him. He might have inquired, sotto voce, where Jonathan's army and navy was—but even a Royal Marine, considered by sailors and his own officers to be slightly less intelligent than a merino sheep, knew better than to rag anyone on the admiral's staff, American "Jonathan" or no. Luke was very glad he had made no mention of his certainty that the British would be mousetrapped if they invaded. He'd kept his lip buttoned not out of any sudden attack of common sense, but because he felt it would be best to hold silence while he was planning desertion.

Where the hell were the Americans? Five days had passed. The British had met no mousetrapping armies or ambushing navy. Luke had seen from a chart that Washington appeared less than twenty miles away. Washington: Cockburn's target. Luke knew everything. One of the first things Lieutenant Scott gave him to copy was a letter from Cockburn to his superior, Cochrane, dated July 17, 1814:

I consider the town of Benedict in the Patuxent to offer us advantages beyond any other spot within the United States. It is, I am informed, only 44 or 45 miles from Washington . . . The facility and rapidity with which an army by landing at Benedict might possess itself of the Capitol, always so great a blow to the government of a country, as well on account of the Resources, the Documents and Records the invading army is almost sure to obtain thereby . . . both Annapolis and Baltimore are to be taken without difficulty from the land side; that is, coming down upon them from the Washington road ...

It was a very long document. After Washington, Annapolis, and Baltimore were burnt and occupied, perhaps the British might turn their attention to Norfolk and other cities. Even though he was no soldier, Luke did not believe Cockburn's raiders were strong enough to take and hold the entire eastern seaboard. But it was bad enough just for the capital to be burnt. Luke felt a moment of intense selfish delight that, thank God, his grandmother had not taken Mrs. Madison up on her offer to come to Washington back before the war started.

Luke was pretty certain the British were going to accomplish exactly what they wanted, barring a miracle. The only Shannon who believed in miracles was his father— Farrell. Any seaman—especially one as skilled and experienced as he was—appreciated organization. Whether it was a pair of fishermen sculling a dory or all hands cutting away a downed mast, embayed on a lee shore, sailors had to work in unison, each knowing his task. But the British—or at least this man Cockburn—went beyond organization. He might have been a bastard. All of the British might have been bastards, from their crazy syphilitic king down to that sweat-dripping moron over at the scuttle with his red woolens and fixed bayonet. But they knew what they were doing. It felt to Shannon like they were not men, but a great red-and-white centipede, swarming toward Washington.

At first light of the eighteenth, as unlikely as Luke had thought it, the British fleet entered the narrow Patuxent River. There were fewer ships now—Lieutenant Scott had informed him that some of them were making a diversion above Baltimore. Others were sailing up the Potomac itself. In front of the big ships of the line sailed a small frigate. It was the Severn, commanded by Captain Nourse, who'd scouted the river earlier. Lieutenant Scott mused that the tacking back and forth reminded him of a regatta. Yachts . . . hunting . . . bearbaiting . . . horse racing. Luke had never understood the British love for comparing killing people to sport. Maybe a dead fox and a dead American gave them the same sense of accomplishment.

The fleet anchored seven miles upriver, waiting for the tide. Cockburn and his staff, including Shannon, transferred to a small tender: the Resolution. That afternoon, at high tide, they continued upriver, and anchored off Benedict. The ships of the line, and the expedition's supreme commander, Admiral Cochrane, would base here, and the troops would land, with orders to march close along the river. Cockburn had a second mission—there was a flotilla of American gunboats upriver, led by a former pirate named Barney. Cockburn planned to remove their potential threat.

This would mean Cochrane was still commander in chief—but far to the rear. Admiral Cockburn and his army counterpart—a General Robert Ross—would make the moment-to-moment decisions. Shannon got the idea from Scott there was an additional benefit from leaving the heavies where the river shallowed. Apparently Cochrane was a raving lunatic; someone who called Americans "a whining, canting race much like the spaniel who must be drubbed into good manners." It also appeared that Cochrane, like most enthusiasts of the moment, could quickly develop cold feet shortly after a plan was implemented. Cochrane also seemed to be an admiral who came up with a new and different scheme at each sunrise. Shannon gathered that was where all the scuttle rumors came from—at one time each and every one of them had been taken under serious consideration by Cochrane.

Not that any of this was told directly to Luke. After a few hours' dictation, which started with a biographical sketch of Admiral Sir George Cockburn, Luke realized the Bible was in error as to who walked on the waters. And if Cockburn—at least from Lieutenant Scott's perspective—had been around for the Revolution, Britannia's flag would still fly on these shores. At first Shannon thought Scott a toady. That he may have been—he had served under Cockburn for eleven years—but he was also a very clever

Allan Cole & Chris Bunch

man, intending himself for great laurels. This journal, to be published after the inevitable victory, would propel Cockburn—and Scott on his tails—to fame, nobility, and possibly even a royal grant on the long-lost family estate in Scotland.

Cockburn seemed—at least in the brief encounters Shannon had with him—to be disdainful of what the public thought, so long as he was doing his duty. But he'd given Scott leave to do what he thought best; therefore the journal, dictated as Scott's duties and circumstances permitted. And Luke Shannon copied the dictation faithfully. If Scott had proposed an opening line of "I sing of arms and Sir George," Luke would have given him an epic. Luke wanted only to be off the Resolution and as far away from this nightmare as he could run.

On the morning of the nineteenth, when the British soldiers landed at Benedict, Luke felt a slight spark of hope that perhaps Cockburn was not such a naval Napoleon after all. The landing was scheduled to commence at dawn, but it was noon before the boatloads of lobsterbacks began beetling toward land. But after a moment's thought, Luke did not feel reassured. They were landing soldiers, after all, and that was like landing cattle without a dock. Kick them over the side and let them swim for shore. To Shannon, and to most other sailors, there was no difference between soldiers and cattle. At least the river was calm. Luke heard of no boat swampings or drownings—worse luck. The landings had continued through the day and the night. By noon of the twentieth, the four British regiments were ready to move out.

They traveled less than four miles, Cockburn's fleet of gunboats and tenders sailing slowly up the Patuxent as support. From what Luke heard from boats pulling alongside the Resolution, the countryside was abandoned. The people had fled at the first sight of red coats. Cockburn, Shannon noted, had other interests besides being an avenging angel. The troops and boatmen were under orders to look for prize goods. Cockburn had announced intentions to hang or put under the lash any soldier, sailor, or marine found looting. Naturally, the order did not apply to the admiral himself. Cockburn was primarily after tobacco. Hogshead after hogshead went onto the ships. The good leaf would go for five hundred dollars a hogshead in London.

This didn't bother Luke much, other than the loot ending in British hands. Anyone who could plant tobacco was richer than he was, and he had little concern for the well-being of the rich. Besides, prizes and prize money were desirable. He himself had once considered signing on as a privateer, like his great-uncle Isaac. At least Cockburn had the gravel to order that barrels would be provided to each British ship, and anyone who wanted was given as much tobacco as he could smoke.

On the twenty-first the troops moved again. Their destination was Nottingham, where Cockburn had heard Barney's flotilla lay. The land on either side of the river had been tilled farmland. Now it changed to thick, deep forest, heavy timber and dense cedar thickets. The road turned inland, and Ross's column could not be seen from the boats.

At Nottingham, Luke felt hopeful for an instant. Gunfire suddenly spattered at the boats. At last, the American army had materialized! Carronades in the boats returned the fire, and white smoke drifted across the water. Shannon managed to borrow a glass. He focused it on the town in time to see a scattering of horsemen leap on their horses and gallop away. That was the Battle of Nottingham. The hell with them, Luke thought, furious. Washington and the goddamned army could fend for themselves. It was time to do what his grandfather did, and worry about Luke Shannon. The first step was to somehow get ashore, perhaps volunteer for a boat crew or something.

Lieutenant Scott provided a solution of sorts. Admiral Cockburn had decided Barney's boats lay farther upriver, and he was determined to bring them to battle this day. Cockburn and his staff would go upriver in armed boats. "You're an

Allan Cole & Chris Bunch

able seaman, Shannon. You'll suit to pull an oar in the admiral's boat."

"Aye, sir." What the hell. It was one step closer to shore and freedom. Even if it was also one step closer to being on the receiving end of cannon fire.

Shannon took his station—suddenly ashamed to find himself hoping that Commodore Barney and all his ships would turn out to be a false rumor, in spite of the fact that this long-unseen flotilla appeared to be the only possible opposition the British could face. So he shut off his mind and became a rowing machine, falling into easy unison with the other sailors.

Royal Marines went ashore, formed up in scattered lines—Shannon guessed this was some kind of attacking formation—and moved off. Cockburn ordered his boats to row on. At long last, just above the unromantically named Pig Point, they saw Barney's gunboats. They were in a long line near the shore. The lead ship was a large sloop, with some kind of meaningful pennant dangling from its mast. The others were gunboats with cannon forward and aft. Seventeen ships. Farther upriver, Luke saw a dozen or so merchant schooners anchored under Barney's protection. Shannon expected the battle to begin immediately, but there was no sign of life from the gunboats.

A sailor suddenly growled, "Th' lead Jonathan's afire!" It was. Shannon saw flames licking up from the sloop's hold. Seconds later a boil of flame, a gout of smoke, and then splashes as debris rained down. The sloop was gone. Thunderdrums . . . and the other ships exploded, as if cued. Only one gunboat remained undamaged. Shannon saw small boats—each with a handful of men—row ashore, and the men run into the brush. A few paused long enough to fire muskets in the general direction of the British.

"Th' whole damn Yankee fleet went and scuttled itself. Wi'out even a tradin' of shot."

So it was. Luke Shannon, maybe for the first time in his life, felt deeply ashamed of his country. He was near tears.

Another sailor chanced, aloud: "This is no harder'n fightin' Dagoes. Dam' Jonathans have no craw to 'em."

Shannon did not even want to strike the man. What he said looked to be gospel truth. Scott, near Cockburn in the bow, appeared disappointed. An enemy committing suicide would be less than enthralling news in London's Gazette, let alone in the to-be-published journal. But Cockburn seemed pleased. He spoke, knowing his every word would be noted by the boat crew and immediately be passed on to the rest of the seamen.

It was a small speech:

"We'll burn the merchantmen, such as we can't take for prizes. And with Barney a fangless tiger, we can join our brothers ashore. And strike for the heart of the enemy!"

Allan Cole & Chris Bunch

CHAPTER THIRTY-SEVEN

THEY MET AT the Eagle Tavern, which lay a few hours'
carriage ride north of Washington. It was an old place,
catering to quiet wealth. The tavern sat beneath a grove of
sturdy oak. It was long and low and had a broad porch that
nearly encircled it. She saw a tall, slender man testing the
limits of the porch as he impatiently paced back and forth. If
it wasn't John Maguire, it was someone just as handsome,
and Diana's pulse quickened and her mouth grew dry as her
carriage neared the tavern.

Dolly's words echoed in her mind: "If you want to end
this game, look him in the eye and tell him you don't love
him. And send him away ..." She'd determined to accomplish
this when she agreed to the meeting. Although why she let
him choose such a place so protected from city gossip, she
didn't allow herself to question. The pace of her heart and the
dryness of her throat answered it. The symptoms certainly
had nothing to do with fear.

He came off the porch in a young man's bound, pulled
open the door before the carriage had come to a full stop and
leapt inside to crush her to his breast. Reason fled and she
kissed him with a hungry mouth. She might have let him take
her then in full view of the tavern's patrons, but John recalled
propriety first and pulled away with a wild laugh.

"I believe these folks are accustomed to warm greetings
between husband and wife," he said. "Especially in these
times. But I think I was about to test their sympathies."

"Is that what you told them, John? That we are man and
wife?"

He became shy at this and mumbled that yes he had, and
would Diana think him a terrible presumer for hiring rooms
under that fiction? The answer she gave was not the one
originally intended. She went with him to the rooms and they
made love for an hour or more. Afterward she begged a
moment's privacy, and he went downstairs for a drink and to

fetch some supper. She wept awhile, then washed her face, made herself up, and pulled a dressing gown of regal-blue from her traveling kit. The gown called her a liar by its presence. Why had she packed it if bed were not among her plans? Diana cursed herself as a slut. Very well, Mrs. Shannon, if that is your nature, admit it. You've had your whore's fling, now thank the man and send him on his way.

It was in this cold mood that she greeted her returning lover. But Maguire seemed not to notice. He laid out the food and drink and chattered pleasantly about this and that. Eventually, however, her silence won the match.

He sat quiet for a time, until he'd gathered enough courage to speak his mind. "I've done it," he said. Abrupt. "My sons think I'm a worse villain than King George himself." He looked at Diana, expecting her questions for the particulars. When none came, he stifled a sigh and plunged on. "I've freed all the slaves I have the right to free. And I've forced my sons to sell me those they possess, and I've arranged for their freedom as well. It took all my remaining land in Virginia to make the trade. And good riddance to it!"

Diana's breast stirred, but she fought for control and held to her silence. Only a slight hesitation in the flow betrayed John's frustration at her manner.

"I've done my best to provide for those people who don't want to come with me as paid and trusted labor. I can't guarantee their happiness, or in any way compensate them for all the wrongs they have suffered. But at least their lives are their own."

Diana finally spoke. She didn't praise him, for she truly believed there was nothing to praise. His actions showed the strength of his character, but in her mind, right—in this case—was simply right. And no one ought be rewarded for what any human being should do. Instead she simply asked him what he planned next.

"The Mississippi ... if I'm to remain alone."

She did not respond.

Allan Cole & Chris Bunch

This time John had enough. "Have mercy, Diana," he pleaded. "I'd rather face a bullet than this cold silence. What I'm trying to say is that I'm doing all I swore I would. I'm not expecting anything in return. They were my plans. I think you agreed they were worthy ones. Now I'm telling a good friend they have been accomplished. There is no other expectation. Please believe this."

"I believe you, John." This was all she said. But she couldn't help the warmth in her tone. Maguire took courage.

"There is something else," he said. "Speaking as the man who loves you, not just your friend, I want you to marry me. This you know. If you will have me, then my future is in your hands. I'll return to Philadelphia, if you like. To settle into any kind of life you like. If it's Pittsburgh that entices you, then Pittsburgh is my ardent choice. Damn it, Diana, I'll go into the wilderness with an axe, if you ask. And I'll do it cheerfully. Please don't think there is any self-sacrifice in what I'm proposing. I am too old for sacrifice. All I want is a little happiness. In the few years I have left, I expect you are the most happiness I am likely to ever find."

His eyes were flashing as he spoke. Diana badly wanted to take him back to bed. But she was half admitting to herself that the shots he was firing were all striking their mark.

"Will you marry me, Diana? Will you be my wife?"

She wanted to tell him yes, and gladly. She had always wanted to tell him that, she realized now. But there was that wise side of her that had kept her safe for many years. A man was a potentially dangerous animal, empowered by law and tradition to strip her of all she owned and deny her all she yearned for. If it were Emmett himself before her, she was not certain what her response would be. She wanted to tell John this, if only to ease her rejection. But she doubted if any man alive could understand this fear: that if they wed, she would cease being Diana Shannon. Correction, she thought. You are really Diana Jameson. That was your mother's name. Oh, don't be silly. You've been a Shannon too long to shed it now.

Oh. Is that your difficulty, woman? She looked up at John, who was still waiting for an answer. Diana almost asked him if he would mind terribly about keeping the name. It was not such an unusual thing. But she didn't ask. For two reasons: that John would certainly say yes—he would say anything to win her at this point—and secondly, if this weak thought had just popped into her head, then she obviously had not given any real consideration to his request. That was entirely unfair of her, and she was ashamed of herself for letting things get so far. She would correct it.

As gently as she could, she begged John for just a little more time. Not more than a week or so. She promised the delay was not out of fear of humiliating him with a rejection she had already decided, but that her mind really did need some sorting and making up. She returned to Washington primed for thought.

That was on August 22. On the twenty-third she stayed in her rooms at Tomlinson's and purposely heard no news and turned away all requests for her presence. Her only company was Kitty. The girl guessed what her mistress was about and kept as quiet as a little mouse. Well, mostly that quiet. Kitty was excited by all this romance in the air, and she occasionally let slip a dramatic sigh. Diana eventually became agitated and thought if she heard one more sigh, she would shoot the girl and then hunt down John Maguire and shoot him as well for putting her in such a silly position. Kitty survived the day. As did Diana's temper.

On the morning of August 24 there came a gentle tapping at her door. It was John. He was wearing his riding clothes, which were disheveled from being hastily pulled on. There was a countryman's coat thrown over his shoulders and an ancient officer's shortsword belted about his waist. She knew at once he hadn't come for an early answer.

He told her the British were on the march, and that unless Mister Madison hunted up his head from wherever hysteria had lost it, there was no one to stop them. A group of men like himself had determined to throw up fortifications at

Allan Cole & Chris Bunch

Bladensburg, for that was the way they were sure the enemy would come.

"Don't be mad, John," Diana cried. She heard the echo of those shots fired nearly forty years ago. And saw Emmett dead and bloody on the ground.

"We don't intend to fight them, Diana," he said. "There's no time for us to organize such a thing, even if any of us believed we were the ones with hope of carrying the day. We are only going to dig and build the breastworks. After that, even a fool will see what has to be done. There'll be real soldiers aplenty to man the barricades and turn them back."

Diana was so frightened for him she could barely speak. Instead she clung to him and pretended she believed all he was saying. And perhaps she did. It would do neither her or him any good to think otherwise. Events were in control now. It was no use to doubt or weep or pray, for there was no mercy in this life, Diana thought. And no one had ever returned to say if there was any in the next.

She poured them both a brandy to steady their nerves. John took his down in a swallow, but rejected a second. He promised he would return as soon as he could—no later, he was sure, than a day.

"What if they break through?" She asked it flat. Diana was a child of war and knew its ways.

"You're right, Diana," John said, proving once again their similarities. "We should have someplace to meet. If all else fails, and I don't find you here or with Mrs. Madison—"

"Here," Diana said. "I won't be with Dolly." The decision was so swift it surprised even her.

"And if not here?" John didn't wait for her answer. He was putting the military part of his mind to work. A safe place . . . out of the city . . . "The Eagle Tavern? What do you think?" He smiled at her, remembering their previous stay.

It was decided. If the world turned upside down, they would both do their best to end the slide at the quiet tavern under the grove of sturdy oak. Diana said she would dispatch Kitty with a little money to hire rooms and wait for them.

They kissed, and he held her close. She could feel the heart hammering in him, and knew it wasn't love, but peril that drove it. She drew away and looked him full in the eyes.

"You come back to me, John Maguire. Do you hear?" She kissed him again before he made a promise impossible to keep.

He left. She watched outside until he exited. The big chestnut marked with the blaze was being held by a boy. John gave the child a coin, climbed on the horse, and kicked it into a trot. The trot lasted no more than twenty or so paces. Another kick, this one impatient, and the trot became a gallop.

She watched the street long after he had gone.

Allan Cole & Chris Bunch

CHAPTER THIRTY-EIGHT

ON AUGUST 22nd, Luke had felt he knew what was going on. He was eavesdropping in Caesar's tent: seeing the maps, hearing the orders and sometimes even what the legates were saying. Two days later it was ask my arse, for I surely do not know.

The night of the twenty-second, he'd slung his hammock on the Resolution. Before dawn he'd been kicked awake by a master-at-arms and told off for shore duties. He had protested—he was specially detailed to Admiral Cockburn. The master-at-arms had grinned evilly and informed him the good admiral seemed to have overlooked a vital member of his command, so out and down, slacker. Luke discovered that sometime during the night Cockburn had gone ashore in a deal of a hurry, taking Scott and two aides with him. Orders came back later the sailors from the armed boats and the marine artillery were to go forward and join the army. But contrary to Luke's prayers, it didn't seem the British had met with disaster. There weren't even any rumors worth believing for the time it took to pass them along.

Shannon had time to bundle pipe, tobacco, a few chunks of ship's biscuit, plus the all-important pages of the journal-to-be in a borrowed soldier's cartridge box, then was ordered into a line, handed three long metal tubes, and told to follow the man in front of him down into a longboat and ashore. Luke asked what the three tubes were, and was told "Congreve rockets." He had vaguely heard the British had some kind of new device, but had no idea what these things were nor how they worked. He was fairly sure they weren't for signaling purposes—there were far too many rockets being carried by too many seamen. The tubes weighed about twelve pounds each, and had, on one side, thin metal loops. The gunners were Royal Marines, and they carried more rockets, plus bundles of sticks and folded up tripods. Other sailors were dragging the expedition's tiny three-pound cannons and two equally small howitzers.

Luke marched off down the road, following the back of the seaman in front of him like a good obedient sheep, doing whatever he was ordered. He tried to form a plan. Somewhere up there—toward the yet-to-show-its-face American army, would be the admiral and Lieutenant Scott. If Scott spotted him, Luke knew he would order him to set aside the rockets and tear strips from that master-at-arms for stealing one of Scott's men. Maybe. On the other hand, if he was "saved" by Scott, that would put him much closer to the eventual sound of guns.

Luke was increasingly nervous about being so close to Cockburn. The admiral was a hero, and heroes died nobly, according to every legend Shannon had heard. Perhaps he would be better hanging back here with the throng, Luke thought, and being a pack animal until he saw a chance to slip away. Planning did not last very long as the metal tubes began to lacerate his shoulder, and his feet began to smolder.

Sometime that morning they were brought to a halt, given water and rations, and told they were now with the army. At two P.M. the sailors were told the army was moving again. They had not gone very far when Shannon heard the dim thud of muskets. Then louder thuds. Cannon. The column accordioned to a halt and the men stood—waiting. More orders. Keep marching. Then they were told to make camp. What had happened up front, no one seemed to quite know. Shannon felt like an old, weary mule. He noticed the pickets around the camp were most alert. Slipping past them looked a task worthy of Grandfather Emmett, not Luke Shannon.

*****

Five in the morning, August 24. The sailors were roused, hastily fed, and put on the march. Luke, hardly a superstitious man—at least for a seaman—took note of the bloodred sunrise. Red sky at morning, sailor take warning . . .

Allan Cole & Chris Bunch

Luke was concentrating on putting one throbbing foot in front of the other. He barely heard the horse thunder down the dusty road. The rider reined to a halt. "Seaman! You! Shannon!"

Luke looked up. It was Lieutenant Scott, uniform dusty, unshaven, red-eyed. "You were given orders. Why are you not carrying them out?"

"Sir, umm, the master-at—"

"Stop arsing about and follow your instructions, or you'll be for the cat!" Scott kicked his horse into a canter and galloped back toward the rear of the column. That was the Royal Navy. Or, Luke theorized, any other goddamned military service.

Luke found a marine to take the rockets, and stumbled toward the front of the column. He dimly noted red-coated soldiers sprawled to the side being screamed at by corporals or sergeants. Eventually he found Cockburn, his staff and orderlies. True to form, they were near the front.

Shannon was streaming sweat and about to go down. A fortuitous halt was ordered. It was ten in the morning. Someone passed him a canteen. He drank metallic hot water. It tasted better than an iced rum punch. Someone else took Luke's handkerchief and soaked it in more precious water. Luke swabbed feebly at his neck and forehead. His rasping breath became normal. Aware of the world once more, his curiosity started itching. He cautiously set out to scratch it.

Scott came thundering back to the tight knot of gold braid that was Admiral Cockburn, General Ross, and their staff. He dismounted, gave Shannon a fairly black scowl, and joined his fellow officers. Both from inquisitiveness and to keep Scott from having something else to snarl about, Luke sought out the coxswain of Cockburn's boat, who'd been civil to him. For two days now Luke's journal had less information than a back-fence gossip. He asked the cox'n what the hell had happened.

The cox'n, not a rumor monger, said there was nothing but humbug tales. All he knew, for sure and certain, was that two of Ross's aides had boarded the Resolution in the early hours of the twenty-second. Something was wrong— and Cockburn had ridden off posthaste with Scott and the aides. Later, Cockburn had issued orders for the marines and sailors to come up and sent Scott off to report to Cochrane, all the way downriver at Benedict. Scott had returned in the small hours of the twenty-third with some kind of worrisome orders. All the cox'n knew was Cockburn and Ross had spent the hours between Scott's return and dawn in conference.

Had that ass Cochrane downriver changed the orders? Had he gotten cold feet? Or maybe General Ross was getting worried, at least a full day's march from the covering guns of the British navy? The coxswain didn't know. Luke had no theories, beyond the most obvious slander. All he knew of the general was that he appeared good-natured and was considered a good leader by his troops. A soldier had said Ross "was a real gentleman for an Irisher." Shannon had snarled that anyone from Ireland who'd general for the British was a bastard traitor who'd sell his own countrymen for a chance to kiss the British king's arse.

Opinions and rumors and the fact that there'd been some hither-and-yonning did not help Luke with his journal. If there'd been some indecision, he was pretty sure Scott wouldn't want hesitation among the mighty presented to the London mob. This left him with meticulously entered weather reports for two days, and a vague accounting of the British units on land. A clerk estimated four thousand British soldiers, sailors, and marines. Eventually Scott hunted Luke down. Shannon hesitatedly suggested there were certain events lacking in the journal that could be important to a future reader. Scott scowled and said to put down that "our forces were closing with an awful majesty on the enemy capital."

Aye, Lieutenant.

At eleven the column started moving again. The British moved in three brigades, with some distance between each group. Cockburn and Ross traveled with the lead element.

pg. 439

They were the 85th Regiment (Bucks Volunteers) of Light Infantry, or so Luke inscribed the to-him-meaningless name in the journal. Light Infantry, it was explained, was exactly that—soldiers carrying little but battle gear, unencumbered with wagons or artillery, intended as scouts and the first shock wave of an army.

They traveled fast. Luke was relieved that somehow, somewhere, he had found a second wind.

The column moved up the winding dirt road six abreast. The men scattered out on either side of the road. Pushing through the fields were flankers. It would be impossible to set an ambush for the British forces. The flankers carried bugles, and could quickly message the commanders at any sign of trouble. Some of them, Luke was interested to note, were black Americans. Runaway slaves dressed in the red of Royal Marines and given the same pay, plus an enlistment bonus of twenty dollars. They were dubbed the Colonial Corps.

In spite of his newfound patriotic stirrings, Luke wished them no evil at all. The British had renounced slavery, the Americans had not. Even if he had not been raised properly by his father and Diana, so that his first and only use of the word nigger around the family was met with a birching, Luke would most likely have felt the same. Seamen were too democratic, too borderline anarchic, to hold with one man keeping another in bondage. There'd been too many free men of color as Luke's shipmates for him to hold any belief in slavery. Good on you Moors, he thought. Hold a man down, and eventually he'll cut your damned throat— and you're to blame, not him. He hoped the Colonial Corps had a share in the earlier looting of the downriver plantations that would have belonged to their ex-masters.

Ahead of the column was a small, deserted town. It looked to be a village prosperity had once hit and then passed by. At the far end of the village, the road L-turned. The column halted. By now Cockburn and the 85th Foot were far ahead of the other two brigades.

Scott's attention was on the village. "Bladensburg, it's named on the map," he informed Shannon. "And here—if your army has the sense God gave a goose—is where they'll stand. Just beyond should be a bridge, and a river crossing. The Jonathans will be in ambuscade in Bladensburg."

Ross ordered the bulk of the army off the road, behind a nearby hill. The advance guard went into Bladensburg, skirmishers first, flanked by squads. A boot or a musket butt would crash in the door. Three men would scuttle inside, bayonets ready. They would search the house from ground to attic, break a window and shout a report. "Nothin' here, Sarn't." And the next house, and then the next.

The advance guard moved through the village: a killing machine honed in Spain, Portugal, Martinique, and Holland. Shannon saw only the beginnings of this. Then he was scrambling up that hill, trying to keep pace with the mounted officers.

From the crest of Lowndes Hill they saw the American army. Luke had never been in nor witnessed a battle. He was pretty sure that battles, whether on land or sea, didn't really look like the engravings he'd seen where soldiers stood in neat lines and marched forward like toy soldiers across a carpet. But now, looking from the hilltop across Bladensburg and the Potomac River at the waiting army, it was like an artist's sketch.

Just beyond the narrow wooden bridge over the Potomac, now less than one hundred feet wide, was a heaped line of dirt and brush. Luke thought there might be cannon behind that hastily piled dirt wall with a ditch in front of it. Farther back, he guessed a couple of hundred yards, was a rough line of soldiers. Still farther behind that line were more soldiers. To him, they did not look impressive. Some of the dots looked like they were in uniform, others just looked like citizens out for a day's birding in the country. But maybe this was all right. What did he know of battles, after all?

"Do you know what you are looking at?" It was Scott.
"Soldiers, sir. American soldiers."

Allan Cole & Chris Bunch

"Do not take me for a fool. Here, take the glass. I will explain, because I want all of this carefully noted in the journal. Your army is led by a former barrister named Winder. We captured him in Canada and exchanged him. It looks to be a great gift. For us.

"I heard tales that Jemmy, your president, and even that man who heads your Admiralty, are playing at general. Below there you see the effects of far too many cooks. First, your Americans should have held the village as long as they could. Then fallen back across the bridge, into the earthworks. They should have dug them longer, extending farther upstream, because I would hazard the river is fordable there. But perhaps they did not have the time. And they have a negligible anchor with the barn on one side and the rail fence on the other flank. The men to either side of the earthworks are parlously exposed, especially against a charge with the naked bayonet.

"That second line, near that orchard. Too far back to support the front line. Very bad. Also, you should see cavalry somewhere. I know you have cavalry, since they sniped at us near Nottingham. They should provide scouting and, most importantly, cover the flanks of the foot soldiers. Then, you see farther back, beyond that second little bridge, the third line of soldiery? With cannon?

"Well and good. But again, they are nearly two thousand yards away from where the battle will begin. Those cannon will be as likely to fire into the backs of their own men as into our ranks. Can you remember all that?"

"Aye, sir."

"Very well. Put down the glass." Scott indicated the command group. "That man on the gray is Colonel Thornton of the First Brigade. He wants to attack now, with the Eighty-fifth, before your Americans settle into proper fighting positions, rather than wait for the other two brigades to come even with us. General Ross has granted permission."

The colonel touched his hat, wheeled his horse and galloped down to his troops. The 85th, in battle line, moved

442

out of sight into Bladensburg. Luke saw white puffs of smoke from the American earthworks.

"You wonder what they are shooting at?" Scott asked. Then, his answer: "Their own fear."

Finally the Americans had a target. The British infantrymen came out of town, and the line became a Vee, aimed at the bridge. Shannon saw, through Scott's glass, some of the Royal Marines set up those Congreve rockets on their firing stands and touch them off.

"We shall see how barbaric your Americans are. The Congreves cannot hit a barn from the inside. But they are good at frightening savages. At least for a while."

The rockets were frightening, Luke had to admit, even this far behind and away from them. They left long smoke trails as they moved through the air, and puffs of smoke, and, heard seconds later, explosions. But they did not seem to hit anything.

"Not good for your side, Jonathan. See how the lines of soldiery waver? Just from the noise and smoke of those contemptible rockets? Now we shall attack. Straight across the bridge, and overrun those guns in the fieldworks."

Shannon moved the glass, and he saw the attack. Red-coated soldiers, bayonets flashing sunlight, ran forward. He heard their battle shouts. In front was their colonel, waving his sword high. For a moment the engravings looked like they were based on real battles.

The American cannon fired. Tiny red bodies pinwheeled into the air or flopped down like marionettes whose strings the puppet master had suddenly cut. Smoke rose over the American positions. The British charge slowed. Cannons thundered again.

The redcoats broke and ran!

Back into Bladensburg.

Shannon fought his expression into blankness for a long moment, then lowered the telescope and looked at Scott. A grimace flickered, and then the lieutenant became calm again.

Allan Cole & Chris Bunch

"A better stand than we had anticipated," he said. Dry.
"Perhaps the Eighty-fifth should not have chanced the bridge.
Ah, look! Give me the glass!

"Something has gone wrong in your positions. There is a
cannon nosed down over the embankment into the dirt. And
now the Eighty-fifth is flanking through the village and
fording the river. The cannoneers are running. Damn!"

"Sir?"

"You have one man with sand," Scott said. "Stayed
behind his gun, loaded by himself, and fired it. Now he's
going. Run, man, like Hell itself were behind you. Bloody
Hell!"

Scott lowered the glass. "I would that man had lived."
He looked again, down at the battlefield. "Ah, yes. The
hardest thing, I have been told by soldiers, is to hold troops in
order when they must retreat. Your line has broken."

Now Shannon had his opportunity with the glass. The
front line had disintegrated. Knots of men ran, in any
direction except toward the British. The 85th had re-formed
after fording the river, gone on line, and now was moving
forward, the red, inexorable juggernaut, and each man felt all
those bayonets were aimed for his throat.

"The question now becomes," Scott said, "whether
whoever is leading your army can stop the retreat at the
second line. Or even keep the second line itself from— I was
born to be hanged," Scott said in sudden astonishment.
"Damme for a low rascal if I ever speak ill of the Congreves
again. A hit!" Luke saw greasy smoke from the second
American line—and that line shatter into panic as well. "It
could only be luck," Scott said.

"Lieutenant Scott," came the high-pitched shout. It was
Cockburn. "If you would mount, I propose we move forward
and join our soldiers."

If Luke had to be witness to a defeat, he would have
preferred it be from this hilltop, where he could maintain the
perspective—and, most importantly, the invulnerability—of
an eagle. But he went back down the hill, through the village,

444

and across the bridge behind Cockburn and Ross. By then the Second and Third brigades had arrived in Bladensburg and were awaiting orders. Cockburn and Ross and an increasingly reluctant Luke Shannon continued forward, onto the battleground.

The battle might appear won, but there were still Americans fighting. A seaman's jersey turned red, and he staggered away. Overhead Luke heard the whine of canister. Just beyond the body-littered American earthworks, Scott dismounted. In the middle of the road was a body. Scott carefully dragged the corpse to the side, then got back on his horse and went after the others. Luke, trotting and out of breath, glanced at the body. Evidently this was the brave solitary gunner at the earthworks.

He was black. Not all Negroes favored the British.

Luke might have anticipated the gore of a killing ground, and even the blast of the guns and muskets. But there was another kind of noise. Men shouting at each other. Men shouting at the enemy. Men just shouting, as if they were inmates of a Bedlam. Men screaming as they went down into pain and death. The howl of thrashing, wounded horses. And the smells. The burn of gunpowder he knew from shipboard. The dry, stagnant smell of a hot August countryside. The reek of shit and ripped guts from a body nearby. Blood, sharp on his nose like the taste of a bitten tongue.

Cockburn crested a small rise, near that second bridge, which in fact spanned a dry ravine, just as the 85th Foot attacked the third line of Americans. The third line did not break. The ground rolled in front of Shannon as a solid wall of fire smashed toward him.

Shannon dove into the ditch. The British soldiers were stumbling into line of attack. Again the cannon roared. The 85th, most of its officers, sergeants, and fuglemen dead or wounded, hesitated. From that third American line, soldiers charged. Some had bayonets fixed on their muskets, others clubbed rifles, ramrods, or swords. The 85th Infantry fell

Allan Cole & Chris Bunch

back across a field and into the ravine. They held discipline of sorts—none of them broke for the rear.

"If there is justice in the world," Scott observed, "the man commanding those guns and those men will be Commodore Barney. He wanted to fight us at Pig Point, and Jemmy Madison ordered him to scuttle and run. Some redcoats are serving the guns. Your marines, I would venture."

That ass Scott was still sitting his horse in the middle of the road, as were the other British officers. Luke guessed that was supposed to be inspirational, but he wished they would ride a dozen yards farther on and provide inspiration for some other targets.

Ross's horse reared, blood staining its coat. Ross slid backward out of the stirrups, shouting orders, and stepped away as the horse fell dead.

There were soldiers running up the road. And here, more of the rocket men. Cockburn walked his horse back and, in a calm voice, ordered them forward, into range of the American line. He suddenly sagged—and Shannon thought he was hit. A stirrup had been clipped by a musket ball.

But still the admiral refused to jump off his nag and eat ditchwater like any sane man should be doing. He was inspirational, no doubt about it, Luke thought. An inspired marine ran up and began fumbling with the stirrup. Far away Luke heard a blast, just as a hot dry wind swept him. The top of the marine's head was gone. Two of the rocket men collapsed. Grapeshot. Luke crawled forward and wound his handkerchief around one marine's near-severed leg. The pumping blood slowed to a gutter.

Luke had no idea whatsoever what was going on with the battle. Nor did he care, any more than he cared which bullock was to be slaughtered in what order in a slaughterhouse. But staring at that marine slowly bleeding to death was worse. Luke got to his knees and saw a confusion. On the road, freight wagons threw clouds of dust as they disappeared away from the battlefield. Here and there were running men. Stumbling men. Men who'd run out of wind and waited to be killed or captured. Dead men and wounded men. A flurry of redcoats, stabbing and bayoneting, swarmed over the cannon ahead. More British soldiers swept from the right over the final battle line.

Cockburn still sat his horse, amid the carnage, seemingly quite at home.

The battle was over and won. The British now had a clear go for their target. But there were some Americans unconvinced, as a musket ball thunked into the dust nearby.

On a hillcrest, Luke saw an American mounted on a blaze-faced chestnut. He was not in uniform, but wore, over civilian attire, a long, country riding coat. He was waving a sword—some kind of tiny ceremonial blade—and shouting. Still trying to rally the running troops, who brushed past him, heedless.

A Royal Marine next to Shannon knelt and aimed at the American officer. Just as he fired, Luke stumbled sideways. The ball went screaming into nowhere. Probably, Luke thought, the Marine would have missed anyway. But like Lieutenant Scott and the black, Luke wanted this man to live.

A young navy captain—Wainwright, Luke thought he was—hurried to Cockburn.

"Sir. Commodore Barney is down. He wishes to give you his surrender."

Luke got to his feet. Cautious. No musket ball or canister riddled him. He followed the British officers forward until they reached the road as it ran past the third line of American defense. A rather fat old man half sat in the ditch, blood pooling around him from the deep wound in his thigh. Admiral Cockburn dismounted, took off his hat, and half bowed.

Luke began to laugh—and stuffed his bloodied sleeve into his mouth. Laughter would not be taken as seemly. But the behavior of these officers was worthy of a Punch and Judy show. Wainwright formally introduced the British to this fat, angry-looking wounded man who was, indeed, the

Allan Cole & Chris Bunch

famous Commodore Barney. Barney, in turn, looked up at the British officer.

"Oh," he said. "Cock-burn is what you are called hereabouts." He stifled a groan. "Admiral, you have got hold of me at last."

Cockburn was equally courtly. "Do not let us speak of that subject, Commodore: I regret to see you in this state."

Mother of All Souls, thought Luke. These bastards actually did talk this way. It was not always an invention of the history mongers. The conversation went on . . . further apologies . . . the immediate parole of Barney ... a surgeon ordered up to dress the American's wounds ... a party of seamen detailed to carry the Commodore's litter to a place of safety . . . and Luke had his plan. Surely, somewhere behind the lines there would come his chance.

He stepped forward smartly. "May I be of service, sir?"

Cockburn studied Shannon and half smiled. "You are that seaman I detailed as Boswell to Lieutenant Scott's Johnson, are you not?" Without waiting for a response from Luke: "I remember you as being either Irish, American, or both, is that correct?"

"Aye, sir."

"Both races have most willing spirit. But I have found their flesh to be almighty weak." Luke's face must have shown something, because Cockburn's smile broadened. "Besides, we have a sufficiency of strong backs and a paucity of legible hands."

Luke touched his hat and stepped back into the throng. One failure was not the harvest.

Between here and the capital would come another chance.

Or even in Washington itself.

CHAPTER THIRTY-NINE

THE SHOPS AND buildings of Washington were mostly shuttered or boarded up. Not that there were many essentials left to be sold—the panic-stricken refugees, fleeing ahead of the British, had bought anything potable or edible as they rushed through the city.

Soldiers thronged around Capitol Hill. Looking for orders, looking for rations, looking for weaponry, looking for their superiors, looking for excitement. Some had been billeted in the Capitol itself the previous night. Bawling officers moved through them, trying to form the men up.

Diana asked what was happening. A young lieutenant paused.

"Orders from the president, madam. Or from the Secretary of War. The British are at Bladensburg. We're to stop them."

Bladensburg! Fear for John crept out at her. She pushed it away. Diana hurried on as the soldiers grouped into cohesive knots—hardly military formations—and marched away, up Maryland Avenue toward Bladensburg.

The President's House stood unguarded. Two cannon sat outside. There was no sign of the cannoneers. The infantrymen assigned to the President's House had also vanished. Unchallenged, Diana walked up the steps and through the doors. Inside was a hysteria of politicians, bureaucrats, and military. Young and old, uniformed or not, each of them had a disaster to shriek about. And none of them seemed to be listening to anyone else's catastrophe.

A bearded old man who might be a judge: "... with my own eyes! The niggers are burning everything between here and Frederick! And there's worse! Any woman . . ."

A colonel of militia, talking to a major of the regulars: "... issued us our rifles. And then the damnation—pardon, ma'am, I did not see you—man wants to count each flint before he issues it! Twice! My command shall never . . ."

A clerk: ". . . 'course it's poisoned. First thing the British agents did to the wells. Best stick to rum." He obviously had.

A young subaltern: "... second column of British regulars coming at us from the west. My sergeant saw them with his own eyes! The city's in a trap . . ."

A naval officer: "... midday at the latest if the army can't hold. Then, when their fleet in the Potomac closes on Fort Washington ..."

A harried-looking minister: "... agents everywhere. The Tories infiltrated the city days ago. Now, when the signal is given ..."

A man wearing bifocals, sounding reasonable: "Of course, without the correct certificates, I could not issue the vouchers. War or no war, there is a proper system which ..."

Diana thought them all mountebanks, sawing at the air and shrilling with ever-increasing desperation as their audience crept out of the theater and away from the struts and bellows. On the far side of the chamber Diana saw "French John"—John Pierre Sioussat—the Madisons' steward. She pushed her way through the throng to him.

"Madame Shannon, believe me, I am not practicing my gallantry when I say I am most glad to see you."

"What is going on?"

"Why, isn't it plain?" French John said. He indicated the crowd. "The world is coming to an end. Just listen to these windymouths."

"Where is President Madison?"

"Now that is a question. I have not seen him since yesterday, when he rode out for battle, wherever it is to be."

"And Mrs. Madison?"

"Upstairs."

"Thank you."

"Mrs. Shannon? Mrs. Madison is very firm in her duty as the president's wife. Perhaps . . . without sufficient concern for her own safety. Listen closely to her intentions, if you would?"

If politicians were circumlocutory, sometimes their domestics could be worse, Diana thought, making her way toward the stairs. Inside the dining room was a singular sight. There was only one man in it. He was carefully setting the table, as if for a formal party. His name . . . Diana thought she remembered it: "Paul? '

The young black started, almost dropping a plate. "Yes, ma'am?"

"Could I ask what you are doing?"

"Mrs. Madison, ma'am. She ordered the table set for Mister Madison an' some military gentlemen. An' the Cabinet. Said they'd be here for dinner."

"I don't think anyone will be sitting down to a full meal this day," Diana said. "If anyone's hungry, there is enough set out." Quite true—there was the usual Virginian's panoply of cold meats, soups, fish, and relishes. And there were coolers, moisture condensing on their outsides, that would contain ale, wine, and cider.

"Mrs. Madison gave me orders, ma'am."

She left the servant to his task—at least it keeps him from lapsing into panic like those fools in the public chamber, she thought—and looked for Dolly Madison. She found her friend at a window, with a brass telescope to one eye. Dolly turned at the footsteps. Her face was pale and she looked as if a decade had been added to her age. But there was a defiant tilt to her head and a fierceness in her eyes. When she saw who had entered, the look fled and she hurried to give Diana a quick embrace.

"Oh, Diana," she said. "I fear everything is—" She broke off, remembering who she was. Dolly forced control. "Tell me, Diana, dear, is this as bad as the Indians?" She gave a false laugh, but seemed to take courage from it. "I pray you're not going to be like the others," she said, "who are very sure of what I should be doing, or not doing. Anything I decide on my own they say is in error."

"Have I ever done so before?" Diana asked.

Dolly managed a smile. "No. At least not directly."

"I only came to see if I could help," Diana said.

Dolly regained a bit of her humor. "Beyond my husband," she said, "or the late General Washington together with his Continental Regulars—I can think of no other I'd rather have with me. The only people who seem to have their wits about them today," Dolly continued, "are French John and—I hope—myself. Everyone else-" Dolly stopped. Even in chaos, she would mind her words.

"Have you heard from your husband?" Diana asked.

"Only hasty notes," Dolly answered. "The most recent said the enemy is stronger than expected—and I am to be prepared to flee the city at a moment's warning."

"You don't appear to be packed," Diana said, looking pointedly around the room.

"I am not. First, I shall not leave until I know my husband is safe. Second, there are no wagons or carriages to be had at any price. I was told the clerk of the House of Representatives found only an oxcart for his records."

"What of your own belongings, Dolly?"

Dolly shook her head. "I would be ashamed of myself," she said, "if I stuffed a carriage with my clothing and jewels and fled like a thief in the night. Those things can be replaced."

Diana looked at her friend in surprise. She doubted if any fashionable lady in Philadelphia or New York could have made such a statement, let alone the dedicated follower of style Dolly Madison was thought to be.

"What we shall take—that is, if we can find a cart— are the papers of this government and Cabinet. And the president's private correspondence. My husband also promised Mister Custis that the Stuart portrait of General Washington would be saved. Then, if there is room, the silver and furnishings of this house, which belong to the public.

"At least, that is what I'd do if I were proposing to leave. But I am not." The last brought the fierceness back to her

452

eyes. "Not until Mister Madison returns. Or ... or I hear something to the contrary."

Now Diana understood what French John was worried about. Gently, she steered Dolly to firmer, calmer ground. She got her friend to issue instructions to carry to French John. In Diana's experience, any action during times of crisis produced at least a small result. And the small things sometimes piled up to a worthy whole. Diana also found she was gaining a tighter grip on her own fears for John Maguire, as they discussed the fate of the nation. She indicated the spyglass.

"Can you see what's happening in the city?"

"That was my intention," Dolly said, a bit rueful. "And possibly to see our army. My dear husband must be with them . . . But all I can see are soldiers wandering around like cattle. As if there is a lack of arms, or of spirit to fight for their own firesides."

There was no answer to this. Diana started for the stairs. Then she saw something very curious. "That house? I believe it to be Colonel Tayloe's? It's flying a white flag. Isn't that a sign of surrender?"

"You haven't kept abreast of events, Diana, dear," she said with a bitter laugh. " The Octagon House is now the French Embassy."

"What?"

"Some of the better members of this city—those who haven't already decamped—have been befriending the Seruriers, begging them to store their valuables until the crisis is over."

Louis Serurier, the French minister, and his beautiful wife were very popular. Madame Serurier had been born and raised in Haiti, and had somehow saved her parents' lives during the uprising. The Seruriers were also the only people in Washington who enjoyed, thanks to the end of the war with France, diplomatic immunity.

"Colonel Tayloe has stolen a march on all of them," Dolly said. "He asked the Seruriers to move into his house altogether. It now should enjoy the immunity of a diplomatic mission. The Seruriers, amiable people that they are, agreed."

"And where is the good Colonel Tayloe at the moment?" Diana asked, giving Dolly the payoff.

"Why suh," the president's wife said in excellent southern dialect, "his duties in the Old Dominion could no longer be denied. The call came mos' loudly after he perceived the British were actually on our shores."

Diana laughed—and Dolly even managed a chuckle. Pondering how she would convince her friend to get out of harm's way, Diana set off to do Dolly's bidding. She corralled French John to find out what was transpiring. Mister Sioussat told her some state papers had already been packed in Mrs. Madison's own carriage. He had the gardener, Tom Magraw, combing the city for more transportation.

"When—if—he returns, and with what success, I think should determine what we do next."

"Would it not be wise," Diana asked, "to prepare now? And for the worst?"

"I presented such a plan to Mrs. Madison, and was told that even in war some things are not done."

"What . . . exactly ... was your plan?"

"First, I proposed we spike those useless cannon out by the gates. Second, a train of gunpowder should be laid to charges below us, on the ground floor. I have the knowledge to prepare a clockwork fuse. Or else I would be willing to remain myself to fire the train."

"A little extreme, don't you think?" Diana eyed him, speculative. French John was, at least from the various stories about him, a creation of extremism. The tales frequently contradicted each other, but purportedly he had been born in France shortly before their revolution. He had decided to become a priest, in a country and age of anti-Catholicism. Something must have happened, because he then ran away to sea. The ship ported in America, where Mister Sioussat deserted. At that point the tales became fact. He appeared in Washington during President Jefferson's term, and was hired as a servant by the British minister. He not only had the cachet of being a sophisticated foreigner, but was competent as well. Mister Madison had seized on French John as a priceless treasure. And he was. He ran the White House as if he were one of Napoleon's field marshals.

"Extreme times call for extreme measures, Madam Shannon. Although I am hardly the worst. Mister Barker suggested to the president, I have been told, that he would blow up the Congress buildings with his own hands, given gunpowder, a corporal's guard, and a few experienced miners."

"I assume President Madison found that—well, surprising?"

French John nodded. "I was further told that he said if such an event were to occur, it would be best done by the English. It would inflame the nation."

"I doubt the president is that calculating," Diana said.

Mister Sioussat shrugged. "I am merely reporting what I have been told."

A servant approached. "John . . . Tom the gardener has come back. Wi' a wagon. But he's afeared to leave it un-watched."

"Very well. Replace him. If any one of these goats tries to commandeer my wagon, I will personally put a ball through his heart and have you trussed and roasted below-stairs in the Great Oven. Send Magraw to me. I shall need his muscles."

French John turned back to Diana. "You see, Madame Shannon? Circumstances clarify conditions."

But French John's phrase was more mellifluous than accurate, Diana discovered. She went back to tell Dolly that transportation was available. Dolly was listening to the final throes of a rather shrill plea from the mayor of Washington.

Mister Blake was saying: "... and if you should fall into British hands, you cannot imagine the blow it would be. A disaster. A catastrophe. You must leave Washington at once."

Allan Cole & Chris Bunch

"I shall leave when Mister Madison advises me," was Dolly's response. "Thank you, sir, for your counsel. And for taking the time, once more, to warn me."

Dolly turned her attention to Diana, who was about to ask what was to be loaded first, when she heard shouts and the drum of horses' hooves. A group of horsemen galloped past out on Pennsylvania Avenue. They were bent low over their horses' necks, and whipping them relentlessly. The horses were not saddled. Remnants of draft harness flapped from their steaming bodies. The riders must have cut the horses from caisson, cart, or artillery piece in a great hurry. This did not bode well. Then came a trickle of cavalrymen on foot. They were men who had ridden their mounts to exhaustion. The men were stumbling. Diana saw some of them glance back, as if the Devil himself were in pursuit.

A single rider thundered up the avenue and wheeled his mount toward the President's House. It was Secretary of War Armstrong. He tossed the reins of his slathered mount to the servant minding the wagon and ran up the steps. Dolly and Diana met him in the entrance hall.

"Lost . . . lost ... all is lost," he managed. "Our army is shattered! There is naught between the British and Washington."

Diana saw that Dolly was determined not to catch the man's hysterical affliction. But she still had to ask: "The president? My husband?"

"I was with him until the last moments," the general said. "Ah. Thank you. Thank you." Unbidden, French John had brought a mug of cider for Armstrong. He drained it. "The army did not fight! They fled! Mister Monroe turned back to rally them. The president said if the city is lost, we are to meet in Frederick. In the heat of the foray, I lost sight of President Madison. I fear the worst. He may have fallen into enemy hands."

This was almost too much for Dolly. She swayed, and Diana started for her. But then she recovered. She was about to put the general to the grill when a second horse galloped up to the President's House. Its rider was Jim Smith, the president's freedman. He was shouting: "Clear out, clear out! General Armstrong has ordered a retreat!"

Astonished, Diana looked at the general, and realized that her knowledge of chaos might not be as complete as she'd thought.

"Jim!" Dolly shouted. "Is Mister Madison all right?"

"He is, mis'tess." Smith dug a crumpled paper from his pocket, handed it to Dolly.

"Thank the good Lord," she whispered. "James is alive."

"Yes'm. He and Mister Rush 'scaped the redcoats. They're for Salona." Smith now noticed the Secretary of War. "General, sir? I thought you was with the army?"

The Secretary of War didn't answer. Then: "This is not the end."

From somewhere, General Armstrong recovered his bluster. "We shall fight on till the end. We shall fortify the Congress buildings for a last redoubt." He turned vaguely in the direction of Dolly. 'Mrs. Madison, you must leave the city immediately."

Without waiting for an answer, he was out the door and back on his horse. He spurred its sides—but the animal could manage no more than a feeble stagger toward Pennsylvania Avenue.

Dolly was in motion. "John, begin loading that wagon."

"Yes, madam."

"See the portrait is secured. I shall gather other things."

"Yes, madam."

Diana started to follow, then paused. She motioned Smith into the dining room and drew him a glass of ale. The black man blinked in astonishment. "Jim. What really happened?"

"I ain't no so'jer, mis'tess. So I can't say exact. Mister Madison went over the battlefield, inspectin'. Gen'ral Armstrong was actin' like he shoulda been in charge. Mister Madison fin'ly told him things should ought be left to the

Allan Cole & Chris Bunch

commandin' general—Winder, I guess they name him?
Gen'ral Armstrong took that hard. He was mutterin'.

"We was ridin' away, an' heard the shootin' commence.
We saw some men on horseback direc'ly, an' they were
shoutin' the British was killin' us. Gen'ral Armstrong put
spurs to his horse. I figgered first he was headin' for the
battle. But . . . best I not say more 'bout him. Th' president
wrote that note, an' told me to make for Mrs. Madison like it
was my life. That's all I know."

Diana thanked him, then sent the man off to assist
French John. Smith paused at the door. "You'll see no harm
comes to Mis'tess Dolly?" he asked. "Mister Madison
couldn't take it, harm come to her."

"I'll make sure she gets out."

Diana found Dolly in the drawing room. She'd pulled
down the great red velvet curtains and was rolling them into
an awkward bundle. She saw Diana. "Help me," she said.

Diana closed the door. "Dolly!" She said it sharp, trying
to shake her.

Dolly straightened, her face flushed with fury. But only
for a moment. Then she looked at the curtains she had pulled
down. She made a rueful face. "Curtains ... I must be mad,"
she said. She sat down on the sofa, breathing deeply. "When
I was a girl," Dolly said, "my grandmother used to tell me
that when everyone else around you is shrieking like
bedlamites—someone must show they are in charge of the
asylum." She looked at the bundle again. "Velvet curtains,
for heaven's sakes. What do we do with these?"

"Load them," Diana said. "They've already been
dismounted."

"Why not? If nothing else, they'll be a reminder to keep
my wits about me."

Diana left her to see if she could help French John.
There were many things Diana Shannon might have chosen
to take with her if her own house in Philadelphia was in
jeopardy. She doubted if any of them would have been
paintings. Oh, well, better a painting than velvet curtains.

The portrait in question hung on the west wall of the dining room. It was one of the portraits Gilbert Stuart had painted of George Washington. Some said it was the best of the lot. Watching the struggles of French John and Magraw, Diana decided that "hung" was an insufficient description of what had been done with the canvas.

"This," Magraw announced, prying at the portrait from atop a ladder, "is th' first paintin' I've seen that appears to ha' growed roots."

"Get a poker," French John said. Three other men were watching. One was Jacob Baker, the banker who aspired to become a sapper; the second another New Yorker, Robert de Peyster; and the third was Charles Carroll of Bellevue, one of Madison's aides. Mister Carroll was pacing back and forth.

"Mister Barker, this is insane. The British might arrive at any moment. And we are spending ourselves worrying about an imbecile picture."

"A picture, Mister Carroll," came a voice, "that the president of the United States has determined to save." Carroll hastily backwatered. It was Dolly Madison.

"My apologies, Mrs. Madison," he said. "Perhaps my choice of words was in poor taste. But I cannot emphasize how important it is for you not to be taken by the British."

"Do not worry yourself, sir," was the imperious reply. "That shall not happen."

Diana was delighted to see her friend behaving like her old self. Although she too worried for Dolly's safety, at the moment she felt a little sorry for any lobsterback who would dare the wrath of the president's wife.

Mister Carroll, meanwhile, was fumbling on. "Of course not. Of course not. Perhaps . . . since the situation here is well in hand, my efforts would be of greatest value if I convey your words to Mister Madison?"

"An excellent idea."

Carroll went. Quickly. A smile quirked Dolly's lips. "Mister Barker, does Mister Carroll have the slightest notion where my husband is to be found? No one else seems to."

Allan Cole & Chris Bunch

"I am certain," Barker said, "Mister Carroll has consulted his own oracle. And I wager he will begin his search in the direction of Georgetown."

Away from the British advance, Diana thought, but she said nothing. Atop the ladder, Magraw tried to use the fireplace poker as a lever. The soft iron bent nearly in half. French John had disappeared.

"We'll ne'er get the bastard off," Magraw panted.

"Mister Magraw!" The warning was from Dolly.

"Sorry, missus. F'rgot myself."

Mister Sioussat reappeared with a heavy axe. "Mrs. Madison ... do you value the frame?"

"Frames are but wood. Do what you must." Mister Sioussat struck well. Wood crashed and splinters flew. Two strokes and the frame was split at the bottom. He went up the ladder and, holding the axe halfway up the haft, struck twice more.

"Catch it! It's coming down." Barker, Magraw, and Diana had the painting before it hit the floor. Priest, possibly, seaman probably, but sometime in his past, French John must also have practiced the art of a woodsman. They laid the portrait flat and considered what to do next. It was still nailed to its stretcher.

"That," de Peyster observed, "will still never fit in either your carriage or the wagon, Mrs. Madison."

"If we cut it off the stretcher"—French John was examining the painting carefully—"and tried to roll it . . . No. It would certainly crack."

Diana found the situation slightly insane. A British army was descending on Washington, with at least some degree of rapine and ruin in its mind. And here was the wife of the president of the United States and four supposedly adult men calmly discussing how to transport a painting Diana personally thought made the late General Washington appear a numbwit.

Smith broke their concentration. "Mistress Madison, th' wagon's full-loaded. Mos' of th' silver's on. An' there was room 'nough for some of th' papers an' books you wanted."

Dolly came back to the present. All efficiency, she established the driver was reliable—he was. Did he know the safest way out of the city? He did. And his destination? The Bank of Maryland. The driver snapped the reins, and the wagon creaked away. Pennsylvania Avenue was now a solid stream of soldiers and civilians, pressing out of the city toward Georgetown. Almost all of them were afoot—those who'd managed to find a horse or mule had long since passed.

They moved slowly—but occasionally there would come a shout, and frenzy would return. They would break into a run for a few yards before sagging back into a shuffle. None of them appeared armed. Some of the soldiers who'd once been proud of actually having been issued uniforms had shed them in a panic, or else ripped off anything suggesting they were military beings. Diana was reminded of the mindless flight from Philadelphia during the plague.

"Now-"

"Now, Dolly," Diana interrupted, "it's time for you to go." She said this as strongly as she could without insult.

"I still have-"

"These gentlemen and I will secure what else we can," Diana said. Her tone indicated she would brook no further argument. Dolly considered, and looked down at the portrait once more.

"Very well," she said. "Gentlemen, save this picture. If you cannot, destroy it. Do not let it fall into the hands of the British." Very reluctantly, Dolly moved toward the main entrance. She scooped up a handful of silver and tucked that in the netted reticule with the few personal items she was willing to carry. Her carriage waited. Her maid, Sukey, and the coachman, Joe Bolin, were already aboard. She started to get inside, then turned. "Diana, dear. Would you please ask

Allan Cole & Chris Bunch

them to rescue the eagles from the drawing room? And
Mister Madison's papers?"

Diana said she would. Still, Dolly was hesitating. Diana
wanted to throttle her.

"One more thing," Dolly said. She smiled at the
impatience now plainly showing on Diana's face. "A personal
favor? Could you try to see that my macaw is cared for?"
Dolly was very fond of the large macaw—a fondness few
others shared.

Diana grinned. "I know the perfect place. Now go, get
out of here!"

Dolly Madison was barely seated when Bolin snapped
his whip, and the carriage was rolling. Diana saw the stern
profile at the carriage window. She thought Dolly looked far
more like a president than her husband. Then she sagged in
enormous relief. She felt like she had years earlier, trying to
put the young James Emmett to bed through a spatter of
excuses and requests.

Diana went back into the President's House. French John
was putting bottles of wine into water-filled buckets.

"Mrs. Madison said—"

"1 heard her instructions. A question, Madame Shannon?
Where is the perfect place for that vile bird?"

"Why, the Octagon House, of course," Diana said with a
laugh. "The new French Embassy. We'll make use of all that
diplomatic immunity. And Mister Sioussat, you might try to
see that the cage is hung over one of Colonel Tayloe's best
carpets."

French John found that amusing. "Madame Shannon, I
marvel at your calmness. You and Madame Madison put us
men to shame."

"To tell the truth, John, I'm barely able to keep from
screaming and running away like those men and women out
there. In fact ... at this moment I find myself in need of a
restorative." Diana reached for one of the bottles.

"I can do far better than that," French John said. He went
into the dining room and returned with two glasses and a

decanter of brandy. "Mister Madison's best," he said. "And I am sure he would rather see it in our bellies than in a redcoat's."

"What are you doing with that wine?" Diana asked, eyeing the buckets.

"It is what I have heard soldiers call a forlorn hope. Possibly the British pigs will be content with that as their loot, and leave all else untouched."

Diana remembered Emmett had said much the same thing many years ago in New Kent. "A forlorn hope, indeed."

"Yes," French John said. "But it is the best I can manage. And I think it is time for you to take the excellent advice you gave Mrs. Madison. The British should arrive shortly. It would be best if you are out of their path."

"There is still the portrait—"

"Mister de Peyster thinks he knows where a cart might be found. In the colored area. It will be saved, and not destroyed. When that is done, we shall depart."

"Where will you go, Mister Sioussat?"

"Philadelphia, I think. Well away from the excitement. I think I need some time to consider whether this career I have chosen is the most comfortable that can be arranged. I certainly did not plan my life to include encountering any more muskets than I had earlier. But that is for the future. Madame Shannon, it is time to save yourself."

Diana thought him to be right. Dolly Madison was on her way to safety. Whatever happened to Washington next was in the hands of the enemy. Now she was for Tomlinson's.

The wait for John Maguire would begin.

Allan Cole & Chris Bunch

CHAPTER FORTY

THE BRITISH ENTERED Washington at twilight.
Cockburn and Ross halted the army outside the toll-road
gates. The chopped-up First Brigade and Second Brigade
took defensive positions, and the unscathed Third—almost
fifteen hundred men of the 21st Regiment, Royal North
British Fusileers plus augmenting sailors and marines—
marched through the gates and up Maryland Avenue. There
were some muttered comments from the troops that they'd
seen— and burnt—better villages than this sprawling hamlet
the Jonathans called their capital. Luke paid no mind. He was
looking for his chance. Slogging along the dusty road, he had
decided that if he also found a way to tip his British cousins
into the shit before he went, that would be all to the better.

Maryland may have been named an avenue, and laid out
to be a magnificent 160 feet wide, but it looked more like a
cattle drover's trail. Cart tracks veered from side to side,
seeking the path of least ruts. There were cattle grazing near
the road, cattle that had escaped being rounded up when their
owners fled. Washington appeared deserted. Ross shouted an
order, and field snares snarled a question into the silence. No
one came out under flag of truce to begin a parley. Ahead of
them was the Capitol. At first Shannon thought it one
building, then realized it was two, with a wooden, covered
walkway between them. Nearby was a scatter of expensive
houses, taverns, and hotels.

It was getting dark. Ross ordered torches lit, and he and
Cockburn reined in and conferred inaudibly. Musket fire
spattered from a house, and Luke flopped full length into the
dust. Ross's horse sagged, then collapsed. There were
soldiers down, blood draining into the roadway. Shannon
came to his feet. A line of infantrymen formed, aimed and
fired at the nearest target—a house. Luke was pretty sure no
one knew where the musketry had come from. There was no

return fire. Skirmishing squads broke from the formation and began searching the area.

Cockburn spurred his horse back down the column, shouting orders. Twenty Congreve rocket men doubled forward and set up their aiming tripods. They fired, and the rockets crashed through the walls of the house and exploded. Flame rolled through the windows. Then a second explosion roared. Luke did not know if the blast knocked him down or if he ducked. At first he thought the house must have been an arsenal or perhaps a landsman's version of a fireship. No, he realized, as more explosions rocked the earth and fire shot high into the sky from the south.

"They've fired the Navy Yard," Scott announced after consulting a sketch map. The sky was more than light enough for that. "Good that the Jonathans have saved us the gunpowder," Cockburn said, indifferent. Ross stood in the middle of the road. He seemed dazed from his fall.

"Detail four men to find the general a new mount."

"Sir."

"Search all these buildings. If you find the snipers, bring them to me. Stay a moment. Make them prisoner only if they are in uniform. If they are in civilian garb, consider them partisans and proceed accordingly. Any building containing implements of war is to be burnt. Inspect that hotel first."

"Aye, sir."

Partisans and guerrillas had no rights, even though all armies encouraged irregular reinforcement. They could be— and were—shot or hanged without trial. Squads of infantrymen moved out on command. Shannon hoped like hell they would not find the brave marksmen. At least somebody was fighting back.

* * * *

Diana had seen, peering cautiously through the edge of the curtained window, the British column advancing through the growing darkness down Maryland Avenue toward Tomlinson's Hotel. She'd heard the spatter of musket rounds outside. And, just like Emmett centuries ago when the militia

Allan Cole & Chris Bunch

of New Kent had decided to fight back against the British, she had said the first thing that came to tongue: "Christ!" Now, just as in New Kent, the British would have carte blanche. She began refiguring her plans. The past few hours had seen a great deal of that.

There was still no sign of John. He'd not been among the trample of soldiers and panicked civilians that poured down Maryland Avenue and out toward Georgetown that afternoon. Diana prayed he hadn't broken his word and played soldier with his toy hunting sword.

Considering toys, she touched the pistol that lay beside her on the yellow satin couch. She had found a barman, one of the few employees of Tomlinson's who had not fled, and asked him to find a pistol. She offered to pay twice what it would cost from a gunsmith or whomever, without any questions. In half an hour the weapon was delivered. It was not much of a weapon—its tiny barrel was a little more than a third of an inch in diameter. But it was charming, from its rococo silver working on the butt of the walnut grip to the ornate scrolling on the lock itself, plus a tiny pouch of powder and shot.

"A perfect weapon for a lady," the barman had said.

For a lady to shoot mice with, perhaps. Mice that were very close and very somnolent. She should have ordered a brace of dragoon pistols, or a punt gun. But this toy was what she had. Armed civilians, in time of war, were in extreme jeopardy. But the hell with that. She would suffer no indignities to her person without fighting back.

Diana had also planned for the lesser catastrophe of having to flee Tomlinson's. She had sewn up her gold in a linen bag and tied it about her waist with tapes. She wore heavy shoes, and a hooded cloak was on the sofa—not needed for its warmth in the August swelter, but for inconspicuous travel if she had to move by night; or even to serve as a sleeping blanket. She'd filled a small traveling case with spare linen, soap, candles, penny royal for the mosquitoes, a veil, gloves, and the largest flask of cologne she could find. The case also included bread, hard cheese, dried apples, and sausage from Tomlinson's kitchen. She added a knife, spoon, a tinderbox, and a tin cup—she would have to chance drinking the water. Finally a bottle of brandy.

Belowstairs she heard the smash of wood and men shouting. She snapped the pistol's frizzen back and cocked the hammer. A muffled scream. The tramp of boots down the corridor, and the slam of something heavy against her door.

"Who is it?" She kept her voice calm.

"King's soldiers. Open or we break down the door." Diana let the hammer down to half cock, hid the pistol in an inner pocket, and went to the door. Two red-coated men nearly as tall as their bayoneted rifles burst through. They ignored her and swept the room. A third man, in the corridor, looked to be in charge. Diana planned a burst of outraged dignity.

The man spoke first. "Is there anyone else in the room?"

Diana shook her head.

"Your mister around ... or did he run away like the rest of them?"

"1 am a widow."

The man pulled a yellow-toothed smile. Not pleasant. "Widow? Who keeps you in this fancy house?"

That was enough.

"Young man, I am a respectable woman of means. You will escort me to your officer. I shall inquire of him who granted you the authority to insult someone so far above your station." She let this filter through, then fired the final shot. "What do you think his response will be?"

A memory or vision of the cat might have dimly crossed the man's mind. "No need for that, mum. We have orders. The hotel's to be burnt. You're to clear out at once."

"This hotel is not government property. There's no soldiers here."

"We found arms, mum. Orders were, anywhere we found arms, we put everything to the torch."

Allan Cole & Chris Bunch

"Nothin' here, Corp'ral." The two soldiers had finished their search.

"Is that your bag, mum?"

"I shall carry it."

"No need, no need." The redcoat picked up Diana's case and started out. Perforce, Diana followed. Near the entrance, she saw those "arms." A couple of shotguns and a sporting rifle. Probably abandoned by some of the hotel guests. Excuse enough.

Diana caught up with the corporal and took back her case.

"M'pologies for what I spoke. You'll not tell the lieutenant?"

Diana thought, what good would it do? She didn't bother with an answer, but hurried across the avenue. There were twenty or so people there, mostly women and children. Some were crying, some numb with shock, some protesting. The first flames licked from the hotel. Very well, now you are a refugee, Diana thought, just like all the poor bastards who came through Cherry Valley. What next? First get the hell away from the damned British and their damned guns. Then . . . then play the rest of the cards as they're dealt.

She slipped away from the knot of people, into the night.

* * * *

"Shannon!"

"Sir." You bastard, Luke thought.

"Quit gaping. You've seen a building burn before. Listen to my orders. I have been told that there is someone else planning a chronicle of this campaign, an army officer. It behooves us to ensure our account will not only be the most accurate, but appear in the most timely fashion. Do you understand what I am saying?"

I do indeed, Lieutenant Scott, he thought. And somehow I promise that these pages in the pack behind me will end up unread in the shitter. If I face the grating for it.

But he said: "Aye aye, sir."

"So I want you up front with us. Keep a full and careful report of everything that happens. We're moving against the Capitol."

Luke touched his hat and ran toward the open square in front of the Capitol, past the blasting flames from Tomlinson's Hotel and a sorrowing knot of women and children. Caught in the middle, just like me. He spared the sympathy.

The night was flickering fire. The British soldiers were drawn up in battle line in front of the two buildings, muskets leveled. There was no sign of life inside. The order came, and the volley boomed. Glass shattered. The lobsterbacks did not receive return fire.

Axemen ran forward, covered by the leveled guns of the second line, and smashed the great doors open. There was a cheer, and assault parties, like the killer automatons they were, rushed the entrance and took up firing positions. Other squads doubled around to cover the rear. The third wave of troops went in the buildings, leapfrogging the cover element. There were no Americans in either building. The command group dismounted.

"Shannon!"

"Sir?"

"Have you ever seen this city before?"

"Nossir. Been at sea, sir. Been in your navy, sir. I was occupied elsewhere. Sir.'

"Very well. The building on the south there is, I have been told, the same as our House of Commons. That would be . . . ?"

"The Representatives' house. Sir."

"The other is your Senate. The House of Lords. They shall both be burnt. Now stay with me."

Obediently, Luke followed as the command group strolled into the building. Just like that unknown sniper, he determined he had to find a way to strike his own blow, no matter how small it might be.

Allan Cole & Chris Bunch

Admiral Cockburn looked curiously around. Luke saw Cockburn pick up a small book, flip through it, and then slip it into his pocket.

"Sir?"

"Yes, seaman?"

"For Lieutenant Scott's journal, sir. What is that book, might I ask?"

Cockburn took it out. "It appears to be an account of the expenditures your United States made during the year 1810. Prices of pickled fish and so forth. An appropriate memento."

"Thank you, sir." Not only did he not understand the British, Luke thought, but he would never understand an admiral. Lieutenant Scott looked displeased. Possibly he thought his hero should have taken as loot the Declaration of Independence if he could have found it.

He beckoned. "You see that man over there?" Scott indicated a bespectacled navy lieutenant, whom Luke had noticed earlier and thought to be one of Cockburn's clerks. Some kind of scholarly sort. "That is Lieutenant Pratt. He is our expert in incendiarism. Report to him."

"Aye aye, sir."

Shannon explained his duties to the Royal arsonist. Pratt told him to pay close attention, and wandered into the lower story of the House of Representatives.

"You observe, seaman, I have deployed these men as three-man teams. The first is to prepare the tinder, the second to ready the kindling, and the third to strike the match."

Pratt may well have seen what he'd ordered as a scurry of men readying themselves for a bucolic picnic fire. Shannon did not. Marines and sailors used long pikes to rip the woodwork off walls and pull away shutters, window sashes, doors, and bookcases. The wood went on stacked furniture, piled records, books, draperies, and rugs.

That was the tinder, Luke thought.

Others used knives to cut rockets apart and spread their gunpowder charges on the stacks. The "match striker" used a lit, pitchball-tipped pike tc start the fire. Flame flickered unevenly.

"Either these Americans used green wood or else built better than I had imagined. This is becoming an interesting problem. Especially when we consider the exterior stone of these structures. Come with me. Upstairs, where there is a larger room. Perhaps the solution lies there."

They found themselves in a large hall. Pratt stood, humming tunelessly to himself, staring around the chamber. He could have been a slightly interested tourist in a museum somewhere. Then he showed a sudden response. A group of Royal Marines had found—they thought—that instant solution. Two Congreve rockets were set up and aimed up at the roof.

A sergeant shouted, 'This'll fire it, sir." Pratt started to shout but was too late, as the sergeant snapped an order and, like clockwork, the gunners touched off the rockets toward the roof. The roof had been covered with sheet iron. The rockets exploded, and for one small moment Luke knew what it was like to be on Hell's plain under the eternal rain of fire. His eardrums intact, Luke picked himself up amid the smolder. Pratt got up and brushed a spark from his uniform coat.

"No," he observed mildly, "that is not the solution. However, there are possibilities here."

He quietly issued orders to the sailors and marines, none of whom seemed more than surprised by the rockets. All of the decks, chairs, and tables in the hall were piled in the center of the room atop a platform. Casks of gunpowder were broken open and their contents spread over the pile. The redcoats retreated to the hall's entrance. Pratt ordered three more rockets aimed at the pile. The gunpowder exploded. Fire spurted toward the ceiling.

"Very well, that," Pratt said. "There should be no need to concern ourselves with the lower floor. Now, to the other building." There was more in the way of kindling in the Senate; red morocco chairs, more books, more papers.

Allan Cole & Chris Bunch

Maybe everybody made jokes about politicians and their damned papers, Luke realized. But every goddamned one of those papers represented somebody. A widow worried about her farm. A veteran asking for a pension. A merchant needing an examination of a tax law. In sum, they were the government. The government of his country.

Luke spotted a ring of keys on the floor. Maybe they opened a vault. Maybe it contained important papers, or government gold. Maybe nothing. He kicked the keys under a sideboard, out of sight. Christ, what he had done was not much, but it was something.

The United States Senate building fired like dry oakum. Luke watched the fire, then turned away. Beside him was Lieutenant Pratt. Firelight reflected from his spectacles. "By your accent . . . you are American?"

"I am that. Sir!"

"This is an ill night's work," Pratt said, without showing any sign of emotion. "You set a small fire. York, in Canada. We retaliated with this. 'Fire answers fire, and through their paly flames/Each battle sees the other's umber'd face,' " he quoted.

"Look over there." He pointed toward a new spurt of flames, out in the darkness. "The explanation, no doubt, will be that sparks from this building spread to those two houses. Brick, they were. Quite a spark, eh? I wonder what response you ex-Colonialists will find to this? Putting the torch to London, perhaps?"

CHAPTER FORTY-ONE

GLASS CRASHED, AND Diana pulled the cloak's hood over her head and knelt, doing her best to resemble a bush. Three men, outlined by spreading flames, clambered out the back window of the house General Washington had built years earlier. Nearby, a second brick building, built by Dr. Thornton, was already engulfed. The men were cumbered with bottles and other things Diana saw them tuck inside their uniforms. "Come, lads," she heard one say. "Tha sarn't'll be seekin't us." The three British soldiers scurried back toward the Capitol buildings.

Diana went onward. She'd skirted Capitol Hill before turning south. The still unfilled canal had been her first major obstacle, a dark line in the night. She eased down the mucky banks, muttering as mud squelched into her shoes, then, taking a chance that she was not walking into a bottomless mire, splashed through the ground water on the canal's bottom and clawed her way up the far bank. She navigated by the distant firelight, trying to keep the flames from the Navy Yard on her left and the Capitol fire behind her.

A large house and its outbuildings bulked out of the night. She thought it to be the Millses' residence, but was unsure. It had been years since she'd had to travel crosscountry. If it was the Mills house, she expected to find no one home, save perhaps a few servants. If Mister Mills had not already fled the August heat, the British would have certainly sent him flying to safety.

She heard a low laugh and slipped behind a tree. She had the pocket pistol ready.

"Strike true. Just on the lock." The speaker had a very thick brogue. Wood and metal smashed. "Inside with us now Be quick. Take only what you can carry. Or drink."

More laughter. She knew who the looters had to be. A handful of those poor damned indentured Irishers brought in to dig the canal, and treated even worse than slaves, as they had no value. Diana found herself hoping that this was, indeed, the Mills house. She also hoped that what they could carry included coinage and jewelry.

After a dinner party some weeks earlier, Mister Mills had regaled the diners with a "delightful" joke: Q: How is an Irishman to be distinguished from a nigger? A: The nigger does not try to smoke a potato.

Diana crept toward the rear of the house and the carriage building, praying there would be a horse left unattended there. The crossbar was lying in the yard, and the great double doors were closed. She was about to ease one open when she heard a whimper from within.

"Sssh. Ssh, my love. I'll protect you. If those redcoats come back here, they shall have to go through me first."

"I trust you, Noah."

Noah, Diana thought, was not Mister Mills's Christian name. But that second voice was certainly Abigail Mills's. Oh!

"Don't worry, lass. The lobsterbacks are busy with their stealing. If they do not burn the house, we'll go back in and save what we can. The master shall be proud of you."

"But my jewels."

"Mister Mills has friends. He'll be able to petition Congress for redress. Don't worry, darlin' Abbie. Tomorrow, when the sun rises, we'll find horses for the carriage and take you to safety. You will think of this as but a dream."

Diana buried a giggle. Too bad Noah wasn't normally an Irish name. That would have made the looting of the Millses' complete. She moved back toward the dirt track that was called a road, heading south.

* * * *

"This is rather mean for something I have heard called the Palace," Lieutenant Scott observed.

"Yessir," Luke said, "I guess it's because we have not had the chance to steal from anyone except the Indians . . . sir." Scott had the grace to smile slightly.

The President's House was not that impressive, viewed just as a single building. But standing by itself, on a nearly open plain, gave it at least a bit of grandeur. The British column had moved up Pennsylvania Avenue, through the row of poplar trees on either side of the avenue, past a low stone fence, until the troops came abreast of the gateposts. The gateposts were topped with eagles, which Luke thought looked adequately imperial. But from there to the house, the grounds—untended and ungardened—were cordoned with a low wood picket fence. The mansion itself was three stories, with four columns at its entrance. Stone terraces extended to either side of the house itself. Luke had seen far grander in Philadelphia, London, or Paris. But what of that? Who was to say America's leader was measured by whether his dwelling compared to Buckingham or Versailles? Louis was executed, Napoleon in exile, George a madman from whore's pox.

"Without appearing too derogatory, this palace appears to be drawn by a draughtsman, from some handbook of architecture."

"Yessir. If you say so. sir. I'm just a fair copyist, sir. I never lived in a house like this, sir. But Lieutenant? If you want your book to say something such as that . . . would it not reduce your admiral's accomplishment? Sir?"

"Shannon," Scott said, "I wondered why you were so readily detached for this duty. I think I am beginning to understand. You are certainly not afraid to voice an opinion. Now . . . inside with us."

"Sir."

The doors of the President's House were open. Inside was a scurry of soldiers. Perhaps Sir George Cockburn had published admonitions against looting. Somehow they did not apply at the moment.

He heard cheers from a side room, and Scott and Shannon headed in that direction. The room was a dining chamber. The long table was set with linen, silver, crystal, and china. On sideboards were trays of cold meats and fowls. A midshipman was hacking at an enormous ham with his

Allan Cole & Chris Bunch

dirk. Baskets of rolls were beside the trays, as were bowls of jams and relishes. The center of attention was a row of coolers filled with bottles of ale, wine, rum, and whiskey. In the middle of the room stood Cockburn and Ross. Both of them were munching delicacies and sipping wine.

"Find two glasses, seaman. Pour us some wine."

"Sir." Luke managed to knock back half a glass in the pouring. Thinking slightly kinder thoughts of the Royal Navy, he brought the two filled glasses back to Scott.

Cockburn lifted his glass. "I propose a toast," he declaimed. "To the health of the Prince Regent and success to His Majesty's arms by sea and land."

A quiet cheer, and the invaders drank. Luke didn't drink. He felt like hurling the goblet at Cockburn. But that would have been a waste of good wine, and no proper seaman would be guilty of that.

"You know, seaman," Scott said, "by the time our army friend is allowed to enter the city, this snack your Americans seem to have abandoned will have grown into a Lucullan repast."

"Sir?"

"There shall be great spits of boar . . . towering aspics . . . sides of beef. Soldiers' tales, like those of fishermen, grow in the telling."

"Yessir."

And, of course, Lieutenant, Luke thought, you'll be the first to ruin a good tale with the truth when you come to write your book, without benefit of my log. Of course.

"Let us continue our reconnoiter, Shannon. Upstairs. See what is to be seen before the conflagration."

Scott drained his glass and told Luke to refill it. Shannon followed orders, and the Royal Navy officer. In an upstairs room Scott saw a small iron safe.

"See if the Jonathans bothered to lock that, sailor."

The safe door was, indeed, ajar. Luke twitched the door open. Inside were stacks of piled currency. He did not examine them. Instead he pushed the door shut until he heard a satisfying click as the lock caught. As Lieutenant Pratt might have said, Luke thought: very well, that.

Scott was in a bedroom, stripped to the waist. He held up a linen shirt. "I would think this to be the linen of your president. Appears to be just my size." Scott grimaced. "I seem to have strained myself dismounting. Seaman . . . would you mind rubbing this muscle?"

Luke goggled, then recovered. Right, Lieutenant. Just what you need. A massage, and then, just here on the bed of the president . . . Mary's Holy Name, do you think me that dumb just for being an American? On my first cruise I did not want to see a length of the bosun's pipe, either.

"Sir? I heard someone calling you. Downstairs." Scott scowled, then tugged on President James Madison's shirt and hastened toward the stairs.

Luke whistled silent relief and followed.

* * * *

The track led south, Diana estimated. This part of Washington was even more dismal than the rest. Here was a ropewalk, there a cluster of slave dwellings. Standing near a clump of trees was a blacksmith's shop. She was moving without a plan now. Perhaps she would go to the Potomac and hope to find a boat that would take her to the other side. Perhaps the causeway across into Virginia was still intact.

Ahead of her, Diana saw the flicker of torches, ten or more of them. She heard singing. Drunken singing. She looked for a hiding place. There were a few shacks to either side of the road. She thought what was inside might well be worse than the drunken mob in front of her.

She found the pistol and cocked it. I will move into the shadows, she decided. With luck they shall not see me. If they do ... I have this one shot. With further luck they'll be frightened and I can flee.

Looking down the road, she did not see, behind her, the flicker of a candle against a burlap curtaining the shack window behind her, nor that curtain twitch open and then close again.

Allan Cole & Chris Bunch

* * * *

Downstairs in the President's House, the fire lovers were at work again. Furniture was piled in the center of rooms, draperies and carpeting had rocket powder poured on them. In the house's central oval room, Luke saw General Ross stacking red velvet cushions like firewood. A well-dressed gentleman was escorted to him by one of his aides. Luke didn't know who the gent was, nor could he hear what he wanted.

Ross struck a noble pose and emoted: "Sir. The French king's house will be as respected as if His Majesty were there in person."

King? Hadn't the French king, whoever the hell he was, gotten shortened by a head some years ago? Were they talking about Napoleon? No. He'd been put into exile on some island somewhere. So what was this king they were talking about? The French must've found a new one somewhere.

He guessed there was always some king or another, wandering around looking for employment. It figured. Here the English had spent the last thousand years or so beating up on the French, and now this general's protecting some house I guess he owns. Kings got to stick together, he thought. But presidents, now ... he saw Pratt leading torchmen into the mansion. "All troops not on fire detail, clear out. Form up on the street."

Cockburn added an order of his own: "Detail a party for the Treasury Building. The main column will help me deal with Dear Josey." Cockburn seemed to be enjoying himself.

At the door Luke turned around. He saw Pratt thrust a torch into the center of those pillows. Fire gouted. The president's mansion exploded into flames almost at once.

The air was hot, thick, and tasted of ashes. The burning city lay under looming black clouds. The soldiers, in formation on Pennsylvania Avenue, needed no orders to remain silent.

This closely resembled Hell. And they were in its maw.

* * * *

Diana whirled, almost firing, as the shack door creaked open. "Inside, missy." A woman's voice. A second to consider—the drunks were only a couple of dozen yards away. Diana ducked through the pineboard door. Pistol still ready, she found the wall and put her back to it. There was a fire in the hearth against the wall, but banked down to a glow.

"We wait till them drinkin' white folks pass on 'fore I strike a light." The torches flickered against the curtain, and then were gone. "Mebbe they run into the redcoats. Find some 'a th' trouble they seekin'."

The woman crossed to the hearth, blew on the fire and added kindling. Diana lowered the pistol to her side but still held it ready as the fire flared up. There were two people in the shack, a man and a woman. They were middle-aged and shabbily dressed. They were both black.

Diana pulled back the cloak's hood. "Hell," the man swore in surprise. "White!"

"Mis'tess," the woman said, "what're you doin' here in niggertown?"

"Getting away from the British," Diana said. "They burnt me out of my hotel."

"White folks' bi'ness," the man said. "Never leads to good." Diana, feeling no threat, uncocked the pistol and put it back in a pocket of her walking dress.

"You sit down, mis'tess. 'Less you feel it ain't right to be in black folks' homes." There were not a lot of choices— the trundle bed the man sat on, a stool, and a very rickety, very elderly chair. Diana chose the stool.

"I thank you. Give me a moment to get my breath, and I'll be on my way."

"I saw you comin' down the track," the man said. " 'Less you got a secret, there ain't no way to th' way you were proceedin'. Causeway's done cut on th' Virginny side by so'jers. What boats were on this side of the river crossed afore dusk." That option was closed. "Best place maybe Saint

Allan Cole & Chris Bunch

Patrick's. Somebody come through an' said th' priest was keepin' it open. For folks with nowheres else to go."

"Jeptha, you are a hard man."

"Tryin' to help."

"Help ain't sendin' no woman, don't matter what color, back out on them streets with outlaws an' sojers an' guns an' whiskey."

"You sayin' she's stayin' here?"

"I'm sayin' just that. You jus' remember, Jeptha Grant. This is my house."

"You always bringin' that up."

"Bringin' it up 'cause you keep forgettin'." The woman turned to Diana. "Sorry, mis'tess. It ain't civil to have differences in front of strangers."

"As I said, I'll be leaving in a moment."

"Mis'tess, you better start thinkin'. Jus' cause Jeptha never learned his manners, shouldn't cause you to go runnin' out of here, to face Lord knows what. Be easy for a while.

"You had anything to eat?" The woman did not wait for a reply. "We got kush an' I stewed up some fish that Jep' caught. If you don't mind nigger food."

"Right now, it sounds like royal fare," Diana said. She was not sure whether she would be leaving or not—but wanted a few more moments to think. "My name is Diana Shannon. And you?"

"I was baptized Georgia Powers."

"Thank you for taking me in."

"White folks' bi'ness," muttered Jeptha once more.

Diana's temper flashed a little: "I saw some black men with muskets marching out of Washington yesterday. They didn't seem to think this was white folks' business."

Jeptha shrugged. "That's so," he agreed. "Heard other niggers—slaves-—run off to join the British. That's the other side, but the same coin."

"Jeptha, I ain't going to say but once more—this is my house, and you stay civil around my guests. Else I run you out with the hogs."

"Georgia, you been threatenin' that for ten years now."

"One of these days, I'll fool you an' follow through. Wait an' see."

"Do you two always argue like this?" Diana asked.

Georgia thought. Then she nodded. "Seems like it. Guess it keeps the juices flowin'."

"I would be proud to eat with you," Diana said. "But ... I am not from around here. What is, umm, kush?"

"Cooked corn bread that you mush up with raw onions. Pour ham gravy on top."

"Oh."

"Eats a lot better than it sounds."

Diana opened her case and took out the bread, cheese, and sausage from Tomlinson's. "I'll add this to the menu."

"Best not. That food saves. Better keep it for traveling."

Jeptha had a question. "You say you're not from these parts. Where 'bouts' your home?"

"Philadelphia."

"They treat niggers different there?"

"Only a bit. Slavery's been outlawed, at least."

"That ain't me and Georgia's worry no more. I 'us born free. I bought Georgia out ten years an' gone. Not th' question."

Diana answered honestly. "Up north, times aren't that good for anyone. It's a little worse for your people. They say you're free and have some of the rights of white people. We've got some Negro merchants. Mechanics. But—" she stopped.

"But I think I know th' rest," Jeptha said. "The job a nigger gets is one a white man won't touch. An' when times get hard, th' nigger's first to let go. Fine for you t' talk about tradesfolk. But where's someone like me get the money to set up shop? Hard enough findin' work that puts corn bread an' beans on the table. Church talks about good S'maritans. That's all it is, talk. Never seen one yet, an' me an' my woman spent all our lives on that road to Jericho. Nigger's got a hard way to go. An' not a lot of choices."

Allan Cole & Chris Bunch

"I had some friends," Diana said, "helped me farm, up in New York. During the Revolution. When the war ended, they went to Canada."

"Not for us," Jeptha said. "I hear black folks who join up with th' British get sent to Canada. Not for us. My middle name ain't Boone. Other choice, they say, is down to the Sugar Isles. Mebbe you free there . . . but I bet there's still overseers with whips in them sugar fields. I even hear some fools talk about goin' back to Afriky. Sure. Get eat by tigers or can'bals. That'd make the white folks happy. Like I said, nigger got a hard way to go. On'y hope is to plug on, keep your head down an' stay away from white folks' bi'ness."

Georgia turned from the fire. "I get used to one blasted fool around, looks as we got two, tonight. You two . . . sittin' talkin' like a pair Meth'dists worryin' about Judgment Day ... an jus' outside there's those folks in red coats. They goin' burn th' city an' this house down 'bout our shoulders 'fore the sun come up anyway. Mos' likely with us inside. So don't be worryin' about tomorrow. Ain't none us likely to see it."

Jeptha suddenly chuckled. "See why I stay wi' her, missus? Keeps my thinkin' straight." He stood. "Kush ready. I could stand eatin' again."

Georgia was right. Kush wasn't that bad. Over the meal, Diana told them about John Maguire and about her decision to strike for the Eagle Tavern.

"I never see that place," Jeptha said. "Sounds like a far walk. Best you take the mule."

"Two days ago," Diana said, "the government was paying five dollars and more just to rent a horse."

"Heard that. Like I said, don't pay to mess wi' white folks' bi'ness."

"I thought somebody would have just requisitioned your mule."

"Hell . . . sorry, missus. Day a nigger can't hide cart, fine racin' horses, an' harness just under the nose of white folk— that's th' day to holler hallelujah an' go on up to th' Lord."

"Thank you. I can pay for the mule."

"We'll talk about payin' when you bring th' mule back, when all these so'jers stop foolin' around an' go on 'bout their bi'ness. Warn you, payin' then'll be steeper than now."

"That's fair."

"Dam' fool is what I am. 'Scuse me. Got bi'ness outside."

Jeptha rose, peered through the burlap curtain. The track outside was deserted. He slipped out.

Diana smiled. "You have quite a husband, Mrs. Powers," Diana said.

Georgia sighed. "That's Jeptha. Jus' time I'm about to put th' spider 'longside his head, he goes an' does some'at like this. On'y thing I know for sure, ain't no way a woman ever goin' understand a man."

* * * *

Admiral Sir George Cockburn reined in his horse at McKeowin's Hotel. There were three men on the steps.

"You." The man addressed wore the high boots and rough garb of a teamster. "I have a question, my good man."

The teamster spat tobacco juice just in front of Cockburn's horse. "Nope." he said.

"What?"

"I ain't a 'good man' for no one wearin' lace an' ruffles. 'Specially when a red coat goes with it."

Cockburn ignored that. "I am looking for the offices of the National Intelligencer."

"What's that?"

"The newspaper, you imbecile." Cockburn's patience extended just so far.

"Don't write. Don't read. 'Specially newspapers. Never heard of it." A sergeant growled and stepped forward, bayonet lowering. The teamster spat again. "You want to be careful with that toothpick, sonny. Else somebody shove it up your arse an' see if you can dance Yankee Doodle."

Another American came between them. "Wait. The Intelligencer's offices are just there." He pointed across the street.

"Thank you, sir," Cockburn gritted.

Allan Cole & Chris Bunch

The teamster was ungrateful. "Shouldn'ta stepped in, Ambrose. Shoulda waited t'see what come next."

Cockburn dismounted and started toward the Intelligencer's office. Luke followed, wishing he could buy the teamster a grog. A few Americans had their backs up. Rifle butts crashed in the newspaper's door. A soldier came out with a handful of papers. He gave one to General Ross. "The last edition, sir."

Ross started to stuff it into a pocket. "Dammit," he said. "My pocket's full of old Madison's love letters. I've no room for this trash." He cast the paper aside.

"Burn the building," Cockburn ordered. "Dear Josey Gales will print no more libels about me."

The incendiaries moved in—and two women rushed out of the shadows. "Sir. General, sir."

"I am not a general. But what may I assist you with?"

"I am Mrs. Stelle. This is Mrs. Brush. We live on this block, sir. If you burn this building, I am afraid our own homes will catch fire."

Cockburn thought a moment. "Very well. It is drawing late. General Ross, I propose we withdraw from the city. Tomorrow we shall return and complete our work. And we shall not burn this building. But I said Dear Josey will malign me no more . . . and so it shall be. Would you post a guard, sir?"

The guard was posted, and the British formed up and marched back down Maryland toward the city gates.

Luke picked up the paper Ross had dropped into the muck. In the flickering light from the roaring fires, he read the National Intelligencer's final prediction: "We feel assured that the numbers and bravery of our men will afford complete protection to the city ..."

CHAPTER FORTY-TWO

ON FIRST MEETING, Jeptha's mule, who may or may not have rejoiced in the name of Balaam, tried to bite her elbow off. "Jus' his way," Jeptha said, not sounding terribly apologetic, "he don' have much use for white folks neither." So not only am I riding a swayback ass, Diana thought, but one that is a bigot as well. "But he'll do what's 'spected. Jus' don't get too close on his head nor tail."

Jeptha had made a sling for Diana's case from a length of hemp. Rope also made up the mule's halter—and both sections of rope were shiny, new, and unstretched. "Slipped out 'fore you woke up to th' ropewalk. Figger redcoats'll be by wi' their torches bymebye, so it'll not be missed." His eyes shifted to the lean-to behind the shack, and Diana was fairly sure that more than ten feet of good hemp had been acquired against future needs.

"When you come to find your major," Georgia said, "you tell him—from us—he's got himself a right good woman. Best he not mess 'round.'

"An' a'ter you tell him that," Jeptha added, "you get Balaam on home. Don' be thinkin' of this like some long-term loan, now."

Diana clambered up on the mule, using Jeptha's cupped hands for a stirrup. "Thank you. You'll get Balaam back."

"We know that."

"Take good care, mis'tess."

Diana kicked, and Balaam blatted a protest, then ambled forward. During the night a storm had broken, heavy rain driving against the shack's walls. It stopped just before dawn. Diana hoped that not only had the fires been extinguished, but the British enthusiasm for arson as well. She thought the safest plan would be to travel generally eastward, toward the Navy Yard. Then she would turn directly north and head for the Eagle Tavern.

A Daughter Of Liberty

She moved slowly, from farm to building to warehouse, trying to think like a dragoon, spying out the countryside. For a while the mule reminded her a bit of Horse—the dull-witted beast she and Emmett had acquired in the flight from New Kent. But Balaam proved to have a great deal of personality. All malevolent. He would stop—in an open field, naturally—and want to graze. Every now and then he'd turn his head and snap at Diana's leg. Diana reciprocated by kicking him in the head when he did so.

From the north, toward Pennsylvania Avenue, Diana heard the snarl of drums and the blare of a bugle. It could only be the British. After a few moments she saw smoke once again spiral up. They were relighting the fires they'd set the night before. Behind her was Greenleaf's Point, where there was some kind of fort; just ahead, the Navy Yard. She wondered whether her cleverness was leading her into a trap. Sliding off Balaam, she went forward afoot, leading—sometimes dragging—the mule. She heard shouts, laughter, and the crackle of flames. Tying the mule's halter to a board protruding from a dilapidated shed, she readied her pistol and peered out at the Navy Yard.

She saw the British. Some of them were in red uniform, others in the costume of common sailors. They must have gone to the yard just at dawn, intending to resume their destruction. There was not much left to destroy: some sheds and shops, and two houses. One of them, Diana remembered, belonged to Captain Tingey, the yard's commanding officer. The two houses were as yet unburnt, as was, strangely enough, a brand new ship floating at anchor.

At the moment, most of the British were clustered around the Tripoli monument, which commemorated the U.S. Navy's fight against the blackmailers of Barbary. It was a typically Grotesque but Heroic piece of statuary, with figures representing History, Fame, and who knew what-all. A few sailors were atop the monument. One of them had a bronze object in his hand; taken from Fame, Diana thought, who had been carved as covering the deeds of her sons with a palm and crown of glory.

Scared, worried, sore and tired, Diana found herself smiling. She could picture the young mariner arriving home with his relic of the war: An' so ye burnt Washington, m'lad? Didja bring away jewels and gold? No, mum. Better—thae boy took yon plate of copper and tin.

A British officer bellowed, and the sailors shinnied down from the monument, re-formed, and marched off. Diana was puzzled, knowing little of the uses of war. It seemed acceptable to her for the British to burn the Navy Yard— even a ropewalk could be considered a weapon. But to leave unburnt the two houses? Gallantry? Perhaps. But why was the ship left unharmed? This made no sense whatsoever.

Was there something in the air of Washington that encouraged chaos—like the foul summer air of Philadelphia drew the plague?

* * * *

Luke marched up Pennsylvania Avenue with a column of British troops. He had spent a very damp night camped on the stubble of Capitol Hill. Even as exhausted as he was, the smoke from the rain-damped fire had kept him coughing awake half the night. Now, a little past eight in the morning, the day was already searing and humid. This British brigade, commanded by a Major Jones, was under orders to burn out the brick building housing the American State, War, and Navy departments. Luke and Lieutenant Scott marched with them. Thirty black Americans had been pressed into service to lug the gunpowder barrels to be used in the demolition. The fires set the night before were now being rekindled by scattered groups of British soldiers and sailors.

Pennsylvania Avenue was a mire. Luke tried to skirt around the deep water-filled ruts and puddles, and was grateful he was not part of the six-deep centipede of the central column.

Admiral Cockburn pulled even with the column. Somewhere, during the night, he had found a new mount. It

pg. 487

was an old, ungroomed white mare, whose long mane and tail trailed. Behind the horse trotted its perplexed-appearing foal.

"Major Jones. Admire my mount."

"Yessir. Looks pure-bred, sir."

"I'm thinking of bringing her back to London, breed a new line of racing stock." A ripple of mirth from the ranks. Cockburn was popular.

Luke heard a shout. He looked ahead and gaped. The British troops were being charged. By one man on a horse.

Major Jones shouted—a calm, parade-ground shout: "The Eighty-fifth will form line." The column spread out, like a red bird spreading its wings. "Make ready!" The troops' muskets were brought up. Frizzens snapped back from priming pans. "Present." And the muskets were aimed.

The horseman was screaming—Luke could not tell what—and waving a pistol. He shot once, wildly. "Fire!" The volley smashed out, and the man spun out of the saddle. A moment later his horse crashed, head first, into the mud.

"Close up," was the next command. The column folded its wings. "The Eighty-fifth will advance." And the march up the broad avenue continued.

Luke stared at the body as he went by. The man's corpse, whoever he had been, had been sieved by the musketry. A lunatic? A brave man pressed beyond logic? The hell with it, Luke thought. Just call him an American.

* * * *

Diana Shannon felt she was in the midst of one of those French plays where lovers would-be lovers, and cuckolded husbands incessantly pop in and out of every entrance and hide in every closet.

After the British had departed, a party of Americans crept into sight. From his oversize cocked hat, Diana knew the man leading them to be Captain Tingey. This party ran to the waterfront and began making preparations to move that unburnt ship. None of them appeared to notice a second group's appearance. And then a third group of people appeared, went to the two undamaged houses and started looting them. Everyone in the yard, Diana thought, has gone mad. Time for her to be moving.

A thought struck her: if she followed that British column up toward Pennsylvania Avenue, they probably would not notice her. And any Americans aboard would be reluctant to bother a lone traveler. Especially one who was armed. Diana took out the pistol, unscrewed the barrel and checked her loading. The ball was in place and the powder still dry. She reprimed the pistol and put it back in her pocket.

In the wake of the raiders, she started north. Now, for the first time, she was heading directly for the tavern. And toward the British lines.

* * * *

Scott and Luke dropped away from the column as Cockburn dismounted in front of the offices of the National Intelligencer. Luke had decided his best chance for freedom was getting away from the command group and then away from Scott himself. A razing party was waiting, ready with axes, gunpowder, torches, and mauls.

"Gentlemen," Cockburn said, "you may begin." The British poured through the smashed door. Cockburn followed on their heels. Mauls smashed into presses. Sailors carried type forms out and scattered them into the backyard. "Be sure all the letter C's are destroyed," Cockburn shouted. "They'll not be able to abuse my name anymore." Laughter. Cockburn himself collected an armload of books, carried them out the rear of the office and tossed them onto a growing fire. "Dear Josey will be dependent on his own education and memory, such little as they be."

The admiral went back inside for more books. He was confronted by a rather apologetic British major and a completely apoplectic American. Cockburn, ever the gentleman book burner. bowed and was about to ask for an introduction, but the American beat him to it.

"Are you a Turk, sir?"

Allan Cole & Chris Bunch

Cockburn stammered, then, in his high voice: "I am not, sir. But I have sailed in their waters."

"No doubt. Are you aware of the library at Alexandria?"

Cockburn was taken aback and on a lee shore. "No. No, and I am not certain—"

"Exactly my point, sir. There is no library at Alexandria. Because the barbaric Musselmen burnt it. Just as you are proposing to burn my Patent Office."

"This gentleman," the British major explained, "is Dr. Thornton. He is Superintendent of Patents."

"Dr. Thornton, are you the same—"

"The same man who was the architect for the Capitol your Mongols burnt last night? I am he, sir. I assume you are their khan?" Cockburn managed an introduction. "I am not pleased to know you, Sir George," Thornton continued. "At the best of times it would be an imposition. Now it is an abhorrence."

The major interposed: "Sir, you said burn all government offices. We found this gentleman there. He said we were about to burn private property."

"And so you are. Look at this." Luke, peering over a marine's shoulder at the door, saw for the first time that Thornton was carrying a rather peculiarly styled violin. "My invention. One of many. Private property. Patentable private property. As are all those models and plans in the office itself."

"Government property—" the major went on, stubbornly, and was interrupted.

"Admiral, tell this oaf of yours I am well aware of his orders. He need not keep replaying that single note of his. Although why I am attempting to reason with a man whom I observe is standing in front of me, soot from the burning of literature on his hands, I do not know." Cockburn actually seemed taken aback. "However, I shall explain as simply as possible. I am the head of the Patent Office. Our offices are rented from Blodgett's Hotel, a private concern. Beyond a small amount of paperwork, all of the plans and models have been submitted by citizenry. This, I think you would agree, is also private property. Are you making war on this government or on its men and women?

"And even if your barbarism does not permit the correct response, let me add there is an excellent chance some of these inventions will benefit all mankind. Not just Americans, but one day even the poor wights who are forced to live in England. Burn this, and I would be unsurprised to see your name go down in history along with the despicable being who fired Alexandria."

Luke expected to hear Cockburn order a marine to bayonet this impossible man. Instead, after a long pause, Cockburn laughed. "Doctor . . . you argue your case well. Major, the Patent Office is to remain untouched. Post a guard. You see, Doctor, we are not quite the Huns you think."

Thornton looked, rather pointedly, at Cockburn's smudged hands, snorted and stalked out.

"Thank God," Admiral Cockburn observed quietly to Lieutenant Scott, "that man chose architecture and mechanics. If he had gone into politics and become president instead of faltering Jemmy, our fleet might well have been taken at the mouth of the Chesapeake and my name synonymous with that of Admiral Byng." The British admiral Byng had gone before an Admiralty firing squad sixty years earlier for losing Minorca to the French. "We were fortunate the good doctor did not have a cane. He reminded me all too much of one of my tutors."

Scott kept a blank expression on his face, evidently unsure of what his reaction should be. The admiral looked around the ruined newspaper. "We have done enough damage here. Mister Gale will find it very hard to resume publication." For some reason, Cockburn seemed not to take as much pleasure in the destruction as he had previously.

Luke trudged behind Scott, Cockburn and the rest of his staff, as they rode back toward the raiders' headquarters. There, they found General Ross, who seemed in an equally

Allan Cole & Chris Bunch

silent mood. Guilt? Luke wondered. From a British general? Not hardly. Cockburn recovered his ebullience. "Scouts have reported three ropewalks in this city." He ordered, "I want them burnt."

"Sir, may I lead one party?" Lieutenant Scott asked.

Cockburn looked at him. "You may, young sir. I fear there will be little glory won in setting the match to hemp and tar. But go."

Luke faded into the mill of troops outside. Half of his plan was accomplished.

CHAPTER FORTY-THREE

A FLICKER OF red caught Diana's eye. She'd stopped near a creek to water the mule, and had chanced a cup of water herself. Nearby was the long, low bulk of a ropewalk. Diana pulled the mule's halter, forcing Balaam deep into the brush next to the streamlet. The animal started to bray in protest— but did not. Red again—the coat of a British soldier. A scout.

The man broke cover, and two other lobsterbacks followed. A party of men—redcoats and sailors—came after them, laden with small casks and tools. Their formation was hardly military. But they knew their task. At an officer's orders, they moved into the ropewalk. Diana saw them spreading the raw hemp down the center of the building. Some barrels were axed open, and the men poured a black, sticky substance on the hemp; tar. Other barrels were opened more carefully; gunpowder, which was spread over the tar. The men re-formed outside and waited. At each end and the middle, matches were tossed onto the hemp. The ropewalk exploded. Black smoke gouted up into the sky, smoke thicker than the dark, gathering clouds on the horizon.

Diana used the brushline to move onward, farther into the city. Ahead lay a line of shacks; cribs, probably the sorry houses the Irish laborers were forced into. Diana passed behind one shack consisting of little but a shabby roof and canvas walls. She heard a woman's scream, cut off in the middle as if a hand had been clamped over her mouth. It was followed by the sound of a blow, then a voice, very thick with alcohol and lust, and very British: "Y'said y' didn't mind it rough, lass. I paid f'r it, an' I'll have it th' way 1 wants."

"Ye bastard, ye're killin* me!"

"It's just a few cuts. Now be still, wi' ye!" A moan . . . not of passion, but pain. Then another attempted scream. Diana's pistol came out, was cocked and aimed at the center of the shack, just stomach high. She pulled the trigger.

The pocket pistol cracked, and the ball ripped through the canvas. A shout. Surprise? Pain? A crash from the other side, and the sound of running feet. Inside—a woman's sobs, interspersed with moans. Then footsteps, out and away.

Very good, Diana Shannon. You are the savior of womankind. You are also what the British will call a guerrilla. Get moving. No. Remember what Emmett taught you.

She hastily reloaded, spilling powder. Pistol ready, she grabbed the halter and fled. Not far ahead was Pennsylvania Avenue, and the British army.

* * * *

Luke sat outside the house the British had requisitioned for the command group, concentrating, it appeared, on the entries in his "journal." He was actually eavesdropping on a conversation between Cockburn and Ross, on the other side of a hollyhock.

"Sir," Cockburn was saying, with considerable heat in his voice, "I ordered the burning of the marine barracks, the Jonathans' bank, and a house—a house that contained materiel of war. All three of these are legitimate subjects for destruction by the usages of war. You countermanded those orders. Might I ask why?"

Ross sounded very tired: "We have burnt enough, Admiral: their library, that hotel, the house of their president."

"That," Cockburn said sarcastically, "was the avowed purpose of this expedition. Which we discussed fully and completely. You were in agreement with me. But now? I do not understand you, sir. War is to be fought to the knife, and the knife to the hilt."

"You are correct in one thing. I was in agreement with you. But no longer. I wanted, you will recall, to withdraw the expeditionary force when we were camped at Marlboro. I should have followed my instincts."

"Why did you not?"

"Because I was reasoning from the wrong perspective. I was concerned—and you rightly chided me—that we were too far beyond the support of Admiral Cochrane. And that the Americans were drawing us into their heartland to trap us into a Carrhae. The example I should have considered was directly in front of me. Spain. Napoleon fought as you have—to the hilt.

"It took Sir Arthur and British Regulars to drive him out. But perhaps a third of his army never saw the front. They were defending the French rear against those guerrillas the emperor had created. The same thing occurred, I understand, in Russia. Sir George, I shall make a prediction."

"Proceed, Robert."

"My prediction is based on some assumptions. First, that the American forces—if there are any—are not capable of, nor planning, an attack while we are here in Washington."

"With what army?"

"I wonder if General Burgoyne did not make the same jest the last time we fought on these shores. But hear me out. My second assumption is that our expeditionary force continues as planned, and we take and sack Baltimore."

"Which we shall."

"Perhaps that will make the Jonathans sue for peace, although it is my observation that Americans are frequently too stupid in the art of war to know when they are defeated. In that event, we return to London as heroes. Titles. Your estate returned to you. Well and good."

"I do not understand your complaint. What else, save glory and honor, is there to life?"

"Glory and honor, yes. But for how long? Five years? Ten? When Britain's policies change, and they accept this nation—speaking the same language and with many of the same customs—as an ally? Do not laugh. Spain has been our enemy, a neutral, our enemy once more, and finally an ally.

"Say this is what happens with America. Then the historians will remember us as a pair of Alarics. Legend will

Allan Cole & Chris Bunch

add incidents of pillage, murder, and rapine, to make the man who conquered Rome into a gentleman compared to us."

"General, I fear the heat and the strain have affected you."

"Quite possibly. But I feel, increasingly, that the only way we shall keep this glory we both hold so dear is if we fall on the field of honor."

"A soldier's fate."

"You do not understand. Perhaps I do not either—fully. Here are my orders. We shall hold in Washington until nightfall. I want a curfew issued. No one, on pain of death, is to be on the streets. At dusk, we shall begin our withdrawal. We will leave a token force behind us, as a ruse de guerre. They will build and tend fires, shout orders, and move about to create the illusion of an army. Two hours afterward they are to withdraw and join the others. There is nothing left for us here in Washington."

There was a long silence. Then Cockburn attempted a bluff laugh. "Aye aye, sir. Regardless of your, umm, interesting theorization, Baltimore is a far fatter and worthier target."

Luke heard movement, hastily scooped his papers into the knapsack. Shit. So he had less than—he glanced up to estimate the time, but the sun was blocked by the smoke from the blazing ropewalks—half a day to implement his plan.

He would not, could not, chance deserting on the march back. Nor would he, he determined, go back into the clutches of the Royal Navy. He would take his chances on a musket ball in the back.

It was then he heard the screams. It was a woman, stumbling toward the headquarters, barefoot, ragged, disheveled. Her chest was a mass of blood. Her screams became words: "He killed me! Damn him, he killed me!"

Cockburn and Ross ran into the street. Behind them came the American doctor whose house had been requisitioned.

"Damn him! Damn all you Sassenachs!" A corporal grabbed her.

"Dr. Ewell! See to this woman!"

Soldiers led her into the house. The American followed. He was gone but a few moments.

"What in the hell is this?" Cockburn wanted to know.

"The woman is a whore."

"I do not give a damn if she is Jemmy's wife! I asked what happened?"

"She was approached by a sailor."

"British?"

"Uh, yes. She went with him willingly, she said. He did not quarrel with the price she named. But once in her lodgings, she claims the man produced a knife and began slashing at her. The wounds on her upper body are quite shallow, so I would think a penknife. If it happened as she said."

"Pardon?"

"It has been my observation that just like niggers and peasants—whores and Irishers lie for profit, to create trouble or merely as a recreation. That woman fits three of those categories. If you are truly concerned, Sir George, offer her a piece of gold or two, and you will see those wounds heal as rapidly as if Christ Himself had touched them."

"Doctor, treat the woman! Keep your cant to yourself."

"I was merely—"

"Your home remains unburnt. Do not think that situation is graven in stone. She shall have gold, though. And I will see the sailor who did this dance at the yardarm. Parade the men! When the woman's wounds are bandaged, she can identify the villain."

Shouted orders, and Luke fell into line with the British. Far down the avenue he saw a solitary rider trot across the road, headed north. He could not tell if the rider was man or woman, nor if the mount was horse or mule.

Ewell was a bastard Tory—but a good surgeon. The woman was skillfully bandaged, given a restorative, and then helped down the ranks. She glared at each man as she passed, but could not identify the attacker.

Cockburn gave her gold—six gold doubloons, to the whore's astonishment. The admiral's face was black with rage.

Poor man, Luke thought. Did you really think your brave sailors were different from any other man who's been given a sword and permission to use it? Or was it your belief in all these days you have been roaring around like a fiery dragon—burning and stealing all that came before you— that war was a game? And those houses set to the torch or fields trampled down were markers in that game? To be taken, put in the box as a token of victory, to emerge undamaged for the next match?

Ross, Cockburn, and their officers conferred. Finally a captain broke from the group. "Volunteers," he shouted. "To destroy the arsenal at the river. I want two hundred men."

Luke was one of the first to step forward.

CHAPTER FORTY-FOUR

THE HOUSE AHEAD of Diana was unexceptional, except it had been fortified. A cart was turned on its side, blocking the yard's main gates. Two barrels were in front of the door. Possibly, she thought, some soldiers with more fight than most had built a hasty stronghold before fleeing. Then she saw the musket's barrel, steadily tracking her. Diana slowly lifted a hand and knocked back the hood of her cloak. The musket vanished, and the door banged open.

A large, raw-boned woman, almost as big as the Tower musket she held, came out. "How do you do, missus."

Diana pulled Balaam to a halt. "Good morning."

"Teakettle's on. If you have time, light for a spell. Milk's still sweet. There's whiskey, but it's a bit early."

Diana tethered Balaam to the overturned cart.

"Come from anywheres near the Congress buildings?"

"Close by."

"The British still in the city?"

"They are."

The woman escorted Diana into the house. There were two other women inside. They were obviously the older woman's daughters.

"I'm Mister Whitlock's wife. Congressman Whitlock, of Ohio. These are m'two daughters, Rosemary and Clarissa."

"Pleased," came the doubled response from the two women. Mrs. Whitlock looked to be anywhere from forty to sixty, a frontierswoman. The daughters were in their early teens, so Diana supposed the mother was most likely thirty years or so. Frontier life aged you, especially if you were a woman.

The house was adequately if simply furnished. Diana barely noticed. She was staring at the muskets. There were— she hastily counted—sixteen, no, seventeen of them. They were in line, leaning against a wall. Their hammers were at half cock. On the floor in front of them were five long, gleaming-edged pikes. On the wooden table near the fire was a collection of butcher knives and three hatchets.

One of the daughters prepared tea.

"You said the lobsterbacks were still around. Which way they headin'?"

"I couldn't tell. There were great groups of them milling around Pennsylvania Avenue. I saw more of them earlier, down toward the Navy Yard."

"Not comin' north yet, are they?"

"Not as far as I could tell... Umm, Mrs. Whitlock, all these weapons? Are there any of our soldiers around?"

"Hell no. Last group we saw was yesterday afternoon. Came through like Old Scratch was nippin' at their hinders. They were droppin' their guns, hats, what few of 'em had uniforms on were strippin' naked like they'd roosted in an anthill. Me and the girls went out and collected what we thought we'd need."

"Meaning no offense, but. . . this is your house, I take it?"

"Rented. Plan on livin' here till Ambrose gets tired of playing politician and we can go back to Marietta."

"If the British find arms in a building, they put it to the torch. That is what happened to me. I was staying at Tomlinson's."

"Thought that was one of the buildin's got burnt."

Diana's warning seemed not to register. "Also, the man I'm going to—" Diana stopped in mid-sentence. She'd almost said "marry." Well, well, I am, am I? Where did that pop up from?

"You were saying, missus?"

"Pardon. I just realized something. My, my . . . uh, fiancé . . . warned that anyone in possession of firearms could be treated as . . . well, an outlaw."

"Haw!"

"Pardon?"

"Missus, you look to be city stock. We ain't. Where we live, there's Indians. You probably don't know much about 'em, but—"

"I used to live in Cherry Valley. I was there, both times, when the Seneca attacked."

Mrs. Whitlock's eyes widened. "Beg your pardon. You ain't a city milksop. Then you know what it's like. These bastard—and I don't want you girls to ever use language like that—lardassed redcoats ain't tansy tea to a scalpin' party. They come up the road, they'll think chain lightnin' is like a baby's kiss."

"These British are regulars. Not like our militia."

"We don't care if they have four rows of teeth and are related to Satan Hisself on their mother's side. They come up this road, they'll go back down a damn sight faster than they come up. Right, girls?"

Only one of the young women hesitated before nodding firmly, and that for less than a second. They were their mother's children.

"Might I inquire as to where your husband is?"

"Far as I know, back in Ohio. Still speechifyin'. He sent us on forward to get the house ready. Or else he's makin' his way here. He ain't worried. Me an' the girls been in a lot straiter fix before."

Diana, thinking the British would be well-advised to not wander near the Whitlock house, finished her tea and stood up.

"You have to leave so quick? More'n welcome to stay with us till things settle out. Least until that storm that's buildin' out there gettin' ready to show Judgment Day passes on."

"I can't. My fiancé's waiting for me outside town." Diana noted the word was coming easier now.

"If that's how it must be. Thanks for comin' by, an' for bringin' us the news."

Allan Cole & Chris Bunch

At the door Diana turned back. "If there'd been more like you, maybe there wouldn't be redcoats in the President's House."

"Child, don't ever think there ain't a lot like me and the girls. A lot of men too, even. Damned redcoats don't put their behinds back on their boats and skedaddle real soon, they'll find out they went to a bear fight with no more'n a willow switch."

"I hope you are correct, Mrs. Whitlock. Good luck to you."

* * * *

"Any gunners, mates, gun captains, and powder boys for'rd," was the command. Luke stepped out smartly, even though his experience behind the great cannon was almost nonexistent. He was starting to see the possibility of simultaneously striking a blow against his captors—for so he thought the British to be—and a chance to lose himself in what he hoped would be the ensuing confusion.

The British troops had marched down to the arsenal at Greenleaf's Point on the Potomac. Evidently the Americans had already made some attempt to prevent the British from seizing the arsenal—the cannon were spiked, and two of the magazine entries were open, the magazines stripped bare.

Luke and the other specialists were put under the command of a very elderly, very soft-spoken gunner.

"First, lads, if you have pipe and tobacco, or cheroots on you, I want them handed forward. We'll leave 'em with those Royal Marines there, by the gates. They'll be guarding the slow matches, the torches, and anything else some hulverhead might kill us with.

"I rec'nize you're not fools. There's none of you missing more'n the usual quota of limbs. But habit makes fools of us all. Any of you wearin' boots, put them over near that well. Don't need no nails strikin' sparks. We are to destroy this magazine, as you know. It would sadden my poor gray wife to learn her husband, followin' orders on a foreign shore, was ascended to Heaven like a latter-day Elijah, thanks to some ignorant shit sack.

"You men claim experience, you an' the officers'll enter the magazine, stack powder kegs together, cut cartridges apart and spread 'em around the kegs. I'll connect the stacks wi' slow fuse, and run it out the entryport for firin' later. We'll use the seamen to help us near the mag'zines, an' the marines . . . hell, I s'pose the marines can be used to carry anything that's heavy and won't take fire. Turn to."

The gunner's caution was well founded. The Royal Navy still shuddered about the fate of the well-named Thunderer, more than fifty years earlier, when a magazine explosion at night killed or wounded nearly a hundred men. All gunpowder needed was a spark or the tiniest flame to explode.

Aboard ship, the magazine and powder room was built lower than the deck around it, so it could be flooded easily. It was always guarded. The ship's commissioned gunner kept the key, and even then could unlock the door only with the permission of the skipper. The passageway to that room was lead lined, and the room itself covered with a thick layer of copper. All metal, from the door lock to the hinges, was brass or copper. When the ship was firing its guns, heavy, water-soaked flannel screens blocked that passageway. And accidents still happened. The British proposed to destroy the American magazine without any of these accidents occurring.

Luke Shannon had another idea. Inside the pack containing his journal he had flint and steel. He slipped them out and tucked them in an inside pocket of his waistcoat. Possibly he could secure a length of slow fuse, light it, and tuck it, smoldering, out of sight. A long enough length for him to be able to run like hell, but not too long so that his British pursuers could chase him down. Maybe.

Possibly another option would be to get his hands on a pistol. That, with its ball pulled, could start a fire. Once again it would be up to his legs to clear the area before there were

Allan Cole & Chris Bunch

further developments. He was not fully content with either idea. Perhaps something else would come to him.

"You, sailor, drop that damned pack with the others' shoes. Stop gaping like Dick Whittington. What the hell are you doing carrying soldier's load, anyway?"

"M' officer's orders, sir. Aye, sir."

Luke trotted forward, unslinging the knapsack. He dropped it beside the well, started toward the open magazine entry, and then his brain told him what his eyes had seen. He stopped and chanced another look into the well. Christ's Holy Name. It was full of barrels. Gunpowder barrels. Luke couldn't see any gleam of water around them. The powder should be still dry and potent. Did the Americans—his countrymen, he corrected—put them down there to hide them from the British? Or did they think there was more water in the well than there was, and assume they were destroying the powder? Hell if he knew, or ever would.

Inside the magazine he went to work with a will. Piling the smaller barrels in stacks. Rolling the larger ones into a common area. Cutting apart—carefully—the serge cartridges, and dumping powder over the lot. There were tons of explosive in the magazine. When Luke thought the task to be about half finished, he "busied" his way to the magazine's entry. He walked out straight across the yard—a man following orders, conveying orders, directly toward the marines standing guard next to the tubs with smoldering matches and piled pitch-covered torches.

"You," he said to one of the marines at the gate. "Cap'n wants a torch. Over there, to that battery." He gestured vaguely toward the spiked cannon. The well lay between the gate and the cannon.

"M' corp'ral sez m' post's here till he sez dif'rent."

"It's your arse." Luke pretended indifference.

"Dun't see no of'cer anyway." Luke didn't say anything. "Damn," the marine managed, "wish'd they'd make th'r minds firm."

"I'll report your problems to the captain," Luke said, and ran back toward the magazine. He stopped at the entrance. Joyful God, Father of hosts. The marine propped his musket against the wall, picked up a torch, blew a slow match to life, and touched the end of the torch to it. The pitch flamed up. Then he began marching—marching at the prescribed rate, like he was pacing his post to and fro on a quarterdeck—toward the cannon.

It was not necessarily true that marines were born stupid. But their service made them that way. From taking the king's Shilling in the least respected of the British services until the man died, probably violently or of some hellish pestilence, his life was absolutely dictated. From dawn to dusk, drill was endless. Every duty was done one, two, three. Over and over again. Luke waited until the marine was a few feet from the well, then he stuck his head inside the magazine and shouted to the gunner: "Sir! Sir! Quick!"

The gunner may have been old, but he was fast. At the entrance to the magazine he spotted the marine. "You! You arsehole! Put that out!"

Other officers and mates had seen the marine. They were screaming as well. The marine stood next to the well, a bovine trying to pull his load, suddenly beset by bees.

Luke added to the shouting. "In the well, goddammit!"

The marine followed that order—the only one that offered a specific thing to do.

Luke was running, running as fast as he could, running as hard as he had since he was a child trying to get away from his father's anger.

A knot of rank was descending on the poor marine, about to shred him limb from limb. One of the marine sentries saw Luke dashing toward him and stepped out, rifle at the port. Luke knocked him spinning.

"That man! Stop that man!"

Luke put his head down and found greater speed. He heard running steps from behind.

"Halt! Halt or we fire!"

Allan Cole & Chris Bunch

"Sergeant! Shoot that man down!"

Commands, and Luke heard the snap of frizzens. His feet could not stop churning. One musket fired, and the ball spat past his shoulder. But the next ... or the next . . .

Greenleaf's Point blew up. Luke rolled to the ground, let the wind blast over him, then chanced a look. The arsenal was a Hell of explosions, smoke, and flames. His impromptu firing squad had been scattered like leaves in a gale.

The arsenal's gate crashed into the roadway ahead of him. Bricks and cobbles shrapneled. An object thudded into a shed wall. It was a man's leg. Luke got up and ran once more. Running north. And then it began raining. At first Luke thought the storm had broken.

But rain was never red.

CHAPTER FORTY-FIVE

THE WIND GREW to gale force as Luke headed toward Pennsylvania Avenue. The sky was dark, growing darker, and not from smoke. Blow, winds, and crack your damned cheeks, he thought. Blow the streets clear and the British into the river. He tried to move like he remembered the British infantrymen had, dashing from cover to cover. Ahead of him, under a tree, lay a body. Luke thought him to be a British seaman. Certainly he was a sailor. There was a small hole below the man's rib cage, caused, perhaps, by a tiny pistol ball. Maybe your shipmates'll pick you up, he thought. Add you to the charnel heap from the arsenal.

Ahead, a British party debouched from Pennsylvania Avenue and moved toward him. Luke went to ground. The party consisted of very alert infantry flankers, and a tatterdemalion of quickly assembled carts. You have not nearly enough hearses, he thought. A pair of officers rode at the head of the column, and just behind him, seamen dragged one of the expedition's small, wheeled three-pounder cannon.

The wind roared down on the city. Blowin' whole gale, sir. Time to reef sail and run under bare poles. Darkness, nearly night. Rain slashed in. At first Luke thought it was hail, it came so sharp. The British continued moving, but far more slowly. The rain broke for a moment, and Luke saw, from the huge black cloud overhead, a funnel form and reach down toward the earth.

The tornado snaked toward him. The roof of a house lifted and broke into a thousand bits. Luke thought he heard thunder slam in the distance. Lightning crackled, bright and, to his eyes, blue, as the twister howled across the road. Luke saw, through the murk, one of the British officers still on his rearing horse as the funnel closed in.

The roaring was all of Luke's world as he clung to the ground, and then it receded.

A Daughter Of Liberty

The British party was shattered. Men lying still, men stumbling about as if in battle shock. Men running, panicked. The officer was down, lying fifteen feet from his motionless horse. The three-pounder, even though it weighed several hundred pounds, had been ripped from its carriage and hurled into a field. Thank you, Lord, Luke prayed. Not only for missing my unworthy hide, but for giving me the best traveling weather you could.

Barely noticing that the tree he'd sheltered under was now stripped of all its leaves and branches, he went on. The rain swept in once more, and the wind gusted. Bruised, soaked to the skin, exhausted and hungry, Luke could not remember being happier.

He was free—and would never be anything other. His luck had returned.

* * * *

Diana Shannon was just outside Washington when the great storm struck. She found shelter in a barn and waited. Part of her mind wanted to plan the future. If she married John Maguire, would that end her life in Philadelphia? If so, she wasn't sure she cared any longer. Would she be happy in his place along the Mississippi? Who could say? At least they would be together. And this time when she built, she would have someone else beside her.

But for all she knew, John might be lying, desperately wounded, on the battleground at Bladensburg. Or even . . . "Come on, Balaam," she said suddenly. It was time to quit dreaming and put one foot in front of the other. Balaam nipped at her, then, having made his point, started for the barn's exit. Diana clambered up on his back and they followed the winding lane north.

By late afternoon the rain had fined down to a drizzle. She was only two or three miles from the Eagle Tavern when she heard the singing:

"And there I see a pumpkin shell
As big as mother's basin,

And every time they touched it off
They scampered like the nation.
"Yankee Doodle keep it up,
Yankee Doodle-"

The song broke off. Then: "Come on, dammit! Sing!"

She came around a bend. There were about thirty of them, shambling in a mob formation down the road. Militia, she guessed, and from a well-to-do district, since they wore uniforms. Most of the militia she'd seen wore civilian clothes. Their uniforms might have looked very fine at one time, on the village green. Now their boots were shabby and worn through, their uniforms muddy, stained, and torn. Only one was armed: the young man at their head. He also was one of the few still wearing his utterly useless shako and looking like he'd attempted to stay tidy.

Diana pulled her mule to the side of the road to let them by.

"Company . . . halt!" the young man shouted.

The group staggered to a stop, and most of the men fell out to the side of the road. A few—the most tired, most tattered, and most angry-appearing—followed their leader to Diana.

"You men, go back to the column. You're probably frightening this poor lady by your appearance. I'll find what we need to know."

"They are not upsetting me," Diana said.

"Thankee, mum," one of the men said. He turned to the officer: "Best we listen as well. If you wuz my bellwether, you'da been mutton fifty miles ago."

"Be silent! Madam, does this road lead to Washington?"

"It does. But I do not think you should follow it there."

"We are under orders, madam. I am Captain Stanforth. My company's part of the Frederick County Militia. Riflemen, every one of us."

Allan Cole & Chris Bunch

"Hard to tell," a man grumbled, "seein' as how ain't none of us got weapon one. Save that pop gun th' fool calls hisself our captain's carryin'."

"I said silence in the ranks. We'll draw our rifles when we report to our colonel in Washington."

Diana gaped. "Captain . . . the British have taken Washington. They're burning it at this very moment."

It was Stanforth's turn to goggle. "But . . . how . . . when ... we heard the redcoats were going to attack Annapolis. Or possibly even Baltimore."

"That is what was being said a few days ago," Diana agreed. "However, it appears no one told the British that." She told them the rest.

"Where's the president?"

"No one seems to know."

Stanforth slumped, as if his legs had been slashed from under him. "Then what is to be done? What are we to do?"

"Seems pretty obvious to me," one of his men said, and added, with drenching sarcasm, "Captain... We ain't got no rifles waitin'. We ain't got no colonel to report to, let alone any of the luxuries like mayhap rations. Ain't even no army to report to, from what this lady says. Hellfire, ain't no capital to defend. What we should be doin' is goin' home."

"You're a hell of a patriot!"

"Stanforth, keep a still tongue or I'll put you in the ditch. Ain't no patriotism about it. Show me a redcoat, gimme something to do something with, an' I'm as outraged a patriot as the next man. But make me foller you around this dam' country for five or six days, lost, with no vittles . . . that changes things. Turns me, as far as I can tell, into a fool."

"I am your captain, dammit!"

Diana was now ignored.

"That's right. We elected you such. Men, I pr'pose a new election, for comp'ny cap'n. Nominations is in order."

"Nathaniel," somebody asked, "you 'member the route home?"

"Think so. Worst case, can't get you no loster'n this goosecap's done."

And with that the officer was deposed. Without further ado, the men got up and, singly and in small groups, started back the way they came.

Nathaniel turned back. "I'll tell your missus you're wagin' a one-man war 'gainst the lobsterbacks, Stanforth. Mebbe she'll strike a medal or somethin'."

After a moment Stanforth stumbled to his feet and followed his former subordinates into the growing dusk.

* * * *

John Maguire was not at the Eagle Tavern. Neither the innkeeper nor his wife had heard from him. Kitty was upstairs asleep in one of the rooms she had hired for Diana and her party. The innkeeper's wife said Kitty was so frightened, she had finally given her a potion to help her rest. Diana said to leave her be.

Diana declined food, even when pressed. She was not hungry. Though exhausted, she was not sleepy either. The innkeeper's wife thought she was close enough to Diana's size to give her dry clothes. Diana thanked her, but refused. At full dark she paid for torches to be set out. Later it began to rain once more.

Still later, the yawning innkeeper said he and his wife were for bed. Diana should come in and rest. Certainly Major Maguire would appear tomorrow. With the condition the roads were in after the storm, no one who could not walk on the water would be able to travel. Diana said she would retire in a while. She told the innkeeper that on the morrow she would need three men, hunters, woodsmen. She would pay well. They would comb the country all the way to Bladensburg, looking for the major.

"I know who you want," the innkeeper said. "Men who fear not God, the Devil, or the British. In the morning I'll bring them here. But you will be of little good unless you rest."

Allan Cole & Chris Bunch

Again Diana refused. She asked for more torches, to replace the ones now guttering down into gloom. Then she sat on the porch, her cloak pulled close around her. Waiting.

It might have been minutes, it might have been hours. But sometime later a tall man came out of the night toward the inn, riding a blaze-faced chestnut... John Maguire.

He reined in, slid stiffly from the saddle and tied the horse's reins. He patted the chestnut, then walked up to Diana. He stood there, looking her up and down, as if not sure the form before him was real. His face was like a sheet, his eyes deep hollows.

They stood only inches apart. For some reason they were ill at ease. Formal. Not quite knowing what was going to happen next—now that it was apparent both had survived. Finally:

"Thank God," John whispered.

"You are unhurt?" Diana asked.

"I am. But only by the Lord's grace. I broke my word to you. . . . Then I recollected my age and fled with the others. The British were between me and you. I had to ride around them. Balthazar threw a shoe this morning, so I had to walk him. I am sorry that—" He broke off, realizing he was babbling. Then he grinned, looking like a small boy caught out in some mischief.

Diana was off the porch and in his arms. Maguire held her tightly. There was no reason for them to speak any further. All was resolved in the embrace. Neither one felt the rain.

* * * *

Far down the road, Luke Shannon plodded toward the torchlight. An inn. If he were rich, he would stop, waken the keeper, order dry clothes and a meal. Many meals. The cook would be working until dawn. If he were rich . . . Luke had not a copper. And he was too happy that he was free, and too miserable to feel worse, to give a damn about money or shelter.

There would be an end to this road. Philadelphia. Some traveler with a wagon would give a poor sailor a ride. Some other Samaritan would feed him. Once home, he could think of a feather bed, and that meal. Surely Grandmother Shannon would have the finest cook in the city in her kitchen. All he wanted was to eat and sleep for a month. Diana would understand. She always did.

Closer to the torchlight, Luke saw two people in front of the inn's large veranda, holding each other. Damned fools. But it must be nice to be so in love you notice not this downpour. The woman was small—only a little smaller than his grandmother.

One of the torches flared, and Luke saw the horse tied nearby had a white blaze on its face. Hanging from its saddle was a shortsword. The man wore a muddy country riding coat. Would that this were the brave man at Bladensburg who'd tried to rally the fleeing Americans— whose life, Luke wanted to think, he'd saved by knocking aside that marine's musket. Now he had returned to this inn, through battle and storm, to his loyal wife.

Damn you for a dreaming Irisher, Luke thought. Keep moving. Philadelphia and Grandmother Shannon are a long and flinty road away, and the wind's in your face.

He tipped his hat in the couple's direction as he went past, and was lost in the darkness and rain.

THE END

Allan Cole & Chris Bunch

ACKNOWLEDGMENTS

HISTORY, THEY SAY, is written by the victors. In America it also has been written by rich white men. The contributions of women and minorities in the events that molded this nation have been largely ignored. Wherever possible we have searched original sources such as diaries and letters to fill these gaps. Many of the people the Shannons meet in this novel are either real or composites of real people. In many cases their words are the ones they spoke during the events described.

A whole host of people helped us with Daughter, and we would like to thank them, humbly and profusely. In many cases, however, our conclusions/thinking differs from theirs, and they are to be held innocent for any stupidities or errors on our part.

One thing that should be mentioned is the continuing controversy on just how Dorothea Payne Todd Madison preferred to spell her diminutive. We chose Dolly over Dolley, using three sources. First and second are Allen Clark's Life and Letters of Dolly Madison, including the cited letter of August 23, 1814, written by Dolly to her sister shortly before abandoning the White House and signed "Dolly," on the basis that she probably knew what she preferred and was certainly the only relatively unrattled person in Washington that particular day. We also believed the Memoirs and Letters of Dolly Madison, which were edited by her grandniece.

Overall personal thanks are due to Arthur and Margaret Macrae, Craig and Jan Studwell, Rita and Avi Schour, Thomas and Cassie Grubb, Dennis Foley, and too many Irish clans in Philadelphia to list singly.

For general moral support we'd like to thank Susan Beck, Kelsey Ramage; Jason and Alissia Cole; the Cole Brothers, Charles, Drew, and David; Sandy Wilt; Elizabeth Bunch and Philip Bunch.

A Daughter Of Liberty

Once again we want to thank Dick Moretti and Clarence Manetti, of the Far Western Steakhouse, Guadalupe, California.

We'd also like to acknowledge the late Fat Ralph, the real Abigail Fahey.

We also owe Danny Retting of Martin B. Retting, Culver City, California; Ian Shein, free-lance gun expert; Cliff Tarpy and the map people at National Geographic (once again); John O'Sullivan of O'Sullivan Courier and Limousine Service, Shannon, Ireland; the Cherry Valley village clerk, Cherry Valley, New York; Marian Cornelia, Cherry Valley Museum, Cherry Valley, New York; Melissa Savoy, Valley Forge Park Interpretive Service; Edwin Ford, historian, Kingston, New York; John Shelly, Archivist, Pennsylvania Historical Commission.

Also, we owe Robert King and Nancy at Historic Urban Plans, Ithaca, New York; Betty Monkman, the White House Curator, Washington, D.C.; Mrs. Florian Thayne, Architect of the Capitol, Washington, D.C.; Richard Stevenson, Library of Congress; Ranger Scott Sheads, Fort McHenry National Monument; Ms. Paula Murphy, United States Navy Historical Center.

We want to thank Joe Kious, Kious Custom Knives, Kerrville, Texas; Butch Beaver, Butch Beaver Custom Knives, New River, Arizona; Tai Goo, custom knifemaker, Tucson, Arizona; Richard von Doenhoff, National Archives, Washington, D.C.; Jonathan Beaty, Time magazine; Linda Beaty, Los Angeles Times; Kenny Hyre, West LA Book Center, Los Angeles, California.

Institutions that helped include Loyola University Library, Westchester, California; the Los Angeles and Philadelphia archdioceses; and the University of California at Los Angeles's main library.

Allan Cole & Chris Bunch